Bewitching Desires
A Savannah Coven Anthology

By
Rebekah R. Ganiere, Tami Lund, Niki Daninger
Jennifer Ray, Danielle Donaldson, Sheri Williams
Michele Mohr, Maria Arell, A.E. Snow
Andra Shine, Sonja Fröjdendal, Kay Blake

Bewitching Desires Copyright © 2015 Fallen Angel Press

All rights reserved. No part of this publication may be reproduced, distributed, or transmitted in any form or by any means, including photocopying, recording, or other electronic or mechanical methods, without the prior written permission of the publisher, except in the case of brief quotations embodied in critical reviews and certain other noncommercial uses permitted by copyright law. For permission requests, write to the publisher, addressed "Attention: Permissions Coordinator," at the address below.

This book is a work of fiction. The names, characters, places and incidents are fictitious and are not to be construed as real in any way. Any resemblance to persons, living or dead, actual events, locales or organizations is entirely coincidental. Bewitching Desires Copyright © 2015 Fallen Angel press

ISBN: 978-1-63300-009-4
ISBN: 978-1-63300-010-0
Cover art by Rebekah R. Ganiere

Fallen Angel Press
1040 N. Las Palmas Blvd.
Bldg. 24 Suite 203
Los Angeles, CA 90038
www.FallenAngelPress.com

TABLE OF CONTENTS

Kissed by the Reaper	Rebekah R. Ganiere	pg. 1
All's Fair: Love & Warlocks	Tami Lund	pg. 64
Micah's Mess	Niki Daninger	pg. ~~129~~ 139
Love Spell	Jennifer Ray	pg. 193
The Banshee and the Barista	Danielle Donaldson	pg. 240
Promised Magic	Sheri Williams	pg. 297
Drifter's Moon	Michele Mohr	pg. 351
Where the Heart Belongs	Maria Arell	pg. 410
A Stolen Spell	A.E. Snow	pg. 466
Heart of a Hunter	Andra Shine	pg. 513
Running with Magic	Sonja Fröjdendal	pg. 571
Magical Shift	Kay Blake	pg. 604

Kissed by the Reaper
By
Rebekah R. Ganiere

DEDICATION

This story is dedicated to Anna B.

Thank you for teaching me how much fun white polyester Cafeteria uniforms and high heels can be!

Love you forever my friend

CHAPTER ONE

Rose glanced at the crumbling headstones and mausoleums and pulled her duster's collar up against the biting wind. The inky black portal to her right snapped and crackled with electricity, as if trying to swallow her whole. She stamped her booted feet to make warmth circulate within her and checked her watch. Only fifteen more minutes.

When she'd been alive, twenty years ago, All Hallows Eve had been her favorite holiday. But now, reduced to a mere babysitter, she spent each Halloween making sure souls got back to hell after a night of fun on Earth. And this year she was in the middle of Podunk nowhere awaiting her charges, next to a pungent sugar beet factory. She knew she wasn't exactly the boss's favorite after what she'd done to his dog last year, but Idaho? Really? As if being a Reaper had been her life's ambition to begin with. Rose leaned against the century old wrought iron fence of the graveyard, hating her existence.

A shriek pulled her attention to the far end of the graveyard. A group of teenagers entered.

Great! Just what I don't need.

The boys, each dressed as 1920s mobsters, laughed and chased female flappers.

She checked her watch again. She wanted this over with so she could get back to her flat above her store, take a warm bath, and enjoy some hot tea.

The first souls drifted across the surrounding streets toward her. Some slower than others, but none wearing an expression of joy for another year of hell. To her right, a dark shadow shifted under a tree and caught her attention. Someone crouched over a white tombstone. Strange she hadn't noticed him approach. She'd stood in the same spot for over four hours. Her skin tingled as she studied his back. Broad shoulders, light hair. He swept the leaves from the base of the stone and placed a single tulip. An odd choice for this time of year.

"Helllooooo Roooooose." An ethereal voice broke into her revere.

Rose glanced over at the old woman. "Hello, Meredith. Enjoy your night?"

"Nooooot paaaaaaarticularly," she said in her slowed speech. The older a spirit, the slower they got.

"Sorry to hear that. At least you got out for a bit." Her gaze drifted back to the figure at the grave. He picked at the weeds around the headstone and tossed them aside. Curiouser and curiouser.

"Yeeeeees. Thaaaaaat's true." Meredith nodded and continued to the mausoleum serving as tonight's portal. Her hunched form shuffled to the gateway and disappeared through it. A distant wail floated back through the dark void toward Rose. The welcoming wail of the dead, she called it.

With only seven minutes to go, spirits swarmed the graveyard now. No one wanted to be late to the portal. The devil wasn't known for being lenient with tardiness. She'd let out three hundred and two tonight, and if she didn't bring them all back, it was her soul that would pay along side theirs. Lucifer had made his desires for her all too clear, as had his personal bodyguard Drix. They both would make any excuse to use her as their play toy.

The stranger at the grave stood, shoulders hunched. Something about his posture drew Rose's attention. The hairs on her neck pricked at the sight of his large form draped in a dark leather coat. It was strange that she could even see him under the cover of the trees. Almost as if he glowed from the inside. She took a step closer, her fist gripped tight around her Reaper blade.

Shouting caught her attention.

"Nope! I won't do it! I won't!"

A group of spirits huddled about twenty feet from where she stood. Old Harry plunked down on a headstone, arms folded. Rose groaned and stomped over. Numerous spirits drifted through her, making her skin pebble with goosebumps.

"What's the problem, Harry?" She tried to keep the annoyance from her voice. For as much as she hated her job, the souls in hell had it much worse.

"I ain't doin' it. I ain't goin' back this time." Old Harry harrumphed at her and turned his head away.

The surrounding spirits glanced at her in fright. She motioned for them to go with a jerk of her head, and they dispersed.

Rose yanked her Reaper blade from its sheath "You know how this works. You've been doing it for sixty years. You get one day a year to come up. Don't ruin it by making me reap you."

"I won't go. I don't care what it means. I can't take another whole year in that place." His wrinkly old mouth wobbled, his cataracted eyes not making contact. "Standing in that line. Letting everyone see. They make fun of me!"

"Harry, please," Rose pleaded. "I don't want to hurt you. This reality is crappy for all of us."

"Not you! You get to live up here."

"Harry–"

"Nooooooo!" he bellowed. Turning from her, and ran as fast as he was able in the opposite direction.

"Dammit, Harry!"

Rose tore through the graveyard after the bony old spirit. The curved knife gleamed ice blue in the moonlight. Harry floated through the headstones, aiming for the gate. Rose sprinted for him as he rounded a crypt. At that same moment one of the teen mobster boys slammed into her. She became corporeal and the boy screamed as their bodies tangled to the ground in a heap.

On contact, the boy's face paled as his life force was sucked into her body. His face froze in a silent scream.

Crap! "Sorry," she muttered.

She sprung to her feet. Her body faded back to night Reaper black, and she took off after Harry again. Reaching him moments later, she gripped his spirit form tightly.

"Let go!" He writhed and wriggled in her grasp.

"Not cool, Harry. You made me almost glean that kid."

Behind her more screams ensued. She looked over her shoulder. The teens had gathered around their friend. Unable to see her, they were unsure what was going on. The boy stared straight at her, wide-eyed. Rose's Reaper form only became corporeal at night if she touched the person with her blade in hand. But once one touched a Reaper, they'd never be the same. Always looking over their shoulder. Her solid black eyes and skeletal form would scar the kid for life.

Rose thrust her blade deep into Harry's belly and ripped it straight upward. His spirit burst open with a pop, in a shower of sparks.

His face sagged. "I just wanted more time," he choked out.

The ground shook, a fissure opened beneath him, and Harry was sucked inside.

"Yeah?" she yelled into the fissure. "Well now you won't be allowed back for ten years! Way to go, genius!"

Rose shook the spirit flecks off her coat, cursed, and took a deep breath, trying to shake chills off her skin. She hated doing that. Sheathing her blade, she turned around. *Frick!* The boy still watched on in horror.

"Boo," she shouted, losing her temper.

He jumped to his feet, screaming in terror. His friends followed him over a low fence and out of sight.

The remaining spirits crowded into the open portal, away from her. No one else wanted to the feel the ice of her blade. Rose heaved a sigh as they disappeared.

She hung her head. She sure hoped they all went in, because she'd forgotten to count. *Dammit!*

When the last spirit disappeared into the portal the hairs on her neck prickled again and she glanced around to see who she'd forgotten.

The figure that'd been huddled over the grave stared at her. Rose swallowed hard as her heart pounded in her chest. He shouldn't be able to see her unless she touched him, but his gaze bore into her anyway.

Something wasn't right.

She took a step toward him. In the moonlight she could barely see his form silhouetted against the darkened sky. He wore a hood so she couldn't see his face. But a sudden flash from his eyes sent her senses into overdrive. *A Jumper.*

Rose shot off in his direction. She'd never seen one before herself but she'd heard stories about Jumpers from other

Reapers. Souls that refused to move on and stayed on Earth by jumping from body to body.

The man turned and fled out the graveyard gate. Her lungs burned as she chased him. Even after all the exercise she got as a Reaper, she still hated running. She followed him down a deserted road till he entered the grounds of the sugar beet factory and cut around the side of a giant smoke stack. He darted in and out of the shadows and she had to concentrate to track him.

"There's no use running," she shouted. "You obviously know what I am."

He looked over his shoulder and his hood fell away, revealing a handsome face wracked with pain.

Rose grumbled. Even though she wasn't technically human anymore, her body still felt the burn of the run. Being a Reaper came with several special abilities, but added stamina wasn't one of them.

The Jumper rounded a corner of a boarded up building. Rose skidded around the corner a moment later and ran into the back of a large guy dressed like a rock star. He reached out and grabbed her by the hand, steadying her. He yanked his hand away and looked down at his palm where he'd touched her.

"Damn that stings. Your hands are frickin' cold."

The others in his group looked around, but couldn't see her.

She scanned the area. There were people everywhere. Music blared over a DJ system that she hadn't heard before due to the pounding of her heart in her ears. A Halloween party.

"Are you the grim Reaper? Too cool," he asked.

Rose shoved her blade back into her coat. "You see a man in a long coat run around this corner right before me?"

"He went that way." The rocker pointed into the crowd.

"Who are you talkin' to?" asked a girl dressed like a hooker.

Rose cursed under her breath and started in the direction he pointed. She weaved through the mass of bodies, trying hard not to touch anyone, but it was difficult. The smell of alcohol and pounding bass made her nauseous. She'd never been one for crowds, even while alive. Now that merely touching a human too long could kill them, she liked them even less. She scanned the crowd for signs of the Jumper. She couldn't let him get away. Bringing in a Jumper might just get Lucifer off her back for a couple years.

She pressed forward, making sure to keep her hands tucked in her coat. After a few minutes she spotted a hooded man in a long leather coat with his back to her, several yards away. Rose shoved through the crowd, touching people left and right. More than one screamed and fell to the ground. The sting of life forces as they entered her body made her move faster.

When she reached the Jumper she grabbed him by the arm. He turned and screamed. His face went ashen and his life force coursed up her arm. She released him and searched his eyes.

The Jumper had moved on.

Rose spun in a circle. "Damn."

A hundred souls or more, and one of them had just acquired a new guest. Jumpers could only move into a new host body by physical contact. Surely someone would notice if one of their friends suddenly took off for no reason.

The music stopped. Everyone groaned and looked around. The screams of the humans she'd touched had hit a fevered pitch and people backed away, unsure of what was happening.

She looked to the DJ platform. He was gone. Rose ran toward the building behind the DJ's set up. Out back was a huge meadow of farmland. Someone raced through the rows of corn, leaving an open trail behind them.

Rose smiled and tore into the field at top speed. Dead stalks whipped through her hair and grabbed at her coat like a toddler's sticky fingers.

"Nice job with the jump back there," she called out. "It doesn't matter where you hide, I will find you."

"You should leave while you have the chance," a voice called.

Rose smiled again. He wasn't that far ahead.

"You're hiding from someone, otherwise you wouldn't be jumping. My boss, perhaps?"

"Or perhaps my boss," came the response.

Rose slowed and her smile fell. "And who would your boss be?"

There was no reply. Rose stopped and listened. The field fell silent except for the sounds of the wind and the people at the distant party.

"You know you can't run forever." She rolled her blade around in her hand and stepped as quiet as possible, trying to hear him.

"But I can run for now," came a silky voice close to her ear.

Rose spun around. There was no one there. "Show yourself!"

"I already have." Again the voice was near her ear.

She spun back the other direction. Fear crept up her spine. Something was off. "Coward. What, are you afraid of little Rose?"

The man appeared from the corn right in front of her. His form was taller than the last had been. His bright blue eyes held an inner glow. He was well built and tan, dressed like an old western cowboy. Blond wavy hair hung loose to his shoulders. It was sexy as hell and made Rose swallow hard.

"So your name is Rose, is it?" The smooth tenor of his voice bounced around in her head. She licked her lips and blinked several times, trying to concentrate. Something about him was overpowering and oddly familiar.

"You aren't supposed to be in that body." She tossed her blade from hand to hand. "Why don't you come here and let me help you out of it?"

"You're right, I'm not." He pointed at her. "But you aren't supposed to be in that body, either."

It was true. The loaner body had been given to her to use as long as she was a Reaper. She pointed at him with her blade. "I was put in this body. The one you're in belongs to someone else."

"Yours belonged to someone else."

"She was brain dead and her spirit was already gone."

He shook his head. "You don't know that. She could have come back."

Why was she even with a Jumper?

His expression became conflicted as his jovial smile wavered and then his façade crumbled. He looked at her pleadingly. "Rose. Go. Please. Go and forget you ever saw me." His voice held a familiarity that struck her deep inside.

"I need your soul to get my boss off my ass."

He shook his head. "I'd do anything to help you, except that."

She lunged for him. Her blade arced downward so she could reap his soul from the human body. He moved to block her and a flash of light descended on her from above, knocking her away. Rose flipped to her feet and a tall, regal-looking female with long, blond hair and eyes like sunshine stood between her and the Jumper. The woman's all white ensemble was almost too blinding to look at. A Celestial.

Rose ran at her immortal enemy. The angel twirled sideways, her mighty white wing slicing toward Rose. Rose ducked and rolled on the ground under the wing and kicked the woman in the back. The angel growled and rolled on the ground before springing back to her feet.

Rose was nose to nose with the Jumper.

He smiled, revealing a dimple on his left cheek. "Impressive. I don't remember you being able to do stuff like that."

The angel used the momentary distraction to grab Rose by the back of her coat and fling her through the air. Rose sailed thirty yards and hit the ground with a crash. Corn stalks stabbed her through her coat. The air whooshed out of her lungs. The angel landed with her feet planted on either side of Rose's head. Her sunlight stare bore deep into Rose.

Rose laughed. "I don't have a soul to burn into, Angel. It was bought by someone else years ago."

"That's not a problem." The blond Barbie doll grasped Rose's shirt and pulled her close. At the same moment Rose struck out with her Reaper blade and slashed Barbie in the face. Golden blood gushed from the wound and she released her hold on Rose. The blood splashed the ground causing the corn stalks to sprout green leaves.

Slashing again with her blade, Rose caught the woman in the stomach. The Barbie cried out and spun away. Her powerful wings knocked Rose down but Rose hopped to her feet and prepared the killing blow.

Strong arms grabbed her from behind and lifted her off the ground.

"Stop," the Jumper yelled. He trembled as his wrists locked around her arms and their skin came in contact. A warm tingle pulsed through Rose and a hum sounded in the air. There was a crack of lighting and suddenly the two were thrust apart, both hit.

Rose's nose smashed into the freezing ground and gushed blood. The earth beneath her withered from her blood drops.

The angel stepped up to Rose, her sword at the ready.

"Don't!" The Jumper got to his feet and stepped between them. Lightning crackled closer in the sky.

The angel stalked closer. "You saw what happened when you touched her, Elijah. The others are on their way now. We should save her now."

"No! You'll leave her alone." Elijah stood his ground.

"What the hell is going on?" Rose wiped the blood from her nose and advanced on Gabriella. "Why are you protecting a Jumper? You're a Celestial. We're supposed to be on the same side in this. And why the hell are you trying to help me?" she asked Elijah.

"I do want to save him. But not in the way we angels usually save souls from you Reapers."

Rose tried to wrap her head around the fact that an angel helped a Jumper and it was the Jumper who tried to save *her*.

Gabriella looked between them and her mouth fell open. Her icy stare landed on Elijah and her face fell. "Aw hell,

Elijah really?" The disdain in her voice was more than apparent. "No! This is the one?"

Elijah took a step closer. "That's enough."

Gabriella looked Rose up and down. "You have to be kidding! She isn't even pretty."

"I said, that's enough." His entire body glowed with light, from the hairs on his head to the toes of his boots, as if someone had suddenly plugged him into an electrical socket.

"No way! You're an angel?" Rose's mouth fell open.

Lightening cracked closer illuminating the field and giving Rose the first full glimpse of Elijah's handsome face. A chord of recognition struck inside her and a memory bubbled just below the surface of her mind, but she couldn't grasp it.

Gabriella turned. "Storm's coming. You need to go, Elijah. I'll hold them off till you can make your escape."

Elijah's gaze caught Rose's. The memory of his touch shot a chill down her spine. Again she was struck with the feeling that she knew him from somewhere. But it wasn't possible. Celestials and Hellspawn didn't mix.

"I'm not going until you two promise not to reap or save each other." He looked between them.

At that moment the ground shook and a fissure opened up a foot from where Rose stood.

"Doesn't seem like that's going to be a problem," said Gabriella. "Looks like her daddy is calling."

Rose's jaw clenched. "He's not my father."

"Sorry, your master then." Gabriella crossed her arms over her chest.

"He may own my soul," said Rose. "But he doesn't own me."

Gabriella gave her a wide beauty queen smile. "Of course not."

The lightning flashed closer.

Gabriella's smile fell and she looked to Elijah. "Run."

He stared at Rose and she could swear he had a million things he wanted to tell her. Instead he took off in the opposite direction.

Gabriella watched another closer flash of lightning. "I may have promised not to hurt you because Elijah asked me not to, but my brothers and sisters are as likely to save you as they are to save him, so if I were you, I'd jump in that hole and go home." She looked at Rose and shook her head. "You don't deserve him."

Gabriella lifted into the air and sped into the storm.

What the hell just happened?

Rose's gaze followed Gabriella's form till it was lost in the clouds. She blew out a breath and looked down at the hole. If Lucifer was calling, he wasn't pleased.

She slid her blade into its holster and took a deep breath. What was the worst Lucifer would do to her? She stepped up to the hole and shivered. She was about to find out.

CHAPTER TWO
One Year Later

"Thank you." Rose grabbed the bag full of fast food goodness and shoved it into her messenger bag. She sipped the cup of cola big enough to quench the thirst of a dragon and walked out the door.

The muggy air cooled and moistened her face, making her glad she wore her leather coat. She didn't like being sticky. Walking five minutes out of her way to grab food that was bad for her was silly. But, it wouldn't kill her and she liked the way it tasted, so she didn't mind.

She sipped her cola and stopped in front of her shop on River Street. The stairs leading to the front door were packed with people like it was freebie day at a brothel. She sighed. Well, it was Halloween, what did she expect?

She walked around the corner and headed to the back entrance. A dark skinned man leaned on the wall by the door, stopping her in her tracks. Hazel eyes peered at her from under his black hoodie.

"Entrance is in the front." She held her keys tight in her fist, ready to strike if he tried anything.

The closer she got the more an unsettling vibe wafted off him. One hand was hidden within his hoodie and a bead of sweat trickled down his cheek. She stopped moving.

He looked down. "I apologize. I just need–"

She held up her palm. "Sorry, dude. We don't sell weed here. Or any other illegal drugs for that matter."

"No. I'm looking for something else."

Rose searched his face. It held pain, but not malice.

"Do I know you?" She continued toward the door. He backed up a step so she could get her key in the lock.

He stared at her for a moment. "I need angelbreath." He winced and grabbed his side.

She looked him up and down, wishing she was in her Reaper form so she could get a better read off him. "That's a powerful healer. Are you sure you know how to use it?"

He nodded and fell forward, leaning on the building for support. His limbs shook.

"Hey, you don't look so good. Are you sure you shouldn't just go to a doctor? Maybe an emergency room even?"

"No emergency room... just the angelbreath."

She was pretty sure the man needed a doctor, but magic users could be funny about having to resort to traditional medicine.

"I don't usually let people in this way, but since what you're looking for is closer to the back I'll let you this once. But next time you have to use the front door like everyone else."

He nodded and again she could swear she knew him, but with how many people came in and out of her store, it was hard to remember them all.

She pushed open the door, kicked a line in the salt, wiped at one of the wards and then pointed. "It's there on the right." She pulled her keys from the lock and let him in.

"Thank you." He stumbled in and she closed the door behind him. He staggered to the first shelf and gripped it.

She kicked the salt back in place. Balancing her drink in the crook of her arm, she pulled a wax stick from her pocket and retraced the ward onto the door.

"Is there anything I can do to help you?" She placed the stick back in her pocket.

He turned and his face looked conflicted and then he shook his head. "I think this should suffice. Thank you, Rose."

She sipped her soda and headed to the front of the store. The smell of herbs and magic skittered through the air. Immaculately organized shelves were lined with bottles, cans, books, papers, parchments, and every other occult item that anyone could possibly need.

She made it through row upon row of supplies, appreciating the last moments of quiet before she opened the floodgates for the next several hours.

Everything in its place, she knew every item by name and where it went. No one worked the store besides Rose and her occasional friend and Supreme Witch of the local coven, Adanna.

Rose checked the mahogany wooden gate and wards on the winding wrought iron staircase that lead up to the more ancient and dangerous books and parchments. No one went upstairs without her permission. No one.

She turned in a circle, surveying her small kingdom. Every polished wooden surface, every perfectly aligned book, every dust free bottle, they were all as they should be. She walked to the large, glass front, wrap around counter and set her bag down, along with her soda and food.

Someone rapped on the stained glass of the front door and she glanced over.

Out the large picture window with the words "Reap What You Sow" painted in black script, where her beautiful belladonna snaked up the side of her shop. The line of people now stretched down the block. She stepped to the window and surveyed her balcony greenhouse garden. Her plants were doing well, mostly due to her earth witch patrons who refused to see them wither from Rose's black thumb. Deadly nightshade, rosary peas, oleander, hemlock, angel trumpets, wolfsbane, and many other beautiful but deadly plants. Luckily for her, people knew better than to try to enter the small greenhouse or touch anything that grew there. Every surface of Rose's shop was warded, spelled, and even hexed in case someone got stupid.

Another louder knock rattled the door.

"Really?" She shook her head.

An angry looking, tall man in a crisp, gray suit stared at her. She looked over at the ancient three-foot iron and aged copper clock in the shape of a pentagram that hung on the wall. Two minutes till opening.

She took one last gulp of her cola and sauntered over to the extra narrow wooden door. She'd purposely designed it that way making it slightly harder on the crowds who felt it was their right to push their way into her store. Like the jackass who stood front and center right now.

She cocked an eyebrow and folded her arms over her chest. He glared at her for a moment more before his expression softened and he inclined his head.

The large clock intoned the hour; eleven a.m. She unlocked the front door and opened it a crack.

"Really, Alaster?" she asked. "You think that's a good way to get me to let you in?"

"I'm in a hurry." He took a step forward but bumped into an invisible barrier, which rippled with blue light like a stone thrown in a pond. He was lucky she hadn't double re-enforced it for Halloween or he'd be flat on his back.

"I'm sorry, what did you say?" she asked.

His jaw clenched and his Adam's apple bobbed up and down twice before he relaxed. "I apologize, Rose."

"Yeah, sure you do." She kicked a divide in the sea salt and sage that protected every outlet of her store and then laid her hands on either side of the doorframe over the wards and swiped them with her palms.

She stepped back and opened the floodgate. People streamed in, scattering like cockroaches in different directions. Good Morning, Halloween.

Rose thumbed through a vanity magazine and took a huge bite of her hamburger. There was a rattle and a screech from behind her.

"Shut up," she called over her shoulder to the black glass curio cabinet.

The cabinet rattled again and a green glow emanated from it for a moment, before it went dark again. She hated keeping dark magical items behind the counter, but the paranormals of the world had somehow designated her to be one of the keepers of dangerous and deadly books and objects. Things she couldn't put out on the floor for just anyone to pick up.

The bell tinkled over the door and three Goth-looking girls walked in and looked around. "Do you sell any black candles?"

Black candles were no joke. "What do you want them for?"

"We're having a séance tonight."

Rose looked the girls up and down. "Do you even know how to do that?"

"Of course," one of the girls huffed.

She was tempted to throw them out.

"Well?" asked the leader, a sarcastic frown on her face.

Let them learn their lesson the hard way. "Left shelf on the back wall." She smirked.

The girls mumbled under their breath and sauntered off.

Several customers brought their items to the counter and Rose rung them up.

"Do you have any more sage?" asked an older female.

"Let me look in the back for you."

She bagged everyone's items and then jumped over the counter and headed into the storeroom, passing through a heavy, navy blue, velvet curtain. Boxes stacked from floor to ceiling on the right side of the room left only a small path between them. It was a hoarder's dream. The left side of the storage area was partitioned off by an identical blue curtain. She pulled it aside, revealing the staircase leading to the basement. The coven would be arriving soon, so she wiped the wards off the stairs, allowing them free access.

She wove through the stacks of boxes till she reached her drying cabinet. Opening the door, she was struck by the scents of herbs and flowers. She found her last dozen bundles of sage and reminded herself to ask Adanna to bring her more.

She shut the cabinet and headed toward the front. She'd barely made it through the curtain when she was accosted by three women who grabbed every last bundle and then rushed off.

"Well, okay then."

She brushed off her clothes and jumped the counter again.

She rang up the customers. Some regulars, some not. Some running out before she could even say, "Have a good day." Most paranormals lacked the manners of even a bridge troll.

She was just finishing up with the last customer when the three Goth girls reappeared, laden with candles, herbs, and a parchment.

They looked at each other nervously and she rang the items up extra slow in an effort to ascertain what was going on.

"Fifty-two ninety-one," she announced.

The girls nodded and pulled out their wallets.

"Did you know there's a black guy slumped on the floor in the last aisle?" said one.

"What?" Alarm bells went off in her head. "Shit." The guy from the back door. She'd completely forgotten about him.

Rose rushed to the side of the counter, threw the separator up and raced down the last aisle. The bell tinkled for the front door, but she kept moving.

She found him splayed on the floor, face down. "Dammit." She knelt by his side and rolled him over. "Hey. Hey, wake up." She patted his cheek.

His eyes fluttered open and went from hazel to golden and then back again. "Rose."

Her heart pounded. A Jumper. "Elijah?"

He nodded. No wonder he knew her name.

She threw his arm over her shoulder and helped him into a seated position.

"How did you find me?" She glanced around while trying to get Elijah to his feet. A Jumper, especially a hurt one wasn't the norm for her. As a Reaper it was her job to play bounty hunter and send Jumpers to hell. They didn't usually come asking for help. Someone was on his tail.

"I've known all year." Blood dribbled down his chin.

She laced her fingers between his, got him up, and leaned him on the shelf. She needed to move him out of sight and get everyone out of the store. No! She needed to get *his* butt out of her store. She still bore the scar from her last visit to Lucifer's pad a year prior when she'd let him slip through her fingers.

"Did you take the angelbreath?" she asked.

He nodded. "The whole container."

"You gotta leave. Now. At sundown I'll have to reap you."

He gaze connected with hers. "I've missed you."

Her gut tightened and the feeling that she knew him from somewhere rushed through her again. All year she'd tried to forget him, but it was hard to forget an angel Jumper. Especially one who looked at her the way he did.

"Ah, damn. Come on." She half dragged, half carried him toward the front of the store. It was slow and he stumbled several times but they finally made it to the curtain separating the store from the back rooms. She glanced toward the front counter. The goths were gone. So was the merchandise. Stupid girls. They'd pay for stealing from her.

She used her hip to nudge the curtain aside and helped him through the box maze over to a large red chaise lounge. She threw him down on it. He grunted and tried to pull himself into a sitting position.

"What the hell happened to you?" She looked around and located a box of tissues. Pulling out several, she dabbed his mouth, wiping away the blood.

"Reapers."

She stopped dabbing. "Reapers plural?"

"Three."

"Reapers don't work together."

He gave her a winning smile. "I'm a special case." He coughed several times and then took in a deep breath.

"I bet you are. Are you cut?" She looked him over, but found no rips in his clothing.

"No. Just bashed around a bit. Human bodies are so fragile."

"You really should get to a hospital."

"Can't. If they try to open me up... They could get quite a surprise."

She blew out a breath and threw the bloody tissues in a box. "So what do we do?"

He squeezed her hand, sending her stomach twirling like a dandelion seed in the wind. She hadn't been able to touch people for over twenty years outside of Hellspawn. The slightest skin to skin contact was too icy, even for paranormals. The thought that her touch had no affect on him sent her mind whirling. Part of her expected them to be thrown apart again, but nothing more happened. What did it mean?

"I need somewhere to rest so I can heal the body."

She cleared her throat and pulled her hand away.

"You could've done that anywhere. Why did you come here?"

"Because you're warded against everything and no one can find me here."

"Oh, wonderful. And here I thought you just wanted to have another chance at our cat and mouse game."

"Darling, there is nothing I would enjoy more than having you chase me again."

Damn that arrogant smile of his. No matter what body he was in, she could still see it.

"Instead you're using the person who chased you, as a bodyguard from other beings chasing you. Interesting. What makes you think I won't reap you when night falls?"

His eyes sparkled and he gave her a crooked smile. "I trust you."

"I'm touched. So do you want to explain to me what—"

The bell rang over the entrance door and a chill swept through her like a bolt of ice.

Elijah's gaze moved to the curtain.

"Stay here," she whispered.

Rose set down the box of tissues and headed for the store. She'd just gotten the curtain parted when she ran smack into a solid chest. She looked up and up, until her gaze met a pair of blood red eyes.

"You want to step back, Drix?" She shoved him. The Hellguard more than gave her the creeps.

He took a step back and she let the curtain swing shut behind her. She looked between the Drix and Lamor, Satan's personal guard. Between them they were seven feet of muscle and malice. Of course, if one was the devil's personal pet, one had to be a tad more than just tough.

"Lucifer would like a word," said Drix.

"It's the middle of the day and Samhain at that."

The two stared at her through pitch black eyes. Drix licked his shark-like pointed teeth and gave her a smile that cut like razorblades.

"Are you saying no? Please say no." He raised a large inky black hand and cupped her cheek. "We didn't get to finish playing last time you said no."

She swatted his hand away and whipped out her Reaper blade from inside her coat. In a flurried spin she had it at his throat. Reaping may be only a nighttime gig, but that didn't mean the daylight hours left her defenseless.

Rose gave him her most winning smile. "I can reap you like the rest, lover. From what I understand it's not an experience even you would enjoy."

Drix growled deep in his chest. Not a rumble of vocal cords like dogs, but more like a vibration of anger from deep within.

"If you two are done with the foreplay," said Lamor. "Boss wants to see you. You have one hour."

"I'll be there." She sheathed her blade. "See ya soon, boys."

Drix stepped around her to the curtain and slammed into it.

"Sorry, hun, you'll have to go out the way you came, no shortcuts today. The Supreme will be here any minute to start the coven meeting."

Drix rumbled again and then turned with Lamor and headed down the aisle to the rear exit.

"Sorry," she called. "Not that way either."

The guards turned and she pointed to the front door. They lumbered past her spewing curses at her as they passed.

An elderly woman waited at the counter. "Are you done talking to yourself yet? I'd like to cash out."

Next to the register sat a pile of cash along with a pile of item tags. She glanced at the curtain and shoved both the cash and the item tags into the register. She'd have to settle up later. Right now she had to figure out what the hell to do with the angel in the storage room.

Fifteen minutes later Rose bit her nails and stared at the sleeping Elijah. He couldn't stay in the store, it was too risky. The coven would be here within an hour and she couldn't chance them finding an angel Jumper in her shop. Who knew what they'd do.

"Rose?" called a female from the other side of the boxes.

She raced around the boxes to find Adanna, the Supreme Witch and good friend, looking for her.

"There you are. I rang up a few people for you." A cute guy stood at Adanna's side. She'd never seen the guy before and he made the hairs on Rose's neck stand up.

"Thanks." Rose eyed the guy up and down.

"Oh, this is Anton. He's come to help me out." Adanna smiled and pushed her hair behind her ear.

Rose stuck out her hand. "I'm Rose."

Anton shook and sucked in a breath. Rose allowed her Reaper grip to spread its icy tendrils up his arm. A jolt of energy shot back at her. He held power beyond what he let on.

His face paled and he pulled away. "It's… nice to meet you," he said.

Adanna turned to him. "Can you wait downstairs for a minute?"

Anton nodded and headed down the dark staircase. When he was out of earshot Adanna turned to her. "What was that about?"

"Nothing." Rose filed it away to talk to Adanna about her new friend later. "Look, I need some help."

"What's wrong?"

"I need you to try and heal someone for me."

Adanna looked leery. "Who?"

"A friend. He's been hurt by Reapers."

"If Reapers hurt him, why is he your friend?"

Rose didn't want to explain. The less people who knew about him the better. Even Adanna. "It's a long story. Come on." She pulled Adanna by the sleeve, leading her back behind the boxes.

Adanna's eyes widened when she spotted Elijah. "He's cute."

"Can you help?"

Adanna scanned him. "Is he cut or is it something else?"

Rose bit her thumbnail. "It's all internal."

Adanna nodded. "Okay, I'll see what I can do." She walked over to Elijah and placed her hands on his abdomen. While chanting, she prodded him with her fingers. "Oh man, it's bad in there. They really did a number on him."

There was a flash of golden light and Elijah's body lurched from the lounge. Adanna fell on her butt and scrambled away.

"Crap, Rose! You should have told me he was an angel."

Rose rushed to Elijah and pressed his body onto the lounge. "Easy." Instinctively she reached out and smoothed his hair.

He relaxed and the light died away. His eyes remained shut and his breathing shallow but the blood stopped trickling from his mouth.

"He's not an angel," Rose lied.

"Sorry, but you can't lie to me." Adanna got to her feet and brushed herself off. "My magic won't work on an angel. They're different."

"It'll work. His body is human." She stroked a bead of sweat from his brow.

"But how– Oh no, Rose. Please don't tell me you're helping a Jumper."

Rose turned to Adanna and leveled her gaze. "Help me get him to my flat?"

Adanna shook her head. "Lucifer is going to marry you for sure this time."

Rose turned to look at Elijah again and something stirred inside her. "He's worth it. I can tell."

Adanna grabbed Elijah under one arm and Rose grabbed him under the other and together they dragged him to the back door and then out to the alley. A few feet from the back door to the shop Rose unlocked a second door covered in wards and sigils. They hauled him inside and Rose closed the door, pouring the warding mixture back over the threshold.

"Couch?" asked Adanna.

"My bed will be better."

Adanna gave her a knowing smile.

"Oh, please. It's only for him to heal."

Adanna nodded. "Sure it is."

They carried him up the stairs to the sparse bedroom and lay him on top of the comforter.

"Should we strip him down? He might be more comfortable that way," suggested Adanna.

Rose punched Adanna's arm. "Don't you have a coven to run?"

Adanna blew out a heavy breath. "Yeah, I do." She turned and headed out.

"Adanna," Rose called, never taking her eyes from Elijah.

"Yeah?"

"That new guy is powerful. Be careful."

"Thanks."

The stairs creaked as Adanna headed back to the shop. Rose's gut twisted with both dread and desire. His beautiful form lay splayed on the bed just ready for her to pounce on him.

Focus! She had to focus. What was wrong with her? Most likely the fact that she hadn't been with a man in more years than she could count and there was now a gorgeous one laying on her bed.

She bit her thumbnail. He looked comfortable enough, but maybe Adanna was right, maybe he'd be more comfortable naked. Angels like being naked, right?

"Oh for heaven's sake, seriously?" She turned and walked into her kitchen, pulled a beer from the fridge and threw the cap into the trash. She assumed she hadn't been much of a drinker as a human, but now that she couldn't die she'd picked up all kinds of nasty vices.

She gulped down the yeasty brew, her eyes on the muscular form of the man on her bed. She wiped her mouth with the back of her hand and sat the bottle on the counter.

"There's an angel in my bed." She laughed. Sounded like the title of a bad romance novel.

Crouching on the floor she hung her head in her hands. "Dammit, Rose, what are you doing?" There was an angel in her bed and her boss had summoned her back to hell. It couldn't be a coincidence. She should go down now, but she couldn't. The coven meeting was about to start and if the witches knew what was really under the carpet and table they sat at, they'd hop on their brooms and fly to another state.

She blew out a breath and stood. Her guest obviously wasn't going anywhere. The best thing she could do was wait till the coven meeting was over and then head to the basement.

Adanna called to say she'd closed up the store for the coven meeting and then Rose spent the next hour reinforcing the wards on her flat. She pulled out her ancient tome and wrote every single sigil she could find. If Reapers were looking for Elijah, there was a good chance angels weren't far behind. And she didn't want Barbie from the year before knocking on her door. It'd taken her weeks to recover from the last fight.

She walked into her bedroom and stared down at the angel wondering what he really looked like inside that gorgeous shell. He had to be even more amazing to behold.

"Hey?" She shook his shoulder. "Elijah?"

His eyes fluttered open. "Rose?" he croaked.

"I have to go see my boss. I'll be back soon. Don't leave."

He grabbed her hand, his eyes still glassy. She rubbed her thumb over his knuckles.

"You're safe here. I'll be back."

"Thank you." His words came out croaky and slurred.

"Stay here."

His hand dropped and his eyes closed.

She stared at his handsome face. Something about him called to her in a way no man had since she'd become a Reaper. She blew out a solemn breath. No! No way was she getting involved with a Jumper. Especially an angel Jumper!

CHAPTER THREE

Rose glanced at the clock as she entered her shop. It was almost three in the afternoon. Just a few more hours until trick-or-treaters would scour the streets looking for candy while she shepherded souls to and from hell for the night. A feat that always got old too fast.

She wasn't sure where she'd end up this time, but she sure hoped it would be somewhere fun, like Vegas or Los Angeles. Not much luck in that though, especially now that she was thirty minutes late getting to hell.

Adanna had already locked up and turned the sign to closed but she checked it anyway. Rose shored up the wards and headed to the basement. She stomped down the dark wooden staircase, past the pictures of all the Supremes, to the coven room door. Her stomach turned in knots as she entered. She had no idea what Lucifer wanted but it couldn't be a coincidence that Elijah showed up and less than an hour later so did the Hellguard.

"A Jumper? Nope haven't seen a Jumper." She pulled the ornate, unique chairs away from the large, black, wood table. "Angel, what angel?" He was the father of lies, how she would out lie him was anyone's guess. He'd questioned her to no end just one year ago about the Jumper she'd found. Fortunately, her lack of information had been from honesty last time. He and Drix had still enjoyed the hours of torturing her before coming to that conclusion.

She placed her palm atop the wooden table and it split in two, each long half separating and moving to either side of the room. The carpet underneath rolled away as well, revealing a large helltrap ward. A circle encased pentagram inside a pentagram. With every ward known on Earth etched into the free space in between the lines. It was one of ten permanent openings to hell on Earth. Each was highly protected from anyone exiting without Lucifer's knowledge. And opening one without permission was a one-way ticket to a place so low even she hadn't seen it.

She pulled out her Reaper blade and stabbed it into a slot in the floor. The stone surface shook and then split apart. Small sections twisted and fell away like puzzle pieces. She shoved her blade back in its holster.

A grinding sound emanated from within the widening hole and stone stairs expanded from the wall and spiraled up to where she waited, sending chills up her spine like icy fingers brushing her neck. She ground her teeth. Going down to hell was like tiny spiders crawling over one's mind.

"Not gonna get any easier." Rose took a deep breath and headed down the steps. Lanterns flickered on as she passed. The smell of Lucifer's favorite air freshener failed to mask the sulfur and brimstone that burned her nostrils Vanilla mixed with ash. Not the kind of scent one could just pick up at Bath and Body Works.

She continued down the narrow, cold, stone, spiral staircase, past portrait after smiling, smug portrait of Lucifer. He'd had one done every five years since he'd lived in hell. She passed them in a dizzying spiral until her stomach turned and her head spun.

"A zig zag staircase would be better than this carousel," she moaned.

Finally she came to the hallway. She stopped at the end, her eyes still going in circles. She leaned heavily on the wall and sucked in a deep breath, in an effort to clear the dizziness.

Cream damask wallpaper met black wainscoting half way up the walls. Beautiful sconces bestowed a gentle golden glow down the passage. At the end of the long corridor was a single ruby-red door and in front of it stood Drix and Lamor. Drix smiled widely at the sight of her.

She took a deep breath and stormed down the hallway, head held high. The further she walked the longer the hall became, like a funhouse. She stopped after several minutes and stared at Drix.

"Knock it off, jackass!"

Drix chuckled and she walked forward again. She closed in on him and his sinister grin deepened. "You're late."

"And you're still ugly, so I guess we all have our problems."

He ran a finger down her cheek to her throat. "I'll be more than happy to teach you a lesson in punctuality."

Rose grabbed his finger and jerked it backward. The digit popped as she broke it in half.

He sucked in a shuddering breath and shifted closer. "That tickled. I have nine more just waiting for your attention."

The door behind Drix opened. "Are you quite done?" asked a smooth voice.

Drix flexed his fingers and the broken digit cracked back into place. He stepped out of the way and Rose was met with the strikingly handsome face of Lucifer. His bright blue eyes glittered with mischief, but the grim set of his deep red lips told her he wasn't in the mood to play.

He held the door open for her and she entered the luxurious penthouse apartment. Lucifer spared no expense in making sure his home was as comfortable as possible. White marble floors stretched the entire open area, leading past a massive gourmet kitchen where Anna B. slaved over a savory meal that made Rose's stomach growl.

Anna B. lifted her heavy head and nodded at Rose. Her extra large bug-like eye stared unblinkingly. You'd think Lucifer had tortured her enough making her don an ill fitting white polyester cafeteria lady uniform and uncomfortable high heels. Who the heck wore high heels all day to serve food? Anywhere else Anna B. would have sent patrons running in fear. But Rose knew all to well the quiet, motherly spirit that resided inside the Hellspawn.

"Smells good, Anna B."

Anna B. gave her a lopsided grin and went back to stirring.

Rose followed Lucifer through his living room. A polar bear rug stared at her, ready to gobble her up. Lucifer crossed to the picture window that wrapped the entire living space and beckoned her over.

Rose swallowed the boulder-sized lump in her throat and stepped up to the floor-to-ceiling window and looked out over the expanse beyond.

If you looked straight out the window, an artificial sun hung lower in the sky exactly where it would be topside.

But it was what was happening below the horizon that made Rose want to race back to her apartment like she was being pursued by hellhounds. She tried not to look but it was impossible to tear her gaze away. Like the time a tarantula had crept near her in a graveyard and she'd tried so hard to not crush it with her shoe. Inevitably, she gave into the impulse and smashed it.

She breathed deep and looked down. Souls, billions of them, waited their turn in a never ending line that had no beginning and no end. Simply waiting and waiting and waiting until it was his turn to relive his own personal hell and then get back in line to do it all over again. As if that wasn't bad enough, all the TVs down there projected everyone else's personal hells to witness like the world's most terrifying reality show.

She'd been down there once. Only once. It was a living horror movie.

A wash of panic swept over her limbs as a scream clawed its way up the back of her throat and threatened to unleash.

"This is my kingdom, little sister. All that you see is mine." Rose glanced over at Lucifer. A contented smile played at the corners of his mouth and a glass of red wine appeared in his hand. He unbuttoned his lavishly expensive gray suit jacket and stuck one hand in his pocket. A swirl of dark chest hair escaped his open white collared shirt. A black angular tattoo of a ward she didn't recognize peeked out from his left peck.

He sipped the wine, staining his soft lips. He stared out the window. "I like what I have," he said.

From the look of him, one would think Lucifer was a billionaire playboy. No horns, no tail, Lucifer was the Prince of Deception, the master manipulator. To be that, one had to be sexy and charming. Sexy people always got what they wanted.

She'd learned a long time ago that it was best to be in a good mood when dealing with Lucifer.

She tried to keep her gaze on the horizon as she waited. He sipped from his glass every minute or so till it was finally finished and then disappeared.

"A Reaper is missing," he said. "And the Jumper you let escape last Samhain is responsible."

Rose bit the inside of her cheek. It wasn't her fault Elijah had gotten away, but arguing equaled pain where Lucifer was concerned. So she took the reprimand.

"I want you to find him and bring him to me." Lucifer turned and looked directly at her. His icy stare commanded her attention.

She swallowed and turned to face him. His tanned skinned stood out against his bronze colored hair. He held a casual air, but with Lucifer, he was never casual, at least not that she'd seen.

"Where do I find him?" she asked.

Lucifer chuckled and stroked her cheek with his manicured hand. "Little sister, if I knew that I wouldn't need you, now would I?"

"True. But do you even know where I start?"

"He's hidden from me. Cloaked somehow. That tells me he's warded. I suggest you start looking anywhere that might have a ward." He dug into his pocket and pulled out a silver amulet. "This'll help you get around faster. No soul duty for you tonight. I want you to start as soon as the sun goes down."

She took the heavy piece of metal and slung it around her neck.

He stepped in so close, their bodies almost touched. He scanned her face and then leaned in and sniffed her hair.

"The invitation still stands, you know. I do so wish you'd be my bride for a decade. You'd have so much more fun in my bed than as a Reaper." He ran a finger over her collarbone and licked his lips.

Rose had to admit that his seduction was a most tempting offer. If he'd been any other man in the world she would have let him take her right there on his bear rug. His broad shoulders and smoldering eyes were enough to make a woman go weak in the knees. But Lucifer wasn't someone one wanted to tangle with. He chewed women up and spat them out for his own selfish pleasure.

"I might have loved you, Rose." His hand caressed her neck. "I still could."

He hadn't been this nice to her since their first meeting. It made the alarm in her head chime like cathedral bells. She tried to swallow the bile that threatened to spew all over his crisp business suit.

"Thank you," she managed. "But I just don't think I could get used to the view."

His eyes flickered red and then blue again. He smiled and backed away. "Ah, well, you're the best Reaper I have now anyway." He rubbed his stubbly chin and strode toward the kitchen. "Find him. Bring him and your debt will be fulfilled."

Rose's heart thumped like a million rabbits running around in her chest. "What?"

He paused. "If you bring me the Jumper, I'll hold your sentence fulfilled and set you free."

Was he serious? She still had thirty-five years left.

"Go. The sun sets soon." He removed his coat and slung it over a barstool. Anna B. set a crystal plate in front of him and he removed his cufflinks and rolled up his sleeves.

She didn't need to be told twice. Rose grabbed the amulet tight in her fist. A small pin pricked her in the middle of her palm. "Reap What You Sow," she said.

She was pulled upward, through the ceiling higher and higher till her hands and knees hit the floor of the basement. The seal had closed and the carpet and table had rolled back in place.

Rose sucked in a deep breath and got shakily to her feet. If she turned Elijah in, she'd move on. She pushed the chairs back to the table, one by one.

A million questions swirled in her mind. And she intended to get answers.

CHAPTER FOUR

Rose trudged up the stairs to her studio flat as the sun began to set. The sounds of water running perked her ears. She stood in her kitchen and looked toward her bedroom. Elijah no longer lay on her bed, but his clothing and shoes sat in a heap on her floor and steam poured out of her bathroom.

She opened the fridge. Inside sat a lonely box of herbs from a member of the coven, a four pack of beer and a hard-boiled egg. Her stomach grumbled. She needed to eat before the sun went down fully and she was no longer corporeal. She closed the fridge and walked into the bedroom. The water stopped in the bathroom. She lifted her hand to knock, but before she could, the door opened and Elijah stood bare chested, with only a towel wrapped around his waist.

They stared at each other for a minute. His deep fawn colored skin rippled with hard packed muscles underneath a light swirl of black hair. His hazel eyes contrasted against his dark skin in an amazing array of color.

"Hey," he said.

"Hi," she managed. Her body thrummed with desire at the sight of him. It'd been years since she'd been held by a man. When one's very touch caused icy pain to shoot through someone, it tended to be a turn off in the sex department.

"I'm sorry I used all your hot water."

"Not a problem. I already showered."

He smiled a warm, sheepish smile that rocked her to the core.

"So I was going to go get some food–"

"I'm starving."

"Okay, cool." She broke eye contact and stepped toward the door. "I'll be back in a few."

"I'll be here."

She glanced back to see him watching her walk away. She wanted to tell him to stay perfectly as he was, but, instead she shook her head, cursed her hormones, and headed for the door.

Ten minutes later Rose returned, food in hand. There was only a half an hour left till sundown. Kids had already begun to stream into the streets. Ghost walks were already lining up and the buzz coming from the cemetery two blocks away told her a portal was ready to open the flood gates and let the spirits out for the night.

She checked and rechecked the wards and sigils on her store and then headed up to the kitchen. The apartment was eerily quiet. She slowed her steps and set the burgers and fries on the small table. She glanced around but there was no Elijah.

"Hello?" she called. "Elijah? Food's ready."

No answer.

Her chest squeezed and her pulse kicked up. She pulled her Reaper blade from its holster and headed to the bedroom. She glanced around and tiptoed toward the bathroom. There was a creak from inside. She switched her stance and headed for the door.

Her heartbeat pounded in her ears. She pulled the door open the same moment someone stepped out. She was propelled backward in a tangle of arms and legs, onto her bed.

"Whoa! Hey!" said Elijah, his face inches from hers. "I thought we were friends." He stared at her Reaper blade. The weight of his hipbones on hers sent a thrill through her. His lean muscular body pressed her down into the plush comforter.

"Elijah!" She closed her eyes and sighed. "Freak. I called you but you didn't answer. I had no idea what I'd find in there."

"Sorry. I was cleaning up the mess I made. I didn't mean to knock you down." His gaze searched her face, his lips inches from hers.

Her brain fogged with desire, making it hard to think straight. "Um… there's food."

"Right. Sorry." He stood, leaving her body too cool, solitary, and alone.

She sheathed her Reaper blade and closed her eyes. This was stupid. She shouldn't even be helping him, let alone allowing him to lie all over her like a personal electric blanket. Lucifer wanted him. If she turned him in, she was free. No more reaping. No more torture. No more death.

"Which burger is mine?" he called.

"They're both the same." She sat up. Get answers and then turn him in. That's what she had to do. He wasn't supposed to be in that body anyway.

She joined him at the small table.

He'd already dug into his food.

She picked at hers.

"So you were attacked by three Reapers, huh?" Subtle.

He stopped chewing and looked up. He took a giant swig of soda and nodded. "I was just hanging out, minding my own business, and they popped up out of nowhere."

"No Gabriella to help you out?"

His expression darkened. "Do you want me to go?"

"No, I want to know what the hell is going on. You were attacked by three Reapers. One of them is missing, yet you survived. How's that possible?"

"He's not missing."

"What?"

"The Reaper, Timothy. He's not missing, he's moved on."

"Moved on? What do you mean moved on? Reapers don't move on without Lucifer's permission and he never gives that permission."

"They can move on but they have to choose to."

She snorted. "If it was that easy, every Reaper would've moved on by now."

"Really? After what you've done. The things you've been forced to do by your boss, would you really choose to move on right now? To face judgment?"

She swallowed. He was right. Her penance wasn't yet complete for the unforgivable act she'd committed right before dying. She couldn't remember what that act was, but she remembered how it felt.

"How do you know all this?" She swigged her soda.

"I'm an angel."

Rose snorted and gulped her soda. "Yeah, you *were* an angel. Now you're just a Jumper."

Elijah sat down his burger and stood. He closed his eyes and looked as if he were praying. Slowly his entire body filled with light. The mortal body that housed him fell away and she saw him for who he truly was. She saw the soul within. He was amazing. A Greek god complete with eight packed abs, chiseled chest, and powerful, muscular thighs. His wheat colored wavy hair would have even made Fabio cringe in shame. He stared at her through bright aquamarine eyes.

"Wow. You're seriously hot." She clapped her hand over her mouth.

He chuckled and his light faded, but she could still see his true form.

She had so many questions for him. "How can I still see the real you?"

"Because I'm letting you."

"And *your* body is..."

"Somewhere safe."

"So what's the deal? Why is everyone after you?"

He looked away. "I've... gone rogue."

"What do you mean?"

"I mean I don't play by the rules anymore. I help those who need help. I don't wait in hopes that another human will help. Humanity has fallen too far for that. But most of all, I don't take orders."

"And so you were what? Cast out?"

His eyes turned hard. "I left."

She nodded. "Your Father must not be very happy."

"Yes, *our* Father is not too happy. I have a few brothers and sisters, like Gabriella, who believe as I do. They try to help or protect me as much as possible, but they have their own problems right now."

"So you've been living here, on Earth this entire last year?"

"Longer than that." He sat down and bit into his hamburger.

"Doing what? How do you live? Eat? Where do you sleep?"

He shrugged. "I travel around the world helping people."

"Quite the saint." She swirled a fry in ketchup.

"And I spend a lot of time here in Savannah."

Her heart thundered. "Here? Why?"

"For you." His angelic gaze bore into her, making her insides turn to gelatin.

"Me?" she croaked.

He held out his hand and without thinking she slipped her palm onto his. Again his touch caused her body to tingle all the way down to her toes. The action so natural, it was like they'd done it a thousand times before.

"Because you're special. You should never have been made a Reaper. You weren't meant to be one. You should have been like me, an angel."

She snorted. "An avenging angel maybe."

"No." He pulled her to her feet and stepped close. "I've watched you for the last year. Seen you with the witches and with other people. I see how it pains you to reap them. How you only want to go back to the way things were."

His hand caressed her cheek and she focused on his plump lips.

"How can you touch me and not feel my Reaper's curse?"

His body compressed into hers and his arousal pushed hard and long against the flat of her stomach.

"I don't know," he whispered. "How is it you can make me feel something besides apathy for the first time in a thousand years."

Her mind fogged with desire. "My boss wants me to bring you in. He said if I do, he'll set me free."

His eyes flickered for a moment and then he ran a gentle thumb over her bottom lip. "I'm right here. Your blade is inches away. Reap my soul. Take me to him. Set yourself free."

Her fingers twitched at the thought. To be free. No longer at Lucifer's beck and call. No more watching the light go out of people's eyes as their souls fade. No more silent pleas that they would see their loved ones in heaven, while she knew where they were really going. Down into the line.

But the way Elijah looked at her. No one had looked at her that way in so long. Even Lucifer didn't look at her that way.

He leaned in close and the scent of her soap wafted off his skin.

"Elijah–"

He pressed his lips to hers, soft as a whispered promise and twisted his fingers in the hair at the base of her neck. Their lips parted and tongues met in a twirl of heat. She wrapped her arms around him and pulled his body into hers. The contact lit her up inside.

Too long, it'd been too long.

She pushed the hoodie from his shoulders and he lifted his arms as she slid his T-shirt off. She kissed over his chest, reveling in the feel of his skin on her lips. He drove her duster to the floor and unstrapped her Reaper blade with one hand. It clattered to the linoleum as he hefted her up, and she wrapped her legs around his trim waist.

Their lips met again and he carried her into her bedroom, his hands on her rear. In a flurry of movement they stripped their clothes off and he lay back on the bed, covering her body with his.

She moved her hands up and down the firm plains of his body. The contours of his muscles, the silky fine hairs that covered his chest and trailed downward, were a delight to her senses. She'd not realized how much she missed touching another person till then. He kissed his way across her chest nipping at her erect buds. Her body flushed with heat, making her thighs tingle. She trailed her fingers down his happy trail, and finding him hard, she wrapped her fingers around the length of him and stroked his need. His head fell to her shoulder and he moaned her name as he kissed her flesh.

His hand moved between her thighs, teasing her sensitive nub and making her suck in a sharp breath.

She stopped moving suddenly and he looked at her. "What's wrong?"

All desire fled from her as reality crashed down around her like a crumbling pile of cinder block. "Do we... I mean... can you have children?"

He stared at her for a minute. His mouth opened and closed. "Yes," he finally said. "I can. And this mortal body can."

"I assume this one can, too," she said.

His face fell onto her chest and she let go of him, digging her hands into her hair. All dressed up and nowhere to go. After several seconds of silence, he kissed her breasts in turn and then trailed kisses down her side to the flat of her stomach.

"I take it you don't have any protection?" she asked.

He chuckled. "It's been a long time. Really long. I don't even think condoms were invented the last time I was with a woman." He looked up at her. "You don't either?"

She shook her head. "My touch is usually protection enough."

They stared at each other and then both burst out laughing. What more could they do?

"I could still–"

"No," he said. "I didn't want this because I wanted to get off. I want you." He kissed her softly. "It's been you forever."

Her body quacked at the need that wound tight inside her. "I could head out to get some condoms and come back."

He shook his head. "The sun'll be down any minute."

"Well, this sucks."

He rolled off her and pulled her into his arms. "Sure does. I've wanted to make love to you for a long time."

"Really?" She smiled and laid her head on his chest, drawing a circle around his nipple. "Well I haven't thought about you once in the last year."

"Oh really?"

"Nope," she lied. Being held by him felt better than anything since becoming a Reaper. Fact was, she had thought about him. Every single day since they'd met the year before. She'd searched for him dozens of times in the customers that came to her store or a stranger on the street and in every graveyard.

"I know you've thought about me."

"Conceited much?" She laughed and looked into his eyes. "How?"

His expression grew serious. "Because I feel it. I feel you."

He kissed her again. Gentle and tender, allowing his tongue to lap at her mouth. Her body heated again and she pulled away.

"What is this?" she asked. "You and me? Mortal enemies, yet we can touch without killing each other. Is it because we're both housed in human bodies?"

He shook his head. "It's bigger."

"Bigger like what?"

He licked his lip. "I don't know."

She kissed his chest and ran her tongue over his skin. He moaned and arched toward her touch. She wanted to feel him inside her so badly she'd even be willing to stand in the line in hell to have him.

He pulled her mouth up to meet his and ran his hands down to the small of her back. Lifting one of her legs he wrapped it around his waist, cupping her rear and kneading her flesh.

His tongue plunged into her mouth hard.

"Elijah." She panted. "I want you."

He stopped moving and kissed the tip of her nose. "I want you, too. But who knows what would happen if you got pregnant."

She groaned. "Well, there's a buzz kill."

"Sorry." He pulled her close. "Guess I need to stop riling you up."

She looked at the clock. "The sun will be down in a few. My skeletal features and pitch black eyes should be enough to dampen your enthusiasm." Painfully she extricated herself from his grip and slid her panties on. "Will you be here when I get back?"

"I should go. I don't want you to get in more trouble."

She laughed. "Seriously? My boss is Satan. I killed his dog. I'm always in trouble."

He raised an eyebrow. "You killed a hellhound?"

"The damn thing wouldn't stop humping my leg."

He smiled. "Remind me to never do that."

She'd just clasped her bra when the first frosty grip of the Reaper change hit her. She stood and leaned on the wall for support. It shot through her heart, spreading outward through her veins, buckling her knees.

"Rose." Elijah jumped from the bed.

She held out her hand. "It's okay. It's just the change. I'm used to it." An icicle punched her gut like being stabbed with a saber. "Okay I lied. I'm not used to it."

He knelt next to her, took her hand in his and placed his other hand on top. Warmth trickled up her arm, spreading over her body like a liquid blanket, removing the worst of the pain. She sucked in a deep breath and locked eyes with him.

He smiled and held her hand as the change continued to take over. Her body turned glacial and her vision morphed into to the unusual soul searching reddish haze.

"Does that happen every night?" he asked.

She nodded and looked away, self conscious of her eyes. "Wouldn't be any fun if it didn't hurt."

He pulled her chin up so she met his gaze and then kissed her. "It isn't you," he said.

A thought struck her. "You don't even know what I really look like. You just see this body. I can't show you my soul the way you show me."

"Not true. I see what's inside. I've seen your soul since the first time we touched. Your soul is as amazing as the rest of you." A sly grin spread across his face. "I hope you like what you see."

She chuckled. "Every last inch. This body you're in pales in comparison. Which is saying a lot because it's pretty damn fine."

Her Reaper blade cast an icy glow through the kitchen and into the bedroom. "I have to go."

He nodded.

"Will you be here?"

"I'll always be here."

CHAPTER FIVE

Rose stepped over the threshold of her apartment into the alleyway; careful not to disturb the salt line. A heavy hand fell on her arm. She slammed the door shut and ripped her blade from its sheath before spinning and holding it to Drix's dark throat.

"What do you want?"

"Let me in and I'll show you." His pitch eyes gleamed in the moonlight.

She stepped away in disgust. "Not on your life."

He glanced at the door. "Lots of wards on your house."

"I don't like visitors. Again, why are you here?"

"Boss wants me to help you track the Jumper."

"I don't need a babysitter."

"Considering your last meeting with this Jumper, I'd say you do."

Rose cursed loudly and swung her blade several times. "Fine, let's go."

"Where?"

"We'll start in the cemetery where I found him last time."

Rose sheathed her blade and then squeezed the amulet Lucifer had given her. She grabbed onto Drix's sleeve. "Nampa, Idaho cemetery."

Together they moved through space and time faster than thought. She used the opportunity to punch Drix in the gut several times, on accident.

They slammed to the ground and Drix fell to his knees but Rose stayed on her feet. She leaned on a headstone and took a deep breath. All around spirits floated out of the cemetery toward the streets. Several waved as they passed.

"Where did you see him?" asked Drix.

Rose glanced around and located the spot where she'd seen Elijah the year prior. She spotted the row of headstones and walked to it.

"There." She pointed.

Drix crouched and wiped the leaves and debris from the piece of marble set into the ground. "Rose Anna Dawson."

Rose sucked in a sharp breath and stared at the stone. Born 1972. Died 1992. A memory stirred.

She was driving in a car. Laughing, she glanced at the person in the passenger seat. A handsome guy with long, wavy, blond hair and striking blue eyes. Elijah. She turned back to look out the windshield. A little girl rolled her bike onto the road. A screech of brakes. The smell of pavement. A shower of glass.

Rose stumbled.

"What?" asked Drix. "You know her?"

Rose swallowed hard and tried to calm her pounding heart. "Nope."

He stood and looked around. "Well, it doesn't look like he's here."

"Why does Lucifer want this Jumper so bad?" Rose tried to keep her voice calm but the tremble of her hand wasn't so easily concealed.

Drix eyed her. "Not my place to question. Yours either."

There was a flash of light and a clap of thunder. The spirits in the cemetery scattered like smoke on the wind. The light focused on them like a spotlight.

"Well, what have we here? Two of Satan's pets?" Gabriella hovered five feet off the ground in all her glory, her bright, white wings spread wide.

Rose groaned. "What the hell do you want?"

"Same as you looks like." Gabriella tossed her gigantic holy sword from one hand to the other.

"Well, guess we're both disappointed."

"Are we?" Gabriella stared at her.

Rose's stomach lurched. "I don't follow."

"Don't you?" She lifted an eyebrow.

Rose's gaze slid sideways to Drix. How did the angel know she'd been with Elijah?

"I think I'll just wait and see where you pop up again," said Gabriella. "He and I have business to discuss."

"What's the haloed harpy jabbering about?" asked Drix.

"She's afraid we're gonna find the Jumper first."

"We are. And she can't have him." Drix rushed Gabriella.

Gabriella wielded her holy sword and the two met in a battle of dark and light. Drix whipped out the black katana strapped to his back. Gabriella met the weapon with precision. Rose held tight to her Reaper blade, unsure if or who to help. She wanted to warn Elijah, but if she ran and Drix won, he'd show up at her door, with the boss.

Drix kicked Gabriella in the stomach. She flew back and slammed to the ground. He jumped on top of her, but Gabriella thrust with her sword at the last second and ran him through.

"Damn," said Rose.

Black blood dripped down Gabriella's sword, staining her white jumpsuit. Drix's body exploded into a million shreds of black goo and showered the ground killing all the grass in a ten foot area. Drix was immortal, but even Hellspawn weren't immune to a holy weapon.

Gabriella flipped to her feet and brushed herself off. "Well, that was fun. Except for him ruining my outfit. Now, where were we?"

"Why do you want him?"

"You're a smart girl. Figure it out."

"Are you on his side?"

Gabriella hung her head and blew out a breath. "I'm not on anyone's side. But that doesn't mean I want to see Eli hurt. He's my brother. And I'll be damned if I'll let him go down for a Reaper."

The words stung like a chainmail glove to the cheek. "What do I have to do with anything?"

Gabriella backed away. "Nothing. Forget it."

Rose advanced. "Tell me!"

"Look." Gabriella stopped. "It's not my place. You forgot your human life, chose to be a Reaper, just do that okay. And do Elijah a favor. Tell him to get lost and find me."

Gabriella's wings spread out full and pearly white. She took to the sky in a whirl of wind that almost bowled Rose over.

The spirits had long since fled. The only sound that remained was the zap and crackle of the portal on the other side of the cemetery. She stared at it, confusion swirling in her mind. Another Reaper waved to her from across the expanse.

Rose shook her head. Just another typical Samhain.

CHAPTER SIX

Rose unlocked her front door and walked inside. It was almost dawn. She'd spent the entire night going from place to place in case she was being tracked. She'd spent an hour in Paris on top of the Eiffel Tower, trying to figure out what was going on.

She reaped half a dozen souls to hell and still had time to stop at an all night convenience store for a Super Gulp.

She walked up the steps, sore and exhausted.

Elijah stood in the kitchen. "Hey."

She nodded, unanswered questions swimming around her like a thick school of fish.

"How was your night?" His voice held concern.

"Interesting." She sipped her soda.

"How so?" He leaned against the doorjamb to the bedroom, his arms crossed.

"I went back to where we met." She scooted past him into her bedroom. "Tried to pretend I was looking for you."

"Smart."

She laid her leather duster on the bed, unstrapped her Reaper blade, and then walked to her wardrobe and hung it inside. Sitting on the end of her bed, she untied her boots.

"You know, it was funny. I took a look at the headstone you'd been crouched by when I spotted you. It was for a woman named Rose Anna Dawson."

He shifted his position and his gaze darted sideways. "You don't say?"

She stared at him till she caught his gaze again. "Gabriella says 'hi' and to find her. She also said she didn't want to see you go down for a Reaper. What'd she mean?"

He ran his palm over his head. "I should go."

"You owe me an explanation."

"I never should have come. I'm sorry." He turned.

She raced to the door and shoved him in the chest. "You aren't going anywhere till you fess up. I lost my memory when I lost my life and became a Reaper, but that grave. That Rose Anna Dawson, it gave me flashes."

He refused to meet her eye.

"You know, don't you? You know who I am."

"Please don't do this."

"Did you know me before I was a Reaper?" She pushed him into the kitchen wall. "Tell me!"

"I know you, okay?" he yelled.

"How?"

"Because…" He threw his hands over his face.

"Because what?"

"Because I was your guardian angel! I was there and told not to interfere and you died."

She backed away. "You… were my angel?"

He hit his head on the wall. "It's dangerous. It's why I kept away and haven't looked for you. I didn't know you were going to be in the cemetery last year. The coincidence was overwhelming. I didn't realize it was you at first, but when you touched me I saw your soul."

"What does it matter? You did your job. You didn't interfere. I died."

He stared at her and then touched her face. "I broke the rules."

"But you just said you didn't save me."

"Not by letting you die. By falling in love with you."

"I'm sorry?"

"Do you really want to know?"

Did she? She nodded.

He blew out a breath and reached for her breast.

She swatted his hand away. "Uh, hello?"

He snickered. "I'm going to show you." He placed his palm over her breast. A white light filled her vision and then she was flooded with memories, like flashes at lightning speed. Their first meeting in the park. Going to the movies. Dinner at a beautiful restaurant. Snuggling on her couch. And dozens upon dozens of other memories of them together. More than six months of memories.

He pulled away and she fell forward. He grabbed her arm, steadying her.

"Us. Together. You and me."

"Yeah."

The memories stormed through her mind again, bombarding her. "Months and months."

"I'd been your guardian angel since your mom died when you were seventeen. I didn't show myself to you till a year before you died. I couldn't hold back anymore. I knew it was forbidden, but I loved you already. I just wanted to be with you. In your life."

"You were in the car with me when I hit that little girl on the bike."

His eyes held immeasurable pain and guilt. "It was my fault. I'd finally told you I loved you. You looked over at me." He fell silent and gazed off into the distance. "I held you while you bled out. I wanted to intervene, but one of my brothers showed up. He wouldn't let me and then while we argued your soul slipped away. I was too late to grab you before a Reaper took hold and dragged you down. I tried to save you. If I'd just held on to you a little bit longer you would've stayed with me."

All the memories swirled in her head and she was flooded with feelings of love, desire, and hope. Things he'd given to her.

She stepped up to him and melted into his frame. Every hard line and flat plane etched into her memory. From the dip of his shoulder joint where she used to lay her head, to the sharply cut V of his hipbones. They were different on the new body he inhabited, but in his arms, it all felt completely familiar anyway. Pressed against him she saw past the body to the soul inside. She saw him. Her Elijah.

"You gave up everything for me."

He cupped her face in his palms. "I'd do it again a thousand times over. In all of my lifetime I've never felt for another the way I feel for you. I only wish I'd held on to you that day and not let go. Your heart was pure. You wouldn't have been held accountable. God would have forgiven you."

"Then why am I Reaper?"

"Because Lucifer beguiled you and you accepted his words and took on the role of Reaper." His eyes held immeasurable pain. "Now I spend every day making sure the same thing doesn't happen to others. I'll never forgive myself for what happened to you."

She kissed him lightly. "It wasn't your fault. I made my choice."

He ran his fingers through the length of her hair and kissed her forehead, her eyelids, her cheek. "I don't ever want to lose you again, Rose."

"You won't." His voice was a soothing wash of warm water over her skin. The sound that brought her home and made her feel safe.

She kissed him and their lips met in a soft blending that had her head spinning and her knees weak.

"Wait." She pushed away from him. "We were together for six months?"

"A bit more, but yes."

She wracked her mind, scrolling through the memories of him. "But we've never had sex."

He gave her a roguish smile. "I told you I'd been waiting a long time for you."

"I think we've both waited long enough." She kissed him hard and he twisted his hands in her hair. Her lips parted as heat surged between their bodies and their tongues tangled in a mixture of need and love.

He ripped her shirt over her head and kissed down the side of her neck to the tops of her breasts. Unclasping her bra, he suckled her sensitive skin.

"Elijah," she moaned. She grasped his jeans and fiddled with the button and zipper, trying to get them off.

She pushed them to the floor with her foot and he kissed his way down her torso to her belly button and stripped off her pants and panties. Standing once more, he wrapped his arms around her waist and hefted her off the floor, his mouth meeting hers once more. The scent of him swirled around her, flooding her with need.

He carried her to the bed, lay her down and then flung his boxer briefs to the floor. She kissed him hard and he slid his hand down between her thighs, teasing her flesh and making her arch against him.

"Rose. I can't hold back this time. I have to be inside you."

She nodded and felt around on the bed for her duster. "Pocket," she moaned as his arousal slid down her belly and poised to enter her.

"What?"

She tried to make her brain form coherent sentences. "I stopped at the store. In my pocket." She gripped him tight and stroked him.

"Stop." He kissed her. "You have to stop or I won't make it."

She chuckled and he ripped a small box from her duster pocket and tore it open. Condoms flew everywhere. He grabbed one by her head, bit it open and rolled it on. Before she could speak, he thrust inside her.

She gasped and cried his name. He kissed her hard and thrust again. Her body shuddered. His rhythm picked up and her core wound tight. She flipped him on his back and leaned down to kiss him again. She rode him, pushing herself back and forth.

He grabbed her hips, helping her, and Rose threw her head back, reveling in the feel of him. He moaned her name and she ground into him harder and faster. Tingles raced up her spine and down her thighs. Her entire body grew sensitive. He spread her thighs wider and drove in deeper. She sucked in a breath and then she spiraled down, down, downward, pulled by ecstasy to that nameless place she couldn't explain. Her breathing stopped and the sensations raced through her. Her muscles pulling tight around him, griping him and bringing him over the edge as well.

After a minute she fell on top of him, completely spent. He tilted her chin and kissed her softly with his full lips.

"That was so worth waiting for," he murmured.

"Yeah." She focused on breathing. "It was."

He looked deep into her eyes and the repercussions of what they'd done slammed into her.

"What do we do now?" she asked.

He smiled. "Well I don't know about you, but I plan on making love to you over and over and over. Then maybe getting some sleep."

She smiled back. "I like that plan."

She let all doubts slip from her mind. She already belonged to hell. She'd deal with the repercussions later.

The sound of breaking glass pulled Rose from her sleep. She sat up suddenly and glanced around. The room had grown dark and she was alone. Crap! She'd slept all day.

Her Reaper sight pulled everything into red hot focus. Keeping the sheet wrapped around her, she ran for her blade and wielded it in front of her. Heavy footsteps pounded up her stairs.

She scanned the room for Elijah, but both he and his clothes were gone. She shifted from foot to foot waiting for the intruder to enter her kitchen,. The intruder neared her bedroom door. She jumped into the kitchen and swung. The man caught the blade in his hand, his red eyes glowing. *Lucifer.*

He scanned her up and down and broke into a wide grin. "If I'd known you slept naked, I'd have come by sooner."

She pulled her blade from his grasp. "What are you doing here and how did you get in?"

His eyes flashed and then he chuckled. "Really, my dear? You think those wards can keep *me* out? There's only one person who can keep me out and I don't think He'll be willing to lend you His power."

Her heart pounded. Elijah could return any second. "What can I do for you?"

"Drix didn't come home last night. Thought you might know something about that."

"An angel got him."

Lucifer's face hardened. "Who?"

"A blond Barbie doll. I don't know her name."

Lucifer swore and fire flew from his fingertips, hitting her cabinets. Rose stomped over and threw a glass of water on the smoldering wood, smoke filling her nostrils.

"Look, I'm sorry about Drix, but you never said he was my responsibility."

Lucifer was in front of her in a blink. "What did the angel say to you?"

Her mind worked fast deciding what to tell him. "She was looking for the Jumper, too."

Lucifer shrugged. "They want his soul as much as I do."

"But why? What's so special about this one?" She held her breath. Would he really tell her?

"Nothing, except for the fact that he's saved two Reapers and got Drix obliterated as well. I have a special place in my palace just for him." He stroked Rose's cheek and down her throat to her shoulder. "Bring him to me, Rose, and I'll set you free." His slender hand cupped her throat and squeezed. "Betray me, and I'll make you my bride forever."

Rose's stomach squirmed like she'd eaten worms. She'd seen Satan use up and burn out two wives already. An eternity in his bed would be a torture beyond standing in the line.

He gave her a wicked smile. "Though, you might like that." His gaze travelled her body and she slapped his hand from her throat.

"Not on your life."

His smile dropped and his gaze turned more glacial than her own touch.

"Then find the Jumper and reap him. You have one year from tonight to bring him in. And that's me being beyond generous." He kissed her cheek and hugged her tight, pressing his firm and aroused body into hers. "I'm trusting you," he whispered.

Then he was gone.

Rose's stifled a sob. He wanted Elijah, the one thing she wasn't willing to give him.

Thirty minutes later she stepped out into the alley and walked around to the front of her shop to check on her plants. Someone had perked them up. Probably after the coven meeting.

A large box sat next to her shop door. She opened the lid and inside found a wad of cash along with a dozen half burned black candles and other items. She picked up the hand written note that had been scrawled in a shaky hand. It begged her forgiveness and promised to never return to her shop. It was signed by three girls.

Rose chuckled and shook her head. There was a reason people never stole from her more than once.

She grabbed the box, stuffed the money in her pocket and headed to her trashcans. After she threw it inside, a hand landed lightly on her shoulder.

She spun to find a tall, strapping blond male. She grabbed his arm and twisted it behind him face planting him into the wall.

"Rose. Rose, it's me." The voice was different but he twisted to look at her and his eyes flashed golden.

She let go and he shook out his arm, rubbing his shoulder.

She looked him up and down. "Nice body. Almost as good as your real one." She caressed his chest. "I was worried. I woke up and you'd left."

"I stepped out to exchange bodies. "I try to not be in the same one for more than a couple of days. It's not fair to the human. When I got back your door was blown up. It was pretty obvious who was inside with you." He cupped her cheek. "He didn't hurt you, did he?"

She snorted. "Who, him?" She glanced away.

He held her face in his hands and forced her to look at him. "What happened?"

She swallowed hard.

His golden glow emanated from within.

"Okay, okay, stop that before someone sees you. I don't have my trashcans warded. Though now that I think about it, maybe I should."

He stared at her. "Rose."

"He wants you bad. Barbie killed his favorite pet bodyguard, Drix. He blames you. But it's more than that. I know it is."

He searched her face. "He threatened you."

"He gave me a year to bring you in, or else–"

"Or else what?"

"Or else I become Mrs. Lucifer."

Elijah's face hardened. "I'll never let that happen."

"You say that, but be serious. You're a Jumper on the run. Because of me. You're no match for him."

"Not because of you. Because I made a decision that wasn't popular with my bosses. I'll go back if I have to. Repent. Beg forgiveness. Whatever it takes. If I'm not a Jumper, he can't grab me and you won't be forced."

"If you go back he'll just blame me and you'll be punished for disobeying anyway. Plus we'd never see each other again." The thought wriggled in her mind and jammed its meaty hooks into her gut.

He kissed her hard and pulled her into him. "I'd lead all the armies of heaven down into the bowels of hell to get you."

She smiled and took a few minutes to revel in the feel of being held by him. "I have to go. You should, too. You have people to save and I have evil to reap."

"I'll be back as soon as I can."

She gave him a tight smile. "You know where I'll be. At least for the next year."

He kissed her again, long and slow. Her body ached and memories of their lovemaking flooded her.

"I love you, Rose."

She ran her hand over his stubbly, hard jaw. "I love you, too."

"I'll return soon." He backed slowly down the alley.

She nodded.

"You just wait. I'm going to figure out a way for us to be together."

She raised her hand and waved.

He didn't turn around till he rounded the corner.

Her ribcage squeezed like a vise grip and she swallowed hard. Seeing him again wasn't the worry. The question was, how long till they were caught?

She headed out onto the streets of Savannah. That, she couldn't worry about.

Right now… she had souls to reap.

Thank you for taking the time to read
Kissed by the Reaper
If you enjoyed the book, please take a moment to leave a review on your favorite retailer.

Look for other books by Rebekah R. Ganiere
Fairelle Series
Red the Were Hunter
Snow the Vampire Slayer
Jamen's Yuletide Bride
Zelle and the Tower
Cinder the Fae (December 2015)

The Society
Reign of the Vampires
Rise of the Fae (Nov. 22 2015)
Vengeance of the Demons (May 2016)

OtherWorlder Series
Saving Christmas
Cupid's Curse (Feb. 2016
Haunted Halloween (Oct. 2016)

Dead Awakenings

Shifter Rising
Promised at the Moon (Apr. 2016)

To find out more about **Rebekah R. Ganiere** or her other Upcoming Releases, or to join her Newsletter for Swag and Freebies, Please connect with her in the following places:

BOOKS WITH A BITE
Newsletter: www.RebekahGaniere.com/Newsletter
Goodreads: www.Goodreads.com/VampWereZombie
Twitter: www.Twitter.com/VampWereZombie
Facebook: www.Facebook.com/VampiresWerewolvesZombies

All's Fair: Love and Warlocks
By
Tami Lund

DEDICATION

Witches, Wenches, whatever. You know who you are. And you know I love you.

CHAPTER ONE

"Why the hell am I here? Why me?"

"Talking to yourself, even for a witch, is generally thought to be a bad sign. Unless you're casting a spell."

Adanna jerked her hand away from the wooden door handle and glanced over her shoulder at the person who was speaking. The curtain of her hair obscured her view somewhat, but she saw enough to know she did not recognize the handsome warlock with thick, dark hair and gray eyes. At least, she assumed he was a warlock. Most covens frowned upon making their supernatural selves known to humans, even though they all lived in the same world.

"Not casting a spell. Do I know you?"

"Probably not." He offered his hand. It was a human custom, but most were.

"Anton Burke. I'm from New England. Salem, to be exact. Weather's certainly nicer here at this time of year."

Salem. Humans, of course, were obsessed with the town, as so many (non) witches had been executed there, several centuries ago. It was a particularly troubling period in their history. And witches, despite their disdain for humans, were just as enthralled with the area.

"It's pretty mild in Savannah, with the exception of July and August. Your coven is the one that's taken over all of New England, isn't it?"

Something akin to a grimace darkened his face but did not dim his handsome features. He had the kind of rugged good looks that screamed bad boy, the kind that caused red-blooded women to tumble into his bed and ask questions later. Her grandmother's lessons to always read people before interacting echoed in her head. She pushed away the memories, the reminder of who she was, what she was.

"Yeah. It's easier that way, I guess. So many small covens; it just wasn't, you know…"

"Personal?"

He smirked. "Economical. Hard to support all those mini empires. Made more sense to create one mega-coven. More money, more control over issues and stuff."

"I heard your coven now stretches all the way to South Carolina."

"You sound suspicious."

Adanna shrugged. "I've belonged to the Savannah Coven my whole life, and we've always been pretty small-town. Seems hard to believe all those covens were willing to be swallowed up by Big Brother, so to speak."

"Times are changing. Most of the covens were run by older witches. They were tired, wanted to retire. And there aren't enough marked Supremes to take their places. What else were they supposed to do?"

Adanna ran a hand through her long locks and focused on steadying her temper. Why it flared at the mention of the conglomerate of covens along the east coast, she had no idea. What did it matter to her if an abnormally large group of witches and warlocks wanted to band together under one Supreme? Everybody knew witches needed someone to manage them, or at the very least, help when they ended up in hot water, which happened more frequently than it ought to. Harboring magic and keeping others from becoming aware was difficult, even for the most learned of witches.

Adanna forced a smile and asked, "So what brings you to this part of the country, Anton Burke?"

He looked up at the sign hanging over the entrance of the occult shop. It was decidedly creepy, which helped to discourage humans. Yet the wards and negative impressions did not deter the otherworldly foot traffic she knew kept Rose, the shopkeeper, well stocked in handmade silver and rhinestone jewelry.

"There's a coven meeting today, right?"

"Yes, but you don't belong to this coven." She glanced at her watch. "And it doesn't start for another hour."

She made it a habit to arrive early, so she could chat with Rose, collect her bearings, and mentally prepare herself for the task at hand. Although truthfully, the coven meetings weren't usually difficult to run. In fact, they were more often than not little more than social gatherings, and she liked most of the witches and warlocks who were members.

Tonight's meeting, in particular, should be an easy one. Her objective was nothing more than to remind everyone to be diligent, to report any zombie or spirit sightings directly to her, and to be careful using magic while imbibing on alcoholic beverages. Using magic while drunk was, by far, the most frequent transgression in her coven. Since a witch's magic was significantly more powerful during Samhain, Adanna suspected she would have her work cut out for her on this, her first Halloween as the Supreme.

"I'm visiting. Here to meet the Supreme Witch. Adanna Grandier."

"Why?"

"I was told to seek her out. Help her adjust. I understand Vesna's death was sudden, and that this Adanna might not be prepared to take over as Supreme Witch."

You can say that again. Adanna self-consciously tugged at the front of her lime green tank top. "I didn't realize she knew I felt so unprepared."

Anton's gray eyes flared as his gaze swept over her person, no doubt taking in the bright tank, black yoga pants, rhinestone studded flip-flops, and her black toenail polish, before coming to rest on her face. She imagined she looked more like a college student than a Supreme Witch, though she was closer to thirty than twenty, and she'd been studying for this position for damn near her entire life, whether she had wanted to or not. She lowered her head so her hair obscured her features, as was her habit. But he reached out, tentatively at first, then pushed at the dark waves, revealing proof positive she was the person he sought. She took a chance and glanced up, and was surprised by what she saw in his eyes.

Hunger.

"Beautiful."

She touched the side of her face, where a black vine twisted along her hairline, from her temple to her cheek. The scrollwork she'd been born with had been called a lot of things by a lot of different people – witches and humans both. *Beautiful* had never been one of those words.

"It's the mark of the Supreme Witch," she muttered, hating it, as she had for most of her life. Her father had been human, and while her grandmother had trained her and prepared her to someday take over the coven, Adanna had always preferred the human side of her nature. Less responsibility. Less chance of failing. Knowing from birth that one was destined to be a ruler was a heavy burden to bear.

Her brother, Micah, hadn't been born with the telltale markings, but he'd coveted the position for as long as she could remember. If only she could give it to him. Then they'd both be happy.

"I know. 'Only the one whom carries the mark may rule.' Would you believe our own coven had to import a Supreme from another state? When the last one died, there was no one to take over. In Salem, of all places."

"That is kind of ironic," she admitted, then paused before saying, "How is it you're connected to my grandmother?"

"Synthia Montgomery is the Salem Supreme. We convinced her to move from Texas. She knew your grandmother. Even though her death was sudden, Vesna seemed to have anticipated it. She paid a visit to Synthia a few months ago and asked her to send me to help with your process of taking over."

It was exactly something her grandmother would do. Although, like Anton said, her death had been sudden. There had been no advance warning of the heart attack that had taken her from them, just a few short months ago. Still, Vesna Grandier had always been a planner, had always thought ahead. Adanna had started Supreme Witch training before she could speak, let alone comprehend what it meant to take over such an important position.

"Why would she send *you* to help me?" She didn't mean to sound ungrateful, but she well understood the importance of her position. Hell, half the time she suspected her own brother was brewing up an idea to steal the title and what he considered the prestige. He didn't understand how thankless of a job it often was.

"Synthia sent me. I'm kind of, I don't know, an admin of sorts, I guess. She figured I'd be able to use my experience working with her to help you get settled into your position here." His smile was charming, almost self-deprecating. She considered again reading him, but figured all she'd get was a healthy dose of sexual attraction.

Which she was woman enough to admit was most certainly two-sided.

"Does Synthia do double-duty as your girlfriend, too?"

His smile widened, and Adanna felt her face heat. Geez, could she have been any more obvious? Okay, yeah, she was attracted to him. He was hot, after all. That thick, dark hair made her fingers itch with the urge to run through it, maybe tug it to encourage him to drop his chin so she could access his full, kissable lips. She wondered what the shadow covering his chin and cheeks would feel like rubbing against the inside of her thigh. She wondered what *his* thighs looked like, out of those just-fitted-enough jeans. His loose, button-down shirt did not hide the bulges in his arms and chest – bulges she was certain could hold a woman up, while he pressed her against the wall and ravished her body…

Goddess above, Adanna needed a life. Or at least a date. Preferably one that lasted until morning.

"No girlfriend," he said, as if she needed reassurance of that fact. Which she didn't, though it was nice to know.

"So how can I help?" He gave her an expectant look, like she was really going to ask for advice from some random warlock she'd never met before.

"By staying quiet and not asking any questions so this meeting doesn't drag on," she replied, reaching for the door to Reap What You Sow. Anton followed her inside.

As always, the shop was as immaculately clean as it had been on the day it opened for the first time. Rose, the owner, was nothing if not meticulous when it came to her workspace.

Adanna's gaze scanned dust-free shelves loaded with books and vials of potions, baskets of dried herbs, and various other sundry items necessary to the magical community. The place was packed with witches and warlocks and other magical beings, all hurrying to stock up in preparation for the Samhain celebrations that would begin at dusk. Out of this scene, most strange was that Rose, the shop's proprietor and the keeper of the only key to the coven meeting room, was nowhere in sight.

"That sounds easy enough," Anton said, reminding Adanna of his presence and giving her a stab of guilt for treating him so poorly.

"Look, I'm sorry I'm being bitchy. I'm always a little stressed before these meetings. I know how to manage a coven – my grandmother shoved the responsibilities down my throat enough. It's just that I don't *want* to. But I am running them, as you can see. Whether I like it or not, I'm not shirking my duties. So you can hang out for our meeting, I'm sure I can get you an invite to any number of Samhain celebrations for tonight, and then you can go home and tell what's her name that I'm doing just fine. She can have a little séance, report back to Grandmother, or whatever. How's that sound?"

"Sounds like you have a lot of built up resentment."

Adanna heard him, but she wasn't listening. She was too busy looking around the shop, hoping for a glimpse of Rose. It didn't make sense that she wasn't there, tending to her customers.

She swept past a group of teenage girls fawning over vials of love potion, and headed toward the crooked staircase carved from an ancient walnut tree. The stairs led down to the secret coven meeting room, located beneath the occult shop. Before she could make it to the heavy blue curtain hiding the stairs, she was stopped by a gnarled hand on her arm.

Adanna looked down at a hunched over old witch. The lady's head barely reached Adanna's waist, and she looked as though she might have seen the turn of the nineteenth century.

"I can't seem to find Rose," the ancient woman said. "And I need some turmeric."

Adanna glanced around, hoping Rose would make an appearance. While she did occasionally step in and help when the shopkeeper needed her, she wasn't keen to do so only an hour prior to running her first Halloween coven meeting.

"Are you going to help me or not?" the old witch asked. She dropped her bag onto the counter with a thud and began rummaging around inside. Adanna glanced at Anton. He nodded.

"How much do you need, ma'am?" he asked the woman, offering up a crooked smile that sent Adanna's heart fluttering, despite the fact it wasn't meant for her.

"I'll take two bundles. Thank you, young man."

"Aisle two, left side," Adanna said to Anton. She had helped Rose stock the shop enough times that she knew where almost every item was located.

A few minutes later, the happy customer shuffled out of the shop. Anton stood next to Adanna, who stood behind the cash register. "She needs a lot more than two bundles of an anti-aging herb at this point," he remarked. Adanna bit the inside of her cheek to keep from laughing.

Another customer stepped up to the counter, presuming Adanna could help. She made a half-hearted attempt to convince the otherworldly being she didn't work there, but the aggressive man wouldn't take no for an answer, and Adanna reluctantly rung up his sale.

Soon, there was a line at the register, and Adanna tallied up sales, while Anton obligingly played runner, retrieving items here and there when necessary, bagging larger orders when it wasn't.

We make a great team. The thought drifted through Adanna's mind as soon as they finished wrapping and bagging a large sale of basil and burdock root to a warlock who didn't have a lick of hair on his head, but was convinced the herbal combination would remedy that issue.

She glanced at Anton out of the corner of her eye and he arched a dark eyebrow. "What?"

She shook her head. "Nothing. Thank you for helping. I didn't mean to turn you into my personal assistant here."

"I'm used to that, remember?"

Right. He was the Salem Supreme's personal assistant. *They* were a great team, not Adanna and Anton. She would do well to remember that, instead of think fanciful thoughts of inviting him back to her place after the meeting. Neither flings nor warlocks were her normal preference, and she had no business considering changing that stance just because a hot guy showed up and swore he was only there to help.

"The coven meeting starts in fifteen minutes. I have to get down there. I don't know where Rose is, but I can't stay up here and watch the shop."

"I'll do it."

"Thanks for the offer, but you can't. Rose has this place warded, so only she and I can touch the register. I guess I'd better go—" A waving arm caught her eye and she looked at the doorway to the storage room. Rose the shopkeeper was desperately trying to get her attention. Adanna abandoned her post at the register and hurried to see what her friend needed.

"What's wrong?"

"I need you to heal someone for me," Rose replied. Anton had followed Adanna into the storage room. Rose glanced at him and dismissed him almost immediately.

"Who?"

"A friend. He's been hurt by reapers."

"Reapers? If reapers hurt him, why is he *your* friend?" Rose was a reaper herself. They didn't normally turn on one another or protect those who had been attacked by one of their own.

"It's a long story. Come on." She pulled Adanna by the sleeve, leading her deeper into the storage room. Adanna could hear Anton's footfalls, indicating he followed.

Her eyes widened when she spotted the dark-skinned, dark-haired man lying on a crimson-colored fainting couch. "He's cute."

"If you like that sort of thing," Anton muttered darkly. Adanna had a silly urge to reassure him she wasn't the least bit attracted to the unconscious man. Why would she feel compelled to reassure him of such a thing? It wasn't like she and Anton were an item. They'd only met less than an hour ago!

"Can you help?"

Adanna studied the man lying on the fainting couch. She didn't see any signs of blood or wounds to explain his unconscious state. "What type of injuries?"

Rose gnawed her thumbnail. "It's all internal."

Adanna nodded. "Okay, I'll see what I can do." She crouched next to the man and placed her hands on his abdomen. Chanting, she gently prodded him with her fingers. "It's bad in there. They really did a number on him."

With a flash of golden light, the man's body lurched from the couch. Adanna fell backwards and winced when her tailbone slammed into the concrete floor. She scrambled away, eyes wide. Anton grabbed her by the arms and pulled her to her feet, keeping a hand on her arm in what Adanna determined was a protective gesture.

"Crap, Rose! You should have told me he was an angel."

Rose rushed to the glowing man and pressed him back against the cushions. "Easy."

The light slowly faded and the man's body relaxed. A moment later, the only sign something had changed was the trickle of blood leaking from between his lips.

"He's not an angel," Rose insisted.

"Sorry, but you can't lie to me," Adanna admonished her friend. "My magic won't work on an angel. They're different."

"It'll work. His body is human." She stroked a bead of sweat from his brow. The gesture struck Adanna as intimate. She and Rose were close, but her friend hadn't mentioned a love interest. Yet her familiarity with the man was unmistakable.

"That's no angel," Anton said. "That's a jumper."

Adanna's eyes widened. "Oh no, Rose. Please don't tell me you're helping a jumper." She knew precious little about jumpers, except that they were usually rogue and often sought by beings with significantly more power than Adanna possessed. The idea that Rose's friend might bring danger to the witches and warlocks in her coven did not sit well with Adanna.

Rose ignored Anton and leveled her gaze on Adanna. "Help me get him to my flat?"

"Lucifer is going to kill you for sure this time." Rose was beholden to the scary Prince of the Underworld, and Adanna knew she was counting the decades until she could be set free. If her boss found out she was harboring a jumper, the set date of Rose's freedom could be pushed back indefinitely.

"He's worth it. I can tell," Rose said, her gaze on the handsome, prone man.

With a sigh of resignation, Adanna agreed to help her take him upstairs.

"I'll help," Anton piped up.

"No, you won't," Rose said, her tone flat. "Stay down here." Her gaze travelled the length of him, and Adanna felt her own skin bristling, not from jealousy, but more of a protective instinct. There was no attraction in the way Rose looked at Anton.

"I'll be right back," Adanna promised him, then she grabbed the unconscious guy under one arm while Rose grabbed his other. Together they dragged him out the back door and into the alley behind the shop. Adanna kept him pressed against the wall while Rose unlocked a door and released the wards and sigils covering it. Then they hauled him into Rose's apartment.

"Couch?" Adanna asked.

"My bed will be better."

Adanna smirked.

"Oh, please. It's only for him to heal."

Adanna nodded. "Sure it is."

They carried him to the sparsely furnished bedroom and lay him on top of the comforter.

"Should we strip him down? He might be more comfortable that way," Adanna couldn't resist suggesting.

Rose pinched her arm. "Don't you have a coven to run?"

She blew out a heavy breath. "Yeah, I do." Before she could leave, Rose called her name. Adanna turned and gave her an expectant look. Rose walked over and pressed something into her hand. She looked down at an ancient, gilded gold key with a dark, faintly glowing ruby embedded into the grip. The only key to the coven meeting room.

"That guy downstairs is powerful. Be careful."

Adanna wanted to ask what she meant, but Rose had already drifted back across the room and was fussing with her guest, plumping his pillows and removing his shoes. With a frustrated shake of her head, Adanna retreated down the stairs. Anton waited for her in the storage room.

"What's a reaper doing hosting your coven meetings?" was his first question.

"She's my friend, and this is the only place nearly every witch in town is familiar with. It was sort of a natural pairing."

"What's she doing with an angel? A jumper, no less. They aren't exactly bedmates under normal circumstances."

"I have no idea. Why are you so concerned?" she asked coolly, feeling the need to defend her friend. Rose may have her quirks and she had a lousy job as a reaper, but she was a good person, and Adanna had no doubt her reasons for protecting a rogue angel were sincere.

"I'm just—" His words were cut off when Adanna stumbled over a metal Pandora's box that must have fallen off a shelf when she was helping Rose carry her angel upstairs. The box shook and rattled and bounced around like a living thing, and Adanna would have tripped and collapsed into a shelf stacked to the rafters with goods for the occult shop, had Anton not grabbed her and pulled her into his arms.

She clutched at his shirt, her breasts smashed against his chest, which wasn't yielding a bit under the pressure. The man was solid muscle. Relaxing her hold on his shirt, she wrapped her arms around his waist and smoothed her palms up his back, enjoying the way his muscles twitched as she did so.

"You okay?" His voice sounded gruff, his breath hot against her ear. If she turned her head, their lips would be millimeters apart. She was shocked that she wanted to do it, to kiss him, to lose herself in his taste. She couldn't seem to think straight, and it was his fault.

She nodded, too afraid her voice would crack if she spoke. She didn't release him, but neither did he release her.

In truth, she was surprised at her own attraction – his delicious muscles not withstanding. She tended to date humans, not warlocks, nor any magical beings, for that matter. Considering Adanna herself was half-human, she figured she had every right to shun her own kind.

Although she wasn't exactly shunning Anton at the moment. In fact, she shifted her hips, reveling in the rather *large* lump she felt pressing into her belly.

Before she could shame herself further, a sound pulled her back to reality. She reluctantly extracted herself from Anton's arms and turned toward the entrance to the shop. A forty-something witch with red hair, red nails, red lips, and far too much makeup posed in the doorway, her gaze lapping at Anton like he was an ice cream sundae.

"Yes?" Adanna said, drawing the other woman's attention.

"Coven meeting," she said, her gaze not leaving Anton. "The rest of us are wondering if you plan to actually run it?"

"Yes, I'll be there in a minute." The dismissal was clear, but it still took the other witch a few moments to turn and strut away. Adanna blew out a breath and smoothed the front of her shirt, gaze downcast. "I'm sorry about that."

"About what?" Anton asked.

Adanna flapped her hand. "Tripping. Falling. Into you. Uh…"

"Don't be sorry. I'm actually hoping we can continue what might have happened if that witch hadn't interrupted. I don't suppose you're free after this meeting?"

Adanna's face heated and she lowered her lashes over her eyes, feeling both pleased and flattered by his attention. "Um, why don't we get through the meeting first?" She stalled, because she had no idea how to respond to the man.

He was a warlock. He was from Massachusetts. She knew nothing about him, quite literally. And while she'd been hit on plenty of times in her life, it had never been by a man who was quite as… virile as this one. She was flustered, which was not a good state of mind to be in when she was about to start a coven meeting.

"Deal."

She left the storage room and hurried down the crooked stairs, trying to get her head on straight, as she passed black and white sketches of past Supreme Witches, adorning the wall. She rounded a bend and came upon her own portrait. The artist managed to capture the scrollwork on her face so vividly, the eye was instantly drawn to it, even though Adanna had specifically told her to tone it down. For once, she didn't cringe as she passed the picture. She was too distracted by Anton's presence.

Damn it, why couldn't she have run into him *after* the meeting?

CHAPTER TWO

The meeting was a disaster. Good for Anton's purposes, not so good for the young coven leader. She stuttered and floundered and generally looked like anything but a leader, but damn, she was hot. Smokin'. Shit, after he'd pulled her into his arms and she'd done that little wiggle thing with her hips, he was pretty sure he would have tried to fuck her on the spot. Too bad the cougar had made her appearance at that moment. That witch had lousy timing.

Synthia hadn't mentioned the Savannah Supreme was so young. For some reason, Anton had assumed he would be dealing with somebody more Synthia's age. Or any of the other coven leaders he'd met in his life. The vast majority were old ladies – and occasionally geezers – before they took on the title.

Not Adanna Grandier. Nothing about her was old, except the magic swirling in her blood and the history behind that sexy tattoo marking her as a leader. Every witch born as a Supreme had a slightly different variation of that mark, and in a different place on their body, too. He imagined it had been hard on her growing up, a young child with intricate scrollwork on her face. Or maybe it had been hard on her mother. Humans were so critical, always fast to call someone out for something they didn't believe was right. If only they knew, that tat represented more power than they could possibly comprehend.

And Synthia wanted it.

You have a job to do, boy-o. Distract the Supreme, let Synthia do her thing, then hightail it out of town before anyone connects the two actions. He had no reason, no desire to stay in Savannah any longer than he had to, to do Synthia's bidding.

Good thing she hadn't clarified just how she wanted him to distract the dark-haired beauty. Anton's initial plan of charming her with tea and silly spells, opening doors and rescuing cats from trees went out the window the moment he realized Adanna was the woman he needed to distract. Oh no, there would be no cat rescuing for this lady. Cat *licking*, maybe... Oh yeah, this was going to be the best job Anton had ever taken for the power hungry Supreme Witch to whom he was beholden.

Oh yeah.

He should have taken the opening when she bumbled and fumbled through the meeting, even if he fully intended to get horizontal with her later. But he hadn't been able to do it. When a group of old biddies ganged up on her after she said she had no intention of wandering the streets tonight, searching for zombies and lost spirits, Anton should have goaded them on, should have encouraged others to join their plight. Instead, he defended the young leader, arguing that she intended to make herself available, should anyone have such sightings. If she was out looking for zombies herself, how was she supposed to help when someone else actually did find one?

And when somebody brought up the fact that Rose hadn't been downstairs before the meeting, he suggested she might have been busy with a personal matter and pointed out that Adanna had managed to take care of everyone's needs in the shopkeeper's absence. He hadn't missed the look of appreciation that crossed Adanna's beautiful, porcelain doll-like face. That alone had been worth not taking advantage of the opportunity to ruin the meeting. That and the promise of hot, sweaty sex, later, in his hotel room. Screw Samhain bonfires and Halloween gatherings. He had plans for a party of two, and it was going to last all night long.

That would be distracting, wouldn't it? The idea was sure as hell distracting him at the moment. For some unfathomable reason, he found her casual attire and the black polish on her toes sexy as hell. She was the most attractive woman he'd ever encountered. Probably due to his surprise at discovering she was closer to his age and not an old lady. Or maybe it was the way her curves had felt under his hands when he'd hugged her.

Maybe it was the look in her eyes – a little bit lost, but with a determination to make it through whatever the hell she needed to get through. He wondered at her story. She clearly did not want to be the Supreme Witch. Why not? He'd never met one who hadn't let all that power go to her head before. Adanna Grandier was intriguing, in more ways than one.

He couldn't wait to peel away the layers. Of her clothes, that is. Anton didn't do emotional connections, but physical ones were an entirely different matter…

The meeting lasted an hour, and to him, it didn't seem like much of anything was accomplished. Adanna gave the usual warnings to watch out for zombies and poltergeists that liked to taunt – and sometimes harm – the humans who all thought the last day of October was an excuse to get drunk, dress up, and pretend to be something they didn't even believe existed. When she gently reminded the attendees to use magic responsibly and not imbibe too much before doing so, a cluster of elderly witches took offense and there were some tense moments as Adanna swore she wasn't trying to ruin their fun. Anton had been as shocked as she when he spoke up and pointed out that they managed to perform magic on every other day of the year without getting wasted first.

Another lost chance at ruining her. Was he losing his game, or was he just that desperate to get into her pants? There couldn't be any other reason. It surely wasn't because he actually liked the young Supreme, that he respected her determination to take care of her coven, her own wishes be damned.

He reminded himself that he didn't let emotions get involved and decided his own thoughts were distracted by the idea of the impending hookup. Better for his ego. And, hopefully, the brain below his waist that was far too eager for this meeting to end.

* * * *

When the last witch left the meeting room, Anton and Adanna followed her out into the hall and Adanna locked the door. He hovered near her and caught a whiff of her scent. She smelled like magic and springtime, flowers and grass after a heavy rain.

Jesus, he was turning into a goddamn loon. He definitely needed to fuck this girl, if only to release the pressure that was suddenly building in his chest. And other places.

"Hey," she said, sounding surprised he was still there.

"My place or yours?"

She looked taken aback by his abrupt question. He silently cursed himself. It was hard to change, though. He was used to being an asshole. It was part of his persona. Synthia expected it of him. A fair number of the jobs she sent him on required him to put his own opinions, feelings, and expectations on the backburner.

It's just a job.

But Adanna was not just a job. If she was, he would have ruined her coven meeting, done what he'd been sent out to do, and would already be heading to the airport by now. Back to Synthia, and whatever her next assignment would be. Normally, he felt ambivalence about the start and end of his contracted jobs. Today, he felt relieved this one wasn't over yet.

Get your head on straight, Anton.

"Um, I skipped lunch, and I'm starved. Why don't we grab a bite to eat somewhere?"

Right. Eating. In a public place. Which was smart of her, of course, and he had to respect that. Except it meant making small talk, getting to know her better, and doing his damndest to avoid telling her anything personal about himself.

"Sure. That sounds great."

CHAPTER THREE

He was forward yet polite, confident, and able to handle the naysayers in the coven with an ease that made Adanna jealous. And let's not forget attractive. The man was serious eye candy, and after that hug they'd shared in the storeroom, she knew for a fact all those bulges were muscle. She hadn't wanted to let him go because of it.

Now she was dining with the man, her attraction growing with each nanosecond, yet she knew next to nothing about him. He was from Salem, his coven leader had been imported from Texas, and he was a contractor by trade. He hadn't even elaborated on what he was contracted to do.

I don't care, I still want to sleep with him.

It was crazy, thinking this way. She had literally no experience with warlocks, save those in her coven, who treated her as either a leader or a child, depending on their age and longevity within the coven. She had only ever dated human men, and by dated, she meant literally going out on a few dates before jumping into bed together. She didn't have a specific number she adhered to; her goal had always been to get to know the person's mind before getting to know his body.

Yet with Anton, all she wanted was get to know his body. Up close and personal. With her tongue. Everywhere. Did he have tattoos? Piercings? That V-shaped muscle on his hips that led to the Promised Land? She wanted to smooth her hand over the scruff on his face, run her fingers through his hair. She wanted to strip off his clothes and stare at him. Maybe lick him. Definitely lick him. All over. She could hardly concentrate on their conversation, for all the thoughts running through her head.

"Thanks for your help at the shop. And the coven meeting," she said after the server cleared their empty plates and returned with fresh drinks – mulled wine for her and a pumpkin ale for him. She'd brought him to Stay A Spell, a B&B with an attached pub that catered specifically to witches and other magical beings who, while they lived amongst the humans, preferred to socialize with their own kind.

The pub was quiet at the moment, but Adanna knew it would pick up later in the evening, as local magical beings tended to migrate here after their bonfires and other Samhain celebrations marking the end of the harvest. She figured it was the perfect place to take a warlock she knew precious little about. They could talk freely for now. But if she decided she didn't want to be alone with him, in a few hours the place would be packed. She'd be able to either lose him in the crowd, or at the very least, engage others in their conversation.

Cook, the owner of Stay A Spell, stopped by their booth and spent a few moments fawning over Anton, commenting about how nice it was to see Adanna on a date with, "such an attractive young man," before she wandered off to chat up a lone warlock, slumped over his beer at the bar.

Attractive young man? Anton was a freaking god. Maybe he'd be willing to strip naked and let her paint his image. Or better yet, paint on his body. With chocolate.

"Sorry – what?"

His mouth twisted into a sardonic smile, and Adanna suspected he well knew what he was doing to her senses. She couldn't decide if that was a good or bad thing.

"I said you're welcome, although I didn't really do anything. Oh, and by the way, I happen to be staying right here. Upstairs."

She held her breath, waiting for him to say, "Want to check out my room?" But he didn't, and she finally slowly expelled the air from her lungs.

"That makes sense. This is the only place in town that caters exclusively to the magical community. Most of our kind have one foot in the human world and one in the magical world."

"Do you have a life outside the coven?"

Adanna shrugged and sipped the cooling wine. The mulling spices tickled her nose, but she breathed deep, enjoying the aroma. "Not really anymore. I used to, but since I became Supreme, I've had to quit my job and focus on taking care of the coven. We're set up sort of like a nonprofit organization. Most of the funds we collect are used to support witches in need, and I see no reason to change that. Most of my time as Supreme is actually spent sorting through requests and determining who gets how much of our funds, and then going back to the coven and asking for more." Her laugh was bitter. Her coven was generous, but the need always outweighed the amount of money the members brought in. Even with a portion of Rose's sales at the occult shop and the generous donations Cook made, there was always more that could be done.

The smile he offered was more gentle, sweeter than the last. Adanna had to dig her nails into her palms to keep from grabbing him by the front of his shirt and dragging him upstairs. She glanced down at her drink. Had he added a love potion when she turned her head for a split second? She pushed the glass away.

"Something wrong?" Anton asked, his thick, dark brows knitted into a look of concern.

"No." She shook her head. "No. I just – I just want to have a clear head, that's all."

"For what?"

"Um…" That was a damn good question. Why *did* she need a clear head? "In case I get any calls." She pulled her phone out of her purse and placed it on the table. "As the Supreme, I have to be on call all night."

"A thankless job."

She shrugged. How many times had she thought the exact same thing? "But it's my job. Imagine if a zombie actually got a hold of a human? The consequences to the entire magical community could be devastating."

"Zombies are idiots. Whoever spots one can take care of the problem without calling you."

"Probably. But the rules are, the Supreme has to be notified. I have to document all sightings and send the information up to Salem, actually. Your Supreme keeps the log for the entire country."

"Trust me, Synthia won't let her duties stop her from having a good time tonight."

Adanna smiled. "Are you implying I should do the same?"

His answering grin was full of mischief – and promise. Lots and lots of promise. "That's exactly what I'm implying. I have a few ideas to help you do it, too."

"Is it warm in here?" She fanned her face.

Anton chuckled. "This whole damn town is warm to me."

"Cool. I meant cool. It's cool in here. Maybe we should go up to your room. I bet it's hotter – er – warmer up there."

Anton's eyes flared, and she knew he comprehended what she was trying to convey with her jumbled words, which was good, because she was shocked she'd actually been brave enough to invite herself up to his room.

He kept those pale gray eyes on her face while he slid out of the booth and tugged his wallet out of his back pocket. He tossed several bills onto the table and then offered his hand. She slipped her smaller one into his, and he pulled her close, pushing the hair away from the side of her face on which the Supreme mark was permanently tattooed.

"It will definitely be warmer in my room." His voice was a breathy whisper next to her ear. She shivered and he stroked his finger along her hairline, tracing the mark. "Let's go," he said abruptly, and he all but dragged her away from the booth and up the stairs to the upper level, where the rented rooms were located.

****

Calm the fuck down, asshole.

It wasn't like this was his first time with a woman – or even with a woman of power. Anton had been Synthia's lackey for a damn long time, and he'd done some shady things on her orders – including sleep with women for a specific purpose.

Like stealing their position within the coven.

Okay, he hadn't yet done that exact thing, but it was arguably what he was doing at the moment.

Yeah, right. He was in this for the pleasure, plain and simple. It wouldn't have mattered if Adanna was a homeless woman or the freaking President of the United States – he wanted to fuck her, and he wanted to do it *right now*. He pulled an antique silver key out of his pocket and noticed his hand shook when he tried to insert it into the lock. He pressed that hand against the wooden door and scrubbed the other over his face.

"Damn."

"What's wrong?" Adanna sounded all innocent and concerned – exactly what he didn't need. And exactly what he wanted.

"I don't think I believed you would really say yes."

She sputtered out a laugh. His dick swelled to the point of pain. Over a fucking laugh? What the hell was wrong with him?

"I didn't think I'd say yes, either. But sometimes you have to listen to your, er, gut. And mine is telling me that I'm about to experience the best few hours of my life."

"Damn right you are." He finally managed to stab the key into the keyhole, twisted, and pushed the door open. He had just enough sense left to step to the side so she could walk inside first, then he closed the door behind him and stood there, watching her take in their surroundings.

His room was at the top of the stairs, on the third floor, which was basically an attic converted into an additional source of income. Wooden beams lined the ceiling, and the lone window was round, like what one would experience in the cabin of a cruise ship. When it was turned on, a small chandelier hanging from the center of the ceiling was the main source of light. The bits of glass dripping from the wrought iron configuration made gentle tinkling noises in the breeze drifting in through the open window. The bed was the centerpiece, a monstrosity with an ornately carved headboard and a white quilt covering the sheets, emphasizing the mound of pillows that had been fluffed and positioned just so by the cleaning staff at the inn.

When he checked in yesterday, he had looked at the room as nothing more than a place to sleep, while he was otherwise engaged in doing Synthia's bidding. Now, he viewed it with a more critical eye, and decided it was a hell of a place to seduce the smokin' hot leader of the Savannah Coven.

"It's beautiful," she said.

"It is," he responded, stepping up behind her and grasping her waist.

"I meant the room."

"I didn't."

He brushed her hair to the side and kissed her collarbone. She made a small, erotic noise, deep in her throat. Anton's fingers dug into her flesh for a moment before he sucked in a deep breath and focused on maintaining his equilibrium. Never before had a woman affected him like this. It was frustrating as hell. On one hand, he wanted to throw her down on the bed and fuck her for the fourteen seconds it would probably take him to climax, on the other, he wanted to stretch this out as long as possible, to enjoy the buildup, revel in the seduction.

"I don't usually do this," she whispered, her voice teasing across his senses, making his inner turmoil that much more difficult. Why did she have to be so damn sexy, so damn cute, so damn young? This gig would have been a thousand times easier if his quarry was an old woman with a penchant for doilies and black cats.

"I'm glad to hear it," he responded. She turned her face toward him and he dropped kisses on her neck, up to her ear, where he nibbled on the lobe. A gold hoop with an intricate design sliced through one hole in her ear, a diamond stud through another, and there was a tiny gold hoop stuck through the upper curve. He didn't fail to note that she had plenty of piercings, yet worked so hard to hide the scrollwork on the side of her face, something that should be a mark of pride to their kind.

Dusk had fallen, bathing the room in darkness. He pressed his lips to her ear and whispered an incantation. The candles positioned on various horizontal surfaces in the room flared to life, their shimmering flames sending shadows dancing across the walls. She twisted her upper body so she could look him in the face.

"That's not a common spell. Or an easy one."

He stroked his finger along her hairline again. "If you want, I can turn on the chandelier."

She glanced up at the glass and wrought iron structure hanging from the ceiling. He could tell she was counting the number of electric bulbs.

"That's okay." Her voice was breathy, sexy as fuck. He cupped her chin, capturing her in that pose, and attacked her lips, kissing her, demanding she stop teasing and give him what he wanted.

If only he knew what that was.

He wanted her, of course, but it was more than that. Right now, at this moment, before they even shed a stitch of clothing, he knew it was more than simple physical gratification. Considering this was a job and Synthia was paying him handsomely, he should be appalled, maybe even scared. But he wasn't. All he could focus on was the dark-haired beauty who swore one-night-stands were not her normal modus operandi. And yet she offered herself to him.

He was damn well going to take what she offered.

She tried to twist in his arms, to fully face him, but he liked her like this, his front to her back. He liked the little bit of extra effort it took to kiss her, but how easy it was to touch her in all the right places. He cupped her breasts, rubbing his thumbs over the tight, hard nubs. She arched her back, pressing into his touch, but made a noise of protest when he abruptly dropped his hands to her waist.

Her protest turned to approval when he slipped his hands under her tank top. She gasped when he smoothed one hand up her belly, then her rib cage, until he cupped her breast with only her bra between his skin and hers.

She arched, pressing her ass against his dick. He continued to massage her breast while he dropped the other hand to cup her sex through her tight yoga pants. Even with the cotton material as a barrier, he could tell she was wet for him. Her heat practically singed his hand. He pressed against her inner thigh, encouraging her to spread her legs wider. When she obliged, he returned to her sex, rubbing his thumb in a circle over her clit, causing her to cry out, muttering words that, had she been concentrating, might have been some sort of spell.

His entire body jerked as if he'd been electrocuted when she shifted her hips and cupped his dick.

"Adanna." Her name was a groan. He adjusted his stance, moving his groin out of her reach.

"I want to touch you, too." He could hear the pout in her voice.

"I'm going to lose it if you keep touching me."

She smiled. "Isn't that the point?"

"Well, I figured you ought to get a little pleasure out of it first."

"I'm definitely getting pleasure," she assured him. Then there was an, "Oh," when he pressed his finger against her folds. "I'm hot," she said on a gasp.

"Yeah."

"We're wearing too many clothes."

Christ, could this woman be any more perfect? A freaking angel, sent from heaven. He was the last person on earth who deserved an angel, but he decided that wasn't important at the moment.

"You're right. Let's get out of them."

He pushed her tank up, flipping it over her head and tossing it to the side, before hooking his thumbs into the waistband of her pants and crouching on his haunches to push them to her ankles, dropping a kiss on her hipbone as she stepped out of the puddle of material.

"What about you?"

He straightened and grabbed her hand, kissed each fingertip in turn, then pressed the palm against his throbbing erection. "You do the honors."

She massaged his dick for a few pleasurably painful moments, until she smoothed her hands up, under his shirt, over his abs, and across his chest, curling her fingers so her nails raked across his sensitive skin. He breathed through his teeth and let her do whatever the hell she wanted.

She grabbed the hem of his shirt and tugged it up and he watched as her gaze took in the bare skin underneath. "I love this muscle," she murmured, stroking a finger along the crease over his hip. His body bucked of its own accord, and her lips quirked as she did it again.

"So you're a sadist," he commented.

She laughed. "No. Just enjoying the fact that I can do this to you."

"You cannot even comprehend what you do to me." He grabbed the front of his shirt and jerked it open, sending buttons flying every which way, before pulling it over his shoulders and letting it drop to the floor.

Her gasp caused him to freeze with his hands on his belt buckle. He looked at her face, saw the shock registered there, and followed her line of vision to the scrollwork running the length of his ribcage on the left side.

"You're a Supreme." Her voice was hushed.

He sighed and let her go when she stepped away from him. "No. Just marked as one."

"But – but you said you had to import your Supreme from somewhere else. Texas. I don't understand. Why?" She waved her hand in a jerking motion, indicating the tattoo he'd been born with.

"My dad was the Supreme over our coven before Synthia. I was too young to take over when he died. So Synthia stepped in." It was the truth, although he left out a whole lot of shit in between. But she didn't need the details. They might ruin the mood. "Is this going to be a problem?"

She shook her head. "It just took me by surprise, that's all. I guess I would have expected you to mention it."

"Would you have, if you were in my position?" he countered, knowing damn well she wouldn't. She resented her role within their community, though he suspected she could be really good at it, if she'd give it half a chance. Usurping her would be easy. He didn't even need to sleep with her.

Not that the knowledge was going to stop him.

"No." She reached for him, slipped her finger into one of the belt loops on his jeans, and pulled him closer. He stood there, barely breathing, while she unbuckled his belt and unsnapped his pants.

He groaned and took a few steps backward, until his shoulders pressed against the wall. She came with him, her hands working to free him from his jeans. "You're going to kill me."

"I certainly hope not." She slid the zipper down and pushed the lips of his jeans out of the way so she could stroke his erection through his boxers. In an effort to cool his overheated libido, to make this last, he closed his eyes and tried to think about baseball, but instead of the Boston Red Sox's power hitter, he pictured Adanna, in her bra and panties, holding the baseball bat, a determined look on her face, as she stared down the pitcher.

"Goddamn it." He grabbed her arms, turned her around so she was the one with her back against the wall. He pulled his wallet out of the back pocket of his jeans and tugged out a condom before dropping the folded leather over his shoulder. "You're good to spend the night, right?"

"Um, sure, I guess."

"Good. Because I can't hold out any longer. I need to fuck you. But I swear, this is only the first time. You'll get something out of this. I'll make damn sure of it. I just – *fuck*." He grabbed her panties and shoved them down her legs, waiting impatiently while she gyrated her way out of them. He reached around her back and expertly flicked the fastener on her bra. After flinging it to the side, he reached up and palmed those perfect, creamy globes with rose-colored tips. He bent and licked first one, then the other. His dick gave an impatient jerk when she responded by arching her back and threading her fingers in his hair.

Anton pulled away enough to shove his boxers down his legs, tear open the condom wrapper, and cover himself with the slippery material. Then he was back, pressing her into the wall, covering her with his body, rolling his hips, teasing her by sliding his dick between her legs but not entering her. Goddamn, she was so ready for him. He gritted his teeth, grabbed her thighs, and lifted her off her feet.

"Oh, yes." Her breathy words were like a spell, wrapping around his body, his dick, his heart.

"Adanna." He didn't know what the hell else to say. "Stay with me forever," seemed a bit premature.

She reached between them and wrapped her hand around his dick, stroking until he muttered a few choice curse words. Finally, she positioned him at her opening and he slid into her like a hot knife through butter, then stopped, filling her, his dick pulsing, her inner walls clutching at him. Her breathing was erratic, almost gasping. Hell, he wasn't fairing much better.

"What the hell is going on with us?" he asked through clenched teeth.

"I don't know, but move, damn it."

He obliged. He didn't have a choice. His body was beyond the point of control. It craved release, and he was powerless to stop it. His hips flexed again and again, flesh slapping flesh, while she made encouraging sounds and scored her nails across his back.

The keening sound that burst from her mouth surprised him so much he momentarily forgot he was on the verge of his own release. Did she just have an orgasm? Hell, he hadn't even been trying. He'd been too wrapped up in his own pleasure. And yet she panted like she was running a marathon, clinging to him, her hips pistoning against him. She reached down and squeezed his ass, pulling him closer, while she threw her head back and closed her eyes, her mouth open, gasping for air.

So fucking sexy.

"Adanna!" He called out her name as his own orgasm overcame him and he mindlessly rammed into her until his legs shook so much he was afraid he would collapse.

Slowly, carefully, he lowered himself to the wooden floor, bringing her with him, as gently as he could. He twisted around so his back pressed against the wall and she was curled in his lap. Her head lolled against his shoulder. When she looked up, her eyes were glazed and a smile tugged at her lips.

"Hey."

"Hey yourself."

"That was good."

"Yeah?"

"Actually, it was way more than good. I'm just incapable of coherent thought at the moment, so I can't think of anything more appropriate to say."

He chuckled. "That's okay." He smoothed his hand over her hair, enjoying the fact that there was no awkwardness between them, like so often happened in situations like this, where two people trip into bed together after meeting only hours prior. Or, in their case, against the wall.

"How long are you in town, anyway?"

CHAPTER FOUR

She shattered the comfortable feeling that had descended over them as they sat there, leaning against the wall, him cradling her in his lap, naked, sated after an incredibly erotic sex session.

Stupid, stupid, stupid.

"Never mind. Forget I asked. So, what do you want to do now?" She tried to crawl out of his lap, but he chuckled and held her there.

"I want to do that again, but I need a few minutes for my body to recuperate enough to make it happen."

"Oh."

"And I'm not sure how long I'm in town. My return plane ticket is open-ended. I came here to help you, remember?"

"Right." Boy, had he helped her. Helped her discover she had never before experienced sex the way it was meant to be. Helped awaken her before now relatively dormant libido. Which was good and bad. Good, for obvious reasons. Bad because the reality was, Anton was from Salem and had no intention of staying permanently. She should not – could not – think in terms of relationship or forever. She might only have tonight.

"So I sort of fantasized about exactly what we just did, when we first met."

"Oh yeah?" He sounded – she couldn't tell. Amused? Impressed? Happy? Damn, she was so terrible at this part. And she usually knew her partner a hell of a lot better than she knew Anton, by the time they got to this point.

He nudged her back, so she climbed out of his lap. He stood and then swept her into his arms. She wrapped her arms around his neck and gave a small shriek, the noise ending in an *oomph* when he tossed her onto the bed. "Don't move," he said, and then he disappeared into the bathroom.

When he returned, the used condom was gone, and he carried a handful of new ones. She arched her brows. "I see you have high hopes."

He shrugged and dumped them on the bedside table before picking up the phone. "They're always in my shaving kit. You never know, right?"

"Right."

He turned away and spoke into the receiver, low enough that she only caught words here and there. After a few moments, he replaced the phone and dropped onto the bed. She arched her brow. "What was that?"

"Sustenance. I don't want you to waste away before morning."

"We just ate dinner."

"We also just burned off about a thousand calories. And hopefully we'll burn a few thousand more before daylight."

"While we wait for food, I should check my phone, see if anyone needs me." She started to roll away from him, but he wrapped his arm around her waist and pulled her close instead, positioning her so she was on her back and he lay half on top of her.

"That can wait. First, I want to kiss you. It's been too long."

"It's only been—" The rest of the sentence was lost in the kiss, so deep, so intense, so *passionate*, her brain quite literally stopped functioning. The man had turned the act into an art form. She wondered if he was a master with potions, for surely he should bottle this and turn it into the greatest love potion ever. He was that good. So good...

A sharp knock on the door pulled her back to reality. "Room service," someone called from the hall.

"Damn." Anton pulled away and rolled off the bed, snagging a black robe from the floor and pulling it over his shoulders as he headed toward the door. Adanna looked around, noticed her clothing strewn every which way, and quickly crawled under the blankets, in case the attendant was able to peek into the room. Besides having no wish for anyone else to see her naked, she didn't need anyone in the local magical community to know she was currently engaged in a one-night stand with a warlock from another state.

"...no, no, I got it. I'd be shirking my duties if I left this cart out here in the hall. Let me just – oh. Adanna."

Samona Westwood's dark eyes widened when her gaze fell upon Adanna, sitting in the middle of the giant bed, clutching the white quilt to her breast. Samona was a young witch, a single mom who had stumbled into their coven after the one in which she grew up cast her out for getting pregnant by a human. Considering Adanna herself was half-human, she could certainly understand the poor girl's plight. She'd used the coven's resources to pay the deposit and first month's rent on an apartment, helped the younger witch find decently priced childcare, and arranged for Cook to give her a job at Stay A Spell.

Now, she stood just inside the room, staring at Adanna, who stared back with shock mirrored on her face.

She never should have listened to her inner hussy.

"Um..." Adanna cleared her throat. "Hi, Samona. I see you drew the short straw tonight."

"What's that mean?"

Adanna waved at the cart laden with an array of hot and cold appetizers and a bottle of wine and two glasses. "Working on Samhain."

"Oh. Yeah, well, it's no big deal. Cook let me bring Wendy in with me, and my shift will be over before it gets busy tonight. What are you doing here?"

Adanna decided that question didn't need a detailed answer. Anton clearly sensed her discomfort. He shoved a wad of bills at Samona and shooed her out of the room. He closed the door and then leaned against it and blew out a breath.

"I hope that didn't undermine your authority or something?"

Adanna lifted one shoulder in a shrug and peered at the cart full of food. "Samona is a sweet girl, but she doesn't have a lot of common sense. Maybe I'll get lucky and she'll forget all about this by the time her shift ends. Not that I'm embarrassed to be seen with you, of course."

Anton plucked the wine bottle off the cart and sat on the bed next to her. "I get it. Here." He half filled a glass and offered it to her. She accepted it and slid off the bed, padding over to where she'd left her purse on the dresser next to the television.

"What are you doing?"

"Checking my phone for – hey, that's mine."

He snagged the phone and held it behind his back. "No business. Not right now. Let's just enjoy the evening."

"Give it back. I'm the Supreme, Anton. Tonight of all nights, I can't shirk my duties. However tempted I might be to do so."

He grimaced, negative emotions crawling across his face like a horror movie. Why did he seem so determined to keep her from checking on the coven?

He glanced at the phone, then at her. Their gazes locked for a long moment, until he reluctantly offered her the device. Adanna accepted it and let out a startled yelp.

"Forty-seven text messages and half as many voicemails? Goddess above, what is going on?" Alarm shot through her system as she scrolled through the messages on her phone and then scrambled around the room, searching for her clothes. "What are you doing?" she asked when he did the same.

"Going with you."

"Why?"

He grabbed his shirt, realized the buttons were gone, and tossed it to the floor again, before striding over to a black leather bag perched on a chair near the window. He extracted a blue T-shirt and pulled it over his head.

"For the obvious reason: because I want to make sure you're okay. But also because I'm pretty sure this isn't normal for your coven. If I can help, I will."

"Anton, I appreciate your concern, but—"

"This isn't up for discussion. Now get dressed."

CHAPTER FIVE

Synthia was behind this. He knew it as surely as he knew he was – should have been – a Supreme, leader of his own coven. If only his parents had died ten years later.

If only.

Something had happened to him over the course of the last few hours. Something he could only attribute to – hell, he didn't know what to attribute it to. This kind of shit didn't happen out of the blue – did it?

No way would he call it love. It was too soon for that, and besides, he didn't believe in the concept anyway. Love didn't exist for people like him.

He'd gotten what he wanted – Adanna, unclothed, wanton and naked, with her legs wrapped around his waist. And because of that, because of what she was doing to his heretofore frozen emotional state, the very last thing he wanted to do was finish this job. Unfortunately, unless he was gravely mistaken, Synthia had decided to play interference. She hadn't had faith he could do this one on his own. He briefly wondered at that, considering everything he'd done for her over the years, but there wasn't time to dwell. All he could do now was try to keep Adanna from getting hurt.

* * * *

"I don't get it. We've never seen so many poltergeists in a year, let alone on one night."

"It is Samhain," Anton reminded her.

"That doesn't matter. The most sightings ever documented in one night was seven, and that was in the nineteenth century. This doesn't make sense." Her phone vibrated – again – and she paused to read a text, then shoot off a reply. Anton kept an eye out for evil spirits and a certain evil coven leader. So far, he hadn't seen either.

"Every time we arrive on the scene, there's nothing here, and the witch or warlock who called it in swears they saw something, but it disappears a few minutes before we arrive. Every time."

She gave him a helpless look, and Anton ached to help her. But he had to tread lightly. He should distance himself, leave her to figure this out on her own. But he couldn't. Despite everything he had to lose, he couldn't walk away. Not until Adanna was safe – with or without her position as Supreme Witch.

* * * *

Panic pushed at her brain. Adanna had a headache of epic proportions. Her first Samhain as Supreme Witch, and she was blowing it. Her coven needed her, and she couldn't figure out how to help them. The worst part of all was the guilt threatening to consume her.

If I hadn't given in to the temptation and slept with Anton, this wouldn't be happening.

If she'd been diligent and alert from the very first text, she might have been able to get ahead of – whatever the hell this was.

"I just don't get it," she said for the hundred and fifteenth time since she and Anton had begun answering summons for help. "Why haven't we seen a single poltergeist? They have no idea who the Supreme is. Yet they seem to know I'm coming. How?"

"Maybe somebody's telling them?"

The feminine voice startled her. Adanna stumbled and might have fallen had Anton not grabbed her arm and held her upright. Samona stepped onto the path and waved, a smile spreading on her face, as if it was perfectly normal to bump into each other while out for an evening stroll. Adanna supposed it would have been – at any other time.

"Samona, what are you doing out here? Where's your baby?"

"Cook is watching her. She said you might need some help. What can I do?"

"Um…" Adanna glanced at Anton, but he was scanning the vicinity. Typically, the troublesome apparitions were more annoying than harmful to witches, but as tonight was as far from a typical evening as one could get, Adanna would rather Samona head home, lock the doors, and spend the evening cuddling with baby Wendy.

"Not happening," the younger witch announced when Adanna suggested exactly that. "You've helped me so much in the last year, Adanna. This is my chance to pay you back."

"You don't have to pay me for anything. I was glad to help. The entire coven was glad to help."

"I'm staying. Look – what was that?" Samona stabbed her finger toward the park across the street. The waning moon and street lamps illuminated Spanish moss gently swaying in the trees. Groups of children dressed in Halloween costumes darted around fat tree trunks, oblivious to any wrongdoing that might be occurring that night.

Anton grabbed her arm. "Stay here." He bolted for the park.

"Who is he kidding?" Adanna said as she laid chase. "I want a piece of that damn poltergeist for screwing up my evening." She knew Samona followed because she could hear sneakers slapping against the pavement behind her.

There were so many people – humans, mostly – and trees, park benches, and shrubbery, it took Adanna and Samona long moments to find Anton. When they did, she almost wished they hadn't.

They had run through a stone archway, into a quieter part of the park. The sounds of children laughing and shouting and generally having a great time died away as they slowed their pace and began walking with more care. Something was definitely not right, but she was certain she had seen Anton hurry to this area.

"Over there," Samona whispered, pointing at an area to their left. Adanna grabbed her arm and pulled her behind a tree with a massive trunk and so much Spanish moss draped amongst its branches, it was hard to see through it.

Samona crept along behind her as Adanna made her way through the curtains of dried, wispy tendrils, trying to get closer to Anton and whomever he was speaking with, without them becoming aware. She could only make out bits and pieces of their heated conversation. She caught a glimpse of Anton gesturing wildly.

The person he spoke to was female, but Adanna could not make out her features. All she could see was a woman with dark hair and a tall, thin frame. Samona stepped on a branch and the sound reverberated through the quiet air.

"Oops. Sorry," Samona said in a stage whisper.

Both Anton and the other woman turned in their direction. "Ah, is this the local Supreme, coming out to play?" the woman called out, taunting.

"Don't do this, Synthia." Anton's voice. Anger laced his words.

Adanna took a deep breath and brushed aside the last of the Spanish moss, stepping out from under the cover of trees. She sensed rather than saw Samona move to stand slightly behind her.

* * * *

This wasn't happening.

Yes, it was.

Shit. What the hell was he supposed to do now? Synthia had indeed come to Savannah because she hadn't trusted him to do this job.

"Why?" Anton had demanded when he finally caught up to her, after she'd darted through the stone archway in the park. He hadn't missed it when she waved off the poltergeist floating nearby.

"Because I knew you wouldn't be able to keep it in your pants long enough to do it yourself."

He grimaced. "For fuck's sake, most of the women I've slept with in my life have been on your command."

"Not this one."

"You weren't specific. You said to distract her. I thought I'd done a damn fine job, frankly."

"What I *said* was to ruin her coven meeting. I anticipated a bunch of pissed off witches and warlocks leaving that occult shop. Instead, everybody was so happy it was nauseating. She's practically a kid. And she hates the position. Why do they even follow her? Why haven't they demanded a more seasoned witch step into the role? This should have been my easiest takeover yet."

"Maybe you weren't meant to take over this one. Maybe it's time to stop growing your empire. Why are you so hell-bent on taking over every coven along the eastern seaboard?"

He had never questioned her motives before, and was surprised at his own gall by doing so now.

"What makes you think I intend to stop at the eastern seaboard?"

Anton didn't reply. Synthia waved her hand. Magic shimmered in the air around her.

"See that? Power. That's why. It's like a drug. I came from nothing. *Nothing*. And I'm an exceptionally strong witch. I deserve so much more than what I was given in life. So I've decided to take what's rightfully mine."

He knew her sob story. She'd told him enough times in the past seventeen years, he could recite it by heart. When he'd been a kid, he'd believed her. When he became an adult, he hadn't cared. At that point, it had become all about the paycheck.

But now? Something in him had changed. Adanna. Meeting Adanna. Falling for Adanna. Christ, did it really happen that fast?

The worst part was, as much as Synthia wanted more power, Adanna truly deserved to run the Savannah Coven. She cared about those witches and warlocks, and whether she believed it or not, they cared about her, too. It was her destiny, and one of these days, she'd realize it and embrace it.

As long as he kept Synthia from stealing it from her.

"You're such a bitch. Sometimes I think I would have been better off, trying to manage the coven by myself."

Synthia snorted. "You were twelve. A child. And need I remind you of how your parents died?"

"No." Anton said the word sharply. He lived with it every single day of his life. Every time he closed his eyes, he relived that particular period in his past.

He and Synthia heard the noise at the same time. The crack of a branch. He knew without turning around that it would be Adanna, but he turned anyway. He wanted to drink her in one last time, before his life went to hell in a hand basket.

"Ah, is this the local Supreme, coming out to play?"

"Don't do this, Synthia." To his ears, the warning sounded more like begging, but he didn't care. He would do anything to protect Adanna.

"Don't do what, Anton?" Synthia's voice was too sweet. She was up to something. She was always up to something, but this time, the fine hairs on the back of his neck stood on end. A strong sense of foreboding hit him in the chest.

"Are you saying I shouldn't stop you from destroying this coven?"

He swore he heard Adanna's sharp intake of breath. He wanted to deny it, but Synthia had him by the balls. Adanna would believe he slept with her deliberately, so Synthia could do what she set out to do. Hell, that had been his plan in the first place, hadn't it?

But then he'd gotten to know the beautiful, sweet, giving coven leader, and something changed inside him. Desire to sleep with her for the job shifted to a desire to sleep with her because he wanted to get closer to her. It had been purely personal. Not that Adanna would ever believe it.

"Anton's too nice to do that," Samona stepped out from behind Adanna. What the hell was she doing there? She'd spent a total of five minutes in his company. Sure, he'd given her a hefty tip, but one couldn't base someone's personality on his tipping generosity.

Could they?

"What's going on, Anton?" Adanna asked the question of him, although her gaze was on Synthia. The two women appeared to be having a staring contest.

It's not what it looks like. That's what he wanted to say, to believe. "It's exactly what it looks like."

The look on her face betrayed her devastation. "Did you lie about everything? Was anything you said the truth?"

"Yes. No. Yes, I lied, but not about everything. Not about –" He abruptly broke off, not wanting to confess in front of Synthia and Samona how he felt. How she made him feel. How he wanted to feel.

"What didn't you lie about?" Synthia asked, her voice mocking.

He glared at her but spoke to Adanna. "My father was the Supreme of the Salem Coven. I was slated to take over when he died. Except it happened when I was twelve. An accident…"

"An accident," Synthia repeated, chiding him. He paused, working up the courage to be honest with Adanna. She deserved no less.

"I killed them. I killed my parents."

CHAPTER SIX

Samona gasped, but Adanna worked hard not to react to his words. Anton killed his parents? He was only twelve when they died!

"An experiment gone wrong. I have stronger magic than most witches or warlocks. I did, even as a kid. But I was screwing with spells I had no business trying to master. The potion blew up. I was knocked unconscious. When I came to, I was in the hospital. Synthia was there and told me my parents had died in the explosion."

It couldn't be true. He had been only twelve. But the look on his face told her that was exactly what happened.

"Why you?" she asked, for the first time speaking directly to the other Supreme.

Synthia lifted one shoulder in a dismissive shrug. "Happened to be in the area. Salem is a fascinating place, after all. So much history." Her smile was toothy. Adanna didn't trust a damn thing the woman said.

"I obviously couldn't manage a coven at the age of twelve," Anton went on to explain. "Synthia offered to move to Salem and take over."

"What about your old coven?" Adanna demanded.

"I come from a tiny town in west Texas. There were three witches total. I'd hardly call that a coven," Synthia said.

"Power hungry." Anton spat the words, glaring at the older woman. "After she'd been in charge for a few years, she decided our coven in Salem wasn't enough. She wanted more. So she began gobbling up other covens in the area."

"How?" Adanna asked. "How come no one stopped you?"

Anton answered. "Most Supremes in the area were elderly. Much older and not nearly as strong as Synthia. Some died, some quietly disappeared after Synthia and I arranged some sort of local scandal. Those who didn't had to deal with stunts like she pulled tonight, except usually worse. Synthia can be damned ruthless when she wants something."

"Really, Anton, are you going to tell them my entire devious plan?"

"Actually, yeah. I realize I'm implicating myself here, but I don't care. I'm done being your lackey. Adanna, if you want to reach out to other Supremes, call an emergency meeting, I'll testify. I swear it."

"Don't be ridiculous. You'll be cast out of our society. Stripped of your magic and forced to live as a human." Synthia's voice held a note of distaste – and possibly fear.

"You don't need to testify," Adanna said. "I have enough standing within the community. The other Supremes will listen to me."

"You don't even like being a Supreme," Synthia protested. "I'm doing you a favor by taking over your coven."

Adanna glanced at Anton for the briefest moment. But not for too long. She didn't want her resolve to waver. "My outlook has changed recently. So here's what you're going to do, Synthia—"

Before she could finish the sentence, a poltergeist appeared out of nowhere and flew straight at her face. Startled, Adanna scrambled backwards, trying to avoid the apparition's icy touch. She tripped over a fallen tree branch and stumbled, landing on her ass.

"Adanna!" Both Samona and Anton called her name. Anton looked as though he meant to rush toward her, but was frozen, face etched with concern, one leg and one arm lifted, as if he were running in place. Samona reached down and pulled her to her feet.

"Are you okay?" the younger witch asked as she awkwardly tried to brush dirt and small twigs from Adanna's backside.

"I'm fine." She pushed Samona's hand away.

"Not for long."

Adanna lifted her head when the other Supreme spoke, and was greeted with a clumsy punch to the face.

"What the hell?" She rubbed her cheek and took in her current predicament.

A small army of zombies appeared and surrounded her and Samona with surprising speed. Zombies did not usually move with any urgency whatsoever, regardless of the circumstances. She shoved away the one that had punched her, and grabbed Samona, pulling her close.

"Careful," she said to the other witch, "while they're usually more annoying than anything else, I think that other Supreme is controlling these ones. Which means they could be dangerous."

"How?" The word was no sooner out of Samona's mouth when a zombie broke from the rest, grabbed her arm, and tried to take a bite out of the appendage. Adanna called on her magic and threw a blast of energy at it, sending it flying backwards into a group of other zombies, who all fell over like bowling pins.

Adanna glanced at Anton, who had broken free of Synthia's spell. The two were struggling, almost wrestling. Considering Anton's height, weight, and muscle advantage, Synthia held her own surprisingly well. Adanna turned her focus back to the zombies, sending blasts of energy every which way, while she and Samona inched closer to the other two witches. She didn't have any direct experience dealing with zombies, and she couldn't recall what her grandmother had taught her about getting rid of them, so all she could do was blast them to keep them at bay. She was more concerned with getting to Synthia at the moment, anyway.

"Not so fast."

Adanna was hit with a spell. It felt as though her body filled with cement, rendering her unable to move. Samona stepped in front of her, as if she meant to protect her Supreme, and Adanna couldn't even open her mouth to tell her to run away and save herself.

"I don't think you understand," Synthia said, her malicious glare on Adanna's face. "This coven is mine. You can either rescind your position as Supreme, or you can suffer my wrath." She smiled, but there was no warmth. Only cold, cruel intent. Somewhere along the line, this woman had become so caught up in gaining more and more power, she'd lost sight of what really mattered in life.

Happiness. Pleasure. Friendships. The love and respect of those within her coven. Synthia had probably never experienced any of that, and Adanna had it all. She always had. She just hadn't realized it. Until now.

You aren't taking this from me. Her own resolve weakened Synthia's spell. The cement seeped out of her limbs. But not fast enough. The zombies encroached again, and Samona clearly had no idea how to push them away. Adanna's mouth would not function, so she couldn't even shout a spell at the younger, frightened witch.

You aren't taking this from me. She flexed her fingers, forced the cement further through her body. The zombies kept coming.

This is my coven. I have to protect them.

A group of zombies exploded, bits of undead flying every which way, some of it so big it knocked over the nearest zombies who hadn't been hit directly. The others paused in their march, heads turning back and forth, clearly trying to determine what to do next. Another group exploded, and the rest began a slow retreat.

"What are you doing? How are you doing that?" Synthia demanded, glaring at Adanna.

"She has the backing of her coven."

Adanna had enough control to turn her head to the side. The group of older witches who had been irritated with her during the meeting stood near the archway leading to the main area of the park. As she watched, one of them threw another blast of magic at the zombies, causing another group to explode. A moment later, witches and warlocks began streaming through the arch.

Her coven.

"Fix this!" Synthia screamed. Adanna turned to face her and saw the other witch speaking to Anton.

"Good idea." He grabbed her arms and twisted them behind her back.

She let out a shriek. "Anton, I command you—"

"You don't command shit. Not anymore. Get rid of the zombies."

"No. This is my—"

"Get rid of them or I'm going to let Adanna's coven have their way with you."

Synthia's gaze darted to the group of witches and warlocks standing in a cluster, decimating her army of zombies. After a few tense heartbeats, her shoulders sagged, and she muttered an incantation. The zombies all froze, and then as a unit began a slow, steady march toward the cemetery Adanna knew was just around the corner. She hoped they didn't run into any humans along the way, but figured tonight, at least, the humans wouldn't even blink at a herd of zombies marching down the street. It was Halloween, after all.

"Let's go," Anton said, drawing Adanna's attention back to him. "We're getting on the next plane to Salem. And if you try anything, know that I happen to be a damn good potion master. It's my specialty."

"You can't be serious?"

"Try me."

Adanna watched as he crab-walked the woman toward the marble arch, without so much as a goodbye or even a backward glance. The members of her coven separated and let them pass without issue until they disappeared from sight.

"Well, this is one Samhain I won't soon forget," said Samona.

CHAPTER SEVEN

"Adanna. What are you doing here? I mean, what a surprise. What – what brings you to Salem?"

Anton recalled his manners, held the door open and moved to the side so she could step into his messy apartment. He'd been working almost nonstop for the past six weeks, trying to fix the disaster Synthia had created with her attempt at world domination.

"And Samona," he added when the young room service attendant stepped into view behind her, holding an infant in her arms. "And some other guy I've never seen before in my life," he said when a warlock stepped up and placed his hand on Samona's shoulder.

"Simon Proctar." The kid offered his hand. He was a jolly sort, seemed overly happy to simply be alive. Just like Samona. Based on the proprietary way his hand hovered on her shoulder, Anton wondered if there wasn't something going on between the two of them. He hoped so. Somebody in his life deserved to find a little happiness. It was in short supply for him at the moment.

He resisted the urge to touch Adanna as she walked by. It was hard. She looked damn fine in her red wool pea coat and leggings tucked into knee-high boots. Her dark hair was windblown, and the mark of the Supreme stood out against the pink of her face. The temperature had taken a nosedive the day before. He imagined she must be freezing, having spent her entire life living in the deep south. He could think of a thousand ways to warm her up, but none were remotely appropriate given the way they'd left things the last time they spoke.

"I understand Synthia has been banished and stripped of her magic," Adanna commented. She walked across the room to his sloppy, paper-strewn desk.

"I sent her back to Texas. Figured that was the ultimate punishment."

"I've been doing some serious research over the course of the last six weeks."

"Oh?"

Samona rolled her eyes. "Oh just tell him, already, Adanna."

"How about I show him instead? By the way, Samona deserves a bulk of the credit for this. She refused to believe anything that Synthia said. And as it turned out, she was right. Sometimes, blind faith in humanity is the best option."

She turned toward the door and tilted her head. Samona and Simon stepped out of the way, leaving a man, a woman, and a kid – more like a young adult – standing in the doorway. The older man had dark hair, a full, almost entirely gray beard, and laugh lines around his bright, gray eyes. The woman also had dark hair, although hers was streaked with gray. Her blue eyes glittered with unshed tears. The kid standing between them was a younger version of Anton.

"Mom? Dad?"

"Hey, son." The man lifted a hand and swiped a tear from his eye.

"Holy shit."

His mom laughed. "Is that really the most appropriate thing to say when meeting your brother for the first time?"

"My – er – *brother*?" He shifted his gaze to Adanna, whose eyes were also misty. "I don't understand."

She smiled and nodded. "It's a long, convoluted story, but let's see if I can give you the shortened version. Then you can have your reunion, Simon and Samona can go back to their hotel, and I promise, I'll give you every last detail we've unearthed."

He liked the sound of that, mostly because it gave him the impression she intended to stay with him. He wasn't sure how that would work, given she needed to run her coven, and he still had a long road ahead, cleaning up Synthia's mess. But he couldn't think about any of that at the moment, because his gaze kept straying to his parents, who, although they looked as though they'd aged far more than they should have in the last seventeen years, were, ultimately, alive and standing before him. He wanted to hug them, but he was still too shocked to move.

"The entire thing was a setup," Adanna said. Her voice was sympathetic, not bitter or angry, which was what he would have expected after everything he confessed back on Halloween.

"Synthia deliberately chose to begin her multi-coven takeover here in Salem. She had been researching, looking for the perfect opportunity to get out of what she considered her miserable existence. She was convinced that because she was born with the mark, she was destined for great things. Greater than simply running a small coven in a tiny town in west Texas."

"But the explosion…" Anton didn't understand. The magical experiment he'd received in the mail had blown up in his face. He'd ended up in the hospital. None of that had been fake.

"That experiment was sent by Synthia. It contained a sleeping potion. Knocked out all three of us," his father explained. His father. Alive.

"Sleeping potion?"

"Yep. Apparently, she checked you into a hospital, then banished us. We've been living in this shack on the side of a mountain, along with a dozen other Supremes."

Anton wiped his hand over his face. "I still don't understand."

"Neither did we, at first," Adanna said.

"I found them," The overtly cheerful Simon announced.

"It's not exactly getting any clearer," Anton remarked. When Simon opened his mouth to speak, Adanna lifted her hand and he remained silent.

"Samona and I researched Synthia's takeovers, trying to figure out how it all happened. I don't think we necessarily knew what we were looking for, other than some sort of explanation. It didn't make sense that so many Supremes would have either handed over the reigns of their covens or simply disappeared off the map. That was the caveat, really. The vast majority literally disappeared without a trace. But they had to be *somewhere*, right? Witches and warlocks have magic, but we can't just disappear. Considering we couldn't find any indication they'd left or died, we brainstormed that they might still be in the general vicinity. So we began a physical search in New England."

"You've been up here before and I didn't know it?" He could hear the injury in his own voice, but he didn't try to hide it. He'd been miserable for the past six weeks, thinking Adanna hated him, thinking he'd never be happy again.

She shook her head. "No. I had to stay home and take care of my coven. We found Simon through one of our members who likes to ski."

"I'm a ski instructor," Simon helpfully added. "And a mountain guide."

"I paid to have him fly down to Savannah, so I could read him, to make sure we could trust him, before we asked for his help," Adanna explained.

Anton was distracted from their immediate situation. "You can read people?" How the hell had he convinced her to sleep with him, if she could read people? While he'd obviously changed his spots in the last six weeks, the reality was, he'd gone to Savannah with the express intention of ruining her.

"I deliberately chose not to read you," she said, answering his unspoken question. "I didn't want to. To be honest, I was afraid what you felt for me was more than just physical attraction."

"It is."

"It wasn't then."

"That's not true. Even when I was doing Synthia's bidding, I still—"

"We know, Anton," Samona said, interrupting him. "Can we get back to the story now?"

He snapped his mouth closed and focused on Adanna, on her beautiful face, the scrollwork marking her as a leader. What he hoped was something akin to love in her eyes…

"Simon came to Savannah and I quickly realized he was as honest as the day is long—"

"And I fell head over heels," Samona said with a giggle and a blush.

"As did I," the mountain guide proclaimed, snaking his arm around her shoulder. "I found them," he announced. "Found their cabin. Well, shack, really. Fourteen people – well, fourteen adults, anyway – all living in conditions that were, frankly, deplorable."

Anton's dad raked his hand through his hair. "The conditions *were* deplorable. But we were a determined bunch. We would have made an awesome reality television series."

"Why didn't you leave?"

His dad's gaze cut to his wife. "Synthia had cast a powerful spell and warded the place. We could walk about twenty feet away from the cabin, but no farther. Tried every spell we knew, and nothing worked. We started getting pretty damn creative with luring animals close enough so we could kill them for food. Luckily, the next set of Supremes she banished to the shack were avid botanists, so we learned what we could and could not eat out of the plants growing nearby." He shrugged. "We survived."

"Not that I'm not thrilled you're alive, but why didn't Synthia kill you?"

Adanna answered. "In the beginning, I suspect, it was insurance. If you woke up in that hospital and didn't believe her elaborate plan, she could try something different. Maybe threaten to torture them if you didn't fall into line. Who knows? She had killed a few Supremes, we believe, but those deaths look as though they were from natural causes. It's possible she worried that too many deaths would make the human authorities take notice."

Anton had so many questions, but one was at the forefront of his mind. "My brother?" He stared at the younger version of himself.

His father ruffled the younger kid's shaggy, dark hair. "Your mother was pregnant when Synthia banished us. We didn't know until about a month into our captivity. He's a tough one, though. Takes after his older brother. And you'll be thrilled to know that Andre happens to be a Supreme, as well."

"That's great, but why should I be thrilled to hear that?"

"Well, because I assume you're moving to Savannah, of course," his mother responded. "I've heard it's a lovely area. I can't wait to visit."

"Moving? To Savannah?" This entire conversation was so surreal, Anton had the ridiculous urge to pinch himself.

"Adanna seems awfully attached to you. And she, of course, can't leave her coven. So it makes sense that you move to hers."

He lifted his gaze to the woman standing by his side. "Is she serious?"

Adanna nodded. "She is. We've become quite friendly over the course of the last week or so."

"This is crazy. I can't. I mean, there's so much to do here. I can't just – I want to, I swear, but—" Adanna pressed two fingers to his lips, effectively silencing him.

"What's left to do?" she asked. "We've just found a dozen Supremes, all of whom are eager to get back to real life, including their responsibilities as leaders of their covens."

His father offered a scrap of paper, upon which was a list of names, corresponding, Anton noted after a quick glance, with cities in which local covens were located. Trying to tamp the hope that was now steadily growing in his gut, he compared the list to the one on his computer, checking off names as he matched them to covens currently without Supremes. His face fell.

Anton glanced at Adanna. "There's one left. A small coven in New Hampshire."

His father nodded. "I believe she was one of the ones Synthia killed outright. Damned stubborn witch, if memory serves. Wouldn't have let go of her coven without a vicious fight."

"That was my great aunt," Simon piped up. "We were pretty close. I was fascinated by her position in the coven, and she taught me a bunch of stuff. I could probably manage things until a replacement is found."

"That's very considerate of you, Simon," Adanna replied, smiling sadly. "But I don't think that will work. Coven rules are very clear. They must be led by a marked Supreme, or the guardians of said marked Supreme, in the event a Supreme dies an untimely death." She glanced at Anton.

Had he been aware of that little caveat to the rule, his entire life might have turned out differently. Although there was one pretty damn incredible result. He now fully, truly believed in love. Because he was unequivocally in love with the woman standing before him.

"What if he's married to the guardian of a marked Supreme?" Samona asked.

Adanna frowned. "Do you happen to know a single witch who recently gave birth to a marked Supreme? I mean, other than Anton's parents, of course. And are you really willing to give Simon up to this woman?"

"I would never give up Simon," the younger witch said so fiercely, Anton had to stifle a laugh. "But as it happens, I am guardian to my very own marked Supreme."

"*What?*"

Samona, with a smirk on her perky face, lifted the leg of the child in her arms and tugged down the baby's pink fleece pants. Scrollwork, eerily similar to both Adanna's and Anton's, crawled up the inside of her left thigh.

"Wendy is a Supreme?" Adanna asked, her gaze darting from child to mother and back again.

Samona nodded eagerly and tugged the child's pants back into place. "I never told anyone because I was afraid they wouldn't believe me, and I didn't want them all looking at my baby like she was some kind of freak. Because she isn't. She's just…"

"A Supreme." Adanna breathed the words. Anton could understand. He could scarcely believe what he was hearing. Was Samona solving their problems? Was it really possible that Anton could move to Savannah, that he and Adanna could be together, forever?

"We'll probably email or call every day," Simon said.

"Yeah, I mean, this is all new to us. But you, Adanna – well, and you too, Anton – y'all really seem to know what you're doing."

"We want to do it right. Which means we're going to do it exactly like you. And we'll raise Wendy the same way. We'll make you proud, Adanna, honest. Just give us a chance."

Adanna glanced at Anton. "I think this is your decision. Or your dad's."

"I've always had a thing for southern girls. And southern heat." The look he gave her was certainly full of heat. "As far as I'm concerned, it's a done deal."

"It's…" Adanna couldn't finish the sentence. Anton snaked his arm around her waist and pulled her into an embrace. Heedless of his parents and the rest of their audience, he cupped her face with his hands and kissed her, fiercely, passionately, until they both were breathing heavily.

"It's a done deal," he repeated, gasping, yet steadily looking into her eyes. "We're a done deal. Forever."

Forever.

If you enjoyed that story, you'll probably like the rest of Tami Lund's books, including:

The Bartender
Candy Crush
Love Gumbo
Naked Truth (Tough Love #1)
Undercover Heat (Tough Love #2)
Delicious Deception (Tough Love #3)
Into the Light (Lightbearer #1)
Dawning of Light (Lightbearer #2)
Light Beyond the Darkness (Lightbearer #3)
Of Love and Darkness (Twisted Fate #1)
The Perfect Christmas (part of the Unwrapping Love Anthology)

Tami's books can be purchased here:
http://www.amazon.com/Tami-Lund/e/B00AXJH5MY/ref=dp_byline_cont_ebooks_1

And if you want to stalk her, check out her website:
http://tamilund.com
Be sure to stalk her on social media, too:
https://www.facebook.com/AuthorTamiLund?ref=hl
https://twitter.com/TamiLundAuthor

Micah's Mess
By
Niki Daninger

DEDICATION

This story is dedicated to those who believe in me. To those who encourage, help, and push me. To those who gave me this chance. Thank You.

Marlene,

I can not thank you enough for all you have done ... You are my numero uno Beta Reader! I value your time, opinions and suggestions but above all else, I value your friendship

♡ Mike

CHAPTER ONE
October 22nd

I slammed the empty bottle onto the bar and gestured for another. I was half tanked, but I didn't care; it had been one of *those* days.

Silas stood a full one before me and gave a cautious look. "No trouble now Micah, I got orders to kick you out if you get rowdy."

I gave the guy a wicked grin. Healing was my only manifested power, but at 6'1"- 220, we both knew he had a snowball's chance in hell of throwing me out. "I'm good. Keep 'em coming."

A couple of females walked in, laughing throatily. Stay a Spell was the only paranormal bar/inn in Savannah, which meant all magical beings were welcome. The place was usually packed.

They headed in my direction; their skin tight dresses and flashing eyes caught the attention of every guy in the bar, but I kept my eyes forward. I knew better.

Succubi.

I sighed as one trailed her nails across the back of my shirt, then traced the raven tat covering most of my shoulder and upper left arm.

"Hmmm," she purred in my ear. "When you gonna put those lips on something more responsive than a cold bottle?"

"I don't have enough power to feed you." I didn't normally put myself down, I had a reputation as a badass to maintain, but like I said, it'd been one of those days.

"Oh lover, your body is all I need tonight." She slid her hand down my side as she pressed against me, making sure I felt her curves. "You're the finest thing I've seen in a long time."

"Thanks." It was dangerous to reject a succubus outright. They were known to hold grudges. "Maybe another time."

"Baby, you need to loosen up. Let me show you what these muscles are made for." She slipped her hand up under my ribbed tank and dug her nails into my abs.

"Take a hike Vicky!"

I turned to face the man who'd claimed the seat next to mine. He was older, late sixties, but he had a full head of salt and pepper hair, and his wiry frame looked strong.

Vicky pouted, linked arms with her companion, and walked off.

"Gregor." The man held out a gnarled hand.

"Micah." His grip was overly tight when we shook; I tried not to roll my eyes. "Look, thanks for—"

"You're Adanna's brother, aren't you?" He raised a finger to get Silas' attention.

My back instantly stiffened. "I'm not a messenger service. You wanna talk to my sister, you'll have to hunt *her* down."

I planted my feet, ready to leave, but Gregor placed a restraining hand on my forearm. That's when I felt the jolt of electricity surge up my arm, making my biceps contract. It wasn't painful, but the sensation wasn't pleasant either. "What the hell dude?"

"Have a seat friend. It's not your sister I want. My proposition is for you."

CHAPTER TWO
October 31st

Reap What You Sow was busy, but that was to be expected. It was two o'clock Samhain day, and a hundred teenage witch wannabes were in the shop buying ingredients for love spells or candles to contact the dead.

I touched the focus stone hanging from a cord around my neck as I pushed through the throng. If any of them knew a true coven was meeting in the next room, they'd wet their panties.

Rose, the owner, was nowhere to be seen so I walked through the blue curtains behind the counter and down the stairs to the meeting room. I wasn't late, but three quarters of the members were already present, each one sitting in a unique chair around the ornately carved table.

Mine, a restored electric chair, wasn't comfortable, but neither was my position at the table. I sat near the foot. If fate weren't such a cruel mistress, I'd be at the head. Instead, my sister had inherited that honor.

What a waste.

I dug at my nails, refusing to look at her. She disapproved of my behavior, but to be honest, the feeling was mutual. She was a natural born Supreme, the granddaughter of one of the greatest leaders the Savannah coven had ever known. The filigreed birthmark on her face ensured all knew exactly who and what she was, but did she care?

No.

She'd rather spend her time hanging around humans, pretending she was one of them.

I should have been born with the mark. I was the one who wanted to lead. I was the one who'd spent every moment I could with our grandmother. I was the one who'd practiced for hours on end, forcing myself to learn all I could before she was taken from us.

The last members trickled in, and Adanna gave her typical, half-hearted address. That's when I noticed the warlock standing by her side. I didn't recognize him, but I recognized the look in his eyes, the way his every action mirrored hers. He wanted her. I almost burst out laughing. My sister didn't date warlocks.

"Keep your eyes out for zombies and lost spirits..." she was saying. Blah, blah, blah. It was obvious she didn't want to be there. You'd think a leader would be interested in the lives of her followers, ask questions, offer advice, but the members looking at her only served to remind her of what she was. Why couldn't anyone but me see it?

But someone *did* see it. The unnamed warlock. He knew she was losing control, and he stepped up to defend her when some of the older witches took offense to her comments about using magic responsibly. Yeah, he wanted her all right. I kept my mouth closed, he didn't need me shining his armor.

The meeting, short and simple, was over in no time. As the members shuffled for the stairs, I reached for my phone. Sliding my finger across the screen I stared at

Gregor's number, remembering his words: *You have until Samhain to decide.*

Adanna's gaze settled on me. We both had dark hair, but her eyes were full green, not muddy like mine. Concern creased her brow, but before she had the chance to say anything, I got to my feet and rushed out the door. I'd made my decision.

My sister had to go.

* * * *

"Hey, yeah, it's me." Guilt and excitement coursed through me as I held the phone to my ear. "I'm in."

"Thought you would be." The warlock's slippery voice gave me chills. "I'll send my assistant out tonight. You need to get the book and meet me at sundown on the seventh."

"And just where is this book I'm supposed to *retrieve*?"

"Phoenix."

"Arizona? You gotta be kidding me."

"You have plenty of time. I'll text you the address."

"Fine, but you're paying for gas."

"The spell I give you will be payment enough."

The exchange didn't sound fair, but he hung up before I could say so. My phone binged a second or two later with a location. I don't do heights, which meant flying was out, so I pulled up MapQuest. Thirty-one hours—each way. Damn it.

I knew how I'd be spending the rest of my Halloween: making potions and stocking my travel bag. No way I was gonna travel cross country without being prepared.

I made my way back to Stay a Spell. I didn't *live* there, but I crashed in a small room more often than not. Cook, the owner, let me stay in exchange for the odd favor; healing the odd staff mishap was easier than trying to stumble my way home after a long night.

The restaurant half of the bar was quaint, with exposed brick walls and wrought iron beams. Lit with hanging lanterns and strings of lights wrapped around the indoor trees and foliage, the place felt like a well kept courtyard. It was quiet; there were only a few couples eating in the dining area.

I ignored them and the rich smells wafting from the kitchen as I made my way up the back staircase to the second floor. The communal room was empty, but the door to the magic and potions room was open. I peeked in and sighed with relief. Also empty. I didn't need anyone spying on my grandmother's secret recipes.

I ran down the hallway to my tiny room, grabbed what I needed, then headed back to the magic room, where I closed and locked the door. Time to work.

* * * *

It was quarter past eleven when I made my way downstairs, my canvas duffle slung over a shoulder. My phone had exploded earlier with requests for help. There'd been some mysterious poltergeist activity, but I'd long since shut if off. Adanna was the Supreme, it was time she did some actual work.

In the meantime, I'd managed to restock my emergency potion supply, but I had one last errand before I called it a night. I was running low on Moonflower, which bloomed only at night. It was more potent if picked on Samhain; it was even more potent if the moon was full, but the dang thing was already waning.

Seamus, the massive Dioane Sidhe bouncer, sat on his stool at the bottom of the stairs, surveying the crowd that had gathered.

I walked up to him and set my bag on the floor. I wasn't what most humans expected of a warlock, I wasn't skinny or geeky, and I didn't run around with a wand. I've got a good build, but the red-bearded warrior always made feel like a dwarf. I puffed out my chest, and he laughed.

The brute had lousy people skills, but we had an understanding. A jealous gorgon, hell-bent on turning him to stone, had suffered a nasty separation from her head a few years ago. I still had the silver serving platter I'd used.

"Going somewhere?" He crossed his arms, beefing out his bicepses to full effect.

"I'll be out of town for a few days."

"All right, I'll inform any customers."

I wasn't supposed to conduct *business* at the bar, except for Cook, but Seamus always sent clients my way. Healing on the sly made me good money, and I tipped him well. "Sounds good."

"Hey," he called out. "Be safe."

I knew what he meant. Halloween night, weirdos, ghouls, and stupid humans were out en mass.

* * * *

I stepped out of my 1978 Ford Ranger and into the beautiful night. The Savannah National Wildlife Refuge surrounded me, welcoming me like a long lost friend. It had been too long since I'd last been here.

The refuge was mostly bottomland, and moonflower grew naturally in tropical hardwood hammocks, but my grandmother had planted some in a hidden clearing when she first became Supreme. As far as I knew, she'd never shown it to anyone but me, and possibly Adanna.

I walked amongst the giant cypress, gum, and oaks, feeling the essence of the place, soft as a whisper along my skin. I didn't have heightened senses, not the way humans would imagine. I couldn't hear or see any better than they could, but I was more attuned to the forces just beyond their senses. Energy pulsed around me, life and…

I stopped. Something was off. I sensed magic— and blood.

I spun in a circle, clutching my focus stone. Something dark had happened here. Holding my hand out before me, I followed the trail through the forest and into a thick stand of undergrowth. Shoving leafy branches aside, I came upon a doe lying against the trunk of a cypress.

Her coat was pale for a white tail, almost creamy. There was something familiar about her though, something that had me thinking *shapeshifter*.

"Damn." I looked down at the arrow in her hindquarters. Archery season in Savannah ended today, at sunset. "Bet you thought you were safe."

I turned around, but there was no trace of the person who'd shot her.

"Look, nothing personal." I bent down, unsheathing my hunting knife. "But shifter blood is hard to come by."

I held the blade out toward her, expecting her to thrash, bolt, or shift. Instead, she lay perfectly still. I pressed the knife to her throat, waiting, but all she did was stare up at me, her eyes wide and dark.

"You don't think I'll do it, do you?" I demanded.

She didn't know who she was dealing with. I was the warlock with the chip on his shoulder. The ass who didn't give a damn about anyone but himself. The guy who was plotting to take down his own sister. I pushed the edge deeper, feeling her pelt brush up against my knuckles, feeling the blood pulse through her jugular.

She didn't answer.

"Ah hell," I grumbled. I wanted to do it, shifter blood had a hundred and one uses, but I couldn't.

Being a healer gave me a good under the table income, but it was an ability I'd often cursed. Sure, I was powerful, but I'd trade it for something that didn't cramp my bad-boy style any day.

"All right, all right." I gave in. "I'll help, but if you tell anyone, I'll hunt you down myself and take every last drop of your blood."

I sheathed my blade and grabbed hold of the arrow. Bracing my free hand on her hip, I pulled. The arrow came free, and I tossed it into the brush but not before I noted the chipped silver tip. That's why she hadn't transformed.

Blood flowed from the wound, but the amount was insignificant. "Lucky you, it missed the femoral artery."

I clasped the stone laying against my chest a second, then covered the hole in her leg with one palm while placing the other flat upon the tree's trunk.

I closed my eyes. I was a conduit. I didn't heal the wound by stitching the fibers of her muscle and skin back together. No, I channeled her injuries through my body, feeling the sharp stab of the arrow, the tearing of flesh, sinew, and vein, the ache of straining muscles, and the exhaustion of lungs fighting for breath, slide over my nerves, into the living tree. I groaned as the wound on her leg closed, and a similar one opened in the trunk. Sap slid down the bark, and I knew the process was complete.

Wiping my hands on my jeans, I stood up. The doe emanated a soft, warm glow as her form altered. I wasn't sure why she was glowing; shifters didn't do that. The light brightened, and I shielded my eyes 'til it faded.

Standing before me, in the now dark forest, was the most beautiful being I'd ever seen. Like the doe she had once been, her eyes were big and dark, and the silky hair tumbling over her slight shoulders was tawny colored. She wore nothing but a long, white, sleeveless shift.

She took my breath away. "You're *not* a shapeshifter."

"I am the guardian of this wood, and I am in your debt."

I cursed under my breath. One might think having an angel in your debt was a good thing, but I knew, from second hand experience, they had a nasty habit of checking in at the most inopportune moments to offer 'help'. The last thing I needed right now was a goody-two-shoes watching over my shoulder.

"I'm Micah."

A shy smile pulled at her lovely lips. "I know every person who has stepped foot here."

"Including the one who shot you?"

"That was no *person*." She looked away. "That was a demon."

"And what would a demon want with a low level angel like you?" The darkness I'd felt earlier made sense now.

She didn't notice my dig, she merely shrugged. "I do not know."

"How'd you get away?" I pressed. I didn't want some big nasty sneaking up behind me to finish what he'd started.

"I borrowed power from the forest and cast him away."

"Well you're good now. Next time watch out for the dark boys." I turned to go; I wanted to put as much distance between us as possible.

"Wait," she called out. "I owe you a debt."

"Yeah." I spun but kept backing up. "I absolve you of that. I don't need any help. Go, be free or whatever."

"I cannot, I used the last of my power to take this form."

That stopped me. "What're you talking about?"

"The arrow was poisoned. I cannot manifest my angelic presence."

"Look, I can't remove poison. I can only heal the body." I frowned. "You're gonna have to find someplace to hide 'til it leaves your system."

"I will go with you." She stepped toward me.

"Oh no." I held my hands up. "No way, I am not a babysitter. I have stuff to do."

"I will help," she offered.

I looked down at her slim form, so delicate and graceful as she took another step. Warning bells clanged in my head, but I couldn't leave her there, in the middle of the forest, defenseless.

I sighed. "I'll find you a safe place to stay. That's it."

We made our way back to my Ford, stopping only to gather several moonflowers and their roots, then went to my apartment. There was no way I was taking her to the bar; the wards were stronger, but I didn't know too many paranormals who'd be happy to see an angel in their favorite joint.

I wasn't at my place often enough for it to be messy, but it definitely had a bachelor flare. I held the door open and gestured to the worn couch. "Have a seat."

"Why do you hate your sister?"

I spun and glared at the innocent looking female running her fingers over my grandmother's embroidered pillow. "Don't do that—don't read my mind!"

"I apologize." She put the pillow down. "I have never taken human form. Your thoughts and emotions are stronger than I thought they would be."

Was she saying she'd only ever been a deer? "You can stay here 'til the poison is gone. It's protected."

I made my way to the bedroom but stopped. "And for the record, I don't *hate* my sister."

Without looking back, I slammed the door between us.

CHAPTER THREE
November 1st

I set a plate in front of my guest and dished out some eggs. She gave the lumpy yellow bits a suspicious look. Remembering her comment from last night I prompted, "What's the matter Angel, you never eat before?"

"My name is Isolde." Her expression was wary. "I have nibbled plants, but I have never eaten…what is this?"

"Never mind," I advised. "Here, try this."

She accepted the piece of bacon I offered and took a tentative bite. She tried to hide it, but I caught her little smile. "It is salty."

"It is." I dropped a few more pieces onto her plate. "Look, I'm leaving. Feel free to stay as long as you need."

"I am going with you. You saved my life, I intend to save yours."

"And how do you plan on doing that in your weakened state?" I laughed; the idea of a tiny angel saving me was insane. Hell, taking her home with me last night had been insane. There was no way she was coming with me.

"I am not so weak." She took another bite and held my gaze. "Why do you look at me like that? I sense—"

"You don't know me." I shoved my plate aside. "You wanna come, fine, I'll let you come, but I'm not gonna listen to crap about my sister or how I live my life. You keep your righteous opinions to yourself. Got it?"

She flinched but nodded.

"The first thing we need to do is get you something else to wear. You can't run around wearing nothing but a slip."

Part of me protested. Isolde in a slip was, quite possibly, the most exquisite thing I'd ever laid eyes on, but that was exactly why she needed more clothes.

"Stay put." Not waiting for an answer, I made my way down the hallway to the last apartment. I felt bad breaking in and worse for stealing. Tanya was a sweet girl, in her own awkward, I-can't-stop-staring-at-you way, but she and Isolde were about the same size.

I raided her closet, taking a couple pair of jeans, a bunch of cotton tops, and a pair of sandals. Then, against my better judgment, I scooped a few delicates from her dresser and made my way back to my own place.

Tossing the items at Isolde, I started cleaning up, careful to keep my mind blank.

When the bathroom door closed, I grabbed my duffle and made a silent escape, making sure to secure the door behind me. Isolde would be safe as long as she stayed in the apartment. There was food in the cabinets, and she had fresh clothes. I crept down the back stairway, telling myself I wasn't responsible for what befell her if she chose to leave.

At the end of the lot, around the side of the building, my Ranger waited... with Isolde. She wore a pair of flare bottom denims and a snug Tee with two kissing frogs on the front. The rest of her things were rolled into a ball at her hip.

"You read my mind again," I accused.

"I did not." She had the gall to look hurt.

"How'd you beat me?"

"I crawled out the bathroom window."

I looked up at the fire escape, then narrowed my gaze. She wanted to tag along fine, but I was ditching her at the first safe house. I unlocked her door, then threw her stuff into my pack.

"Where are we going?"

"Phoenix."

* * * *

It was just after midnight, our time, when we got to Shreveport. Thirteen hours was one hell of a trip, but we'd stopped several times to stretch our legs and grab some personal items, like an extra toothbrush, and fuel up on snacks. Isolde had developed a fondness for salted meat, so I'd bought her a large bag of jerky.

I'd been tempted, more than once, to tell her what the strips were made of, but her childish delight in them and every new thing she came across had me out of sorts. She had a naivety and wonder about her that drew me in, and I found myself doing things just to make her smile.

I knew I'd regret it. I didn't need some angel undermining my determination, not now, but I couldn't complain. I'd expected her to throw sermons and Bible quotes at me. I had nothing against the guy upstairs, but I was a selfish schmuck; *I* wanted to be boss. She'd surprised me with quiet acceptance though, which made it easy to answer her never-ending barrage of questions.

"Isa, we're here." I pulled into a space behind a large, abandoned looking building just outside of town.

"This is Phoenix?" She turned her dark, sleepy eyes on me and my stomach clenched.

"No, we're at a safe house. Phoenix is another nineteen hours away."

"Safe house," she repeated.

I held my phone up, showing her the opened app. "Yeah, paranormals have places all over the country. Protected from nasties and humans who'd love to see if we float."

She frowned but followed me up the concrete steps to a heavy metal door.

I knocked five times, in a pattern, over the welded sigil, and the door opened. We made our way through the foyer, decorated in early 19th century style, to the check in desk. The place wasn't well cared for, but it was better than a chain motel.

A female vamp wearing Gothic Lolita walked from a back room and I cringed; she looked like a walking cliché. "We need a room for the night."

"Fifty." She held out her hand. "Cash."

The added comment was unnecessary. I wouldn't have used a hexed credit card on a fellow freak.

"Room 8, upstairs to the left," she drawled. "Bar's in the basement. Mind your manners."

"Yes ma'am." A drink sounded good, but I didn't need trouble. Not tonight.

On the second floor I opened the door to our room and cursed. There was only one bed. I had enjoyed my time with Isolde, but I was *not* going there. I grabbed the quilt and a pillow, threw them on the floor, and stretched out facing the wall. "I'll see you in the morning."

My eyes had been closed no more than a minute when I felt something crawling over my shoulder. I swiped, expecting a spider, but my fingers made contact with Isolde's. I twisted so I could see her.

She was leaning over the edge of the bed, her hand outstretched, her expression sad. In that moment, I had the strange feeling she was hiding something.

"Why did you choose the raven?"

Most considered the bird a harbinger of death, due to its presence on battlefields, gorging upon the fallen. It was an assumption that served me well, but the truth was not so dark. "My grandmother taught me to seek out the deep mysteries. Hugin was one of Odin's ravens; he was sent out in search of knowledge."

"In North American mythology, the raven is known as the bringer of light." She touched the tip of her finger to my arm again. This time I didn't brush her away. "I am sorry about your grandmother."

"I asked you to quit reading me," I growled.

"Yes, but I wanted you to know I feel your pain." She withdrew her hand and disappeared atop the bed.

I had no response. I wanted to be mad at her, to lash out as I'd done a hundred times since the funeral, but I couldn't. Stupid angel was turning me soft. I huffed, then turned my back to her again and squeezed my eyes shut.

CHAPTER FOUR
November 2nd

"Micah." Her voice was soft, almost sensual, and her hands were warm on my skin. "Micah!"

Disoriented, I opened my eyes. Isolde knelt over me, shaking my shoulder. "Hey—"

"Shhhhh." She crouched lower. "Something is here. Something…"

I was up in a flash, shoving her behind me. "What?"

There was a crash and a shout, followed by a bang, as if someone had been thrown against a wall.

"We need to get out of here."

"The window?" she suggested.

I frowned, unlike my apartment, there was no fire escape.

There was another crash, and the hallway filled with angry shouts. I crept to the door and peered around the edge at the chaos. Figures were bumping around in the semi-darkness, bouncing off each other. At the end, the stereotypical vamp from behind the desk held her arms high, chanting something fierce. The space stretched like a horror movie corridor that never seemed to end.

"Grab my bag." I gestured to the duffle on the chair, and Isolde inched toward it. "Hurry."

She brought it over, and I tucked her under my arm. "Hug the wall to the right and head down the stairs."

She didn't have time to answer, someone was thrown into our door, and the force knocked me backward. I was caught up in a tangle of hairy arms and legs as a were transformed atop me.

"You!" Everyone froze as the massive shape in the middle of the commotion pointed at Isolde and smiled. "Found you."

There was genuine fear in her eyes, and it pissed me off. Cinching the were around the middle, I shoved him back into the fray. Not that he minded; 200 pounds of muscle, claw, and fang, he launched himself at the enormous intruder.

"Now, Isa. Go now!" I grabbed her wrist and pulled her after me, down the stairway, through the foyer, and out to the lot.

The wind had picked up; trash swirled around when we reached my truck. A transformer shorted and zapped on the closest electrical pole just as glass rained down on us. The fight had made it to our room. It wouldn't be long before the brute realized we weren't there.

I pushed Isolde into the cab, ran to my side, and turned the engine over. The Ford was old but reliable. She lurched to life, and we sped down the road, toward the interstate, with rain pelting the windshield.

"That was him. The demon who poisoned me." Isolde was pale and shaking. I wanted to pull over and calm her, but I couldn't. The beast would be on our tracks in no time. We needed to find a safe spot. A *true* one. "How did he find me?"

"He must have followed us from Savannah."

"How did he get in? I thought there were spells…" She was nearly hysterical, but it was a damn good question. Idiot owner must have forgotten to ward a window. The ruckus *did* start upstairs. Someone was getting a no-star review.

"Hey." I reached over and held her hand.

She faced me, and her shoulders sagged. "You are not hurt?"

"Me? No, I'm fine." Through all that she was worried about me?

We drove twenty minutes to a cheap motel, the kind I'd been trying to avoid, and hunkered down.

"Will he not just follow us here?" Isolde asked after a long stretch of uncomfortable silence.

We sat on the bed, leaning against the headboard, and I scooted closer. I'd drawn half a dozen runes over the doorframe, another batch around the window, and several on the walls for good measure.

"I don't think the demon *knew* we were there." I'd put a little thought into this. "I think he just assumed we'd hide in a safe house. I bet he checked a few before he found us."

I could see the uncertainty in her eyes. "Are you sure?"

I wasn't, it didn't explain how he'd followed us in the first place, but I didn't want to tell her that, so I offered a false smile. "I'm not the only one who knows how to download an app."

I wrapped my arm around her shoulders, rested my head on hers, and closed my eyes. Seemed I was stuck with her for a while longer.

* * * *

I woke up after seven that morning, with Isolde cradled on my lap. She looked peaceful. I wanted to let her sleep, but we had to get going. I tucked silken strands behind her ear, causing her to stir.

She stretched, then looked up at me, her cheeks blushing when she noticed I was staring. "Sorry."

I wanted to pull her into my arms, but I hardened my resolve instead. "So, why is that demon after you?"

The pink drained from her face. "I do not know."

"He must want something. First he poisons you, keeping you earthbound, then he tracks you thirteen hours to a safe house and tears the place up."

"As you said, I am just a low level angel."

So she *had* noted my comment. I regretted it but wished I didn't.

"All right. Let's get our stuff together and get out of here. We still have a long way to go."

CHAPTER FIVE
November 3rd

Deciding to avoid safe houses, we'd checked into another chain motel last night, just as we'd reached El Paso. Phoenix was only another seven-ish hours away, but by ten o'clock, I'd been beyond exhausted. I'd needed to crash.

Isolde was putting our supplies back in the bag, along with our laundry. She was abnormally quiet.

I'd been hard on her yesterday, throwing out a hundred questions, asking her to re-live every moment from the Halloween attack, but it had to be done. We had to figure out what the demon wanted if there was any chance for us to stay ahead of him. At this point we both knew someone willing to follow us to Shreveport wasn't giving up.

"Look, I didn't mean what I said." I knew why she was upset. I'd lashed out and said she was more likely to kill me than save me. It was true, but I'd said it more to distance myself than to shed light. Every time I looked at her, I felt the urge to protect grow stronger. I didn't need that kind of attachment. "You can read me if you like."

She zipped up the bag then met my gaze. "Are you apologizing?"

"Will you stop moping?"

A slow smile pulled at her lips.

"You played me." I laughed. "Guess I deserved that."

I grabbed the duffle, checked to make sure there were no demons waiting outside, then ushered the devious little angel out. "Let's get something to eat."

We stopped at a diner for breakfast burritos before continuing our journey. We had plenty of time to spare—as long as trouble didn't find us. Seven hours would get us to the location by four. That gave me time to scope things out before coming up with a plan.

Taking a little time to enjoy a meal was my reward for getting this far without doing something stupid.

"So, what does the guardian of a bottomland do exactly?" I eyed her over my glass of OJ. "You help the plants grow and save little animals from alligators?"

She narrowed her gaze. "You mock my purpose."

"I have a hard time imagining life as a deer. Must get lonely after a few millennia."

"I have an angelic form too."

"But you've never been a *person* before, not like you are now."

"No, not like I am now." Her expression fell. Was that regret? "I have watched many people over the years, and I have often wondered…"

"What?" I had to know. What would an angel want?

"You need anything else, coffee, tea?" Our waitress stopped at the table with the check.

"No." My answer was curt. The moment was ruined. Isolde had turned away; she wasn't gonna answer my question now.

I paid the check, and we began the last leg of our journey.

* * * *

For everything I'd heard about Phoenix, I wasn't prepared for how dry it actually was. It wasn't much hotter than Georgia, there was even a slight breeze, but Savannah was humid and full of trees, swamplands, and life. Arizona felt parched, and with the exception of the fancy palm trees planted throughout housing developments, near dead. I wasn't sure how life survived here or why it even wanted to.

Isolde, on the other hand, seemed enchanted. She marveled over the cacti, lizards, wide-open sky, and scrub swept landscape.

Looking through the windshield, I had to admit, there was a wild beauty to the place. That said, I was looking forward to getting the book and leaving as soon as possible.

"Let's find somewhere to stay—somewhere *nice*. We can drop our stuff off, then I'll head into town."

In Arcadia, a suburb just outside of Phoenix, we found a fancy bed & breakfast constructed right into the hillside. The building had the look of a modern adobe resort. There was a courtyard, a wrap-around terrace, and enormous windows that gave an incredible view of Camelback Mountain. There was also an indoor pool surrounded by landscaped rocks and foliage. It was a mini oasis, and the moisture in the air had me thinking of home again.

After checking in, I took out my supplies, and drew runes about the whole room, reciting an incantation to ward against anyone or *thing* not invited. There'd been no sign of the demon since leaving Shreveport, but for all I knew, he was just downstairs. I hoped things would go smoothly from here on out, but the truth was, I was waiting for the other shoe to drop.

Isolde stood staring out the large suite window, her small frame in silhouette against the brightness from outside. An other-worldly feeling came over me then, as if I had somehow jumped into someone else's life. I was most likely channeling the emotions of the man who'd stayed in this room last. Maybe he'd been on his honeymoon, maybe he'd stared at his bride the way I was now staring at Isa.

Without thought, I walked up behind her, bent down and inhaled the fresh scent of her hair. I'd washed, but I hadn't showered since Samhain. I was probably ripe, but she smelled tropical, like a fruity drink served at a beachside bar. I wanted to turn her around and pull her against me. I wanted to kiss her.

I stepped back.

"I need a shower." Yeah, I needed one all right. An ice cold one.

Isa spun to face me. "You do not have to do it you know."

I frowned. I knew what she meant. "I told you. I don't want your opinions."

"This is not who you are. You do not hurt, you heal."

"I'm not going to hurt my sister. I'm going to cast a spell that will remove her powers so I can lead the coven. She'll probably thank me."

She didn't miss my annoyed tone; she held her hand out as if trying to calm a wary animal. That angered me more.

"I'm not one of your charges. I don't need your help." If my stomach didn't knot at the idea of her being out in the world alone, hunted by a demon, I'd have left her already, but I felt responsible for her safety. Truthfully, I felt more than that, but I wasn't gonna admit it.

"You have wasted too much time denying your true—"

"My true what? Who are you to counsel me? An angel put in charge of...?" I was pissed now, and words left me. Spending two and a half days together did not give her a key to the inner workings of my brain. "You. Do. Not. Know. Me."

"When I said I know every person who has ever stepped foot in my woods, I meant it."

"What are you talking about?"

"I *do* know you Micah. I have known you since your grandmother first brought you to the refuge. I watched you search for plants and dig up bugs. I watched you dip your toes in the water, chase birds, and play in dancing sunbeams." She tipped her head, a questioning look on her face. "You do not remember me, do you?"

The color drained from my face as images flooded my mind, overwhelming my other senses. A pale deer. *That's* why she'd looked familiar. I reached out for something to steady me, but I ended up on my knees, my vision blurred.

"Let it come back to you." Isolde's voice was at my ear—soft and soothing as she prompted, "You were seven. You wandered away, following the water. You found—"

"I found a squirrel," I answered. "He was caught up in the muddy roots of a tree. I thought he was dead but…"

"But he was not. You sensed the life in him. You healed him."

"That was my first time." I could see the scene play before me, as real as the day it had happened. "I lifted him and felt his heartbeat. It was faint but there."

I cradled the scrawny, wet creature to my chest. Its eyes were open but vacant, the chest hardly rose as it fought to draw breath, but I knew… I knew *it could be saved. I sat there a long moment, willing it to get better, but nothing happened. Nothing until I grabbed a hold of the tree's trunk, trying to get to dry land.*

With no warning, a rush of blinding pain surged through me. My chest constricted, and my lungs burned. I was only a child, but I understood—I was dying. The pain was trapped inside me, tearing me up.

*And then there was someone, no, some*thing *there beside me; something that helped the pain pass through. I felt it slide across my body and into the tree with a sense of relief that had me shaking. The squirrel wriggled in my arms, escaped my grip, and took off into the woods.*

"That was you." I blinked, clearing my vision and stared into Isa's doe eyes. The same eyes I'd seen looking down at me in the woods. "You helped me."

"I gave you a way to focus." She placed her hand over my chest, over the black kyanite pendent resting there. "It grounds you."

The deer's face was so close I could see my reflection in its dark eyes. I reached out to touch her, but she backed up. Before she bounded away though, she pawed at the ground. A sliver of hoof came away and lay in the dirt, but when I picked it up, I was surprised to find a fan shaped, crystalline stone.

The same stone that now hung from my neck.

"Kyanite should protect you from negative energy, but you fight it. Your heart is filled with anger, jealousy, and pain."

I pulled away. "Yeah well, a lot has happened since I was seven."

"That was not the last time you saw me." She looked hurt, but I couldn't afford to fall down that hole.

"No, it wasn't," I admitted. Now that my mind had cleared, more memories were surfacing. "I saw you many times while I was young, but then no more."

Isolde dropped her head as if she were unable to look at me. "I was always there."

"Then what, you hid yourself from me? Why?" I wasn't ready to spill, but I'd been hurt by her disappearance. And then I'd put her out of my head entirely.

"You were no longer a child." She got up, walked into the bedroom, and closed the door.

What the hell was that? The deer I'd grown fond of had actually been an angel, an angel who had been looking out for me? My mind ached too much to try and sort things out further. Limping my way to the bathroom, I decided a shower could wait no longer.

* * * *

The coven was located on the second floor of an herbal remedies shop in downtown Scottsdale, sandwiched between touristy gift stores that sold everything from souvenir shirts, and mugs to candy, and antiques. I'd scoped out the location, after my shower, while Isolde was still cloistered in the bedroom.

I didn't want to think about her. Didn't want to remember all the times I'd looked for her, all the times I'd hoped for just a glimpse, hoped she hadn't been killed by a hunter. She was an old wound. One I'd spent the last nine years ignoring, but I couldn't anymore.

I was eighteen when I last saw her. I'd been away a long time, years, but when I returned, I went straight to the wildlife refuge. I'd eventually found her, frolicking in a shallow pool of water.

She'd turned her stunned gaze upon me, then stood frozen a long moment. For a brief second, I'd thought she would let me get closer, let me touch her, but when I took a step forward, she'd bounded off.

I hadn't seen her again, not 'til three nights ago.

I wasn't sure why she'd gotten so emotional, why she'd closed herself in the bedroom. She'd abandoned *me*, not the other way around. There had been something in her expression though, something I couldn't put my finger on.

When I let myself back into our hotel room, she was again looking out the window. Her hair was wet.

"Decided to take a shower too?" It was a dumb question.

She turned and my breath caught; there was a single tear glistening on her cheek. She wiped it away then said, "It was wonderful."

Ignoring common sense, I walked over and placed a hand on her shoulder. "Is everything okay?"

She nodded shyly. "Yes. I just... I wanted to apologize for— "

"Forget it," I cut her off. I couldn't stand the thought of her crying. I might act like a prick, but the truth was, I did have a heart. "The past is the past."

She nodded again. "Did you find the coven?"

"Yeah. It's fully warded though and not just against humans or demons."

"You cannot get the book?"

"Oh, I can get it." I gave her a rakish smile. "But I'm waiting 'til midnight. I want to make sure no one is around."

She frowned. I knew what she'd been hoping—that it was beyond me, that I'd give up and go back home. But she was out of luck, I had a plan.

"Can I go outside?" She walked back to the window, which overlooked Camelback's solitary peaks.

"Not a good idea."

"You think the demon is here."

"I think it would be a foolish risk." I hadn't wanted her help, hadn't wanted to take her with me, and I sure as hell hadn't wanted her butting her nose into my business, but once again, I'd grown fond of her.

I tossed the channel changer at her. "Let's watch a show and call for some room service instead."

CHAPTER SIX
November 4th

I picked the lock to the Mom & Pop hardware store next to the herbal shop and slipped into the darkened interior. Isa was right behind me. I'd tried to get her to stay in our room, but that had been as successful as bathing a cat.

"Wait here." I left her standing by the adjoining wall so I could search the aisles.

"Fat Max, nice." I examined the sheetrock knife, smiling with approval. A little online research told me the buildings in this section had all been fabricated as one big, divided unit. That meant a couple layers of sheetrock and some 2x4s were all that stood between me and the coven. I was betting the doors and window were warded but not the walls. We'd soon find out.

"Here we go." I pulled a metal shelving unit aside and stabbed the knife into the wall. In less than five minutes I'd managed to make a hole big enough for me to fit through. The herbal shop, on the other side of a table displaying scented soap, beckoned.

"Any chance you'll let me do this alone?" The question was rhetorical, but Isa shook her head anyway.

Sliding the table out of the way, I turned sideways and slipped between the studs. The heady smell of fresh and dried botanicals tugged on my heartstrings. My grandmother had always been cooking up some potion or another, and I'd come to associate the smell with her.

Damn it. The last thing I needed, after a nosy guardian angel, were thoughts of the only woman who ever truly loved me. I cleared my throat and took a tentative step forward.

The far wall was lined with shelves holding hundreds of colorful mason jars. In the middle of the room, under drying bundles hanging from the ceiling, stood an island that showcased deep ceramic bowls, each filled with ingredients and tiny metal scoops. There were small dropper bottles filled with essential oils and knick-knacks by the register, but behind that I saw a set of stairs. They went up.

Bingo.

I made my way across the planked floor, around the counter, and up the steps. A feeling of dread came over me, but I knew it was just a glamour—a deterrent to curious humans tempted to snoop. At the top of the stairs, I passed through a sequined curtain hung with charms, tiny bells, and iron trinkets. Apparently they had an issue with fae in Phoenix.

Most covens automatically warded against demons, but thankfully, not too many were concerned with angels; Isa followed me up to an open, second floor loft. Like the space we had back in Rose's shop, there was a large wooden table, with elaborate carvings, centered in the room. The surrounding walls were lined in shelves, like downstairs, but these held books. There had to be a thousand of them.

I pulled my phone out and brought up the sketch Gregor had texted. He'd assured me the ancient, leather bound volume was his and his banishment was due to nothing more than an illicit affair with the Supreme, followed by a subsequent altercation with her mate.

"The prick was jealous," Gregor had sneered. "I took something of his, so he took something of mine."

Did I believe him? Not entirely, but I could still hear the animosity in his voice, see the rage in his eyes. There'd been *some* truth to his claim.

Isa took the phone from me and studied the image. Without explanation, she began checking spines.

I stood unmoving for a long moment. Was this the same angel who'd tried, twice, to change my mind? Was she really helping me, or did she have an ulterior motive?

Deciding it was best *I* find the tome, I took the other side of the room and began flipping books.

After half an hour, we were still unsuccessful. I wanted to switch sides, but Isa insisted she had thoroughly checked all the books. She might be able to keep something from me, but angels couldn't lie. She had not seen the book.

"Maybe they moved it," Isa suggested. It was a valid thought. If the coven members thought Gregor was after the book, they might have hidden it somewhere else.

I leaned against the table, so much like the one in our own meeting room. It wobbled, ever so slightly. That's when the idea came. Rose kept something hidden beneath our table. She never spoke of it, but I'd heard the whispers, the muted screams. I'd sensed its presence.

Crawling under the table, I knocked on the floor, trying to find a loose or creaky board.

"What is this?"

I looked over my shoulder. Isa was under the table with me, pointing to the underside.

"Hot damn!" It was a hidden drawer.

Sliding it open, we recovered a metal lockbox. I shook it. There was something large inside. And heavy. It could easily be a book.

"Okay, let's see what we got." I slid out from under the table and grabbed my pack. Digging around, I found my lockpicking kit, then set to work.

"Would they have spelled it shut?" Isa asked as she scooted next to me.

"My grandmother always said 'sometimes the simplest solution is the best solution.' I imagine most would sit here trying to find the right spell but… Ah." I smiled as the lid popped open. "They'd only have wasted their time."

Inside was a gold bound book with raised symbols and a substantial clasp holding the covers shut.

"You did it!" Isa's eyes lit up with excitement as she leaned forward and hugged me.

I stiffened—instantly. There was no subtlety, and Isa reacted, pulling back so she could look at me.

Her pupils were dilated, and her full lips were slightly parted.

Holy Hell.

She touched my cheek, thumbing four days' worth of stubble. I couldn't help myself, I pressed my nose to the inside of her wrist, taking in her scent.

"Micah?"

Her soft plea undid me. I slid my hand into her silky hair and pulled her mouth to mine. She was beautiful, loyal, pure, and delicious—everything a good guy would lay his life down for. Why on earth was she kissing a jackass like me?

I would have deepened the kiss, drawn her closer, pressed her body against mine, but something thudded to the floor. Startled, I twisted away, only to find a calico cat, fur bristling as it hissed.

"Pssssss, Pssssss." Isa twitched her fingers, and the feline padded closer, twining itself around her arm. She saw my scowl and offered an apology. "I have a way with animals."

"Yes, you do." I got to my feet and offered my hand.

Isa placed the cat atop the table and gave it a loving scratch before turning to me. She looked uncertain, like she wanted to say something but didn't know what.

I didn't give her the time to figure it out. "Let's get out of here."

I placed the empty box back in the hidden drawer and replaced it. Then, because this wasn't the first thing I'd stolen, I mumbled a complicated incantation, obscuring all identifying evidence. We didn't need a demon *and* a coven of angry witches on our tail.

We crept back downstairs and through the hole in the wall. A minor glamour would hide it for a few days; just long enough for our trail to go cold.

Isa's fingers dug into my arm as she sidled up against me. Something was wrong.

Standing behind us, his mouth stretched wide in a cocky smile, was a demon. He was not wearing a human form. I felt confident he was *our* demon.

"Damn boy, you can't be showing your ugly like that. You might scare someone."

The demon laughed, a horrible bone grinding sound that had me cringing. "I thought you were a smart one—valued power, not beauty. Give me the bird and I'll be gone."

Oh hell...

"Say, just for the sake of curiosity…how'd you find us?" I hoped the beast was proud enough to brag 'cause I planned on getting out of there. I didn't know how, but I was taking Isa with me.

The demon stepped closer and narrowed his eyes. "You left something behind. In the woods."

I made a motion behind my back, Isa needed to get out if I was to have any chance with this bastard. I should have known better though. She grabbed my hand and squeezed. She wasn't leaving.

"Quit your stalling. This is a one-time offer. Hand her over or I go through you."

Lightening flashed outside, illuminating the small shop, just before a loud crack of thunder shook the floor and rattled the windows.

I had one chance to use the distraction. My hand went to the front flap on my bag, where I kept a vial of Holy Water. I pulled the stopper and threw the contents into the demon's face.

He howled in rage and charged blindly, knocking me back against the metal shelving unit. I grunted but was thankful Isa had managed to get out of the way.

I twisted in the monster's grip. He was powerful as all hell, but he didn't have a good hold of me. Sharp talons raked my side, shredding my thin tee and my skin. I was more than capable of putting down a normal human, I'd seen my fair share of brawls, but this was something all together different. Claws slashed me again, this time they went deep. I felt the hot, wet flow of blood soak the front of my jeans.

"Isa run!" I didn't know where she was, but I couldn't hold out much longer. Despite the pain, I placed one hand flat upon the demon's chest and grabbed hold of my focus stone. Using all the strength I had, I transferred my injuries into his burly form.

He squealed like a stuck pig and bucked as more lightening flashed. The sight was horrific; the contrast between light and dark making it hard to see clearly.

There was a loud clang, and when the beast collapsed atop me I realized it hadn't been thunder. Isa stood over us both, a large shovel in her hands.

"Ugh!" I pushed the creature's dead weight aside, grabbed the book that had fallen and handed it to her.

"What are you doing?"

"Looking for something…" I riffled through the demon's clothing. There was nothing in his pockets, but under his shirt, strung on a long cord, was a canvas pouch. I felt the familiar shape within, yanked it free and shoved Isa out into the downpour.

"What the hell, is the weather following us too?" I was pretty sure thunderstorms were rare for Arizona. We ran for the truck but didn't go back to the B&B. Instead, I pulled up my app and looked for the closest safe house. The demon could find us there just as easily as anywhere else, but there'd be more capable bodies to get in his way. I know what that made me, but I didn't care. I had to get the tracker out of Isa, and I needed time to do it.

* * * *

We ended up at a safe house in Buckeye, forty minutes west. It was the wrong direction, but I hoped that would confuse the demon. We had wounded him—worse than he'd wounded me, but I had no doubt he'd be after us again. Soon.

Shucking my torn clothes, I pulled another pair of pants and a fresh shirt from my pack, stuffed myself into them, then pulled out the small pouch I'd confiscated. If I was right, inside I would find…

"Is that the arrow that shot me?" Isa looked at the chipped, wedge-shaped object on my palm.

"The head, yes." It made sense. Silver aided in connecting astral and physical bodies. If the missing piece was still in her leg, then the demon could use it to find her almost anywhere.

"I'm gonna try to remove the broken bit, just in case he has another way to track it." I gave her an apologetic frown. "You're gonna have to remove your pants."

Surprise, but not suspicion, flickered across her face. Without a word, she undid her zipper and slid her jeans to the floor. I did my best to ignore the feminine curve of her bare legs, the way they folded daintily beneath her when she sat on the bed.

"I'm not very good at this, it's gonna hurt." Spells were not my forte. I'd only perfected a few basic wards and the few glamours I used to keep my butt out of trouble.

"I trust you." That's all she said, but those three tiny words ate at me like a cancer. No one had ever said them to me before, no one had ever had cause to. If she'd known I planned on ditching her, she wouldn't have either.

Sitting down beside her, I took one long, steadying breath, then placed the broken arrow tip against her skin. Grasping the black kyanite at my chest with my free hand, I closed my eyes and concentrated.

It was subtle at first, an urge to slide the bit of silver up along her thigh, but the urge turned into a need, and I let my hand drift upward. I wasn't directing it so much as allowing it to be pulled along. It came to a stop a hand span below her hip, just where the arrow had pierced her. I'd found it.

"Now for the fun part." Pressing the tip into her flesh, I mumbled a spell of completion. I wanted to coax the chip out of her, convince it to join the silver it had been forged with, to once again form a whole. It was resistant, but I had determination on my side.

Isolde gasped but didn't cry out. She was in pain, I could all but *feel* the sharp bit tearing its way through her muscle. Thankfully, it hadn't been embedded in bone.

I could've gone slower, given her more time to adjust to the sensation, but speed was what we needed. I wanted to get as far from there as possible. I spoke the words with more force, compelling the chip, drawing it out with a final demand.

With a sigh, Isa collapsed onto the mattress. I wanted to let her rest, hell, I wanted to join her—I was wiped too, but I couldn't. We needed to leave.

Grabbing the potted ficus I'd pilfered from the lobby, I healed her leg as fast as I could then placed her jeans on the bed as I walked to the bathroom. Dropping both pieces of the arrow into the toilet, I flushed. "Hunt that down, you bastard."

I packed up our stuff and hauled Isa back to the truck. "You can sleep while I drive."

"Where are we going?" She sounded half asleep already.

"Oklahoma City. It's about sixteen hours north and east of here." The demon knew we would be heading back to Georgia. I was counting on him thinking we'd take the quickest route.

"You can not go that far." She made an effort to protest, but I dug another small vial from my pack.

"With this I can, it's like caffeine on steroids. I'll have to seriously crash once we get to the next safe house though."

CHAPTER SEVEN
November 6th

"Unh, I feel like I was hit by a train." I tried to work out the stiffness that had settled in my bones, then looked over at the clock; it was a little after eight in the evening. We'd arrived at the safe house around six the night before, and I'd gone comatose as soon as my head had hit the pillow. Twenty-six hours of recovery did as much harm as good, but magic had a price. Always.

Isa sat next to me on the ratty double bed, a channel clicker in her hand. There was a contented smile on her lips and for a brief moment I pretended we were a normal couple away on vacation. There were no witches, no warlocks, no angels or demons. And in that moment, I understood my sister.

My mind immediately rebelled—I didn't want to empathize with Adanna. I wanted her position, the one she didn't care about. Before Isa could guess my intentions, I sat up and kissed her. Fiercely. I needed to show her I wasn't a good guy. I wasn't the type to save angels, fight demons on their behalf or take away their pain. I wasn't loosing focus, I was a selfish, Grade A ass. I needed to convince *myself*.

She responded, sagging against me and parting her lips so I could taste her. But when I demanded more, pushed her up against the headboard, she squirmed.

Damn it! I cursed, releasing her. I wanted her to know I wasn't worthy of her trust but there was no way I would force a female.

Annoyed and confused, I stormed out of the room, down the hall, and out into the damp night. The misting of rain felt good against my heated skin. I let it accumulate and drip down my face, drenching my clothing and calming my soul. I was running way too hot lately, and I couldn't blame that entirely on Isolde.

I stood outside a long time, letting my frustration run off and puddle at my feet. When I was sufficiently chilled, I wandered back to our room.

Isa had packed our things and was waiting. I thought she'd hang her head or avert her eyes when she saw me but she didn't. Her gaze sought mine right away, making sure I understood.

I did, and I wanted to scream. She had no right insinuating herself into my life, making me question my motives, uncovering memories I'd successfully buried, telling me she *knew* me.

I snatched the bag from her outstretched hand, turned and headed for the truck, all without saying one word. We had two days to get back to Savannah; I wasn't gonna waste another minute in this hole.

CHAPTER EIGHT
November 6th

Atlanta was only three or four hours from Savannah. We'd made good time, arriving at a luxury inn before noon. I had reasons for stopping though.

One: I needed another shower. A hot one this time.

Two: I needed a break. The amount of traveling we'd done in the past six days was enough to kill a person. I was positive my backside was permanently imprinted with a ribbed texture that matched the vinyl seat of my truck.

Three: If the demon knew we were from Savannah, that was the *last* place I wanted to be. We'd sneak in, as close to the meeting time as possible, then sneak back out once it was over.

I hoped the poison would leave Isa's system soon. I didn't know what we'd do if it didn't. Hell, I didn't know what we'd do if it did...Would she stay with me? Did I want her to? Did she still owe me a debt? She *had* smashed the demon with a shovel.

And what about me? Would I have to go into hiding and forget about leading the coven? The demon knew who I was, he'd have no trouble hunting me down.

Too many thoughts crowded my mind. I shoved them all aside and stepped under the hot spray of water. *Ahhhh*, there was nothing like a scalding shower to numb one's body and brain. I stood in the tub, letting the spray burn my skin, breathing in the steam 'til the water ran cold.

Scrubbing my head with a towel, I walked into our lavishly decorated room. Done in dark jeweled tones, with thick curtains hung about the bed and velvet accents, it looked like the set for a vampire love scene. I tried not to cringe.

Isolde was asleep. Curled on her side, one hand dangled over the edge of the plush mattress while the other hugged a feathered pillow close.

The curtains were drawn back, so I knelt down before her, studying the way her lashes fluttered as she dreamed. What did angels see in their minds when they closed their eyes? Did they see images of heaven?

Wow.

I pondered that. Isa had seen heaven, it existed. Why would she want to spend a single moment here on earth, protecting trees and animals — protecting me?

I'd have to ask her, when she woke. For now, I was content to let her sleep. In fact, I was content to climb onto the bed behind her and pull her against my chest.

She wouldn't be here forever. Someday she would leave me. But not right now.

* * * *

It was dusk when we woke from our nap. I stretched, giving Isa her space. I wanted her to know I wasn't gonna pull a stunt like I had yesterday.

She looked down at me. There was understanding in her eyes and something playful. "Would you think ill of me if I told you I was starving?"

"Would you think ill of me if I told you I'm gonna use a hexed card? I'm out of cash." She blushed a lovely shade of pink. I wanted to pull her back into my arms but resisted. "Come on. I know where to go."

We drove into the heart of Atlanta, to a high-end steak house, where we relaxed over warm buttered rolls and laughed over salads. I even ordered a bottle of champagne. Isa was timid about trying cow, 'til I told her what bacon and jerky were made of. She stared coyly at me, her dark eyes sparkling in the candlelight as she tasted her drink.

Even in jeans and a simple cotton top she was stunning. More than that, I was coming to see her as a ray of light in my otherwise dismal life. If I wasn't careful, I might do the unthinkable— fall for an angel.

Behind my mask, my mind waged a brutal war. Deny my feelings and continue 'life as usual' or admit them and do everything in my power to hold onto her?

I tried to cover my inner turmoil by stuffing a large hunk of meat in my mouth. Isa had said she wouldn't read me, but I was sure she sensed my dilemma.

"Is something wrong?" she asked, confirming my suspicion.

"I'm trying not to think about the future," I confessed. She could take that any number of ways. I hoped she didn't zero in on the most obvious.

Isa nodded but said nothing, and I feared things would be strained for the rest of the evening. After an uncomfortable minute or two, she placed her pale, cool hand over mine. "You are stronger than you think."

Her comment was as vague as mine, but I had the sinking feeling she knew more than she was letting on. Before I could respond, two large slices of chocolate cake were set down before us.

Isa tested the caramel sauce with a dainty finger and smiled brightly.

Like that, all other concerns vanished.

* * * *

Back in our room, I sat on the edge of the bed, flipping through channels on the enormous wide-screen TV, while Isa showered. Dinner had gone well—better than I could have dreamed. Conversation had been light and fun, at times it even bordered on flirty, and the food had been delicious. When I closed my eyes, I could still see the joy on Isa's face as she relished her dessert.

If my life were a chick flick I knew what came next. But it wasn't, and once again I was reminded of Adanna, trying to live her life as a normal human, trying to pretend she could have *The American Dream*. This time I didn't get pissed, this time I felt weary.

"I think I am out of fresh clothing." Isa stepped into the spacious suite, holding a towel chastely about her.

Holy Hell.

The sight of her long, slim legs, stretching out from under the damp cloth, was enough to render me speechless.

"Micah?" She walked closer and tipped her head. There was concern on her lovely face. "Thinking about the future again?"

What could I say…?

Stopping before me, she offered a sympathetic smile. "It is not too late to change your mind. You do not have to meet with him."

My anger flared anew. "I don't need you to save me—from demons, warlocks or myself. I am not the little boy you helped twenty years ago!"

Isa stood calmly, unaffected by my reaction or words. "No. You are not."

Before I knew what I was doing I blurted, "Why did you leave?"

"You left first," she murmured.

Again, I was left without words. It was true.

I'd lived the first fourteen years of my life not knowing who my father was. Hell, my own mother hadn't known. Just after my birthday, he'd shown up, a burly warlock with muddy hazel eyes—just like mine. He'd insisted it was time he stepped up, time he raised his son to be a man, not a 'pansy witch' who mixed potions with his grandmother.

I loved my grandmother, more than anyone alive but adolescent boys want what they want when they want it, and I was no different. If anything, lacking a male role model, I wanted it more. I wanted to be treated like a man.

I went with him.

I was eighteen when I realized I would never be the warlock my father wanted me to be. To this day, healing is my only innate ability, even with two empowered parents. I also realized his only reason for taking me was to get back at my mother. A plan that might have worked, had she given a damn about me...

When I left him, it was to move in with my grandmother. For good.

"You know why I did." I had no doubt she'd read me the first day I'd gone back to the refuge. She'd admitted as much. "Now answer my question."

Isa shifted before me. "You were different. There were dark, ugly thoughts I had never seen in you before."

"Yes, he changed me." I couldn't deny that. I'd recognized what my father was but not soon enough. He'd poisoned me as surely as the demon had poisoned Isa.

"And so had time." She paused a long moment. "You were a man."

I narrowed my gaze. "What are you saying?"

"I am saying, despite the darkness, I was drawn to you."

"You stayed away because you were..." But I suddenly understood, at least I thought so. I tried a different approach. "Why are you here now? Why are you with me? I absolved your debt."

Isa stepped even closer, then reached out to caress my clean-shaven cheek. "Because beneath this dented suit of armor, you have a beautiful soul."

I opened my mouth to protest but no words came, and then Isa dropped her towel. It pooled around her feet, and the blood drained from my face. She was too beautiful, too pure. Sure, I'd imagined— what red blooded guy wouldn't have? But this, this went beyond fantasy. I couldn't...

Isa lifted my hand and placed it at her waist. I felt the angle of her hipbone beneath my palm. Damn that was sexy.

She slid her hands up into my hair and lowered her lips to mine. In all my life, I had never experienced such a kiss. There was no selfishness, or lustful greed, no judgment, and no pity. There was only acceptance as she slipped between my knees and pressed her body to mine.

"Wait." I pulled back. If I'd held off a second longer, I wouldn't have been able to. "Isn't there some law against this? I really don't need a heavenly host coming down here to toast me with holy flames."

A playful smile pulled at her luscious lips. "You humans need your words, your promises, your ceremonies—none of them binding. An angel's love is true. It is eternal. I have made my choice."

"Isa, I—"

"There has never been, and there never will be anyone but you. That is enough."

I pulled her down onto the mattress, cradling her under me as I covered her mouth with my own. And with that I was truly lost.

She was slim but her curves were soft and her skin slid beneath my hands like fine silk. Her hair, more gold than buttery when wet, splayed across the bed, filling the air with her intoxicating scent.

I dropped my head to her neck. I had to taste the flesh that had me so heated, had to explore the perfect body that had my insides twisting into knots. She arched beneath me, and I prayed this wasn't a cruel dream.

Did she really love me? Did she really think my soul was beautiful? Was she really giving herself to me?

In a rush, my clothes were removed and tossed aside. I needed to feel her skin, warm and smooth against my own. I needed to feel her breath on my shoulder, her hands on my chest, on my back, her nails in my biceps when I eliminated the last bit of space between us.

I lifted her, and with eyes pressed tightly shut, Isa threw her head back against the sheets, rising to meet me. I marveled as a drop of sweat settled at her collarbone. In that moment, there was nothing else, the world and all its problems ceased to exist. There was only the two of us, and we had become one.

CHAPTER NINE
November 7th

Isa and I sat in my truck, a mile away from where I'd first found her, waiting for Gregor to arrive. I looked at my phone again; it was five thirty-six. It would be full dark any moment now. I was anxious; things had a tendency to go wrong in my life. We'd managed to escape the demon, but the hairs on the back of my neck rose every time I heard a rustle outside.

Isa squeezed my hand in reassurance. She hadn't said a word about changing my mind all day. She'd shown me last night that she trusted my judgment, trusted me, who I could be. I wasn't worthy of such trust, but I was ass enough to accept it.

I looked over at her and returned the gesture.

We'd spent most of the day at the Georgia Aquarium. I figured an angel who'd lived most of her life in a bottomland forest, who'd spent the better part of a week traveling through some of the US's most arid states, might appreciate a different view. I'd figured right. She'd pulled me along behind her, a smile of pure elation plastered on her lovely face as she took everything in.

The exhibits were breathtaking. I had several pictures of Isa standing beneath the Ocean Voyager tunnel, amazement sparkling in her eyes as thousands of fish swam over her head. I'd only had eyes for her. She'd unpacked her white shift dress, and as far as I was concerned, she shouldn't wear anything else. Ever.

Every so often, she'd turned around, offering a coy smile. A smile that told me she had not forgotten last night. A smile that heated my blood all over again. She had no regrets.

Neither did I. I'd slept the whole night with her tucked in my arms, her legs twined with mine, oblivious to everything but her amazing fragrance and the soft sound of her breathing. When morning came, I hadn't wanted to get up—yet here we were.

An SUV pulled off the road, and a pair of headlights shone on us. Gregor had arrived.

"It's time." I grabbed the book from the seat between us and stepped down.

The vehicle stopped, the older warlock got out and walked toward me. He left his engine running though, using the headlights to illuminate the diminishing space between us.

The wind picked up, stirring the leaves in the surrounding oak and tupelo. Moisture filled the air; seemed it was about to rain. Again.

A door slammed behind me, and Gregor's eyes went wide. Then he burst out laughing.

That was not a good sign; I held the book tight against my chest. "What's so funny?"

"Boy, you impress the hell out of me." He rubbed at his grizzled jaw. "Not only did you retrieve the book, a feat in itself, but you managed to find the key."

I turned to see what Gregor was staring at and frowned. The only thing I saw was Isa, her dress fluttering about her legs as she walked toward me.

"Yyamuth, come see what he brought us!"

The passenger side door opened, and out stepped the very demon who had been pursuing us; he wasn't in beast mode but I recognized him from the Shreveport safehouse. Isa ducked behind me, clutching my shoulders in fear.

"Look, I don't know what the hell is going on," I commented, "but I fulfilled my half of the bargain."

"And I am about to fulfill mine." Gregor gave a wicked smile.

I held the book out, noticing tiny drops of water on the cover. "I don't want the spell, just take the book and leave."

"No?" He drawled. "Don't tell me...the angel has shown you the error of your ways."

Six days ago I would have insisted he was wrong, I would have gotten angry and lashed out. Now I tossed the book at Gregor's feet and nudged Isa backward. "We're going."

"*You* are welcome to go. The angel is not. I need her blood to open the book."

"I said I don't want the spell." I continued to retreat.

"That is your choice. I *do*, however, along with every other spell I have been denied for the past thirteen years!"

I knew better than to turn my back on a warlock, let alone a demon. My father had taught me that much.

"Find another key." I tried to sound sure of myself but if Gregor knew as much about me as I thought he did, he would know I didn't have much of an arsenal. I remembered the jolt of energy he'd sent up my arm at the bar. No, a fight with him would not last long.

He laughed again. "Ah, I can see why you favor the bird, she is exquisite, but the answer is no. Has to be her. Has to be now."

"Micah?" Isa's voice behind me sounded as shaken as I felt. "Can you stall?"

"What the hell do you think I'm doing?"

"I feel something."

I spared a quick glance, we were still several yards from the truck, her face was near white. "What?"

"The poison," she whispered. "I think it's finally wearing off."

"Get her!" Gregor commanded.

I spun back, just as Yyamuth strode forward.

Crap...

I stepped up to meet him, hoping I'd be able to give Isa the break she needed. I might not survive this night, but there was a chance she would. I guess I *was* the type to fight demons on an angel's behalf.

He glared down at me. "I know your tricks now boy. I'm gonna kill you nice and fast."

"Forget about him," Gregor yelled. "She's getting away!"

Yyamuth grunted and threw me aside.

Yeah, that wasn't embarrassing. I watched in horror as he transformed, dropping his human guise to advance on Isa. Grotesque, knobby protrusions sprouted from his head, and his shoulders expanded as matching growths ripped through his shirt.

With no concern for my own safety, I leapt onto the demon's back. Wrenching the steer-like horns that had erupted from the sides of his skull, I tried to turn him aside. I could see Isa, she had made it to the truck, and she was emitting a subtle glow.

Yyamuth bellowed in anger as he shook his head. The gesture was savage, but I wasn't giving up that easy. I reached around and dug my fingers into one of his eyes, igniting more rage. He bowed his head and charged sideways for the nearest tree.

I had no intention of getting pinned; I jumped off the beast's gnarled back but landed badly. My ankle gave out, and I went down even as the demon crashed into a young cypress.

Cursing, I scrambled to my feet but a pair of hands gripped me from behind, sending a bolt of electricity reverberating through my body. I dropped back to my knees.

On all fours, gasping for breath, I heard Gregor's mocking laugh. "You've got heart, I'll give you that much. You'd have made a fine leader. Too bad—"

I wasn't about to sit around mincing words, I attacked, knocking him to the ground. Wind, debris and fat raindrops swirled around us as the storm picked up, but I could see the fury in his eyes easily enough. I didn't know how much energy he had, but I couldn't risk another charge, my muscles were still twitching. I slammed him in the face with my fist. His magic was more lethal than mine, but I had him beat in the bare-knuckles department.

I pummeled him without mercy, but his fingers dug into my thighs and another shock ripped through me. I was thrown backward.

Gregor stood over me as lightening slashed across the sky. I could see the branches overhead thrashing and the tiny sparks that danced along his fingers as he wiped the blood from his mouth. "That's gonna cost you boy."

I couldn't take another. One more jolt and I was sure my heart would explode. Still, I held his gaze, there was no way I would show him weakness. All I could hope was my life gave Isa the chance she needed to escape.

I lifted my chin, ready for his next assault, but it never came— an eerie flash of light caught us both off guard, and we shielded our eyes. When the brilliance dimmed, I saw Isolde, in her pure angelic form, locked in mortal combat with Yyamuth. The two had radiant, magical weapons crossed, and the opposing forces flashed like a cut electrical cable.

"Do you love her? Of course you do." Gregor chuckled as he turned back to me. "Do you know what I'm going to do with her once Yyamuth contains her? I'm going to drain every last drop of her blood over the book and break the binding."

He stooped over me and laughed harder. "And then I'm going to let him play with her lifeless body."

I saw red. Literally. In my mind's eye, Gregor's face exploded and bloody pieces littered the forest floor. Lightening forked through the sky again, followed by a concussive clap of thunder. This time I felt the storm's power coursing through me, not over me. It was a *part* of me, like the blood flowing through my veins.

I planted my hands on either side, clutching at the wet vegetation. Touching the sliver of kyanite helped me focus, but it wasn't necessary. Not any more. With a burst of force, I sent the damage my body had sustained into the growth beneath me. I could almost feel it traveling down through the dirt, into the vast network of interconnecting roots. In a matter of seconds, I found myself sitting in a blackened patch.

Gregor sneered. "That's not gonna save you."

"Maybe not." I conceded and rose to my feet. He must have sensed the change in me, the surety that I now felt. He backed up a step. "But this might."

I raised my arms, and the sky lit up with a fireworks display to rival any Fourth of July celebration. I felt the drain. I knew this was not something I could keep up, but I'd be damned if I didn't use every last bit of my strength to take this bastard down and go to Isa's aid. The thought of her fighting that hideous demon alone, of him touching her, dead or alive, filled me with more dread than I cared to acknowledge.

Gregor's sneer turned to fear, and he ran for his vehicle.

I dropped my arms, raising them had just been for show anyway. A new sense had awakened in me. I could see the wind currents surrounding us, the way they swirled around, faster and faster, picking up leaves, dirt and detritus. I nudged them a bit with my will, directing them at the warlock's fleeing backside.

He reached his SUV, but as he pulled at his door, a large branch crashed into it shattering the window. Gregor skidded away, trying to shield his face. I had him then. Rushing forward, I slammed him against the back panel. His eyes bulged as I rammed my forearm under his jaw. He was either too stunned to shock me or he knew how I'd respond.

"Call off your goon."

"You're a fool," he managed. "You would've been leader of your coven, we could've been friends. I could've taught you, mentored you—"

"Sorry, the coven belongs to my sister, and one asshat father is my limit." I pushed a little harder to let him know I was serious.

"Have it your way." Gregor's expression turned murderous. He twisted in my grip, but when I shoved him back I felt the sharp sting of a blade slicing into my side.

I grabbed his wrist. The wound wasn't fatal, but I couldn't let him stab me again. Boxing up the pain, I set my mind on one singular action. Gregor had to die. I would *not* let him have Isa.

Inside me, the power of the storm rose. It churned with my anger, need, and fear. It swelled and pulsed under my skin like a living thing, fighting to be let free. I let it build, gaining power until it reached the fevered point where I could no longer contain it. Bowing my head, I stepped back, letting all the fury of my newfound power loose.

Thunder, so violent the earth shook, rocked the SUV. Gregor's face paled. With no further warning, a bolt of lightning shot through his body, charring him instantly.

And then the storm was gone.

We fell to the ground at the same time. Blood seeped between my fingers, but I had neither the strength nor the willpower to heal myself. I had to find—

A roar like nothing I'd ever heard erupted from the woods and I turned in time to see Yyamuth bearing down on me. The look of malevolence on his face was enough to catch my breath.

Where was Isolde? I couldn't see her… was she…?

"You killed him!" The demon's accusation rang in my ears, filling me with dread even though I'd already accepted my fate. His burning gaze swept over Gregor's corpse, and he growled deep in his chest. "I will end you now."

Reaching down, he hauled me to my feet, only to toss me up against the SUV. I braced myself in the very spot Gregor had met his demise, feeling the scorch pattern in the paint behind me.

I looked for Isa one last time, but she was nowhere to be seen. I was defeated. When Yyamuth pulled his burning blade back, ready to run me through, I stood without protest. "Just do it already."

With a growl, the demon thrust his sword forward. I braced myself.

In a flash of gleaming light, Isa materialized before me, and the flaming tip of Yyamuth's blade slid through her. Without pause, she swung her glowing weapon down through the demon's collarbone— all the way to his chest. The beast toppled to the dirt even as Isa fell back against me.

"No!" I shouted. *No. This can not be happening.* I sank to the ground, pulling her into my arms.

She smiled up at me. "I saved you. I have fulfilled my promise."

"No," I repeated. "No, hang on. I can heal you."

"You can not." She reached up to touch my cheek, and I knew she was right. Even if I had the energy, this wasn't a mortal wound.

I clasped her face between my hands. "Isa, please don't go."

"There has never been...and there never will be...anyone but you."

"That's not enough," I whispered, but it was too late. She was gone.

I clutched her to my chest, but I felt nothing. Absolutely nothing. I was numb. Totally and completely numb. Somewhere, buried deep, I knew I should be begging, pleading, bargaining, hell, I should have been praying, but nothing came. I sat there, in the middle of nowhere, rocking back and forth, my hands wound in her soft tresses.

Memories of last night filled my mind.

She stood before me, her hand on my face, a look of acceptance in her eyes. She was beneath me, a seductive smile on her beautiful lips. She slept next to me, her feathered lashes caressing her silken cheek.

I saw us together, and hot tears slid down my face.

I broke.

* * * *

Soft light crept between my lids. It was dawn. I blinked, feeling my body awaken. Many bad things had happened last night, too many to dwell on, but I was in the embrace of my beloved. I had been blessed with a second chance. "Micah?"

The arms around me stirred, and I was lowered to his lap. Staring down at me were the most stunning eyes I had even seen—warm brown with flecks of olive green, like the leaves that danced above our heads.

"Isa? How?"

I lifted my hand to his cheek, where streaks of sorrow dirtied his face. I did not care, he was beautiful, inside and out. He was the man I always knew he could be; the man I wanted to spend my life with. My *mortal* life. "He heard your prayer."

Micah shook his head. "But, I didn't—I couldn't…"

"Then call it magic," I winked and ever so slowly he smiled.

There was no more need for words. His head lowered, his lips met mine, and I tasted the salt of fresh tears. I did not need to read his mind to see the truth.

He loved me too.

You can find Niki Daninger on Facebook:
https://www.facebook.com/nikidaninger
On Wordpress: https://nikidaninger.wordpress.com/
And on Pinterest: https://www.pinterest.com/ndaninger/

Love Spell
By
Jennifer Ray

DEDICATION

To the Wenches for all the laughs. To my husband whose love and support is endless. And to my children, my greatest blessings.

CHAPTER ONE

Keira stuck her bottom lip out and blew a puff of air to move her bangs out of her eyes. They always fell in her eyes when she tried to pour her potions. "Dang it! I've added too much." She shrugged and referred back to her book. "Do you have his blood, Lucy?" She looked up from the spell book and studied the short, plump, middle-aged woman.

"Um..." Lucy rummaged around in her purse. "Here." She handed Keira a blood-stained tissue. "Will this work?"

Keira pinched the tissue with tweezers out of Lucy's grasp, her nose scrunching at the wadded crunchiness.

"I guess it will have to." Thank God she wore gloves today.

Tearing the tissue apart and using one big red stain, she shoved the piece into the tube with the tweezers and swirled it around to dissolve it. She added two drops of mint flavoring, swirled again, and then poured it into a glass vile.

"Okay, have Jimmy swallow this in one gulp first thing tomorrow morning on an empty stomach. Wait an hour before he has anything to drink or eat, and that should be it." She smiled at Lucy and handed her the vile.

Lucy shoved a wad of cash at her. "Thank you, Miss Weathersby."

"Anytime. Let me know how he's doing in a day or two."

The little woman waddled out of the shop door.

She checked her watch. Nine-fifty. "Shnizzle! I'm going to be late." Untying her apron, she turned in circles in the small, single garage she called her shop to find her bag. She got down on her hands and knees to search under the tables. Organization was the key if she wanted to continue to mix her potions and work at the pharmacy. Life without her craft or medications wasn't an option. Her dream ever since she was a little girl was to help cure people of what ailed them. Both body and heart.

A knock at the door made her jerk her head up and slam it against the table edge. "Fudge!" She carefully crawled out from underneath the table, crossed to the door to open it an inch, and peeked out at her visitor. Greeted with a pastel pink dress, matching clutch, and bleach blonde hair styled in thick curls as a tissue was dabbed at the watery eyes, Keira swallowed back a wave of nausea. "Anna, what's wrong?" She shoved the door wide and ushered in her client.

Anna glanced around outside before she stepped into the shop. "Keira, something went wrong."

"What happened?" Keira tied on her floral apron.

"I gave the potion to Connor like you said, but nothing happened. He hasn't changed at all. No I-love-yous, no I-need-you-in-my-life-forever, and no here's-my-fraternity-pin." Anna flopped down in the single chair that graced Keira's shop, her curls bouncing and falling into place perfectly. "Why didn't it work?" Her green eyes welled and she dabbed at them.

Keira's shoulders dropped and she released a deep breath. She kneeled before Anna and gently proceeded. "I hate to ask, but are you sure he loves you?"

Anna brought her hand to her heart, eyebrows raised. "Of course he does, silly. What kind of question is that?"

"A foolish one, obviously," Keira mumbled as she stood up.

"What did you say?" Anna demanded.

"Oh, umm... I was just wondering out loud what might have gone wrong." Keira nibbled her lip under Anna's hawk-like scrutiny. "Let me consult my potion book."

Keira opened the book to the love potion index and slid her finger down the listings until she located the *Love Profession* potion. She turned to the page and scanned the directions, the side effects, and then the troubleshooting fine print. "Was he drinking when you gave him the potion?"

"No."

"Hmm... Well, we can try the potion again and see if it works this time. Maybe he's just a hard sell." Keira giggled, but swallowed it back at Anna's frown. "Some people are harder to influence with a potion, and it takes a second dose to ensure success."

"Fine, but I'm not paying you again," Anna rolled her shoulders back and sat up straighter, if that was even possible. "You should list the side effects and not guarantee your work." Her statement emphasized with a humph.

Keira sighed. "Anna, these are potions and spells. It's not like they're FDA approved. There is no guarantee, just like in life."

"I'm still not paying. Besides, I don't have the money. I've already used up my allowance. My father will want to know why I need the cash. Do you want the district attorney questioning what you do back here?" Anna folded her hands in her lap.

Keira slammed the book shut and crossed her arms.

"Please, Keira. I promise, if this works, all of my sorority sisters will be banging down your door." Again with the water works.

"Fine, but please don't send your sorority sisters here. I don't think I can take the neediness." Keira reopened the book and sorted the ingredients.

"Whatever you want, as long as you can get me that fraternity pin."

* * * *

Wade glanced over at the commotion in the back room. "Thank you for joining us, Keira." He pushed his glasses up and winked. Trying to concentrate on the slip of paper in his hand, his attention was repeatedly drawn to the awkward, frazzled woman as she dropped her bag and struggled with her lab coat.

"Sorry. I had, um, car trouble." She pulled her long, dark brown hair into a messy bun and combed her bangs with her fingers. The gesture drew his attention to her baby blue eyes.

Wade blinked and refocused on the paper to fill the prescription. "Mrs. Robbins will be here in half an hour. Can you get her prescriptions together?"

"Sure." She started up the second computer and tapped away.

He cleared his throat. "Do you need a ride home tonight?" At her blank stare, he continued. "You said you had car trouble. I'm offering you a lift home if you needed it. Unless you already have one."

She blushed. "Oh! No, thank you. I was able to get it started and got here on my own." She turned back to print labels for the pill bottles.

Wade handed off the amoxicillin for Sara to give the customer. He tried to busy himself with the next prescription. Keira breezed by him to get more pills. A scent of mint and honey tickled his nose. She always had unique fragrances, like she chose a different perfume every day. No two days the same, unlike Ginny whose blood probably reeked of Chanel she wore it so often. Ginny even wore her perfume to the beach. He bet Keira smelled like saltwater and suntan lotion at the beach. He smiled at the image of Keira in a polka-dot swimsuit and floppy hat, all curves, and with her nose stuck in a book. Oh Lord, what was he thinking? Ginny in her designer bikinis and sunglasses, sipping her expensive bottled water, and tapping away on her phone should be foremost in his thoughts, not Keira. Shaking the image out of his mind, he focused on the prescriptions.

There was loud smack, and then, "Oh fudge!" Keira knelt on the floor picking up medication. "I'm sorry, Wade. I spilled the thyroid pills."

Wade chuckled. If she wasn't such a great employee and pharmacist, he would have sent her packing a long time ago. At least, that's how he convinced himself.

"Which ones?"

"Armour thyroid."

"There's more. Don't worry." He went to the back and pulled out the new shipment. Mint and honey accosted his nose again. He grabbed the bottle and held it over his shoulder. "Here you go."

She grabbed the bottle and mumbled, "Thanks."

He thrust his hand through his shaggy hair, took a calming breath, and went back to his computer. There was no way he would let Keira get under his skin. Ginny was his girlfriend, and he wasn't about to change that status. Right?

"Keira Weathersby? Nell Weathersby's granddaughter? Is that you?" Mrs. Robbins called out from her spot at the counter.

She stiffened for a moment and then plastered a smile, which didn't meet her eyes, onto her face. "Yes, ma'am, she's my grandmother." Keira stepped down from the pharmacist's private upper level.

"All these years I've been coming here, and I didn't know you worked here. How are you doing, child? Are you getting on okay since she's passed? You two were always two peas in a pod, what with your parents being so busy lawyering. Are you practicing the craft?" Mrs. Robbins was a little hard of hearing so she, naturally, shouted all of her words to compensate for the listener's obvious hearing loss.

Keira glanced up at Wade, then turned Mrs. Robbins away to speak to her privately. "Come with me Mrs. Robbins while Sara takes care of your insurance."

Wade frowned. *What did she mean by craft?*

The two women had an animated discussion and gave each other a hug. Keira retrieved Mrs. Robbins' medication and walked her out. After seeing Mrs. Robbins off, Keira strode back to her computer and glanced over at him. "Sorry about that. She's an old friend of my grandmother's. I think she gets confused sometimes." She smiled at him and went back to work.

He pushed his glasses up and cleared his throat. "What did she mean by craft?"

Keira stiffened again and busied herself with work. Was she hiding something?

"Hmm?"

"She asked if you're practicing the craft." He turned and faced her, leaning his hip on the counter.

She blew at her bangs. "Oh. I think you misunderstood her. Um, she meant still doing crafts like my grandmother. I, uh, used to help her with her quilting." She gave him a quick smile and darted to the shelves to grab a medication, ending the conversation.

There was something going on with the woman, and he wanted to learn about all of her secrets. Unfortunately, he would have to leave that to whomever she ended up with.

CHAPTER TWO

Keira tried not to stare while Wade gave instructions to Sara as he removed his lab coat. He was an enigma. His attire a complete contradiction to the facade he showed the public. From the waist up, he was all business. He wore a button down shirt with his lab coat, but below revealed colorful pants and Converses. If he was really going all out, he'd break out the bow tie. Paired with his black, thick rim glasses; shaggy, brown hair; and charming, lopsided smile, he was probably the sexiest, goofiest, and geekiest man she had ever met. Perfect and totally adorable. She sighed. Unfortunately he was with a miserable, snobby, judgmental, gorgeous southern belle. "Ugh!"

"What's wrong?" Wade looked up from his paperwork.

Her cheeks warmed. "Um, nothing. I remembered something I need to take care of at home." She put her headphones on and turned back to her work. "Have a good night," she called over her shoulder. When Wade touched her, she almost jumped out of her skin, knocking her headphones off.

"Sorry. I just wanted to say have a great night." Wade smiled and handed back her headphones.

Her heart pounded. She really needed to find another pharmacy to work at. It was only a matter of time before Wade proposed to Ginny, and she couldn't watch the two of them get married. *Nope, not gonna sit back and watch that.* Shaking her head, she counted pills.

"Keira?" Sara leaned in and waved her hand in front of Keira's face.

Keira pulled her headphones off. "What is it?"

"Ginny Baldwin needs to speak with you." Sara pointed down at the frowning woman at the counter.

Keira sighed and walked to the counter. "Hi, Ginny. Wade just left if you're looking for him."

Ginny squared her shoulders, which caused her short, light blonde waves to jiggle. "I know." She quirked an eyebrow. "I came here to speak to you."

"Me? Whatever for?" She shoved her hands into her coat pockets.

Ginny sighed and rolled her eyes. "Can we speak somewhere in private?"

Keira glanced around. "Um, we can go in the back." She gestured with her thumb over her shoulder.

Her boss's girlfriend breezed past her and strolled to the back with perfect posture. Keira became overly conscious and tried to elongate her spine, but had the sinking feeling she walked like a penguin rather than with anything resembling grace. Giving up, she followed Ginny.

Once she entered the back room, Ginny turned to face her. "I need to discuss Wade with you. I have some concerns."

Keira's stomach lurched. "Oh? What concerns?"

"As you know, we've been together for some time now. It's only natural that the next step in our relationship is to get married. But every time I bring up weddings and marriage, he changes the subject or pretends to ignore me. I think he needs some urging because, obviously, we are meant to be together. That's where you come in." She clasped her hands together and gave Keira a tight smile.

"I... I don't see how this involves me. I think this is between the two of you. I don't think I can help." But she couldn't stop there. "Besides, don't you think he'll propose in his own time when he's ready? He may even be planning something already and is ignoring you to not ruin the surprise. Or something." Lord help her, why was she being dragged into this?

Keira had celebrated when they went to different colleges, thrilled to be rid of her. Unfortunately, the joke was on her when Ginny walked into the pharmacy on Keira's first day as Wade's girlfriend. It was definitely time to find a new job.

Ginny giggled in an annoying high-pitched tone. "Oh, Keira, don't you think I know my Wade better than you? Trust me, he's not planning anything. But it's high time he did. Don't bother playing coy with me. Anna told me all about what you're doing for her and how it worked for Connor. I can't possibly be beaten by my little sister to the altar." She smoothed out her pink dress and gently patted back her hair. "The very idea that Anna would get a ring before me. The nerve of that child. I could just– humph!" She quickly shook her head and folded her hands back together as her regal calmness returned.

"I'm not sure what you're asking me to do, Ginny." Keira turned and glanced out of the doorway, hoping someone or something would interrupt them.

Ginny groaned. "Honestly, Keira, do I have to spell out everything for you? I need you to do your witchy thing and make a potion or spell or whatever it is that you do and get that pesky boyfriend of mine to propose. Do you understand me?" She said the last sentence with a childish stomp, then closed her eyes and took a couple of deep breaths. "I'll pay you whatever you want. Just get me the damn proposal."

Keira stared at the woman before her. She had gone from queen-like control to fidgety and pacing.

"Is everything okay? Is there a reason you need him to propose now?" Keira gasped, glanced out the doorway, and whispered, "Are you pregnant?"

"Bless your heart, Keira Weathersby. You honestly think I would tell you if anything was wrong?" She threw back her head and cackled. "I am trying to make a business proposition. I guess I can take my business elsewhere." Ginny brushed past her and headed out of the pharmacy.

"Wait," Keira called after her. "Let me think about it, okay? I'm not a big fan of doing spells or potions on my friends. In fact, I have a policy that I won't, but seeing as you're determined to do this with or without my help, I'm not sure I want you to go somewhere else. The wrong spell or potion could have adverse effects. Give me until next week to think about this and decide on what I want to do. Okay?"

Ginny gave her a proud smile. "No, you've got until Friday. I want him proposing to me at my family's Halloween party Saturday night." She turned on her heel and waved over her shoulder as the sliding glass doors opened to the night.

CHAPTER THREE

The screen door slammed shut behind her as Keira kicked the house door closed. Dropping her bag on the closest chair in the living room, she carried the brown paper grocery bag to the galley kitchen. After she emptied the contents and put away everything, she grabbed one of the frozen meals.

"Pizza it is." She tossed the plastic container into the microwave, swung the door shut, and typed in the cooking time.

She toed off her shoes and slipped on her flip flops. Switching on the outside lights, she made the short trip to her garage shop and unlocked the door. If she was going to do what Ginny wanted in three days she had to find the right potion.

Too many times her grandmother had told her, "The wrong potion can have severe consequences." Every potion and spell dealing with the heart and emotions was like playing with fire. An individual's personality could be completely altered. Permanently. Wade deserved better, but she had to protect him the best she could.

She skimmed through her alchemy book. Was there an engagement potion? Love, family, friends, love lost, forgotten love, and on it went, but no potion to get someone to propose. Since Wade already loved Ginny, she could do a simple love profession potion, and it would push him to propose. That may work.

Yanking one of the table's drawers open, she grabbed a vial. "Dang it! I'm almost out of honey." She made a note on her shopping list to stop by the local beekeeper and gathered up the rest of the ingredients.

After Anna's complaint this morning about the potion not being strong enough, Keira doubled the potency for this one just to be sure. She didn't want the wrath of Ginny Baldwin. The woman may look the part of the sweet southern belle, but she held a grudge as long as the Mississippi. And Ginny wasn't above revenge if Keira's bald Barbie dolls from their childhood play dates were any indication.

She twisted the vial's top closed, cleaned up, and marched back to the house. "Let's get this over with." The house door slammed shut behind her as she strode to the living room and dug her phone out of her purse. She scrolled through her contacts and found Ginny's.

"Hello," a female voice said on the other line.

"Ginny, this is Keira. I have your order ready. Can you come over tonight?" She peered down at the vial in her hand and sighed.

"Perfect," Ginny giggled. "Yes, I'm on my way. Do you still live at your grandmother's?"

"Yes."

"I'll be there in fifteen minutes." Ginny hung up on her.

Keira shoved the phone back into her purse and sank to the couch behind her. She stared at her favorite painting on the wall across from her of a cottage tucked away in the woods. A heavy sigh escaped her lips. Living far away in the cottage sounded more appealing than dealing with Ginny.

She laid her head back against the couch and stared at the ceiling. "I hope this works."

CHAPTER FOUR

The day couldn't end soon enough. Even though Wade had taken painkillers, his headache still throbbed at his temples. He slapped a label onto the pill bottle, shoved the bottle into a paper bag, and handed it to Sara. Beer and solitude sounded good right now.

"Good morning." Keira breezed by him on her way to the back.

"Morning." Well maybe not complete solitude.

She returned to the pharmacist counter pulling on her lab coat. "How was your evening?" Perched on her stool, she turned and studied his face with those all-seeing pale blue eyes. Her dark eyebrows creased together, and she nibbled her bottom lip. "Everything okay?"

"Everything's fine." He ignored her worried expression and pulled up the next prescription.

"Oh, okay."

Maybe it was the hurt he convinced himself he heard in her words, but he opened his mouth and the words tumbled out. "Ginny and I had a big fight last night. She has her heart set on getting engaged, and I just don't know yet. I don't want anything to change. Why does she?" Heat burned at his cheeks. What had come over him? Why was he sharing this with Keira?

"I take it, you didn't propose then? No burning desire to ask her to marry you?" Her gaze widened.

Was she holding her breath? "What? No. Hell, we don't even live together. Not that I want to change that situation either." He always imagined a little cottage and a garden, but Ginny wanted one of the old mansions like the one she grew up in for their future. Having household staff and large stuffy parties with people he didn't know or like wasn't high on his list of future achievements. Keira would probably like a cottage. He groaned.

Her shoulders slouched and she released a breath. "Are you feeling okay?" She worried her lip again.

Those pink lips taunted him, eliciting an urge to kiss them which he ignored. "I had a headache earlier..." His attention focused back on his temples and the lack of pressure. "But that seems to have disappeared."

She gave him a sunny smile. "Good."

He couldn't help it, he smiled back. Damn it.

* * * *

"It didn't work." Ginny slammed her purse down on the counter.

"I know." Keira fished out the small vial she had in her pants pocket. "Here's another potion." She handed the vial to Ginny.

"If you knew the potion wasn't going to work, why did you give it to me?" Ginny stomped her foot causing her meticulous, bleach blonde ponytail to swing back and forth.

Keira rolled her eyes. "I had no idea it wouldn't. I don't know if that potion," she pointed at the vial now in Ginny's hand, "will work either. When Wade told me about your fight last night, I knew you would be paying me a visit. I went home at lunch and made a different potion. It's another profession potion. It works in a different way. There isn't a proposal potion, so I'm doing the best I can with the tools I have."

"Wait. Wade told you about our fight?" Ginny's question ended on an extremely high note.

"I kind of fished it out of him. Look, just give him the potion tonight, and hopefully, that will be the end of all of this." She crossed her arms in front of her, waiting for whatever Ginny would spew at her next.

Ginny arched a perfectly sculpted eyebrow at her and put her hands on her hips. "Fine, but it better work this time." She lifted one of her hands and pointed at Keira. "Do you understand me?" She grabbed her purse and shoved the vial in. Turning on the toe of her designer flats, she glided out of the building.

Keira dropped her arms to her sides. "You have no idea how much I want this to be over," she mumbled. Wade's lost, sad expression fluttered into her mind before she had a chance to stop it from forming.

* * * *

"Some witch you are," the female voice on the other line said.

"I guess the new potion didn't work either?" Keira studied the ceiling of her living room.

"No. It made him sick. I'm beginning to think you're doing this on purpose. I found another witch. She said not only could she do a spell to get him to propose, but she's even had experience using this spell with great results."

Keira sat up. "Please, give me one more chance. Then, if it doesn't work, you can use the other witch's spell. Okay?"

Ginny sighed into the phone. "Fine. One more chance. That's it." The line went dead.

Keira headed to her shop. She really needed to find a love spell.

CHAPTER FIVE

The rustle of his bag indicated Wade was moments from leaving. Now was Keira's last chance. She pulled the little slip of paper from her pocket and turned to face him.

Her Latin chant was barely above a whisper. She crammed the paper back in her pocket and tiptoed to the back room. With his back to her, Wade stared at the wall, paused mid-shove of his plastic lunch container.

"Wade?" She reached across and tapped his shoulder.

His body gave a little shiver. He flipped the flap of his satchel closed and slipped it over his head to cross his body. Shoulders straightening, he turned to her. His blue eyes sparkled at her from behind his black-rimmed glasses. Crinkles formed at the corner of his eyes.

Her gaze slid down to his mouth. His tongue darted out to moisten his lips, and he smiled.

"Yes, Keira?" He stepped up to her. Their bodies inches apart.

She swallowed. "Wh– What?"

His arm brushed hers as he pushed his glasses up. The heat of her skin had her craving a cool drink. Heck, a cold shower.

His smiled widened, and he leaned forward. "You said my name." He brushed a lose tendril behind her ear.

In spite of her being on the brink of sweating through her blouse, a chill ran straight up her spine. "Oh, I, um... Right. Have a nice weekend." She stepped back and fanned herself.

He frowned and straightened up. "You too."

Once he disappeared through the door, she ran to the refrigerator and grabbed a bottle of water. She didn't put it down until it was empty. What the heck just happened? She flapped the front of her blouse.

* * * *

What was he doing here? Wade stared at her front door, his hand raised, poised to knock, but he hesitated. *You should be over at Ginny's.* He slammed his fist on his thigh.

Movement from the window caught his attention. Keira sat down on the couch and turned on the TV. Her dark hair was up in a bun, exposing her creamy neck. A repetitive knock surprised him. It was his own fist demanding an audience with her.

She jumped up and glanced out the window. He smiled and waved. "Damn it. You're an idiot."

The heavy, wood door opened. "Wade? What are you doing here?" A loose wisp of hair hung down and drew his attention to her low cut, v-neck t-shirt.

He jerked his gaze up to her face and cleared his throat. "Can I come in? Please?"

She stepped back and opened the door wider, gesturing him in.

"I wanted to talk to you about something." He glanced around her house, more like a cottage. It suited her.

"Okay... What is it?" She leaned back against the closed front door.

How could an old stretched out t-shirt, pajama pants, and mismatched fuzzy socks turn him on more than the elegance of Ginny's satin robes, ornate slippers, and perfectly coiffed hair?

"Ginny."

"What about Ginny?" She eyed him and kept her hand on the doorknob.

He shook his head. "No, not Ginny. You." He stepped up to her, and although he wanted to grab her, he kept his fisted hands at his sides.

Her eyebrows rose. "Me? Did I do something wrong at work?" She moistened her lips and brought her hand up to her chest.

What was one little kiss? He grabbed her cheeks and lowered his head to hers. His mouth brushed over hers, but she didn't push him away. He traced her lips with his tongue. She parted them for him, and he deepened the kiss.

Her hands rested on his chest. He caressed the back of her neck to hold her in place while his other hand braced him against the door.

Their tongues tasted and caressed. She was sweet and salty. He couldn't get enough, he needed more.

He broke the kiss and kissed down her jaw line to her throat. The honey he had come to know her by filled his senses, but her skin was salty. He could lick, kiss, and taste and never be satisfied.

She pressed her hands against his chest. Finally he pulled away and looked down at her.

"What are you doing?" She brushed her bangs out of her eyes with one hand while the other remained on his chest.

"I'm not sure. I had to see you tonight, and I don't know why. When I saw you, I needed to kiss you. I'm sorry. I should leave." He pulled his hands away from her and waited for her to step out of the way of the door.

"Oh fudge!" She started to pace. "I messed up again." She continued muttering to herself, but he couldn't make out what she said.

"No. It wasn't you. All the blame is on me." Wanting to stop her pacing, he reached out and grasped her arm. She turned and gave him a weak smile.

"No, it really was me. I botched up my spell." She gasped and clamped a hand over her mouth, her eyes widening.

"What? A spell?" Savannah was full of people who swore witches existed or believed they were witches, but he'd never come face to face with someone who actually admitted it to him.

"I... I... I come from a long line of witches, but it's not something I usually advertise. Only the people who know my family or knew my grandmother know about me." She tugged her arm from his hand and went to sit down in the living room.

He followed her and sat in the chair next to her. "You actually believe in that hocus pocus stuff?" He shoved his hand through his hair. He'd never pegged her as a believer. "Wait. What kind of spell?" If this was even remotely true, what had she done to him?

"Um, you see, the thing is Ginny and I grew up together. She's heard of my family, and I'm helping her sister. So she asked for my assistance." She clasped her hands in her lap, but wiggled her fingers like she couldn't hold still.

"Anna? What in the world would you be helping her with? A new dress?" He snorted. Anna was one of the silliest girls he had ever had the misfortune of knowing. Even more silly than Ginny. "What does Ginny have to do with this?"

"Well, she wanted to nudge you in the matrimonial direction." She dipped her head, refusing to meet his eye.

"That explains a lot." He slammed his fist down on the chair's armrest.

"It does?"

"She keeps leaving wedding magazines and pictures of engagement rings at my place. Then there's the fight the other night." He rubbed his temples.

"Why don't you just propose to her? It's not like you have to marry her the next day. You can work on a long engagement. I'm sure it will take her at least a year to plan her wedding."

He heaved himself up and paced. "You sound just like her. I'll propose when I'm ready. I'm not ready."

"But–"

"No."

"Wade, why can't you just–"

His pacing came to a stop in front of her. "Damn it, Keira. It's because I'm in love with you."

Her mouth formed a perfect little O and her eyebrows shot up.

He knelt down in front of her and held her hands in his. "Please tell me I have some chance with you."

Her expression softened and she nibbled her lip. "Wade, I don't think you really mean that. The spell…"

"Yes, I do. I know I do." He reached up and pulled her head down to meet his lips. When she refused to open up to him, he kissed her closed eyelids, her nose, and then gave one of her ears a nibble. Giving in momentarily, she sighed, her hands caressed his cheeks, and she melted into him.

She groaned, pulled away from him, and stood up. "Wade, I can't do this. It's not real. What about Ginny? Have you given that any thought?"

He fell back and sat on his feet. "What do you mean it's not real? Are you talking about the witch stuff? I don't believe in that. Besides, whatever you did didn't work." Standing up, he blocked her path. "And yes, I have given thought to Ginny, and I'm going to end it with her tomorrow." He reached out for her, but she stepped away.

"That's the thing, the spell did work. Well kind of..." She rubbed her temples. "I don't think you should make any rash decisions like breaking up with Ginny right now.

Frowning, he stepped toward her and grabbed her arms. "I'm not engaged nor do I have the desire to be engaged to Ginny. So I would say your little potions didn't work."

"No, you don't understand. There isn't a potion or herb or spell to get someone to propose marriage that I know of. There are only love potions and spells." She stared at him, worrying her hands.

"Love spells to make someone fall in love?"

She nodded.

How could what he felt for her not be real? He never fantasized about Ginny or daydreamed about kissing her. He never rushed to be with her just so he could watch her smile or brush her bangs out of her face or nibble her delectable lips. Could this really be only smoke and mirrors? He grabbed her hand and rubbed the smooth skin on the back of her hand with his thumb. His pulse thudded in his ears. This was definitely real, and somehow, someway, he would prove it to her. Raising her hand to his mouth, he fluttered a kiss across the creamy skin. "All right. What do you suggest we do to fix this?"

"I need to undo the spell."

CHAPTER SIX

Keira locked the shop behind her and met Wade at the side door. She held the book up to show him she'd gotten what she needed.

He grabbed the tome from her hands. "This old book holds the power to break the spell you have over me?" He gave her a dimpled grin.

Oh goodness, she was in trouble. His kisses alone about did her in. But if he wanted to confess his love for her, he needed to do it spell free. It had to be the real thing.

Unfortunately, when she reversed this spell, it was guaranteed he would run screaming back to Ginny and all of her perfectness. Someone like Wade didn't fall for someone like her.

"Do you want a beer?"

He stopped mid-stride and gaped at her. "You have beer?"

"Um, yes. I drink it too." She yanked open the fridge and grabbed two bottles of beer. She used the bottom edge of her shirt and twisted a bottle open, handed it to him, and then opened one for herself.

He watched her take a swig off the bottle before he lifted it to his mouth. "You know, you could just forget about reversing the spell and leave things the way they are." He winked.

She snorted. "I'd rather be loved for more than my beer drinking abilities."

He shrugged.

She led him into the small dining room next to the kitchen. He brushed past her and pulled a chair out for her. She paused and looked at the chair.

"Don't tell me you've never had a man pull a chair out for you? There are still gentlemen around." He gestured toward the chair.

Sitting, she looked up at him. "I'm sure there are still gentlemen, but I don't seem to find any." She opened the grimoire he laid before her. The paper marking the page peeked out the bottom, and she carefully turned to the page.

Wade leaned in to look at the page too. "What language is that? Latin?"

"Yes." She reread the translated information. There wasn't any mention of undoing the spell or another spell that would counteract it.

"Do you know what it says?"

"Um, no. But it wasn't necessary. I had to do the spell in Latin anyway." She flipped back to the beginning to find the list of spells.

"You chanted a spell and had no idea what it meant?" He frowned at the book.

"I knew what the spell was for and the gist of what was said just not the exact translation." She went back to reading the list of spells as he chugged his beer.

"Thank God I didn't sprout a second head or something." He set the empty bottle on the table. "I think I need another beer. Do you mind?"

Not looking up from the book, she nodded. "Help yourself. My boss pays me a decent salary." She smiled at his choked cough.

The refrigerator door opening and the pop of the cap twisting off echoed through the silent house.

"What the hell do you eat?"

"Food. I'm not a vampire."

Wade chuckled. "You would never guess it from the contents of your fridge."

"Check the freezer."

One door slammed shut and another opened. "Good Lord. I need to take you out to eat. Hell, I need to cook you a real meal." The freezer snapped closed.

He sat down next to her, as she slammed the grimoire shut. "There's nothing in here that can help." She laid her forehead on the book.

"So now what?" Wade lifted the beer bottle to his lips and guzzled the contents.

She sat back up. "I don't know. I can ask my group tomorrow."

"Your group?"

"My coven. We're meeting tomorrow. I'll ask them."

Wade's eyebrows rose. "A coven? Where do you meet?"

She smiled. "Now that, I'm not allowed to tell you. You should probably go home in case Ginny is looking for you."

He sighed. "She's not looking for me. She's over at her parents' place helping set up. I'm not quite sure why since the party planner and caterer are doing most of the work. But she's staying the night there. Is it all right if I stay a while longer? I promise to keep it platonic, for now." He gave her a lopsided grin.

Keira took a gulp of beer, giving herself a moment to overcome the fluttering in her stomach his smile created. "Um, okay. Want to watch a movie? I can order us a pizza."

He tucked a loose strand of hair behind her ear and searched her eyes. "Are you sure we have to undo this spell?"

* * * *

Wade laid a piece of bacon on the hot skillet. The sizzle made him yank his hand away before the grease burned him. The coffee and cooking bacon aromas filled the small kitchen. Heaven knew the last time this kitchen was used properly. He added more bacon to the skillet and went back to chopping the vegetables he'd bought. A creak of the floor interrupted the rhythmic clack of the knife on the cutting board.

"What's all of this? It smells so good."

He scraped the chopped onions and green peppers into an empty bowl and grabbed a coffee cup. Once filled, the sugar and cream added, he turned around to Keira. "I thought I would make us some breakfast. You do know what that is, right? It's not something frozen or that comes out of a box."

She sipped her coffee, and a brief "mmm..." escaped her lips before she answered him. "Very funny. I know what breakfast is. I just don't bother making it." She walked over and inspected everything on the counters. "What are you making?" She grabbed a strawberry out of the colander and popped it into her mouth.

"Everything. I love big breakfasts. We're having veggie and cheese omelets, bacon, fruit, grits, toast with jam, orange juice, and the nectar of the gods, coffee." He turned the bacon on the skillet.

Glancing down at her mug, she frowned. "How did you know how I liked my coffee? It's delicious by the way."

"I've known you for over a year. You take it the same as me. Now find me a saucepan to make the grits."

She leaned down and fished out a pan.

"Thank you for letting me crash on your couch last night. I apologize for passing out. One of the unfortunate side effects of drinking beer, extreme sleepiness." He busied himself with cracking eggs.

"No big deal. I hope it wasn't too uncomfortable."

He whisked the eggs and added everything else. "I was pretty comfortable, surprisingly. Can you pull the bacon off the skillet?"

"This..." She gestured around the kitchen. "This is amazing. I haven't had a cooked breakfast, unless you count toasting a PopTart, since my grandmother died. We used to make pancakes every Saturday morning." The corner of her mouth lifted as she carefully laid out the cooked bacon.

"You were close to your grandmother?"

"Yes. I lived with her most of my life."

"What about your parents?"

"They're too busy working to be bothered with me. My mom is in Charleston and my dad is here."

Wade flipped the omelet closed. "Aren't they attorneys?"

"Yes, they're divorce attorneys. They've always been too career focused to be involved with me. Once they divorced, ironic, I know, I started staying with my grandmother because they both threw themselves into being better than the other."

He slid the omelet onto a dish and cracked more eggs for the next one. "Can you make the grits, please?" He pointed at the package and then went back to work. "So was your grandmother a witch too?"

"Yes. She taught me everything I know. She's the reason I became a pharmacist. We work with a lot of potions and herbs. It only made sense, and witchcraft doesn't exactly pay the bills." She chuckled.

"What about your parents? Are either of them witches?" He slid the spatula under the omelet and turned it over to finish cooking.

Keira added the grits to the boiling water and stirred. "My father is, but he doesn't practice. I'm not even sure he knows how to do any potions or spells. My grandmother tried teaching him, but according to her, he was always more interested in his friends and girls. He's very money driven." She shrugged her shoulders and turned off the burner.

He stared at her. Even with her hair in a messy wet bun, no make-up, and wearing old worn out comfy clothes, she was beautiful. She never seemed to worry about her clothes or appearance, and the comfortable confidence which glowed out of her flawless skin dazzled him.

"What is it?"

He blinked out of his reverie. "Sorry, your story had me thinking of my family." His cheeks warmed at the lie.

She grinned. "Tell me about your family."

"There's not much to tell that you probably don't already know. My dad, grandfather, and great grandfather were pharmacists, and my family pretty much owns all of the non-chain pharmacies from here to Charleston. My mom is a doctor and my brother is supposed to be going to med school. We're a close family. That's us in a nutshell." He slid the second omelet onto a dish. "Everything's ready. Let's eat." They both filled their plates and sat in the dining room.

"This is fantastic," she mumbled with a full mouth.

"Thank you. So what's the plan for today?"

"I have my meeting, and I'll see if one of them can help me out. Are you going to be around? I may need your presence to undo the spell." She finished off the omelet and bacon and was now putting a dent in everything else.

"Yes, I will. You sure I can't come with you to your meeting?"

"No. Sorry. Want some more coffee?" She grabbed her mug and stood.

"Please." He held up his own mug, but before she moved away, he grasped her arm and pulled her down. Face to face, his lips captured hers. A brief, sweet kiss which would, he hoped, leave her head spinning. "You still sure you want to undo your spell? Because I'm quite content where I am." He winked and released her arm.

She tripped to the kitchen in pursuit of their coffee.

He had to convince her that all of this was real. The spell may have pushed him to finally do something, but it was still real. If only he could show her somehow.

CHAPTER SEVEN

"Adanna," Keira called after the dark haired supreme witch. Adanna stopped mid-stride in front of the store counter before leaving the store, and Keira caught up to her. "Can I talk to you for a minute?"

"Sure. What's up?" Adanna glanced around and then turned back to her.

Keira focused on the head-witch's eyes ignoring the intricate scroll work on the side of her face. "I kind of messed up. I cast a love spell on someone, and now I need to undo it. Do you know what I need to do?" She chewed her bottom lip.

Adanna frowned. "Um... I don't know."

Warmth crept up Keira's face. "I have to fix this." She blew her bangs out of her face and tried to ignore the panic churning in her stomach.

Adanna sighed. "My grandmother knew this old witch. Everyone calls her Old Maggie. I'm sure she'll know. In fact, I think your grandmother knew her as well. Keeps to herself, but all the old-timers are friends, I guess." She reached over to the counter and scribbled something on a scrap piece of paper. "Here's her address. She lives outside of Beaufort." She held out the paper.

Keira took it and mumbled, "Thanks."

"No problem. Good luck."

* * * *

Keira inched down the gravel road. "I think this is it."

"Creepy. Do you have any idea who this witch is?" Wade watched out the front windshield.

"No. Adanna said my grandmother knew her and her grandmother knew her, but she mostly keeps to herself. I'm sure it'll be fine."

The tree-lined drive opened up to a small cottage tucked against the surrounding woods. Despite the ivy that grew over the house, almost blocking it from the casual observer, it seemed oddly familiar. The door and two front windows the only things peeking out from the camouflage.

Once parked, Keira covered the short distance to the door. She took a deep breath and knocked lightly.

"What if no one is home?" Wade whispered into her ear sending a shiver down her spine.

Before she could answer, the cottage door creaked open. A petite, hunched-over, elderly woman stood before them blinking her pale blue eyes as if the daylight stung them. She smiled and stepped aside to allow them in.

"Maggie?" Keira hesitated before taking a step over the threshold.

"Good afternoon, Keira. How can I help you?"

Keira gaped at the woman. "How did you know who I am?" Wade's body pressed up against her back and he grabbed her hand, giving her strength.

"I knew you would find me one day, and here you are." The woman shut the door behind them and smiled again.

"Adanna said you were a friend of my grandmother's, but I don't remember her ever speaking of you." She stayed near the door in case they needed to leave quickly. There must be a reason her grandmother had failed to mention Old Maggie.

"Of course you wouldn't have heard of me. Nell and I had a... We had a falling out many years ago. It was before she married your grandfather. We disagreed about how we were going to run our matchmaking business. But you didn't come here to reminisce, so tell me how I can help you." Maggie sat down at her kitchen table in front of them and folded her hands in her lap.

Keira pointed over her shoulder. "His girlfriend hired me to get him to propose. I don't know of any proposal potions or spells, so I tried love potions. Those didn't work." She glanced back at Wade and smiled. "Then I tried a love spell. I thought that since he was in love with his girlfriend, I could chant the spell and he would profess his love to her and hopefully propose. Um, that didn't work. He's in love with me now, and I don't know how to undo it."

Maggie glanced between the two of them. "Interesting. First of all, there is a proposal spell, but you won't find it in any of Nell's books. One of our points of contention. Second, the love spell you used is not meant for a witch to chant and then the spell receiver to magically fall for whomever the spell was done for. This is what I call a "nudge" spell. The person who chants it must care about the person she or he is saying it to, and the recipient must care for the spell chanter. It nudges them together because they already care about each other."

"I don't understand. He loves his girlfriend, not me."

"Ahh, there lies the intriguing part. He must have true feelings for you." The woman stood up and shuffled over to Wade. She reached up with her gnarled hands and pulled him down to face her. "Yes, there's very little spell in his eyes."

"I already told her that I was in love with her, but she won't believe me unless we break the spell," Wade said.

The woman sighed. "Very well. Unlike most spells, this spell is really quite basic. Chant it backwards and it will lift."

She crept over to a bookshelf and withdrew a dusty tome. Opening it, she handed it to Keira.

It was the same spell. Keira read it backwards, and once done, she studied Wade. Nothing had changed. He gave her a goofy grin and raised his eyebrow daring her to admit she was wrong. "It didn't work."

Maggie reached back up with her arthritic hands to bring his face down to her level and studied his eyes. "It's lifted, so anything he tells you about his feelings are genuine."

"I still love you." He stepped toward her to grab her up in an embrace, but she held her hands up.

She turned to Maggie. "You're sure?"

"Yes, yes." Maggie waved her hand to shoo off the question. "Now remember, not all spells are this simplistic. Some spells require more power to undo than was put into them." She sat back down and breathed heavily. "I will admit that Nell had a point in not wanting to truly change people's feelings. She only wanted to nudge people in the direction of their heart. I only wish I had come to that realization before she died. But where she went wrong was not teaching you all of this so that you were fully informed and prepared for if something goes wrong or if you need to really help someone."

"I guess I still have some things to learn." Keira wrapped her arms around Wade.

"Will you let me show you the things Nell left out? Not to change you, but to make you a better witch. It can be my apology even if it's a little too late."

"That would be great. I would love to learn more and to find out about my grandmother as a young woman."

Maggie stood and walked over to her bookshelf. She removed a large book that had the least amount of dust on the entire bookcase. "Take this grimoire and study up. We'll meet soon."

"I look forward to it. Thank you for your help today."

Wade opened the door and she walked out. Looking at the cottage, she frowned. "This cottage seems so familiar. Are you sure I haven't been here before? Maybe as a child?"

"No, your grandmother never returned here. There was a painting made of this cottage over a hundred years ago. Nell loved the painting and took it with her when she left. Although it didn't have this ivy on it."

"Oh my goodness. I know exactly which one it is. I love that painting too." She pictured the cozy cottage before her with a little less ivy, and it was the living room painting.

"I have always planned to leave it to you because I have no one, and I know that's what Nell would have wanted. It was her dream, not mine."

"Wow. That's... I don't know what to say." Keira walked back to the doorway and hugged the old woman. "I'll be in touch."

CHAPTER EIGHT

"All right. Meet me at the park in two hours. Okay?" Wade leaned down and kissed Keira on the forehead.

"Okay."

"I'll see you in a little bit." He climbed out of the car. Once Keira drove away, he released a deep breath and his shoulders slouched. How do you tell someone you have been with for four years that it's over? Ginny had to have some clue or she wouldn't be trying to find a witch to make him propose. That's the other thing, how could someone who supposedly loved you force your hand on something you weren't ready to do? He walked up the wide staircase to the double front doors of Ginny's parents' house and rang the doorbell.

"There you are. I've been looking for you all afternoon." Ginny grabbed his hand pulled him over threshold. "Come on. I have your Halloween costume all ready in one of the spare bedrooms."

He pulled his arm from her hold. "Can we talk for a minute first?" He had to get this over with now before she roped him into staying and he had to do it later.

"Of course. Is something the matter?" She frowned at him.

"No. We just need to talk."

"All right. Well let's go outside to the back patio out of the way of everyone." She led the way through the parlor, formal living room, and then through her father's study. Smiling, she opened the door to a small patio framed by a pergola with flowery vines growing over it.

He pulled out one of the chairs circling the glass table and waited for her to sit then sat across from her.

"Something has been bothering me lately, and I couldn't figure out what it was at first. But I know what it is now. I really don't think we're the same people anymore, and I don't think we want the same things. What I'm trying to say–"

Ginny began reading off a slip of paper. The words didn't make sense.

"What are you saying?"

She didn't look up from the paper. The nonsense words kept falling from her mouth.

"Ginny? What is that?" Haziness blurred the edges of his mind.

She finished reading, slid the paper back into her pocket, and finally looked up at him. She smiled. "You were saying?"

He blinked away the fog. "Oh, yes." Standing up, he walked over to her chair, knelt down on one knee, and grabbed her hands. "Virginia Katherine Baldwin, will you do me the great honor of becoming my wife?"

* * * *

Keira sat on one of the park benches across from the Baldwin home. The Halloween party was in full swing, and it was finally dark enough for children to venture out in their costumes. The first trick-or-treaters bounded up to the door. Chatter, laughter, and music spilled out of the front door when someone opened it with candy in hand. It had been two and a half hours since she dropped off Wade, and there was no sign of him. Time to check in on him.

She followed a larger group of older children up the sidewalk. The double doors stood wide allowing guests to see when the trick-or-treaters came up. Wade and Ginny, dressed as Romeo and Juliet, were framed inside the doorway chatting with another young couple. The man slapped Wade's arm and shook his hand, shouting his congratulations over the noise. She froze on the spot in the doorway. Why were people congratulating them? Wade caught her stare and excused himself from the group.

"Oh hey, Keira. You're still here? I thought you would've left by now." He took a sip of the amber liquor from the small, crystal tumbler in his hand.

She glanced around. "Wade, you knew that I was waiting outside for you. What's going on?"

Another guest slapped Wade's arm as he walked by. "Let me know when the bachelor party is." The man winked and walked on.

Wade turned back to her. "Ginny and I got engaged. Isn't that great?" He grinned.

"But–"

"Keira, what are you doing here?" Ginny turned and smiled at Wade. "Excuse us, darling." She grabbed Keira's upper arm in a tight grip and pulled her out of the house to the furthest corner of the large front porch. "Since you can't seem to do your job, I had to go somewhere else," she hissed.

She glanced over Keira's shoulder and stared off at something or someone. "As you can see, my plan is starting to work. Now I just need the finishing touches."

Keira turned to look at whatever Ginny stared at. An unfamiliar man in a gladiator costume watched the two of them from the opposite side of the porch. Even from this distance in dim light, his frown and clenched jaw line were visible. She turned back to Ginny, who still stared back at the man. "W– Wade proposed? I don't understand."

Ginny rolled her eyes and turned her head back to Keira. "Of course he did. One little spell and it was over. Word to the wise, you really should give up practicing witchcraft. It's not your strong suit." She glanced at Keira's comfortable attire and frowned. "Make sure you never mention any of this to anyone. Do you understand me?"

Keira nodded, blinking back tears.

"Good. Now run along. You're not..." She gestured to Keira's body. "Appropriately costumed, nor were you invited." Ginny brushed past her, her gaze lingered on the gladiator for a moment, and she disappeared into the house.

CHAPTER NINE

The home phone began to ring in the kitchen. Keira threw off her blanket and got up from the couch. She needed a chocolate milk refill anyway.

"Hello?"

"Keira? It's Maggie."

"Oh, hey Maggie." She sat on the stool that was just below the wall-mounted phone.

"I wondered when you would be available to come back out here so that we can work together? Unless you and that pretty boy are too busy making eyes at each other." Maggie chuckled.

"No worries about that. He's too busy making eyes at someone else." She stood up from the stool and crossed over to the freezer to grab the chocolate chip cookie dough ice cream. Pulling a spoon from the drawer next to the refrigerator, she leaned back against the counter and held the phone between her ear and shoulder.

"What? What happened?"

She swallowed a mouthful of ice cream. "Ginny, his fiancé, went to another witch and got a proposal spell. It worked, and now they're engaged like she wanted." She shoved in another spoonful of the cold delight.

"Hmm... That's a powerful spell if she was able to overcome his love for you." The rustle of pages echoed through the receiver.

"He obviously didn't really care." She reached into the fridge and grabbed the chocolate syrup.

"That's crap. I know just the spell that little, lying chippy used. I also know how to break it. You need to profess your love to him. He needs to hear it. If he truly loves you, it will break the spell."

Keira squirted chocolate syrup into the carton, tossed the syrup back into the fridge, and scooped up a spoonful of chocolate covered ice-cream. "And if he doesn't love me?" She licked the spoon clean.

"If I'm wrong and he doesn't love you, you will have made your situation a little awkward. It may be time to find a new job, but I'm rarely wrong."

Keira dropped the spoon into the carton and placed it on the counter. "I don't know. If they're meant to be together, then I don't want to ruin that for them."

"Honey, if they're meant to be, nothing you can do will undo that spell. You have nothing to lose. Just trust me and do it."

Keira sighed. "Okay. I'll try it tomorrow. Maybe."

"Tomorrow it is. I'll expect a full report after work."

CHAPTER TEN

Keira ignored Wade for as much of the day as she could. She kept busy filling prescriptions and answering questions. It was the third day she had to work with him and his apparent happiness, but after Maggie's call last night, today she would try and set things right. Could she admit her feelings? What if he didn't feel the same? She couldn't think like that. He would want to be out from under this spell if he truly didn't want to be engaged to Ginny, and it was her responsibility to help him. Nobody was around and he was about to leave for the day so now was her chance to talk to him. She took a couple of deep breaths and walked over to him.

"Wade, can I talk to you before you leave? Privately."

He looked up from his computer. "Sure. Let's go to the back." He gestured for her to walk ahead. "What do you need?"

Once in the back room, she turned around and faced him. She cleared her throat. "I don't think it's working out here. I am giving you my one month notice. If you need me to help train or anything, I'll be happy to do it."

He frowned. "This is awful. Why didn't you tell me earlier you were unhappy? Is this because of this weekend?"

"You remember? You haven't said anything to me about it."

He took off his lab coat and hung it up on the hook. "I'm sorry about everything that happened Friday and Saturday. Like you said it was just the spell. Please don't let this get in the way of our friendship and work relationship." Grabbing his bag, he slipped it over his head and onto his shoulder.

She crossed her arms and frowned. "I just can't do this."

Wade walked up to her and grabbed her upper arms. "Okay. Thanks for offering to help train. I'll let you know if I need the help. But I want you to know, I'm sorry to see you go." He released her and turned to leave. Before he opened the door he turned back to her. "Can you tell me why?"

She unfolded her arms and let them hang at her sides. Now was her chance. Turning away from him, she looked out the doorway toward the counter. "Because I love you, and I don't think I can bear to see you with someone else anymore." Not wanting to hear his response, she left the room. At her computer, the tell tale creek of the back door signaled Wade had gone.

* * * *

"He left? He didn't say anything to you, and you haven't heard from him?" Maggie called for Keira's report on her love declaration.

"Nope. Nothing. I told you it was the love spell." She wrapped the blanket tighter around her as a loud rumble vibrated through the house. "That storm is getting pretty bad out there."

"Thunderstorms are wonderful. Can't you just feel the electricity humming through your body?" Maggie started to hum.

Keira chuckled. "Thank you for making me feel a little bit better. I'm not looking forward to tomorrow. It's going to be awkward at work. Maybe I'll call in sick." She watched the sky from the front window as another spider web of lightening lit up the darkness.

"I'm sorry I can't do more for you. Chin up my dear. We'll find you someone else."

The rumble from the lightening was joined by a knock on the door. Keira sat up and tried to see out into the darkness of the night. "Someone's at my door. I'll talk to you later. We'll make plans for meeting up again. Okay?"

"Sounds good, my dear. Goodnight."

"Bye." Keira ended the call and got up to answer the door. Whoever it was had to be drenched because she didn't have an overhang or anything to protect visitors from the elements. She opened the door and stared at the soaking wet man before her.

"Is what you said to me today true?"

"What?" She couldn't believe her eyes. Wade stood in his white button down shirt, light green slacks, and Converses, drenched. His normally floppy, dark blond hair was plastered against his face and head.

"Do you love me? Or was this some kind of spell thing again?" Lifting his glasses, he wiped away the rain that ran into his eyes and replaced his glasses.

"Does it matter?" She wrapped her arms around herself.

He stepped toward her, grabbed her shoulders, and began to shake her. "Keira, answer the damn question."

His shaking had pulled her out onto her front stoop, and the rain began to tickle her scalp. "Yes," she whispered.

He brought his face down level with hers. "What? I can't hear you."

"Y–" She cleared her throat. "Yes, I love you."

Not even a second later, he swooped in and captured her lips. His hands slid down her arms and to her hips. He clasped them, pulled her to him, and then wrapped his arms around her waist, effectively crushing her to him from toes to lips. Nothing remained dry with his wet body so efficiently wrapped around hers.

Her lips parted and he deepened the kiss. She snaked her arms around his neck. Thunder crashed and lightening brightened the dark world around them. He tasted like rain and something uniquely him. The cool rain barely chilled the heat or the hope flooding her body.

He broke the kiss and rested his forehead on hers. "I love you too. I don't know what came over me. Do you forgive me?"

Pulling back, she looked up at him and framed his face with her hands. "There's nothing to forgive. You didn't have control. I have to admit, I was sure that if you really cared for me this wouldn't have happened, but Maggie said you were under a powerful spell. The only way to break it was if I confessed my true feelings to you and if you returned those feelings." She searched his eyes making sure it was really him and not some version the spell created.

"I do. When you told me you loved me today, I was so confused. Nothing made sense. I wanted to be with you, but I felt obligated to be with Ginny. I knew Ginny must have done something, so I went to find her. Do you know where I found her?"

Keira shook her wet head.

"She was in bed with another man. A married man. It was quite a scene, but she admitted that she used witchcraft to get me to propose. The worst part was she only wanted me to propose to make that man jealous so he would leave his wife. I really don't know how she got away with this for so long. I rode my bike over here as soon as I left Ginny's, and it started to rain. I had to know what was really going on. I had to be with you, to see you." He grabbed her again and stole another kiss.

Completely soaked through, her body shivered uncontrollably. One part cold rain, one part electricity, mixed with the sheer happiness radiating through her.

He rubbed his hands up and down her bare arms. "You're shivering. I'm sorry. Let's go inside."

Not wanting to let go of him, she dragged him over the threshold.

He shut the door behind them and wrapped her up in his arms again. He kissed down her chin to her neck while licking at the small rivulets of rainwater on her skin. Lifting his head, he tucked a wet tendril behind her ear and smiled.

"You did it again. You put me under a love spell." He whispered and gave her lips a light kiss. "But this time I won't let you break the spell. It's forever."

You can find Jennifer Ray on the web at
www.jenniferraybooks.com,
on Facebook at www.facebook.com/JenniferRayAuthor,
and on Twitter at @JentopiaWrites.

The Banshee and The Barista
By
Danielle Donaldson

CHAPTER ONE

It had been three days since Jenny last spoke aloud. It wasn't the longest she had ever gone but she was pleased with herself.

Adanna, the Supreme Witch, said that Jenny was a Banshee. She could sense impending death. In myth, she's supposed to wail, and anyone who heard her scream would die soon.

That's not how it worked for her, at least, not so far. Jenny could dream a death. She could feel the darkness in the world. It was a heavy black aura that fell over her mind and into her bones. She sensed the light in people that was quickly burning out, the light in their eyes dimming, the heat of their body growing colder even when their heart was slowly stopping and she didn't have to scream. Jenny whispered and the person died. Anytime she spoke, Jenny was afraid that someone nearby would perish.

One time, she noticed that the bus driver was on the verge of a heart attack. She perceived a dark hole in his chest that nobody else could see. Though she was desperate to say something, before any sound came out, he hunched over the steering wheel and stopped breathing. At least the bus was at a stop when that happened.

The last thing she'd said three days ago was goodbye to her co-worker, Maggie, at the spa she worked at. Halloween was here now, so she couldn't keep her mouth shut any longer. Too many witches were around. Too many friends that she had to smile at, and say hello to, and ask about their day. Jenny wanted to chew her lips off but couldn't. She breezed into her favorite coffee shop. The barista always knew what she wanted, a large Earl Grey tea with a splash of milk. She didn't have to order.

Jenny put her money on the counter and a buck in the tip jar.

The skinny guy behind the counter smiled widely and chattered on about how the weather was so bright for Halloween. He wouldn't quit rambling that the sunny outlook ruined his holiday happiness. Eventually, Jenny stopped listening and just stared. He had a satin red cape around his neck that looked like it was made for children and a super hero shirt on. Jenny stared and chewed on her bottom lip, stifling a laugh. He looked ridiculous in his baggy jeans, worn skater shoes, and a makeshift costume.

"Oh, you like my costume? It's not much, I know. But my boss doesn't let us wear real costumes. He said I have to stop overwhelming the customers, and he totally shut down my vampire idea. He said the dripping blood would scare people, especially the kids, but I told him that he couldn't kill my holiday spirit." His smile was wide, and he ran his hand through his long, jet-black hair.

Jenny nodded and tapped her fingernails on the counter top. He didn't turn to get her tea. Instead, he pulled an empty paper cup from behind him but kept up the smile.

"Jenny, right?" he said. "I'm Mac. I work here." He pointed at the name tag on his shirt and laughed at his own joke.

Jenny nodded and sighed. The Coven meeting started in ten minutes, and she didn't want to be late. The coffee shop was supposed to be busy. There should be a line of people behind her, pushing Mac to shut up and move onto the next person, but it was empty. She studied the hipster art on the brick walls, hoping that someone would walk in behind her and distract Mac. But the café remained deserted. Just Mac and Jenny.

Usually, Jenny would choose the corner booth by the window and study her herbs and crystals, do some finger stretches, and drink her tea in silence. It was nice to sit around other people but not say a word.

"You don't talk much. I know you come in here a lot, but you don't say much. You keep to yourself." He gulped and his throat bobbed up and down. "But I don't mean that in a stalker kind of way. You don't need to call Dateline on me or anything. I'm saying that you come in a lot when I'm working, and you're kind of hard to ignore. I've noticed–"

He must have seen her grimace. *Oh great, Jenny. Get it together. You're supposed to be friendly to people. Quiet. Mute even, but friendly. People don't ask questions of friendly people.*

"I didn't mean that you are like freaky or something and that's why you're hard to ignore. It's that I think you're amazingly beautiful and you never talk to anyone, especially me..." He turned away from her and poured hot water in the cup. He dropped the tea bag in, poured a quick dash of milk, and splashed a bit over the edge. He pushed the top on and slid it across the counter toward her hands. His cheeks were rosy and flushed. His black eyelashes were long, and his deep brown eyes stared into hers for a brief moment. It took her breath away.

Great, Jenny. Now you made him uncomfortable and weird. You probably can't come back into this place again. You ruined it. She screwed up her face in a frown.

"H-h-h-h-have a good day." The words stumbled out of his mouth. She could practically see them in front of her. Even with his thick beard stubble, his jaw clenched.

She nodded again and took her tea. She stopped for a moment and opened her mouth, but no sound came out. *Come on. You can say something. You have to say something, anything. One word. Use your words. I can do this. I can say something.* She warred with herself. She couldn't do it. *Don't say anything. It could backfire. It'd be like that one time at the Perez house. All you said was 'Good morning' and the parrot dropped dead. Like that. You dreamt it. You said words. It happened. You can't say anything. You could kill him. Remember the nice librarian lady with the purple cardigan. You asked her where a book on lions was, and she had a heart attack at the zoo the next day. Keep your mouth shut.*

She shuffled to the front door. Mac groaned behind her.

CHAPTER TWO

Mac whimpered and punched his fist onto the counter top. He threw the white towel that hung from his apron, onto the floor. Jenny's long red hair flowed behind her as she shuffled down the street in the direction of Reap What You Sow.

Mac had seen her head that way before. He went in the store on his break once to see if he could catch a glimpse of her. He hoped she worked there. He tried to browse around the shop, which was overloaded with a bunch of old books and plants in jars, and a few weird things he didn't look at too closely. But a mean-looking blond woman stared at him from behind the counter. He got out of there pretty quickly after that. It seemed amazing. Mysterious and weird and everything that drew him to her in the first place. He had tried a few more times to go into the shop but was intimated by the idea of it before he could get in the front door.

"Yo!" Kristen said as she walked in from the back room. "You done talking with your one and only true love?" She giggled as she bent down to scoop up the towel and tossed it into the dirty linens bag.

Kristen brushed a hand over her purple buzz cut hair before washing her hands in the sink behind the espresso machine.

"Please don't say that. She's hardly knows I exist, and you make me sound like the creepiest guy in the world." Mac shivered and crossed his arms over his chest.

"I know. I know." Kristen dried her hands on a clean white towel and handed it to Mac. "You make these adorable puppy eyes every time she comes in here, and she never says anything to you. It's kinda sad."

Kristen's multiple nose piercings flashed in the afternoon light that poured through the front windows. It warmed the shop nicely for late October.

"If you want sad, you should've seen the completely depressing side-show act that was my attempt at making conversation a few seconds ago."

"That bad?" Kristen winced.

"She practically backed out of here like I was a bear that wanted to bite her head off, or worse, a baby deer that she was afraid would run into oncoming traffic."

"Ouch. To be fair, you look more like a baby deer than a menacing bear." Kristen smirked.

"I told you for the millionth time, this costume is totally bad ass, okay? I'm working with what I got, and you should get in the spirit." Mac struck a superhero pose with his feet firmly planted apart and his fists on his hips.

Kristen bent over in her laughter. "Dude. Admit it. You have no game with the ladies."

Mac placed his hand on his chest and scoffed. "How dare you! You know nothing of my *game* with the ladies. Besides, there's only one lady I'm interested in."

"I've warned you about that too. You can't put her on a pedestal. You can't put all your eggs in the mute-pale-girl-that-has-an-affinity-for-crappy-tea basket. She's pretty but there's plenty of fish in the sea." Kristen started to sort through the pastry case as she talked.

The shop was completely dead, not a soul in sight to distract Mac from wanting to dig a hole and put his head in it.

"Could you possibly use more metaphors to describe my love life?"

"Is that a challenge? Because I can. Don't think that I won't take one of your sarcastic little comments literally one day."

"No." Mac pouted out his lower lip. He replayed his interaction with Jenny in his mind. He couldn't remember half of what he said. It was like he blacked out and his mouth took over whenever she was near. Her silence forced him to fill the void and he'd ramble. He probably scared her away and sounded like a stalker or something.

"You don't understand. Today was the day. Halloween is my favorite holiday. I was finally going to ask her out. It was going to be amazing, and I didn't even get to do that." He hung his head.

Kristen patted him softly on the shoulder.

"Buck up, kiddo. There's always next year."

He couldn't help but notice Jenny. He couldn't look away sometimes. Something drew him. Each time she came into the shop, he noticed a new detail that was different about her. The freckles that covered the tip of her nose to the edges of her lips. Her lips that curved into a perfect cupid's bow and she smiled at everyone that crossed her path. The way she rolled her wrists around like her hands were tired. When she gave up her seat for the tired looking mom with the fussing baby or that she always had spare change for those in line that were short for their order, he nearly swooned. How she only wore loose flowery dresses when the weather peaked over eighty degrees. Or how she slung her worn brown leather bag over her shoulder and across her chest after paying for her tea.

He tried to forget her. Kristen managed to rope him into going out to her favorite clubs to try and find a date. Kristen also managed to forget to mention that all of her favorite clubs featured mostly lesbian clientele.

Yet, each time Jenny strode into the shop, the world stopped spinning for a moment.

"Oh gods, you're doing it again," Kristen said.

"What?" Mac shook his head, trying to shake the thoughts from his mind.

"You're staring off into space like a loon." Kristen furrowed her eyebrows. "Dude, you were thinking about her, weren't you?"

Mac shook his head.

"Don't play me, man. You've definitely got it bad."

CHAPTER THREE

Jenny walked out of the coven meeting as the sun slunk down over the road. It still baked her skin and she breathed in deeply. She had said 257 words during the coven meeting, mostly to acknowledge the other witches. She even snickered at a dirty joke about going skyclad in the woods on Halloween night.

She breathed a little lighter, surrounded by the people who understood her. Even if a few of them seemed a bit afraid of her power, they knew her history. They knew what she was. No greater comfort than being around people who get you.

When she stepped off the curb and walked quickly across the street, her legs moved a little easier in the world. Did one of the witches give her a blessing she wasn't aware of? She wouldn't put it past the kind-hearted witches in the coven to take care of her. They worried that she was too sullen.

Maybe it was Halloween. Everyone accepts death around this time of year. It was something to be celebrated and revered in jubilant parties or kids trick-or-treating. The veil between the world of the dead and that of the living was thin as the natural world decayed around them into winter, slowing dying itself. It brought Jenny peace. The fear of death was not breathing down her neck, but she kept her mouth shut anyway in case.

Jenny jogged to her job at Healing Hands, a massage spa, only a few blocks away from Reap What You Sow. She was late to clock-in but wasn't sure if she had any appointments. Either way, with her good mood, she was eager to get straight to work.

Massage therapy paid the bills and gave her a way to give back. After all the death she experienced, she needed to help give life, support life in a way. When a client lay on her table and she put her hands on them, she rubbed at their aches and pains that tingled under her fingers. She could feel and see the aura of their ailments. The glowing deep purple in the abdomen of a woman struggling with her fertility crippled her emotions. When she massaged a man with too much work stress, the angry red aura would burst from his neck and shoulders. She used her magic, what little she'd learned to harvest and control, to ease their sufferings, to help their bodies heal.

"Hey girl, you're late," Maggie said as Jenny rushed over to clock-in.

Jenny nodded at her and shrugged her shoulders in an apology. She washed her hands and put her apron on. She patted the healing crystals in her apron pocket for good luck. By channeling energy Jenny's power had increased, but knowing she had the crystals made her feel better.

"There's already a client waiting for you," Maggie said, "and honey, he is pretty cute. Weird, but cute. Kinda like you." Maggie giggled and went back to flipping through her magazine.

Jenny gently touched the blue paisley headscarf Maggie wore over her naturally kinky black hair. When Maggie turned to her, Jenny pointed and gave Maggie a thumbs up. Jenny's sign for "I like that. It's cute. Please know that I like you!" Maggie smiled and squeezed Jenny's forearm. It was a relief to work with a woman who accepted her non-verbal communication.

Jenny waved goodbye and headed down the small hall to the massage room. For a "spa," the place was pretty small, but for the quaint downtown, it was a luxury.

She took a deep breath before she knock on the door. A man's muffled voice signaled for her to come in. Jenny opened the door to the dimly lit room and closed it quickly behind her.

Maggie already turned on the little fake waterfall machine and put lavender in the infuser. She made a mental note to buy her a gift.

The man lay on the bed on his back, the sheet pulled all the way up to his chin. Jenny couldn't help but scoff a little. At least he was shirtless underneath it. Had he kept his pants on too?

He flinched with his eyes closed and sucked in his stomach as she pulled the sheet down. She shook her head and patted his arm but didn't look at him. All clients were the same after all. They wanted relaxation and relief. Bodies were bodies after all, she saw enough of them to know. *Relax Jeez, he's tense and we haven't even started.*

She turned to get her lotion out of the warmer when she heard his voice.

"Sorry, this is my first time. I mean my first massage. My co-worker, Kristen, said that I should come in here. Said I needed to treat myself or something, and I thought that I would pop in. You had an opening so here I am. Please tell me if I'm doing something wrong and I can change it. Sorry about the sheet. I didn't know—"

Jenny stopped her movements at the sound of his voice. She froze with her back turned to him and rolled her eyes. *Not this guy again. It's the guy from the coffee shop that won't shut up.* She cringed and turned around slowly.

He stopped talking and propped up himself on the table on his elbows. The sheet fell past his waist, and the tops of his boxer briefs peeked out from under it.

His eyes widened when they met hers.

"Oh, God. This is terrible." He groaned and placed his hand over his eyes.

Jenny set the warm bottle of lotion in the holder hooked to her belt and put her hand on her hip. *Are you freaking serious? This guy is stalking me and he thinks this is terrible?*

As if he read her mind, he said, "Please. I'm so sorry. I didn't know you worked here. I didn't mean for this to happen. Let me get dressed and I'm outta here. I'm such an idiot." He collapsed backwards onto the table and his head bounced harshly off the padding.

Jenny rolled her eyes. *Twice in one day? After the guy was so awkward earlier? I can't believe my luck. But, Maggie's right, he's kinda cute and sweet even if he never shuts up.*

"Aren't you going to get out of here so I can get dressed? Or do I have to shamefully change in front of you?" He asked, tilting his head off the bed.

Jenny waved her hands in front of her. *No. No.* She pushed him back onto the table and smoothed out the sheet edges. She curled her fingers into an "okay" symbol. *It's going to be fine. It won't be weird at all. It's Halloween. Let it go. He's not a stalker.*

His dark eyes searched her for a moment. He held his breath, ran his hand through his long hair, and tucked it behind his ears.

"Fine. I guess we're doing this." He laid back. "But I'm sorry about earlier, and I didn't mean for this to happen today." His voice was quieter now as she squirted lotion into her hand.

She took a cleansing breath.

The first moment she laid hands on someone always scared her a little. *What if I see that he has rapidly spreading cancer or that he will accidentally electrocute himself with a toaster? What if I see his mother or brother or best friend dying?*

A memory overtook her for a moment. She watched her parents drive away in their new car. She was thirteen again and tears were running down her face. She told them she hated them. She told them that she wished they were dead. Then Dad's new car was found three days later rolled over an embankment. Both of them dead.

Jenny's hands hovered over Mac's body, over his shoulders. She must have closed her eyes because she opened them when he started talking.

"Are you sure that this is okay? You seem a little hesitant. I get it. Don't worry." He moved to get up again.

Jenny shoved his shoulders down. When her skin touched his full-on, she saw bright yellow behind her eyes. Dandelions in spring. The sun when it first crested over a mountain at dawn. She had never seen yellow so beautiful before.

She drew her hands back a little.

Mac opened his eyes but didn't say anything. His mouth was a straight line.

Jenny tried her best to smile at him.

She put her hands back down. The feeling wasn't as jarring, but it was still there. She massaged him calmly, letting the "Sounds of Nature" CD take over the job of filling in the awkward silence.

He closed his eyes and let her hands work over his body. He had a scar on his right collarbone, Jenny determined it was an old break healed over. When she started to massage his forearm and hands, his body sunk into the bed. The sign of a client starting to relax.

After, she massaged the back of his calves, she noticed the muscle differences between them. He'd skateboarded at one time. One leg was used for pushing.

She worked her way up to his head and tapped him lightly on the shoulder. He didn't respond. His eyes were closed. Had he fallen asleep? She studied his face for a moment. His nose was cute, a little big for his face, but it worked. His mouth was full, and she thought for a moment that it looked perfect for kissing but quickly shook that idea out of her head. She never kissed anyone other than her parents when they were alive. It was too scary to be that close to anyone. As a teenager, it was easy. No boy wanted to be with the creepy quiet girl in foster care. As a twenty-something, she hadn't even tried the dating scene.

She tapped him again on the shoulder. One of his eyes popped open. She signaled that it was time to roll over.

"I wasn't asleep," he told her. "I wondered what it would take to get you to talk. I hoped you would say something." He flipped over quickly while she held the sheet up and turned her head away. When his body was settled face down, she shimmied the sheet over him. His back looked massive. *A swimmer's body. He would be impressive in the water.*

"You know, I don't even know what your voice sounds like." His own voice was muffled from the pressure of the face cradle.

You probably don't want to know what it sounds like. It'd probably kill you. She rubbed his shoulders in smooth, long arcs across the muscles not feeling any ailments, only the usual muscle stress. His heart beat fast and it felt like the center of a rose, deep reds with the softness of a down feather.

Jeez, Jenny. Get it together. You got one semi-naked guy on your table and you freak out? You've done this before. Be a professional.

"You're left handed?" The words tumbled out of her mouth before she realized that she had thought them. Her hands stilled and she snapped her mouth shut. *What the hell? What is wrong with me today?*

"You can tell that?" Mac said, still facing down. The muscles in his shoulder flexed almost involuntarily. "Also, you said something!"

Jenny grimaced. She didn't mean to say anything. She let her guard down. She couldn't let that happen again.

"Seriously, I thought that you were deaf or hard of hearing. I even looked for a couple of videos online to learn sign language, but I thought it would be weird if I walked over to you and started signing and you weren't actually deaf. I'd probably piss you off. Plus, I noticed that you don't read lips so I was pretty sure you could hear me." He used his arms to oddly gesture as he spoke, with his face still down in the cradle of the bed.

Deaf? What? I always try to respond, maybe not verbally, but I try to do something when people talk to me. I'm quiet. I like to keep to myself. I...

As her hands swooped over his left shoulder blade, rubbing at the aching muscles there, she felt his heart almost burst into bright pink and purples. It was warm to her touch, heating her fingers. She'd never felt anything like it. Her own aches in her tense hands and arms melted away. It ignited her own heart, like dipping her toes into a nice warm bath or taking the first bite of rich chocolate cake. She smiled and sunk into the feeling, sighing.

Whoa.

She jumped away from the table. Jenny's long hair flew around her body and into her face. Her backside knocked into the sideboard table behind her. The usually calming sounds of the CD skipped in the little boom box. Jenny reached back and turned it off.

Mac sat up and looked at her. She must have looked like a wild animal. She was a wild animal. She opened her right hand and placed it over his chest. His skin was warm and his body was solid. She splayed her fingers over where his heart beat behind his ribs. Its color aura danced and his heart beat quicker. Her eyes fluttered to a close. The power of him flowed into her hand, soothing her. Her mind became a calm pond, not a ripple of stress visible.

She'd never had the power flow *into* her before. She was always the one pushing energy into someone, healing them.

Mac started to speak, "What's going–" She placed her left pointer finger over his lips without opening her eyes. His lips were so soft and they felt magenta and hot, and she wanted to rub her fingertip over them, but she tried her best to keep her hand still.

He leaned in to her touch even though his breath hitched in his throat.

She reveled in the feeling that emanated from his heart for a moment. It was like caramel on her tongue, the smell of seawater on a summer breeze through her hair, the soft purr of a kitten in her lap.

His eyes went wide and his mouth fell open. She searched his face and her body responded in a way that she had never experienced. There was a hot rush between her legs and her stomach flipped.

"What are you doing?" Mac whispered and his eyes never left hers. His deep brown eyes were tender and they crinkled at the edges as he smirked.

She pushed the energy back into him, showing him what she felt. It was all new to her. She was used to pushing healing or calming thoughts into people, trying to push the visions of death away from her but this was different. This held up a mirror to him and reflected what she experienced by touching him.

She pushed the feeling through her palm and his skin grew hot under her touch. His energy was hot cocoa next to a fire in wintertime, the smooth first taste of pumpkin pie, a bubble bath warm around her legs. For a moment, his eyes widened and he looked far away, but then his eyes closed and his head rocked backward on his neck, a soft smile on his lips. His neck was open to her and she wanted to put her lips on the arch of his muscles and kiss and suck and nibble...

She thought she might have been pushing too many of those feelings into him, because he jumped upright, holding her palm to his chest. His dark, hungry eyes met hers. She was ravenous for him.

She stepped away and pulled her hand back. *You're a professional.* She'd worked hard enough to make sure that she kept her professionalism in a field where she pretty regularly got asked if she was a "happy ending" kind of massage therapist.

Mac cleared his throat and looked away, he moved the sheet over his lower body, to hide the outline of a large erection. It wasn't uncommon for men to get erections during massages, but usually she ignored it. This was clearly different.

This was because of the connection between them, the feeling he showed her.

"Uh...I'm sorry. I'm so sorry." He cleared his throat. "Uh...this doesn't happen. I should go. I definitely should go." He started to swing off the massage bed, wrapping the sheet around him. He reached down to grab his clothes but before he could put them on, her voice cleared through the silence.

"That's never happened to me before. I mean that feeling. I touched you and talked and..." *Nothing happened. He's still alive. He's breathing, well, panting, but he's alive.* Usually, death was around her all the time. She saw when people were going to die and they did. She touched Mac and it felt like he healed her. Not a hint of death on him. "You're okay."

He didn't turn to look at her, and snorted a short laugh as he sorted through his clothes. His back was smooth and she could see the small muscles in them as he bent over. She wanted to run her hands all over his skin and lay her head across its expanse and feel his heat.

She couldn't stand it anymore. If she was in the room much longer, she was going to pounce on him like a cat. She had to leave.

She was out the door before Mac could say anything to her. Jenny ran out of the spa with her apron still on. She had to see someone about this.

CHAPTER FOUR

"I'm a freaking idiot." Mac blew into the coffee shop. Kristen was getting ready to close up shop. A man in a suit awkwardly stood at the counter, shifting from one foot to the other, a five dollar bill in his hand. Kristen rolled her eyes at him and held up her pointer finger to Mac to wait a minute. As Kristen rang up the customer, she smiled stiffly at him. She handed the suit a cup of coffee and followed him to the door. Mac stood in silence, pretending to look into the empty pastry display.

As Kristen clicked the lock behind the last businessman of the day, she turned to Mac.

"Blah. I hate it when they come in right at closing time. I'm in a rush to get out here. There's a killer party across town that I need to get to." She went behind the counter and counted the money in the register. "So what about you being an idiot?"

She whispered the numbers aloud as she counted the bills.

"I'm an idiot. I went to that massage place and guess who I ran into? Jenny! Of all the places after making a complete ass out of myself earlier today, and better yet, I made everything worse. I should be a professional fool." He let the words fly out of his mouth as he paced the floor in front of the cash register.

Kristen raised her eyebrows at him. "Wait, your dream girl works at the spa place?"

Mac nodded his head and chewed on his thumbnail.

"She's the one that gave you a massage?"

Mac nodded again.

"Jeez, Mac, what in the world did you do to make things worse? You're supposed to lay there and relax. Did you run your motor mouth?"

Mac shrugged. He had talked a lot at first, out of nervousness, out of habit.

"Oh God, Mac, did you get a boner?" Kristen dropped the money back into the cash drawer and pushed it in with a bang.

Mac turned to look at her, his mouth twisted into a scowl. His face flushed.

"Oh God, you totally did! You got a boner while your dream girl gave you a massage. What a creep, Mac. I thought you were better than that."

Mac shook his head at her. "It wasn't like that, I swear. I know it's going to sound dumb or crazy or both, but I swear something weird happened."

Kristen scoffed and started to walk to the backroom. "A girl can't even do her job without you and your penis ruining it for her." She muttered under her breath.

"Kris, you don't get it. She touched me and it was like she showed me something with her hands. Colors and heat and feelings exploded inside of me. It was like nothing I have ever felt. It was like I saw inside her head or something, and I couldn't stop it."

"Okay, Romeo. I knew you were a romantic but this is taking things into like a weird level of creepy that I didn't think you were capable of." She continued to walk away. She shut off the espresso machine and clicked off the blenders and coffee warmers. She poured out the lukewarm leftovers while he followed her around the cafe.

"And if you're going to act all frantic like that, at least do something productive. Wipe down the counters."

"This was different. It was...magical." Mac looked up at the dimmed lights of the dining room.

"God, Mac. You're losing it." Kristen shook her head at him.

"Kris. I'm telling you there's something about this girl."

"Okay, well, tell me how you messed it up." Kristen went into the break room to wrap up the close down routine. "I seem to remember it was penis related."

"Oh yeah, that." Mac's mouth fell open. "I got a boner but it wasn't like that, I swear. When she touched me, I swear I felt her thinking about me and her and like...sex stuff."

"I seriously don't understand why girls sleep with guys. I don't get it." Kristen shook her head and hung up her apron on a hook beside the sink. She washed her hands roughly. "Mac, I know you like this girl, but I doubt you can read her mind."

"Don't roll your eyes at me like that. They are going to fall out of your head one of these days."

"Look, Mac. I want to believe that you and your dream girl have a weird mind-meld thing going on, but it's not possible."

Mac shook his head. "I swear this is different. She even talked to me."

"I wish you could hear yourself right now. You sound ridiculous."

"No, I mean it. She talked to me and her voice was so soft and gentle, and I loved it." Mac sighed and placed his head against the doorjamb too forcefully. It thudded.

Kristen winced. "Man, you got it bad."

CHAPTER FIVE

Jenny knocked on the door until her knuckles hurt. Rainbow was her mentor, a close friend and confidante. She was a tiny, older woman and hunched at the shoulders. She always had a kind smile for a stranger and was the first person to take Jenny under her wing when she'd stumbled into Savannah.

The door rattled on the hinges until Rainbow opened it.

"Girl, you scared me. What's going on?"

Jenny rushed into the cute little bungalow house, pushing Rainbow out of the way. She paced around in the front hallway, circling back and forth with her hand squarely planted on her forehead.

"Jenny, sweetie, come sit down. We'll have tea."

Rainbow was used to Jenny coming to her in a depression. When her hairdresser's cat died, Jenny was sure it was because she touched the framed photo of the cat that the hairdresser kept on her station. After Jenny saw on the news that a young boy's body was found in the woods, she thought she had seen him at the mall a few days before he went missing. Whenever Jenny was touched by death, she had a vision, or a whisper in her ear about the impending doom, she turned to Rainbow.

Rainbow put the tea kettle on while Jenny sat stiffly at her kitchen table, tapping her fingertips on the tabletop. The older woman shuffled around the kitchen in a flowing dress and worn slippers.

"Oh, I know that look." Rainbow laid out two mismatched teacups and placed bags in each of them. Her long and delicate sleeves danced as she moved. Her skirts ruffled with her walking around the kitchen. "Do you have man problems?"

Jenny's eyes watered and her tummy gurgled uncomfortably. Her head swam in heaviness, and she was overcome with the desire to lie down.

"Sweetheart, you can talk to me. You know that I'm not afraid of your powers," Rainbow said. The teakettle started to whistle. She poured the steaming water into the teacups and placed Jenny's in front of her on the table. The small cottage was cozy, filled to the brim with cutesy porcelain figurines of babies and cats and knitting projects strewn about it various states of completion.

Jenny wrapped her fingers around the cup. The tea warmed her hands through the porcelain, but she still missed the feeling of Mac's skin beneath her fingers. She took a long breath in and out.

"I think they are man problems," Jenny whispered. She bit at her bottom lip, tearing at the tender skin there.

"Honey, if you think that you have man problems, you most certainly are having man problems. So what's his name?" Rainbow sipped her tea and placed a shortbread cookie on a napkin next to Jenny's cup.

Jenny's teeth worried at her lip until she was sure that it would be bruised the next day. If she dared to say his name, would he be safe? She wasn't sure.

"You can say his name. He is going to be okay."

Jenny nodded. "His name is Mac. I– He works at the coffee shop, and he came in to get a massage and… I don't know what happened."

She swallowed hard and Rainbow nodded, waiting for her to continue.

"And when I touched him, it was like a crazy thing happened. I can't explain it. We connected."

Rainbow nodded and raised her eyebrows. The older woman wasn't magically inclined, but she understood that magic existed and only encouraged Jenny through her life, even helped her get the massage therapist job.

Jenny blushed down her neck and onto her chest. "Not like that. I've never– it wasn't like *that*." Jenny shook her head, clearing the image of Mac lying on her massage bed, the span of his shoulders and the feeling of his tight muscles under her fingers.

"Okay, honey. So you had a connection, not a sexual one, but a magical one?"

Jenny swallowed hard. "Well, it was definitely magical. It was his energy, like his spirit or soul? I could see how he was feeling and I could show him how I was feeling. He pushed something into me, and it was like I could see in his mind and maybe there was something sexual going on."

She remembered the throb between her legs and the darkness in Mac's hooded eyes.

"So, you like this boy?" Rainbow asked.

Jenny thought for a moment. Earlier that day, she could barely stand Mac's motor mouth when she was picking up her tea, but now, his voice was in her head. She liked the sound of his name on her lips.

Rainbow laughed a little. "I think you like this boy. The look on your face is so far away. I think you're in love, baby."

Jenny looked at Rainbow with her short blond bob hair and kind eyes behind her glasses. Rainbow was the closest thing to a mother that Jenny had, and as much as she hated admitting it, Mac stirred something in her that she couldn't ignore. There was a constant throb in between her legs and she kept seeing Mac's face in her mind's eye.

"So, I actually planned on calling you today. I think I found some information that would be interesting to you." Rainbow pulled a heavy, leather bound book down from her sagging bookshelf and thumped it onto the table next to Jenny. Rainbow opened the book to a page that she had marked with an old feather between the pages.

"Look here. It says that Banshees were clan related, meaning that your mother or aunt or grandmother must have also been one."

Jenny thought for a moment about her mother. She had never warned Jenny about the possibility, but witchcraft had to run in families. Her mother was sensitive, sometimes distant, but every time she held Jenny, rubbed her back, Jenny felt calm and safe.

"Maybe my Mom? But, why didn't she say anything?" Jenny whispered, and grounding her teeth together. Tears welled but didn't spill over. The look her mother gave her when she left that last time before the crash was so sad, so mournful. At least, it looked like that in retrospect. *She couldn't have known that she was about to die, could she? Or that Dad was? Wouldn't she had been able to stop it if she did?*

"Maybe, sweetie, she knew what was going to happen to her and your dad because she had powers too, but there was nothing to do to stop it. When it's your time, it's your time. I guess we will never really know. Did she leave you something? A book or resources?" Rainbow asked.

"Not that I can remember. I have a small journal of hers, but I've never opened it. I could never..."

Rainbow nodded. "I understand, sweetie. I know it's been hard on you."

Jenny took Rainbow's hand in hers for a moment, squeezing tightly to hold back the tears.

The older woman refocused on the ancient volume. "There's also something in here about how a Banshee's wail could prevent a death. According to the mythology, if a Banshee prevents a death, she has to suffer pain equal to that of the death but she would be resurrected." Rainbow read from the old book. The pages were see-through thin.

"What does that mean?" Jenny raised her eyebrows. She had never thought about preventing a death outright before. She didn't think that she could stop it once it was coming.

"Maybe you could stop a death once you see it coming, but you'd have to sacrifice the pain in return. Of course, this is only one source, I haven't been able to find anything to support this information."

She started to nod when her body was taken over by a feeling of dread and blackness.

A vision washed over her. Every muscle in her body tensed. Death was coming. Her mind flooded with the images of pale limbs against the front of a Savannah city bus, blood on the windshield, and a crumpled body lying in the street. Blood pooled beneath the head of a young woman. She had purple hair shaved close to the scalp and blood dripped out of her nose from beneath her piercings. Jenny gasped and recognized the woman.

The dark night surrounded the bus, but the street bustled with kids out going door-to-door trick or treating, and adults in costumes walking to the downtown bars. The woman was clothed in her black slacks and shirt from the coffee shop. In the same moment that she saw the woman's broken body in her mind's eye, Mac skid to the woman's side and his face twisted into a grimace. There was nothing he could do.

She pushed her chair back with a crash. Rainbow put her hand up to her mouth in silence.

"I have to go. I'm sorry." Jenny rushed from the room. She had to get to Mac and fast or that woman was going to get hit by a bus. The sun was going down soon.

CHAPTER SIX

"I'm gonna go find her, Kris. I have to. I can't let this go. Tonight is my night." Mac paced back and forth.

"You're going to wear a hole in the floor if you keep doing that." Kristen closed the safe and turned off the lights in the back of the shop. She walked toward the storefront.

Mac shuffled behind her. His eyes on the ground and he bit his thumbnail.

Kristen shooed him through the door and locked up behind him.

"You think I should? You think she'd talk to me? I mean, I know that she doesn't talk much, but she talked to me today. After what happened, I mean, wow. I wish you knew what I was talking about." Mac rested his head on the glass window.

Kristen shook her head and laughed. "I think you're crazy, but if you think this girl is worth all this energy, you might as well try." Kristen took her cell phone out of her back pocket and typed away at the screen. "You better get out of my hair though. I have a date and I'm pretty sure you'll scare her off if you're following at my heels and chattering away about a weird girl touching you."

"She's not weird. She's amazing." Mac's eye turned up toward the sky. The stars burst through the night's darkness.

"Wait!" A woman's voice broke through Mac's daydream. Jenny ran toward them. Her long auburn hair trailed behind her, and she stared at Kristen.

Mac stood up straight and cleared his throat. He couldn't look away. The street lamp above her illuminated her pale skin in a glow that Mac found beautiful. *I wonder what she looks like during a sunrise.*

Jenny gulped for air and placed her open palms on her knees, leaning over and breathing hard. She must have run a ways. Mac opened his mouth to say hello when Jenny yelled into Kristen's face, "You can't! You can't leave!"

Jenny's freckled cheeks were cherry red. She shook her head and waved her hands in front of her face while she caught her breath.

"What? Excuse you." Kristen reared her head back in disgust.

"No, I mean. I'm sorry. Hold on." Jenny gasped.

"Are you okay? You look like you ran a marathon or something." Mac leaned down to look at her face. She looked scared and her mouth was pinched shut.

Kristen started to walk around Jenny. "Look, you need to get this girl in check or something. I gotta go, I'm going to be late."

Jenny stepped in front of her, blocking Kristen with her body.

"What the hell?" Kristen took another step to the side.

"No. Don't." Jenny placed her palm up to Kristen and shifted her eyes between Mac and Kristen. "You're going to die if you go."

"What?" Mac and Kristen said at the same time. Mac placed a hand on Jenny's shoulder tentatively.

The contact between them lit him up immediately. Her fear and pain shot through his veins and made his heart start pumping faster and louder. She chewed on her lip and there was a line of worry forming between her eyebrows.

Please understand. She seemed to be saying. Mac felt the sadness in her from touching her shoulder.

"Kris. She's right. Something bad is going to happen."

"Wait, you're going to believe this nut job?" Kristen shook her head and tried to push past Mac and Jenny. "She doesn't even know who I am."

Jenny grabbed her arm as she brushed by and pulled her in close.

"I'm telling the truth. You're going to get hit by a bus tonight. I saw it. I'm a–a banshee." Jenny blushed deeply. What the hell did that mean?

"Banshee? What kind of crazy is that? Are you going to push me in front of a bus?" Kristen balled up her fists at her sides and looked at Jenny sideways.

"I know it doesn't make sense. I'm still learning myself but it means that I can sometimes sense or see when people are going to die and this afternoon, I saw you." Jenny gestured toward Kristen.

"Wait, after– after the massage?" Mac stumbled.

"Yeah but this was different than usual. Sometimes it's an accident that people seem to die around me but this vision was clear. The clearest that I've ever seen. I need to keep you safe tonight." Jenny straightened her back and steadied her shoulders.

"I have a date," Kristen said.

"Dude, you could die," Mac replied.

"Dude," Kristen said, "do you know how hard it is to find another lesbian in this town that I haven't already dated? It's a small dating pool here. I can't miss this." She looked down and continued tapping on her phone. She walked away from the light of the coffee shop's storefront.

"You have to stop her," Jenny said to Mac, grabbing his fingers and intertwining them with her own. Her fingers felt impossibly cold and darkness spread across his head, up his arm and blazed on his forehead. It burned with how cold it was. He saw Kristen's death for himself. The way her blood dripped down the front of the bus. The gasps of strangers as they stopped to see what happened. How Kristen's eyes open despite his fingers pushing them closed.

"Kris. Don't! You have to stop!" Mac chased her down and stopped her by placing his hands on her shoulders.

CHAPTER SEVEN

"Get off of me, Mac. I'm not playing into this weird Final Destination thing you have going on here." Kristen kept walking. She looked up briefly from her cell phone to getting ready to cross the street.

"No!" Jenny forcefully pulled her backwards from the curb which made them both land hard on their backsides as a city bus blared past them, close enough to the curb to make Jenny's long hair sway in the wind it left in its wake.

"What the hell, man?" Kristen stood and brushed her black pants off.

"That was it! That was the bus. Jenny, you were right!" Mac scooped her into his arms and twirled her around. Jenny gasped from his touch but smiled down at him. He placed her down softly and her feet touched the ground like they were dancing.

"What do you mean that was the bus? That was the bus that was supposed to hit me?" Kristen said.

"I think so. I think that was the bus." Jenny blew her hair out of her face. She slumped her shoulders forward in relief. Mac's arms were still around her waist, her body pushed up against his.

"I still have no idea what you guys are talking about." Kristen started to step off the curb and Mac jerked her back again.

"No, I need to make sure that you'll be safe. We'll walk with you to your date," he said.

Jenny nodded as Kristen looked from her to Mac.

"You guys are crazy people." Kristen shoved her phone in her back pocket. "Fine, let's go. This night has already been weird enough."

Mac threw his arm out to the side of him. "After you, M'lady."

Kristen snorted. "Seriously, ya'll are weird."

"We aren't even in costume." Mac pointed at the children bustling around them and the adults piled into the bars, getting an early start to the Halloween festivities.

"Mac, you have your cape in your pocket. I know you." Kristen said.

Mac rolled his eyes and shrugged his shoulders.

Jenny followed closely behind and to the side of Mac, still on edge about Kristen's safety. *So, she's going to a date. Mac and her aren't dating. So maybe Mac is single?* She shook her head. It didn't matter. She couldn't date. Things like this kept happening to her, especially if she got emotionally close.

Her body hummed near Mac's. He wore a dark colored button up shirt with the sleeves rolled up to his elbows. His tough forearms flexed as he thrust his hands in his pockets. She wanted to reach out and trace the edge of the muscle with her fingertip but held her hand back in a fist. *Control yourself.*

Kristen and Mac speed walked to a bar called The Abington. Mac kept guiding Kristen around the corners, making sure that they weren't going to go into the street for any reason. When they couldn't walk any further without crossing the road, Mac insisted that they wait and wait until all the cars had cleared and then he walked with his arm around Kristen, blocking traffic with his body.

"You believe her, don't you?" Jenny heard Kristen murmur.

Mac looked over his shoulder at Jenny and he smiled at her. Her eyes were dark in the streetlights.

"Yes. Of course. I told you before. You don't understand what happened earlier," he whispered.

Jenny overheard him and beamed. *So he did feel something earlier.*

There was a warm glow in her lower belly at the memory of the tenting of the sheet around his erection while Mac was on her massage table. For a moment, she regretted running out on him and not taking advantage of the situation.

"Here we are." Kristen's words shook Jenny from her steamy thoughts.

The bar was packed with people in costumes that jostled around them in the din of the room. A girl in a short black tutu and a yellow tube top waved at Kristen.

"See you guys, I gotta go," Kristen said, over her shoulder without looking back.

"I guess we're on our own," Mac said, as he shuffled his feet on the ground and shoved his hands in his pockets. Tension rolled off of him but she held back from squeezing the tight muscles of his shoulders.

He gestured at an empty table near the front door. "We should sit and maybe watch her for a while? I'm still a little worried."

Jenny nodded. Better safe than sorry.

Mac tapped his fingers on the tabletop as he looked around for a cocktail waitress. "Do you drink? I mean, we can get drinks. Settle in. If you want, only if you want. I don't want you to feel like I'm pressuring you or something. I'm pretty sure you saved my friend's life, and I don't know how to thank you. The least I can do is buy you a drink–" Mac rambled on until

Jenny placed her hand on top of his on the table. A warm fire lit in her belly, and she clenched her legs together tightly. She couldn't shake the thoughts from earlier as much as she fought it.

She met his dark eyes with her green ones and tucked her hair behind her ear.

Mac froze and his face flushed. Jenny was certain that his pants were growing tight around his erection. She could feel the energy of his sexual excitement through his hand. She tried her best to show him that she was relieved for Kristen through her touch.

"I think she's going to be okay," Jenny said, nodding toward Mac's friend and co-worker.

Kristen stood across the bar, laughing at something the girl dressed like a bumblebee said and gently caressed her date's cheek.

Mac swallowed hard and nodded. "Who are you, Jenny?"

Jenny pulled her hand away from his like it burned her. *Too close. I have to remember that. Don't get too close.*

She shook her head and got up to leave. Mac called to her through the crowd of people, but Jenny didn't turn back. As she pushed her way out of the crowd and through the front door, Mac caught up to her and pulled her into a darkened alley. He pushed his body against her and backed her against the brick. Her breath quickened. The closeness of his body made electricity tingle in her fingers and her head spin.

His mouth was so close that his lips brushed against her cheek as he spoke.

"I know you're special, Jenny. I know that you were as surprised at what happened today as I was. I'm not afraid of you," he whispered.

Jenny met his eyes. They were bright in the darkness.

"Banshee. Magic. Whatever you are. I want to know you." His voice was strained and his breath warmed her cheek. His black hair hung over his forehead and Jenny snaked her hand through his hair to brush it away from his face. His eyes closed at her gentle touch.

"I'm afraid," she admitted.

"That's okay."

"What if I hurt you?"

Mac pulled his eyebrows together and wrinkled his forehead; his heart beat against her. She rested her hand on the swell of his muscles there.

"You're afraid of hurting me? Like killing me?"

Jenny nodded and stared at his neck, too afraid to meet his eyes. She bit her lip until it hurt, ready to cry. She thought of her parents. The last things she said to them before they died. She had power. She could kill the people she loved most.

Mac grabbed her hand. "Let me show you something."

CHAPTER EIGHT

Mac pulled up to the cemetery gates in his busted old Honda. Jenny sat at his side with her hands in her lap. Mac didn't talk much on the ride over, but he had to show her.

He put the car in park and walked around to open Jenny's door. He held his hand out to help her from the car. She took it gingerly. The connection between them was muted, maybe because of the setting.

She furled her eyebrows and tilted her head to the side.

"Trust me. It's nothing too weird. I want to show you something." Mac tucked his hands into his pockets as they walked through the gates. Jenny visibly relaxed when they crossed the threshold. Her arms swung loosely at her sides and her lips curled into a little smile.

"You look happy," Mac said.

Jenny nodded.

He looked at her straight on, standing between two headstones. Her long auburn hair blew gently in the breeze and her green eyes searched Mac's. He ran his thumb across the curve of her cheek and she leaned into his touch.

"Death doesn't scare you?"

"These people are already dead. I don't have to worry about...anything." She stared at his hands while Mac played with the charms on her necklace. The moon lit up Jenny's pale skin, showing the shimmering silver key, sun, and anchor charms on her necklace. He could lean down to kiss her. Her mouth looked so kissable, but he wouldn't. He shook his head and walked away.

"I want to show you something." He knelt in front of the headstone and brushed away loose leaves that had blown about the stone. He straightened the flowers that he had placed in the flower holder a few days before. "Happy Halloween, Mom."

Jenny knelt next to him and waved at the stone.

"Sorry if this is awkward. My mom died a couple years ago– breast cancer. I come here on Halloween. Our favorite holiday." Mac chewed the inside of his cheek.

"Not awkward. Thank you for bringing me," Jenny said quietly. "My parents died when I was thirteen– car crash."

"I'm sorry, Jenny." Mac leaned back on his hands and stretched his feet in front of him.

"It's okay. I mean, it's not okay, but you know what I mean. I'm okay, I think." Jenny wrapped her arms around her middle. Mac leaned over and rubbed her upper arm. Her shoulders relaxed and the tension in her face dissipated. "I think I killed them. We fought before they left. I said I wished they were dead, and then they died. It was all my fault."

Tears spilled onto her cheeks. Her mouth twisted into a grimace.

"Hey. I'm sorry. I don't think it was your fault. I'm so sorry. I didn't mean anything by this. I wanted to make sure that you knew that I'm not afraid of death. I'm not afraid of whatever crazy stuff you have going on or the Banshee stuff or the amazing connection we have when we touch even briefly," Mac said. He rubbed her back and smooth cool feelings passed through his hands from her. She relaxed and the tears dried up. He felt it in the calm light blue behind his eyes. She must have pushed the feeling into him again.

"Why is Halloween your favorite holiday?" Jenny asked when the tears subsided.

"My mom and I used to dress up in matching outfits. She'd go all out, decorating the house, making it spooky for the other neighborhood kids. It was a month-long celebration. She taught me death wasn't something to be particularly scared of. It's just another stop on the journey."

Jenny nodded.

"You aren't afraid that I'm going to kill you?" Jenny whispered.

Mac scoffed. "No. If I can see your smile one more time and die in the next moment, I will die a happy man."

Jenny smiled and blushed.

"So, you're a Banshee? What does that mean?" Mac asked as he leaned back on one of his hands, looking at the sky and trees above them.

Jenny was quiet for a moment.

"I'm not even sure what it means. It means that I can feel when death is coming. I have visions. But I'm also a witch. I can heal people, touch them and make them feel better."

"Witch, huh? You sure this isn't just a big Halloween joke? You find out that this is my favorite holiday, and you're doing this to mess with me?"

"You think that what happened back there with the bus was a coincidence? That this is me messing with you?" Jenny touched his forearm with her pointer finger, showing him the hot passion that made him grow hard under the thin sheet on the massage table earlier in the day. His breath quickened almost immediately. His pants grew tight around his erection.

"No, you're right. I'm an idiot to doubt you." He moaned and adjusted the way he was sitting to make room in the crotch of his pants. Mac rubbed his thumb against her bottom lip. She closed her eyes and leaned into him. He closed the distance between them and placed his lips gently against hers. She sighed against his mouth and he cupped the back of her head.

He threaded his fingers through her hair, tugging at the hairs near her scalp. She tilted her head up and moaned. Their connection was passionate and lovely. Her lips were the soft touch of rose petals, the buzz of a bumblebee as it drifted from flower to flower, the warmth of afternoon sun on his skin

He whispered against her mouth and her face as he placed light kisses on her skin. "Your smile is beautiful. Your voice is beautiful. You're amazing. You're magic."

"So, you believe me?" She whispered.

"Yes, with the weird thing we have going on? Hell yeah I do and I love it." Mac said. His beard brushed against her sensitive skin and she shivered.

"It doesn't freak you out?"

"No way. I mean, it's special. I've never felt this with anyone before. You're pulling me in, Jenny. You're a magnet that my soul needs to be near." Mac smiled in the dim light. Jenny ran her hand over the quirk of his cheek from his broad smile. "I know that sounds cheesy."

"A little bit. A little Mac and cheesy." Jenny laughed, her mouth fell open and her chest shook with the force of her chortle.

"Now, that was definitely cheesy."

She giggled and kissed along his jaw line. His skin was on fire despite the chill in the air around them. Orange and yellow sparks bloomed behind his eyes.

"If you kill me, Jenny, it's going to be from blowing my mind." He laughed.

Her mouth was hot and her tongue traced along his bottom lip. He sucked it into his mouth gently and she squeaked in surprise. She pulled away and her eyes widened.

"Let's get out of here." Mac pulled her to her feet and raced through the cemetery gates with her hand in his. "But I'm going to have some follow-up questions to this witch business."

They crossed through the front gate of the cemetery and Mac let go of Jenny's hand to jog to the passenger side of the car to unlock and open the door for her. She went widely around the back of the car. She met his eyes with a smile but he saw the headlights of something coming at her fast.

"Jenny!" He yelled before her body was flung across the parking lot, a rag doll of a body beyond Mac's reach. Blood spilled from her head that toppled against the pavement. Her lungs whistled with her every breath.

The truck had come out of nowhere and, threw her body across the pavement, her skin looked like it was scraped away by the pavement. Hot blood pooled around her and Mac heard the screech of tires squeal away as her skin turned ashy. Jenny's. Her eyes closed as he struggled to get to her.

CHAPTER NINE

"Jenny! Jenny!" Mac was hunched over her broken body, trying to get her to open her eyes, but too afraid to touch her. There was blood everywhere. He scrambled to get his cell phone out, but his hands were too shaky. His fingers were too wet with blood to operate the touch screen.

"God. Oh God. What the hell?" Mac muttered. He wiped at the screen with the hem of his shirt and wiped the blood on his hands on the legs of his jeans. As dialed emergency services, Jenny's breath came back with force.

She was gasping on the ground and Mac dropped the phone.

"Jenny, oh, Jenny. You're okay. Jeez, we need to get an ambulance. I'm getting an ambulance, okay?" He rambled.

"No." Jenny gasped. She reached up and grabbed him with an arm that Mac was pretty sure was broken a few seconds before. The road rash on her face started to heal before his eyes. The light from a street lamp shone on them as her legs started to straighten out, the crack of bones snapping into place. Jenny moaned with the pain of it, hissing between her clenched teeth.

"What the hell is happening?" Mac threw his hand into his hair.

"Wait." Jenny croaked.

The cuts on her head and hands were closing up, the bleeding ceased. Her breathing came easier; the whistle in her chest abated.

"Are you freaking Wolverine too?"

Jenny caught her breath, propping herself up on her elbows. There was still blood on her clothes and on the ground around her, but there was color in her face and she looked whole.

"Oh. I didn't think that was actually going to happen." Her voice was even and calm.

"What the hell just happened? Why are you so okay about this?" Mac was shaking, certain he'd watched her die and then come back to life.

"Rainbow, my mentor, said that this was possible. If I stopped a death, I'd have to suffer the same pain but be resurrected."

"So, you mean that because you saved Kris, you had to get hit by a freaking truck and come back from the dead?" Mac's voice trembled but tears didn't prick at the back of his eyes any longer.

"I guess? This is the first time that this has happened to me."

"We should take you to the hospital. You were just bleeding everywhere. This is your blood. Your bones were all broken."

"No. I think I'm okay now," Jenny said. "Look, I feel okay." She touched him on the cheek. The blood on her hands was dry and she rubbed her thumb over his jaw line. She pushed peace and wholeness into his mind, clearing it.

"Are you sure? Are you really sure?" He asked again. "You might be in shock. I think I saw that on TV somewhere."

"I'm okay, Mac. I just want to get out here. Take me someplace?"

"Yeah, I can do that." He helped her onto her feet. She was a little wobbly, but not too bad considering a truck just took her out a few minutes before.

* * * *

Mac's apartment was a second floor walk-up, above a florist shop. It was cozy and small. Stacks of books lined the entry way and he tossed his keys into a glass bowl on the kitchen counter.

"I know it's only a studio and it's not that much, but it's home and I like it." Mac toed off his shoes and kicked them beside the couch. "Want something to drink? I can make you something. I'm not sure what I have... I mean, I don't have guests over often so this is a little strange, and I'm not sure what to do."

Jenny laughed quietly. Mac opened and closed the fridge and the cabinets over and over again. She crossed the small room and placed her hands on his shoulders. He relaxed immediately.

She ran her fingernails over his shoulder blades in sweeping circles. He shivered and there was a bit of the passion she saw earlier from him through their connection.

"Let's go wash up. We both have blood on us and you didn't bring me here to stand in the kitchen babbling," Jenny whispered. She squeezed her legs together at the thought of why Mac brought her to his apartment. She had never done this before, stand in a man's kitchen, a man whose body she desperately wanted to see and touch.

"I know I'm babbling. I'm sorry. I think I'm nervous. I've never– you're the first woman that's been in my place." Mac turned to face Jenny. He threaded his fingers through hers and pulled her closer.

Jenny looked around with raised eyebrows. "Thank you. I'm honored."

Mac laughed and nuzzled into the crook of her neck. His voice vibrated into her bones and bright pink feelings burst behind her eyes. She felt– loved. Loved. *So this is what it feels like*. There was a hint of hot white passion beneath the connection between her and Mac, but at the moment, it was gentle like a soft fuzzy blanket brushed against her cheek. It was a cup of her favorite tea and a kitten purring in her lap.

She laughed out loud which made Mac pull away.

"What?"

"Oh nothing. I was thinking that you make me feel like kittens."

"Wait, what?" Mac pulled away even further.

"No! I didn't mean it like that." Jenny tugged on his fingertips, hooking their hands back together. "I meant that you make me feel great and comfortable and this whole connection thing is weird."

"I'm glad I make you comfortable, but I hope that I don't only make you think about kittens, especially when I'm touching you." Mac's eyes turned darker and he gripped Jenny's hips in his hands, pulling her until her body was flush with his. His excitement pressed into her, through his jeans.

She wet her lips.

"I definitely think of other things," she murmured. Where their skin met, white fire flamed in Jenny's chest. She sucked in a breath when Mac leaned down to kiss the bare skin over her collarbone.

"Good," he whispered against her skin.

He scooped her up into his arms and carried her bridal style to his bathroom. He turned on the shower and started to strip. She pulled off her blood stained clothes slowly. Despite their gross coating and that she desperately needed a shower, she was still shy.

"How about I go first? Then you?" Mac said, looking down at her in her bra and underwear. She turned around as he pulled down his boxers, got into the shower and pulled the curtain closed. He showered quickly, scrubbing at the blood on his skin. He reached out and grabbed the towel behind Jenny and wrapped it around him before stepping out of the shower.

"You go. I'll go grab you a towel."

When he left the room, she stripped down and got into the warm spray of water. She scrubbed her skin carefully to get all the blood off and to linger a little and make certain that she was clean. When she was done, she grabbed the towel that Mac had left out for her and wrapped it around her body.

She padded into his room. He was near his bed that sat behind a tri-fold partition. He was pulling a shirt over his head, soft pajama pants covering the rest of his body.

"Hey." She whispered.

"Hey." His voice was soft and the look in his eyes made her stomach flip. "Come here."

She walked over to him only dressed in the towel and he wrapped his arms around her.

"I'm so glad that you're okay."

"Me too."

"And I'm so glad that you're naked in my apartment."

Jenny laughed, throwing her head back. She looked up at him and he pulled her closer to him. She reached up and kissed him gently on his lips. Her skin felt like it was going to burst with the heat from his touch. She gasped against his mouth and he deepened the kiss, sucking lightly at her bottom lip. He picked her up and turned her around.

"Do you want to stay here tonight? I got you some pajamas." Mac held up a pair of flannel pants and a worn black band shirt up for her.

"I'd appreciate that if that's okay?" Jenny asked, wringing her hands in the towel.

"Mi casa es su casa." Mac smirked at her.

"You're such a dork."

"But a totally hot dork, right?"

"Yes." She placed a gentle kiss on the tip of his nose.

He turned away to let her change. She scooted down onto the pillow and yawned so deeply that it shook her chest.

Mac flicked off the light and climbed into the bed next to her. When his arm snaked around her waist, she sunk into the mattress and sleep overtook her quickly.

CHAPTER TEN

Mac trailed his hand on Jenny's rib cage. She was turned away from him, sleeping soundly. Her hair draped onto the pillow and Mac pulled the blankets up to keep her warm. His apartment got cold at night. Mac listened to her breathing and couldn't believe his life. She was magical that much he was sure of. Maybe a little crazy but he didn't care. She made him feel things that he could not even imagine. Her legs were intertwined with his under the blankets and he could feel the warmth from where they touched. Not the warmth of another body, but the spread of comfort that he didn't have the capacity to even imagine.

She was special even if Kristen thought she was a loon. He felt it. He felt Jenny's fear and confusion and saw into Jenny's mind about the bus crash without Jenny needing to say anything at all. Seeing Jenny get hit by the truck and come back from the dead, proved it all. He was still a little shaky from all that.

His eyes followed the slant of her nose and her slightly parted lips and he knew he was a goner.

He leaned back on the pillow and smiled to himself. *Halloween is the best.*

* * * *

Mac opened his eyes as the sun rose above the horizon outside. He reached out. The bed was empty next to him. He sat up and peeked around the partition at the rest of his apartment.

"Jenny?" He called. There was no answer.

He cursed to himself that Jenny bailed on him until he spotted her standing at the kitchen sink.

"Hey." He sighed in relief.

"Hey," she said and smiled at him. She filled a teakettle with water from the tap.

"You're still here," Mac said.

"Yes." She ignited the stovetop and placed the kettle on the flame. "Did you think that I took off in the night?"

Mac scoffed. "No. Definitely not. I'm fine. I wasn't freaking out or anything."

Jenny snickered. "Sure you weren't."

She wore Mac's holey band shirt and baggy pajama pants. Even as covered up as she was, he remember the look of her smooth, milky thighs and the crest of her small breasts speckled with freckles from the night before when she got out of the shower.

He leaned over her shoulder, tucking his head there.

"Hey, turn off the stove," Mac said.

"I made tea. I'm sorry I didn't ask you before, but I don't know how the etiquette of these things go." She turned off the burner.

"Oh, no. That's fine. I meant that I hope that we'll be too busy when it goes off."

"Oh, really?"

She ran past him to the bed with a laugh and collapsed on top of the covers. Mac dove on top of her.

* * * *

He placed her gently on the pillow as he ran his tongue up the curve of her throat, which made her gasp. Her breath came faster. Bright white shone in her mind and threatened to burst from her hands. It was power like nothing she had ever experienced before. Mac saw it too. She tugged on her shirt and yanked it over her head.

She captured his mouth with hers. His lips were plush and he kissed her deeply, trailing his tongue on her bottom lip until she opened them for him. She sucked on his tongue gently. He bucked against her center, making her throb. It was a delicious and new feeling and she only wanted more. She arched her back and thrust against him. Purples and white and red of love and passion were streaming through her now. Too many feelings and colors for Jenny to keep track of. They flowed over her in wonderful waves.

"Jenny, I swear. You're amazing." Mac sucked her bottom lip and nipped at it softly.

"Mac–" Her voice was a breath.

He sat on his knees and looked down at her. Running his hand through his hair, he looked at her like there was no other woman in the world.

"I want to remember this moment forever." He tickled his fingertips on Jenny's exposed stomach. She felt the heat of their connection from his light touches.

"You're so sweet, but I think this is where I tell you to shut up and kiss me." She grinned.

"As long as you keep saying my name like that, I'll do whatever you want." He yanked his shirt off and Jenny squirmed underneath him.

"Come here, I wanna feel you." She ran her palms over his muscles.

"Can I feel you?" He asked shyly.

She blushed and the look on his face made her warm all over.

CHAPTER ELEVEN

Mac was gentle with her and playful. Jenny couldn't remember how many times she laughed and said his name.

She giggled while she said his name, whispered his name, moaned his name, and screamed his name when he kissed down her stomach and licked her from top to bottom. He was still alive, still very much alive on top of her, kissing her and manipulating her body in ways that she didn't know any man could.

When he lay down next to her the sun had been up for hours, she caught her breath.

"Oh boy, we're going to need food and provisions, but I never want to leave this bed. I never want to leave you." He smirked.

Jenny's stomach rumbled.

"We're going to need food. You're wearing me out," she said.

"You're so ready to give up now? We're just beginning." Mac kissed her shoulder and winked at her. If she weren't already lying down, she'd probably swoon at that moment.

"I'm not ready to give up, but I'm going to need sustenance to keep going."

"I'll order something. Do you have any preferences? Vegan or vegetarian or lactose intolerant? I mean, I love me a BLT but I can learn to love broccoli if you need me to. Do you like Mexican? Thai? Chinese?"

"Not vegan or vegetarian. Anything is fine. You don't have to be so accommodating, you know." Jenny traced circles on his upper thigh, tickling the black hairs there.

"Stop. Stop!" Mac laughed.

"Oh! You're ticklish!" Jenny wiggled her fingers at him.

"Stop! I can't handle it." Mac jumped out of bed and grabbed his cell phone from his jeans on the floor.

"And yeah, I have to accommodate the lady's wishes. I'm a gentleman after all. Plus, you basically died. I think you deserve what you want for a few days. I'll get the food. You stay there. Rest. Get ready for more." He winked at her again.

Jenny laughed and stared at the ceiling, tracing a small crack in the paint from one corner to beyond the partition. Mac paced the apartment ordering food.

The idea of him talking on the phone while naked made her smile. Between her legs was deliciously sore so she hung her knees apart under the sheet. She looked around his "bedroom" and studied the stacks of books around her. Mystery thrillers, self-help books, history novels, heavy looking textbooks.

Mac sauntered back and tossed his cell phone on the nightstand.

"So, I went with pizza. I figured it was the best bet. We have thirty minutes until a delivery boy shows up so I need to get to work counting those freckles on your back because I want to be at least half way done before he gets here."

"Pizza is good."

Mac took a deep breath and crawled into the bed next to her.

"I wanted to ask you about Kris. Do you think she's okay now?" Mac said solemnly. He cracked his knuckles and rubbed his hands together.

Jenny leaned up on her elbows; the sheet fell to her stomach and exposed her breasts.

"I think she's okay." Jenny nodded. She hadn't felt any darkness since the night before. When the bus blared by, she relief washed away the panic in her heart and the darkness left her. "I'm not sure how this works. I'm still learning, but I haven't felt or seen anything since last night, so I think so?"

Mac blew his hair out of his face.

"Good. Because I don't think that I could listen to any bad news when you look like that." He gingerly placed a palm on Jenny's breast. Her nipple hardened under his touch and her pale skin flushed with the rush.

CHAPTER TWELVE

"Mac, I'm fine." Kris said over the phone. Mac buttoned up a black shirt for work. Kristen had disappeared for a few days after Halloween. "My date went really well and I was preoccupied but I'm very much alive."

Mac snorted. "Well, that's good. About the girl and the aliveness."

"What about you? You left the bar in quite a hurry with that red head."

"I know. Things are good." Mac smiled widely. He planned on bringing Jenny lunch on his break, but he needed to make sure that Kris was okay first. "Things are really good."

"God, we sound like a bunch of love sick fools."

Mac pulled on his worn Converses as he scooped up his keys from the counter. "I don't know about you, but I'm definitely a love sick fool. She's amazing."

"Jenny?" Kris asked. "That's her name, right?"

"Yes and she's wonderful and beautiful and amazing."

"Enough with all that. Okay, since you are so into her, I'll try my best to forgive her basically threatening my life."

Mac stopped in front of his apartment door.

"Kris, you don't understand. It wasn't like that. We all shared a near death experience. It's bonding," Mac said.

Kris laughed on the other end of the line. "I don't see it that way, but I'm happy that you're happy."

"Thanks. That means a lot."

* * * *

Mac carried the flowers to Jenny's front door. Her apartment was equally small but she placed small potted flowers by the front door. The aroma of garlic and tomato tickled his nose. He knocked lightly, the number 3 that hung from a small nail on the door swung slightly.

Jenny opened the door and Mac's breath caught in his throat for a moment.

She wore a skirt that fell beneath her knees and a v-neck light green sweater. He wanted to plant kisses along her collar and chest, a kiss for each freckle.

"Wow," Mac managed.

"Speechless?" Jenny smiled. "I can't believe it."

She pulled him into a hug, wrapping her arms around his neck.

"I'm so happy to see you."

Swirls of magenta burst behind his eyes when she kissed him. The feeling of love settled into his heart.

Danielle Donaldson writes from Southern California where she lives with her husband and young son. Her novels are stories of hope. The smallest candle is still fighting the shadows. Every person has their struggles, their darkness but the cycle of life continues and the light might be around the next bend. Check out more of her work including her poetry and short stories at WriterDanielleDonaldson.com. She'd love to hear from you.

To hear more about her upcoming work, sign up for her newsletter!

Promised Magic
By
Sheri Williams

DEDICATION

To my wenches, I keep trying to leave romance behind (not purposely) and you keep pulling me back in. Don't ever stop doing that.

To Betty, thanks for letting me use your name. I am still going to write the rest of your story.

To Anna, I quite like knowing I wrote the "most romantic thing ever."

CHAPTER ONE

Opening his eyes, Brior found Elena towering over him. Her breasts, unaffected by gravity or age, bounced with her enthusiastic fucking. She raked his chest with red tipped fingers. Her groans and grunts should have been sexy, they should have had him close to exploding, but they didn't. He had no chance to think about it. The next thing he knew she leaned down, whispered in his ear. "I want all your power, Brior. Stop fighting me."

Shocked awake, with eyes wide, Brior's breath caught in his throat, he pressed against the tabletop and flexed his fingers against the hard, cool surface, to pull in the energy of the now dormant wood.

Stop fighting, my ass.

He scanned the darkened room, making sure there were no other customers paying undue attention to him, as he started to come down from the dream. The owner of the B&B overlooked him crashing at the table in the pub. She didn't fuss anymore since he kept a room there. But if he started disturbing customers, she might tighten his reigns.

The mug of ale he'd been nursing had long since gone flat, but he still chugged it down. The dream had been particularly vivid this time. There was a telltale bulge in his pants to prove it. While the fear overcame his lust in the dream, in real life he couldn't stop the natural reaction. Fucking Elena. He should have known better. No one that good looking could truly be interested in him. She'd caught the scent of magic on him and sunk her claws in deep. It had taken him more time than he'd like to admit to realize she didn't want him for just his body.

Fucking blind that's what I was.

Berating himself didn't work, but it took a lot to stop once he'd started. *Blinded by her breasts and her willingness to get naked everywhere.* Brior rubbed his face, the stubble from his jaw scratchy. He covered his face with his hands. Something had to change. Talking to the wood through his fingers didn't help. It was time to bite the bullet and just do it. Pulling a worn card from his shirt pocket, he rubbed his thumb over the picture.

The Wheel of Fortune card. The fortune teller he'd gone to in a drunken stupor said he was supposed to find Savannah Rose. Well, he was in Savannah, he just had to find Rose. It was weird how clearly he remembered that reading. He'd been going all his life, most of the time not paying any attention, but that night, despite being drunk off his ass, the tarot had called to him. He'd found the first reader he could and sat there as she drew the Wheel. "Changes for the better," she'd said.

It was the "for the better" part he was having a hard time with. His life had been in shambles since his parents' deaths. He'd been put into care as a naïve sixteen year old, no extended family to take him in for two years. Not even a family friend that he could remember. His parents had kept him fairly insulated his whole life, up until the night they died. His fists clenched involuntarily. There was no use getting mad about it now. He scraped the bench along the floor as he pushed out of the corner. Boots that had seen better days barked out an echo as he crossed the floor over to the bar to pay his tab.

"G'nite, man."

The bartender didn't look up from the book in his hand, just said, "Yeah, man."

And people say I suck at being social. He stopped at the stairway, on the way to his room. *I have got to stop talking to myself. Shit, I did it again.*

Thunk! Brior knocked his head against the stairway's wall and groaned. He knew he needed to start making a go at being an actual adult. Not drinking himself stupid and falling asleep at the bar would be a good first step. Maybe then he'd find someone to talk to instead of arguing with himself.

The tarot card felt like it was burning a hole in his pocket. Stripping out of his shirt, he dropped it to the floor of his room. Next came his boots and jeans, leaving him buck-naked as he fell on the bed. If anyone robbed him, that's how they would find him. Dead to the world, bare-assed and snoring like the devil.

Hours later when he woke, he shivered. At some point in the night the window in his room had come open. Autumn in the south wasn't particularly cold, but there was a slight chill in the morning air.

He dragged his pants on and went to close the window. No use in scaring any passersby. His foot caught something on the floor, and bending, he scooped up a letter. A dusty rose colored envelope with his name and the B&B scrawled across it. Brior almost dropped it. Dammit, first the magic on his eighteenth birthday, and the tarot card inviting him to a coven meeting, now a window opening on its own accord to deliver an envelope out of the blue? His life was turning into a freaking Harry Potter novel.

He left the envelope on the table by the window, and flipped the lock, lest any more magical letters arrived. Brior dug through his clothes, found his least beat up jeans and tee, and brought them to the tiny bathroom with him. After a quick shower and shave he was dressed and ready. There were still a few hours before he had to be at the coven meeting. His stomach rumbled as he shut the door to his room on his way out. Food. Yes. He could probably talk Cook out of some of the scraps from breakfast, since he'd missed it again.

He ran his fingers along the gnarled wooden banister as he meandered down the hall, the faintest of tremors flaring through his fingertips. Latent magic. That's what Elena had taught him. Even just thinking her name brought a bad taste to his mouth. He'd spent two years with her, during which she had taught him very little, and groomed him to be her boy toy, all while hatching a plan to steal his magic. Busy muttering under his breath, Brior almost slammed into one of the bartenders, Silas, as he turned a corner.

"Damn, kid, get out of your head." Silas rubbed his elbow where he'd hit the wall.

"Yeah, sorry, man. Hey, wait, why are you here this early? You were still here last night when I went up."

"I'm aware." Silas was fluent in sarcasm. Brior could appreciate that. "Cook sent me looking for you. Wants you to play gopher for her this morning."

"Yeah, okay. Thanks, I was headed that way."

Silas nodded and turned to duck out the side door now that his mission was completed.

The noise of the kitchen was boisterous as Brior approached. Cook's outbursts weren't new. She was always shouting at someone. He'd caught the brunt of it a few times since he'd started working for her casually for room and board.

"Gods be blessed, you idiot. I asked for chives! What are these?" Cook brandished a handful of what looked like dandelions. A young kid quivered in front of her. "Chives, boy. Go find me some chives."

"Morning, Cook. Busy scaring the help, I see."

She raised a grey eyebrow. "What, you think I won't smack you with this spoon, too?"

"No, ma'am." Dropping into a bow, Brior grinned. He knew she couldn't resist his charm, and sure enough when he straightened, her green eyes lit up and she smiled.

"Boy, you're lucky I knew your parents. Come here," she gathered him into a hug, "Blessed Samhain to you."

"And you also." Brior tried hard not to choke up, but it was difficult. The loss of his parents still tore at his insides. When he'd made his way to Savannah, Cook had been the only person he ran into that he knew from growing up. She'd been friends with his parents when he was a kid, but he'd forgotten about her since she left when he was young. One of the very few people who'd been in their inner circle. She'd known about the magic. About his legacy. And she'd never said a word because she had promised his parents. One of the few times she'd talked to him about his family that had come up.

After the mess with Elena he'd stumbled into Stay a Spell, and Cook had come running. From the back of the kitchen she'd recognized he was there. A part of her decision to let him stay and work off his room and board was her guilt about not being there when they'd died. She told him how she cried when she heard he'd been lost to the system and she couldn't do a thing about it. Mumbling through tears, she apologized over and over. She'd nursed him back to health after Elena was finished with him, and she spent the better part of that time berating him for not coming straight to her.

They'd come to an accord, though. And for Brior she was family and he loved her. "Silas said you needed me. You want me to fetch Chives?"

"No, silly boy. I need you to bring something to Rose for me."

"What...wait." Brior leaned on the cutting block. "How did you know about that?"

"You think I don't know what is happening today? Coven meeting. Has been the same for years. I was going to go over myself but with help like I've got, I don't feel safe leaving my kitchen." There was a good bit of love in her voice when she talked about her kitchen. It was her special kind of magic. It might have been a simple B&B and pub, but the food was spectacular.

"Okay, okay. No problem. Is this Rose woman expecting me to have something for her?"

"I'll call, remind her that it'll be today. Now sit down and eat. You're too skinny." She pushed a plate full of sausage and gravy under his nose. The peppery aroma sang to his senses. "Yes, ma'am." He dug in, the food warming him through. He ate with gusto, trying his best to think only of the meeting he would attend that day, and not the envelope that sat on his side table.

CHAPTER TWO

Brior made it to the meeting early, left the brown wrapped package on a side counter, and then hung around to check things out. Unsure about the idea of joining the coven, he kept his senses tight, just in case any of the people here were like Elena. The owner of the shop, Rose, the one the fortuneteller had pointed him to, wasn't even there.

After two hours, he left the meeting unsatisfied. There was still a ton he didn't know. The last four years since his abilities had kicked in had been an exercise in frustration. Every time there was a chance he had a lead, or some new information, it turned out to be a dead end. There had to be someone out there who could help him, who could teach him.

With his plans to question Cook dashed, Brior wandered the streets of Savannah. The early evening sky was dancing with colors. Blue to purple with a few shots of orangey-pink to keep it interesting.

This was his favorite time of day. When the air was cool, he could get lost among the people taking advantage of the lovely weather. As just one of the crowd, Brior liked pretending to be normal. A feeling he hadn't had in a while. He had magic that he didn't understand, he was working part time as a mechanic to put spending money in his pocket, and helping Cook out at the B&B to keep a roof over his head. It all seemed dull. Aside from the tenuous relationship he now had with dirt and nature in general, he wondered if there wasn't something else out there.

The one thing he had gleaned from the coven meeting was the existence of a loose community of others like him. Did he want to be a part of it? He had the offer; a family connection allowed him a seat if he wanted it. But did he? He'd been on his own so long now, the idea of family seemed foreign.

It was times like these he really wished he had his mom there to talk to. She'd know exactly what to tell him. But since he couldn't raise people from the dead, or at least not as far as he knew, he'd go to the next best thing. Cook.

He walked back to Stay A Spell faster than when he left, and with purpose. Cook could tell him about Rose and the coven. They seemed to be good people, a few of the folks at the meeting had been friendly enough to him, though a group that diverse was bound to have some squabbles. There was a good chance he was overthinking joining. He tended to do that.

The kitchen was dark by the time he returned. Cook must have gone home early. Maybe she was out doing her own Samhain rituals. In all the talks they had had since they were reunited, he'd never had the guts to ask if she practiced. He wanted to, but it never felt right. She'd offered some tidbits in conversation, but not a lot. Not enough to show him what he needed to be doing. With nothing else to do, Brior went up to his room.

The second he hit the light switch, the envelope lying on the table grabbed his attention. The sweet, cheery color stood out in the bland, ordinary room. In a few quick strides he held it in his hand, the texture between his calloused fingers odd, as he slid them across the envelope. Turning it over, he studied it. There were no other markings aside from his name and the address of the B&B. He wondered if that meant it had been hand delivered. The idea that someone had been in his room creeped him out more than if it magically had appeared.

He plopped down hard on his bed. The creaking of wood shook him out of his reverie. There was no point putting it off.

He lifted the unglued flap, his breath shaky. He didn't understand why he was nervous. It was just a piece of mail. Except deep down he knew that this letter might be life altering. From the envelope he pulled a folded page. One more short breath before he opened it, and then he held his breath altogether.

> *Dear Brior,*
> *I know you don't know me. It bothers me to know you have gone your whole life waiting for this day, just like I have. As you are aware, my twenty first birthday is a mere month away. I wanted a chance to meet you before we say our vows...*

There was more, the author seemed to enjoy putting pen to paper, but Brior stopped paying attention to what he was reading after those five words. "Before we say our vows." That couldn't possibly mean what it implied. Once he was able to control his breathing he read and re-read those few words. Vows. What the hell? Was he supposed to be getting married?

It was on the tip of his tongue to curse his parents. How could they not have told him about something as important as this? In the long list of things they had kept from him when he was kid, this one was critical. Right up there with forgetting to mention he was a witch, and letting him wake up feeling weird one morning. The letter fell to the floor. He hadn't gone his whole life waiting for this. Dammit. How was he supposed to find this person? More fucking questions, and this one was almost laughable. He tugged his hair until his scalp protested. Lifting his head, he zoned in on the dropped envelope.

He swiped it off the floor and checked inside. That letter couldn't be it, could it? Sure enough there was one more scrap of paper inside, tucked down into one corner. It was an address in Bucharest, Romania. What the...*Romania*? His supposed lifelong intended wife lived in Romania? Land of vampires and such? Wait, were vampires even real? He was driving himself insane, thinking in circles. Of course they were probably real. He was a freaking witch, wasn't he?

"I need a drink." Shaking his head, he tucked the slip in his shirt pocket, nice and safe next to the tarot card, and went down to the pub. The bar was mostly empty except for a few tables in the back, occupied by magical people. You'd think it wouldn't surprise him anymore, but it did. The strangeness of his new life weighed him down. He sat at the bar and ordered a Guinness.

"Brior." Silas slid the glass across the bar with a nod of his head.

"What's up, man?"

"Not much. Pretty dead tonight. Most likely will be until after midnight. Then we might get a few."

"Everyone's busy celebrating Halloween, huh?" Brior took a deep pull off his beer, the dark liquid coating his dry throat.

"Most folks round here are celebrating Samhain, but yeah the kids are doing the Halloween thing."

"Yeah. I forgot. Big community of that here, magical folks I mean."

"Of that? You are *of that*, you know that, right? No use pretending you aren't." The guy's tone turned to disgust and he stalked off.

Dammit, I can't talk to people. I'm better off talking to an empty room. Brior left the half empty glass on the bar top next to a few bills.

Leaving the B&B behind him, he strode out into the night. In the darkness he came across kids running and screaming, enjoying their freedom, even if it was just for one night. He carried on through the night, his brain a jumbled mess, running around in circles going over the coven meeting, the envelope, and the mystery girl he was supposed to be marrying in a few days. None of his thoughts left him with anything that resembled a solid idea of what he should actually do.

A park bench under an antique reproduction lamp called to him. A quiet space for him to think. Close to open earth. The mixture of dirt and clay he'd come to recognize in a whole new way. With his boots kicked off and his socks balled up on the bench next to him, he wiggled his toes in the dewy grass. The tension slipped away, his shoulders relaxed. He hadn't yet learned how to use his magic, or abilities, or if he even had any. He did know the fresh earth settled him. Cleared his head. And that moment, he needed calm.

The slip of paper in his pocket felt like a weight. He pulled it out and held it up to the light. A simple piece of paper with an address on it. He stared at it, hoping that something new would come to him, but nothing did.

Romania. He kept coming back to that. His dad's family was from Romania. That was the only thing he knew about his ancestry. It looked as if his and his dad's lives were going to intersect there. Unsure of when he made the decision, he only knew that he would go. He owed it to the girl, the one who expected to marry him on her twenty first birthday. He'd use the computer Cook had in the office for ordering. He'd book a flight to Romania, it would take a good chunk of his emergency cash but it was worth it. He was sure the answers were there.

CHAPTER THREE

Cook was understandably worried. She made him take money, as he didn't have much after the price of the ticket. She'd told him to call at every layover and when he landed, but had no answer to the most obvious questions. Who was this girl and why did she expect to marry him? Brior merely nodded at her for a solid hour of her worrying at him. Then he hugged her before he climbed into the taxi and headed to the airport. She was his surrogate mom, and despite his aloof act, he was going to miss her.

The airport was huge. Brior stood awestruck. He'd never been anywhere like it. When his parents had been alive they'd lived on a farm in the country, which was almost completely self-sustained. Savannah was comfortable, but Atlanta made him feel small, it wasn't a feeling he particularly enjoyed. Check in was a quick and painless process. Except for the one attendant who almost made him strip but wouldn't say why.

Brior collapsed into his seat, drained. All the steel and glass around him tugged at his magic. This was yet another reason his childhood in the country made sense. If he inherited earth magic from his parents, they too would seek proximity to fresh earth.

The takeoff was a new experience for him. There was a moment when he dry retched, but the lady next to him rubbed her hand across his neck in soothing circles. She was a stranger, yes, but there was something about her that calmed him, and her actions helped soothe his fear of crashing to earth in a ball of fire.

When they were in the air, flying smooth, he turned to thank her, but she cut him off.

"I totally understand. Air is my thing, my element. If I could I'd be flying out there with the birds and the clouds."

Brior's jaw dropped and she laughed heartily.

"How did..."

"I can smell the earth on you. It's strong. Anyone who has basic abilities can generally spot another witch among the crowd." Brior pulled back, his face devoid of emotion. She couldn't possibly know how bad that made him feel. Her blasé attitude only proved how little he knew.

"Oh, yeah."

"Well, shit. I've upset you. Sorry. Big mouth. My foot is perpetually in it. I'm Betty, by the way." She took his hand even though he didn't offer it, and shook it forcefully. "So my earth friend, how come you don't know your own powers yet?" Again Brior was taken aback by her boldness. But what did he have to lose? He was stuck next to her for the length of the flight and then he'd probably never see her again. It was worth the risk to uncover information about his powers. Giving her a once over, noting her open expression, he spilled his whole story. He told her about those two years in foster care. About his eighteenth birthday and how he woke up knowing something was different. He even told her about Elena.

Once finished it was Betty's turn to be taken aback. "Wow. That's some life story."

"Tell me about it."

And she did. The two of them spent the rest of the flight hunched together. She told him all she knew about witches with earth powers, which wasn't near as much as she knew about air. But it was more than he did and it gave him hope he would find out more, eventually. Betty scribbled her number down on a piece of paper, as they landed in Russia for a layover.

"Call me if you make it back to the States. I'll help if I can."

"Thanks Betty. Seriously. You're the first to tell me anything useful. I appreciate it more than you could ever know." He leaned in to give her a quick hug.

"Hey good luck getting married." She walked off laughing, leaving Brior standing there shaking his head. That had been interesting; she'd been loud and open, but had given him more information in a few hours than he'd learned in the past four years. She also gave him a list of books that he should read. She'd laughed at that. Sending him off to a dusty old library to find books that contained actual magical knowledge. According to her, he would learn a lot on this journey.

With her phone number tucked safely in his wallet, he strode through the airport, trying to find the terminal for his connecting flight. She wasn't from Georgia, but Tennessee, and that was close enough. She'd be a future ally, and he needed that in his life. *Who knew what would come of this trip?* His next flight boarded after what seemed like hours in the terminal, but eventually he was on his way. He landed in Romania after an uneventful flight. Brior had been away from the ground for too long. His balance was off. His first goal after finding his way out of the airport was to find some bare earth for him to ground to.

"Keep yourself grounded," Betty had told him, "It'll be important for you to keep your energy up. To keep your head clear."

He'd asked her if all witches were like that. If they needed their element the way he did. She didn't have an answer, but she did tell him that his raw power was stronger than she had seen with anyone else. That she felt it come off him in waves. "How the hell am I supposed to take that?" he'd asked her. She never had answered. She just shrugged it off.

By the time he broke through the doors to the airport he was searching desperately for earth, any dirt would work at that point. At last he found a small grassy area near a parking garage, he yanked off his boots and socks and stood there, the grass tickling his feet. The weather surprised him, it was strangely close to what he left back in the states. A woman passing by raised an eyebrow at him, but he didn't care. It was worth the strange looks; his energy came back, his mood lightened, his heart rate slowed. When he was more himself, less frenzied, he tugged his boots back on. It took him a moment to find his bearings, but when he did he found a taxi stand.

He pulled the slip with the address out of his shirt pocket one last time. He'd memorized it, but he liked the touch and the weight of the paper. A taxi pulled to the curb in front of him, and he got in rattling off the address to the driver. And then he was off to meet his intended.

The back of the taxi was oddly comfortable and Brior settled in for the ride. Out the window he caught his first real impression of the city. It had an old-world feel to it, which made sense, as that's what it was. He could see the wear on the bricks of the buildings as he went by. They had to stop by a church and Brior looked up to see the gargoyles guarding an old church steeple. The grey stones were partially blocked by scaffolding, but even the basic wood and steel couldn't mar the beauty of the proud building.

They passed a sidewalk cafe, a bakery and a bookseller. Brior made a mental note to come back to that street later, it looked welcoming, a good place for him to melt into the crowd. Nerves settled in his stomach. Right then, driving past that bookstore it hit him that he was there to meet a girl who might turn out to be his wife. The absurdity of it had his stomach clenched. Bile rose up the back of his throat. He fought the urge to throw up in the taxi. Through the haze of his turmoil he barely realized the driver was speaking to him.

"What's that?" Through gritted teeth he didn't even recognize his own voice.

"I said we're here mate. That'll be twenty three lei." Brior took out the money he was glad he had the foresight to get exchanged at the airport. When his boot hit the cobbled street, his ankle almost turned under him.

"Dammit." He tested his weight on his foot as he tugged his bag out behind him. The door slammed shut of its own accord as the driver sped off. "Okay then."

The street was empty. Not a sound in the air, not even the call of a bird or the bark of a squirrel. Which was odd as there was a gated park directly opposite where he stood.

He had to tilt his head to take in the whole of the building in front of him. Old-world indeed. It was the same grey block of the church he had passed, and even more beautiful. How the builder created the curves and the twists of the turrets amazed him.

Turrets. That was a weird thing to see on a residential house, although maybe not now that he was in Romania. He took a deep breath and straightened his shoulders before he stepped up to the door. In front of him was the strangest doorknocker he had ever seen. A gnarled fist jutted out, in that fist was a tarnished brass ring with a hammer hanging from it. The brass was cold in his hand when he knocked.

It reverberated louder than he expected. There was no immediate response, no sounds of life behind the great wooden door, but as he went to lift the knocker again the door opened. A short man peered up at him.

"Sir?"

Brior had to stop himself from staring. The man holding the door was a dwarf. And he spoke English.

"Yes. Uh. I'm here to see...well, I don't know who exactly. I received an envelope with this address on it."

"Ah yes. You'll be here to see the master then. Please do follow. Leave your bag, I'll handle that."

Brior had a split second where he almost changed his mind; his pulse jumped, a bead of sweat rolled down the back of his neck, but he stepped over the threshold. Through the great wooden door he walked down a short hallway and into a lush garden. Fruit trees lined the brick walls, tempered by beds of flowers, some strange to Brior. It was like walking into a wonderland. The peace of the earth enveloped him. His powers had never been urgent before. His fingers itched and heart raced, the urge to toe off his boots and step into the lush green grass overtook him.

"Do it." The voice was timid, almost a whisper. Brior stopped, searching through the foliage for the speaker. "I do it every time I walk through the door. The verdant grass, the cold dirt, it calls to you."

"Why do you hide?" A pivot to either side didn't show the girl. Her voice was a song on the wind. Just like the cool earth, it called to him.

"I won't harm you." Brior said.

"I know you won't. You are Brior. We are to be wed." From under an apple tree, she glided toward him. Her feet were bare, small and slender. He let his gaze travel up the rest of her. She was exactly like her feet. Slim, petite, and pale. Her hair was amber, shiny and long. There were round brass glasses perched on the tip of her upturned nose.

"And you are?" Brior couldn't continue to stay silent. This wasn't the best way to start. He wanted to kick himself. Instead he stepped forward, reaching out as if to calm a frightened animal. "I'm sorry. From your letter I gather you grew up knowing about me. I just found out when I got the letter."

"What about your parents?" She asked the question with a compassion he wasn't used to.

"Died when I was sixteen."

"My father...he didn't know. The spell on the letter was to get it to you. Our families haven't been in contact since they signed the contract years ago. If he had known, things would have been handled differently." She sat on a low brick wall he hadn't noticed before and waved him over.

The girl stared at him until he went and sat by her. The silence stretched between them but it wasn't awkward. After a few minutes he gave in and slipped off his boots and socks. Toes wiggled in the grass, the power in him drew the power in the earth to him.

"Wonderful yes? It soothes me."

"It is." He didn't look at her face, instead studied her toes. From this proximity he could see they were painted a pale pink color. "I guess I should ask; what's your name?"

"Astrid."

He rolled the name around his tongue, trying it out. To see how it fit. "Astrid. A lovely name. So Astrid, what do you do?"

"Do? I study. I tend the gardens. I make tea." Not only did her family live in an old city, but they lived an old fashioned life it seemed.

"What do you study? Do you want to work?" Her eyes grew wide, the pale green became almost clear.

"Work? No. I'm to wed and take care of the house. The children. Carry on the legacy."

He laughed. He might as well have landed in Victorian times.

"We are both young. I'm only a year older than you. How are we supposed to support ourselves?" It hit him then. Children. Legacy. Shit. "Whose legacy? I barely know how to use my powers. I didn't find out about them until my eighteenth birthday when I woke up with muddy feet. Four years and I can barely do more than absorb the energy from the earth."

"Your parents didn't raise you with your powers? The match between us was made because we are both of the earth, and from powerful families. My father would never have agreed to it had he known this." Worry etched across her face, tiny lines around her eyes and mouth made her strangely more attractive.

"I don't know what they were thinking. If you're shocked, you can only imagine my reaction."

Where his feet touched the earth, his skin tingled. It was a pleasant feeling, tempting him to stay there. He shook it off. Things weren't going to work out between him and the lovely Astrid. If her father weren't satisfied with his meager abilities, he would find a way to break the contract. The idea left Brior feeling weirdly distraught.

"Father will have to be told. I'll go with you. I fear he'll not be happy."

"I don't want him taking it out on you."

She reached out to touch him, but hesitated, then with more determination rested her hand on his arm.

"He would never make a move against me. I'm stronger than he is."

"Wait, what?" Brior's head spun. "You are stronger than your father? How does that happen?"

"I'm unsure. I'd say luck, but it's not really. My whole family walks on eggshells around me. Worried I might go crazy or something. I don't know what they think I'm going to do, throw a tree at them?"

She laughed at her own joke. A solid, hearty laugh sounded strange coming from the lovely, ethereal girl next to him. A rolling mass of conflicted emotions fought in Brior. The energy of the earth beneath his feet called to him, but the girl with the green eyes did almost as much. When he made the decision to make the trip he hadn't known what to expect, but it never crossed his mind that he would have an immediate connection with her. The one thing he desired was more information about the magic inside him.

"I know you said your dad would be upset. What do you think he's going to do? I was really hoping to learn more about my powers here. There has been a sad lack of facts in my life."

She tightened her grip on his arm. Her obvious compassion for him warmed his heart.

"I know he will take no umbrage with that. He believes in knowing about your powers, and using them, I am sure he'll be willing to help." She'd danced around the other subject that had him worried. Their union. The connection that sizzled between them, he wondered if she recognized it too. If it was normal, their magic recognized the match?

"Let's go and see him. He'll be in his study. No point in putting it off." Her dress billowed as she stood, a quick twist to settle it about her. Brior was mesmerized. Even Elena had never affected him like this. What was happening wasn't a surge of schoolboy lust, but a shimmer in his soul. She held her delicate hand out for him to take. He stood, slid his hand in hers, and moved toward a door he hadn't noticed before.

"What about my bare feet?"

"Dirty feet are practically expected in this house. Even my father, in all his stuffiness, goes barefoot the majority of the time."

CHAPTER FOUR

Brior tried to discreetly take in his surroundings. The interior of the house was only a tad more modern than the exterior. The trek to Astrid's father's study felt like the walk to an execution. Sweat settled at the base of his hair, and threatened to drip down his forehead. It was all he could do not to gulp audibly when they stood in front of the door. This one was ornate like the front, only without the giant weird hammer knocker.

"I'd tell you not to be nervous but it would be hypocritical. I will tell you not to let him intimidate you. His bark is much worse than his bite."

"You know I never understood that metaphor. I don't like a dog barking at me anymore than I'd like one to bite me."

Her head tilted, revealing shadows under her eyes. She studied him.

"I think you'll be fine. Father does like a pragmatist."

"Then it's probably best not to tell him I dream of running a unicorn farm." Straight-faced he delivered that line and was not disappointed in her boisterous laugh. The door in front of them opened. The dwarf butler stood to one side; the same blank look on his face.

"Master Black will see you madam and sir."

"Thank you Reggie." Astrid skirted around him, and dragged Brior with her.

"Father. There is much to discuss." Brior admired how she handled her father. All business.

"This is Mister Pyke, I presume." The man stood to shake hands with a firm grip and sat back in his chair. He looked like a man who was used to getting his way, which Brior supposed he was. "Sit, sit. Would you like some tea dear?"

Brior had expected animosity. Either Astrid had exaggerated her father's attitude or he was a great actor.

"No thank you father. You might want a glass of something stronger though. There has been a, shall we say, kink, in your plans."

"What do you mean?" Grey eyebrows shot up, the nice facade gone.

Astrid laid it out for him. Everything her intended had told her, she relayed to her father. He stopped the discourse a few times to badger Brior about details, but Brior did what Astrid instructed and held his ground. By the end of it, the study was more of an interrogation room.

Her father had waved them away, rubbing his temple. It was clear to Brior that his plan to have a major place among the magical families in Romania had been wiped away without any chance of recovery. He'd asked why no one had told him when Brior's parents had died. Brior wished he knew. Hand in hand the betrothed returned to the walled garden.

The instant his feet hit the luxuriant grass, he calmed. As long as he could have access to the earth he would be okay. That was a truth he knew to his core. Along with the knowledge that the girl next to him, affected him in ways he never expected.

"Do you find me attractive?" Her question came out in a whisper. The vulnerability in those four words was like a knife through his heart.

"What...why? Why ask that? Yes. Of course I do."

"Why would you say of course? I know I'm not a great beauty." And there was that knife in his heart twisting, ripping it to shreds.

"Who on earth have you been talking to? A lovelier lady I have never laid eyes on. I can promise that."

"I'm not overly endowed. I'm aware that is what men like."

"This is by far the strangest conversation….look, it's not about the size of your, um, assets. Your face is lovely; a beautiful smile, enchanting eyes, hell, even the freckles are cute."

"I think you flatter me, because you feel you have to." There was a crack in her voice. Enough to let him know she wasn't just fishing for compliments, but that she really believed her assertions.

Moving to straddle the low wall they sat on, he drew her around to face him. He tilted her chin so that she was looking at him.

"I hate, with a raging fire you would think that. I hate for any woman to believe that. There is always a guy that will tell you those things. Make you feel less than you are. And that is not a real man." His shoulders were tense, his blood pumping. "There are a lot of things people who know me could say, but I do not lie. I do not flatter people. The truth is important to me."

She squeaked like a mouse.

Brior had to rein it in. He knew that he could get loud when pushed, and the idea that any man would tell this lovely creature that she was less than beautiful horrified him.

"I'm sorry. I shouldn't have raised my voice."

"It's...it's okay. I can tell that you are a passionate man." She blushed when she realized what she had said. "I meant, it's easy to see that you have very strong feelings. I don't, sadly."

"I'm sure you do, you simply need to find what makes you passionate." His wink had her smiling again, and it made Brior happy. He loved to be the reason she smiled.

"This garden. I am passionate about it. My sanctuary."

"How long are we going to keep up the passionate talk, eh? It's a tad weird being this open about my desires in your father's house."

"You don't need to worry about father. If he has a headache he'll not be seen for the rest of the day. He'll go to his spot, a private garden outside of his study to be among the earth he is closest to."

"Speaking of earth magic, why does he have less power than you? If you don't mind me asking."

"We don't know, truly. My older brother is like him, and my mother has even less power. He has tried for years to figure it out but hasn't been able to. It bothers him a great deal, but there doesn't seem to be anything he can do about it." The proverbial light bulb went off over Brior's head. It made sense, she didn't know many people, wasn't allowed out of the house, and her father had the power to make her feel less.

"It was him, wasn't it? The guy who tears you down. Why do you stay in his house?"

"Where would I go?" Tears threatened to spill down her cheeks, and Brior did the only thing he could do. He gathered her up in his arms. She fit perfectly, and he had to check his urges.

"Forgive me. Please, I do not want to be the reason you cry."

"You...you think it's easy, but it's not. Our world is not like yours. I have nowhere to go, I would be shunned by my whole community for daring to leave my father's house before I am married."

"Let's get married then."

She pushed back so hard he fell over and landed on his ass, on a bed of newly crushed flowers.

"What? Why would you say that?" There was a hint of a screech in her question and Brior couldn't help but smile.

The more the idea blossomed, the more merit it had.

"We are supposed to anyway, aren't we? And it could be beneficial to the both of us. You get out of this house that has you living like a Victorian nun and I get knowledge about my abilities."

"Maybe you're the crazy one."

"It's a win-win situation." He climbed off the flowers and straddled the low wall in front of her. Only inches away. "Do you really want to live in this house forever? Never experiencing the outside world?"

"He won't allow it. Father will decide he was cheated in the deal."

"What if we make him believe it's a love match?"

"What?" Astrid coughed a few times, and then it turned to a fit and Brior had to hold her close to pat her back. A few minutes later and she was under control. "How could it be a love match? I've known you all of a half a day."

"What, you don't believe in love at first sight?" He gripped her arms and pushed her back with a gentle touch, to see her face. "I've never met a woman who didn't believe in that."

She stiffened under his touch.

"It's not that I don't believe. It's that I've had no experience with it."

"Ouch. Okay, I see what you're saying. Let me use one of your questions. Do you not find me attractive?"

"I suppose. You are pleasant to look at. And you don't smell."

"I don't smell?" He had to hold back a grin when he noticed the slight lines near her eyes. She too was holding back a smile. "It makes me wonder what kind of guys you've met if that is complimentary."

"I've not met any men. Aside from a few of my brother's friends who have come to see father, or his associates who come for meetings."

"What? You've not had a date? Ever?"

"No. I have known since I was five years old that I would be marrying you."

"Shit." His heart leapt to his throat. "You've never?"

"Never what? There are so many ways to end that question."

"I have the distinct impression you're baiting me."

For a split second she looked at her feet, the shy girl overtaking. But then she was back, the sweet, funny and much more open version of Astrid.

"Maybe I am, should you say shit again?"

I think I need to have my head checked; I like it when she baits me like this. He couldn't stop the thought, though it didn't worry him. He'd already warmed to the idea of marriage to her. The elephant in the room, the topic they were currently dancing around, her virginal status, made it more interesting.

"I can be blunt. Do you know anything about the, uh, nighttime aspects of marriage?"

"That's blunt?" She giggled, and Brior was drawn to the movement of her breasts. They were very close to his hands.

"Yes I know about sex. No I've never had it. No I've never kissed a boy. I have been waiting for you, like I was supposed to."

"That is strangely stirring."

"Now that is blunt. Tell me the truth Brior, since it is so important to you. Would you really be happy spending the rest of your life with me? Not knowing anything about me besides our magic is compatible?"

"Truthfully? The idea suits me more than it should. Which is a strange mix of scary and stupid. I'm twenty two. You're twenty one. We're so young." He paused to run his fingers through his hair, which left it sticking up. "The thing is, something like fifty percent of marriages fail. You're saying we have a fifty/fifty chance. I like your spunk. I think you're pretty. The white knight inside me wants to take you away from this and show you the world."

"White knight?"

"Yeah, who knew?" Moved away from her and repositioned himself on the wall. "You've prepared for this your whole life. I haven't. But I think it could work."

"Yes."

Brior thought he was hallucinating. Wait, what? She said yes?

"Yes to wha...what?"

"Yes. We should go through with it. Get married. Move somewhere else." Amazed that she was able to say that with her voice quivering, Brior stared at her. Despite living her whole life in this house, and garden, she was quite self-possessed.

"Just like that?" He arched his eyebrow.

"Have you changed your mind already? One second you're proposing, the next you're backing out. Men are fickle creatures."

Before Astrid had a chance to protest, Brior tucked his finger into the collar of her dress, pulled her to him and kissed her full on the mouth. At first she didn't move. Didn't breathe. But Brior kept up the pressure and slowly she opened her lips a bit. When her body started loosening up he pulled back.

Her cheeks were flushed pink, her chest slightly heaving, being kissed looked good on Astrid. And Brior reveled in the fact that he had done that to her. He and no one else. It was a heady feeling.

"What...what was that for?"

"You have such a smart mouth. I like it. It needed to be kissed."

"I can, uh...I can smart off again."

He chuckled before he leaned in to drop a quick, chaste kiss.

"We have time. When we get married, we'll have all the time to kiss."

"Yes." She straightened her hair. "We merely need to convince my father it is a love match. Despite us meeting, you know, today."

"Insta-love."

"Insta-love? What is that?"

"I have this friend back home, she reads tons of romance novels. They are full of insta-love. You know. Man meets woman. They fall in love. Have mad monkey sex. Live Happily Ever After."

"Mad monkey sex?" Her eyes took on a glazed look.

Hello! Brior's thoughts interrupted. *She is interested in sex. Despite never having it. I can work with that.* His brain went into overdrive with that look in her eyes. He needed to be reassuring. "Maybe not to start off with, but we can certainly get there. If that is what you want." It was hard for him to not go into super lust mode. Her reactions were not making it easy for him.

"I've read about it. The practical and the flowery, but never mad monkey sex." Every time she said those three words, her eyes lit up, and Brior knew that she would be fun to educate.

"I can teach you. I'm fairly certain I would love to demonstrate."

"When do we start?" The breathless tone of her voice had his pants tightening. This girl was doing a number on him. She was snarky, sometimes confident, at times shy, but definitely into sex. He might not actually believe in the idea behind those romance books, but insta-lust that was happening as he sat there.

"We should probably be married first, so your father doesn't have me killed."

"We can elope." Her eyes dilated, and she covered her mouth.

"Eager much?" While they talked his hands made their way up her legs. Though the delicate fabric of her dress shimmered between their skin, the heat was tangible. She might not have realized it but she was turned on. Her mind was probably a little fuzzy; he knew it was best to not take her idea seriously. "Again, I think I'd rather not have your father kill me. Maybe we table that idea for a contingency in case he doesn't buy the love-at-first-sight act."

"Oh yes. That makes much more sense. Of course."

It hurt him, almost physically, to see her lose that sparkle. The shine that came from having lusty thoughts. He figured he could get her there again, easily, if her reactions to him were honest.

"When do you think we should approach him?"

"He'll be away for at least a day. I think it best to let him see us together, really sell it, and then give him the good news."

"How? Does he watch you?"

"Yes."

One word and it broke his heart. If he hadn't already wanted to help her get free, that would've done it. No one should be a prisoner in their own home.

"We need to sell it huh?"

"Yes. I know, you'll have to kiss me again. I'm sorry about that."

Brior studied her face, and ah...there it was. Her left eyebrow arched again. She was baiting him. Who was he to deny her?

"Come here." She didn't move. "You kiss me."

Her pupils dilated as she leaned in, her eyes open. She laid her lips on his. Brior's hands gripped her legs, held them still and under control. It was important to Brior that she find her own way, even if it was going to kill him.

When she fluttered her eyelashes she really moved into him. She gripped his shoulders as her mouth met his. With his eyes closed, he fell under her spell. A breath later and her tongue tentatively darted out to trace the lines of his mouth. Despite admonishments to let her lead, he couldn't refrain from testing the waters and pulling it into his mouth. She gasped and he drew back. Now it was his chest heaving. His heart thudded in his ears. A simple kiss and she had destroyed him.

"Wow."

"Yes. You can say that again."

"Wow." Her fingers danced along her lips.

"I didn't mean... hell. Yes, wow."

"Is it all like that?" She blushed but looked at him straight on.

He admired that quality in her. Hell, he admired everything about her.

"Better."

"Oh." The blush spread and Brior's stomach dropped. The edges of his desire were already starting to fade. Admiration and affection, throw in a metric ton of lust and he was close to having real feelings. The other four letter word that started with L. He was in so much trouble with her. Playing at insta-love might actually turn into actual love, and who could have dreamed that possible after one day? *He thought of the people who write romance novels.* He'd have to tell Cook about this; no way he could pick on her for reading those books anymore. He was living one.

CHAPTER FIVE

They'd had to leave the garden. Brior worried if they stayed there much longer he'd have taken her right there in the flower bed, and that was no place for a virgin. But hell was she tempting. Who knew that innocence could be such a turn on? Maybe it was his way of scrubbing Elena from his mind. From his body.

They'd made a plan for Astrid to show him her library. A whole room of books all about magic, and more specifically earth magic. He was finally getting the chance to learn. They spent the better part of the evening pouring over books. She helped him find some of the books Betty told him about, because with a library that size she was destined to have a few.

With books between them he learned about calling the forces to him. How to control the earth if he needed to. It was heady stuff to finally be inching toward actually being able to use his magic. Even more interesting was the way his whole body crackled and spit when Astrid used even the smallest amount of her power near him.

Then, when it was time to go to dinner, Brior made a point of holding Astrid's hand as they walked behind Reggie. It was a simple show of affection, but by the sharp look of the butler, Brior knew it would get back to Astrid's father. And that was the whole plan.

At dinner they kept it up. Brior would lean over to push a lone strand of hair from Astrid's cheek, and she repaid him by giving him tastes of the food on her plate. The whole experience left Brior dazzled. When they adjourned to the formal dining room he hadn't known what to expect, and he couldn't have guessed if he tried. A full buffet was set up along a sideboard and the table seemed to stretch for miles. Astrid led him, pointed out food he didn't recognize, and they each picked something different.

When they finished dinner, a maid entered to clean the table, another brought out a dessert tray. It was all so opulent; Brior could understand how Astrid had lived in the house without arguing. Everything she wanted was brought to her, except freedom.

After dessert, Brior was stuffed more than he'd ever been in his whole life. They spent time in the garden before breaking apart for the night.

"Why weren't your mom and brother there?" They'd been sitting in the garden a few moments, each of them lost in their own thoughts when Brior's curiosity got the better of him. He knew not to expect her father; she'd already mentioned that he wouldn't show himself for at least a day after they'd given him a headache.

"Mother is ill, she's been in a home for a while now. Father spares no cost to get her the best care, and my brother is at university."

"Why aren't you at university?" He could imagine the answer, and already the anger was boiling.

"Father believed I was getting married, no reason for me to further my studies." She shrugged a shoulder and Brior itched to punch something. Anything. Preferably her father.

"Besides, my brother is really just getting drunk and whoring around, which are my father's words, and if he doesn't shape up Father will stop paying tuition. I can study just fine in my library."

It bothered him how nonchalant she was about her situation. But maybe she really didn't know any other way.

"I imagine you are a voracious learner."

"I am. What makes you say that?" She had tilted her head in a way that made her hair fall to one side; it left one perfect ear exposed to the light rain that had just started. That little piece of flesh taunted him.

"I've noticed that when you put your mind to something, you don't hold back." Her cheeks reddened, and Brior could have kicked himself. Her blush was lovely, but he was supposed to be putting on a show for her father, not flirting because it felt good. A sneaky thought entered his mind. *I like being the reason she blushes.*

"Are you arguing with yourself?" Astrid compared their hands, studying the differences, before looking back up. "I know that look, my father does it, and I've been told I do as well."

"Maybe not arguing. Maybe scolding."

"Why would you scold yourself?" Her thumb pressed the soft spot between his thumb and pointer finger, a strange sensation poured through him. The same crackling he felt in the library, but different, softer.

"What are you doing?"

"I'm sending you calming energy. From the wet grass through me, into you. There was tenseness around your eyes. You are too hard on yourself."

And here I was thinking I was saving her. Well I can let her save me too.

"You're doing it again, arguing with yourself, or scolding yourself."

"No, that time I was giving in to the inevitable."

She tried to slip her hand from his, but he held on, and moved her closer to him. They'd been close before but they now they were inches apart.

"Inevitable?" Her eyes closed and her lips parted.

"Yes..." Brior spoke on a sigh as he covered his mouth with hers. This time he didn't hold back. Fingers that itched to touch her, thread in her hair, angled her head to get better access. Not breaking the kiss, Astrid scooted closer so she was sitting across his lap.

She moaned. Or he did. The contact jolted both of them and he yanked back, regretting it in an instant. Her lips were red and glistening, almost bruised from his kisses, and his lust kicked into overdrive. Slowly she opened her eyes, big and green, they brimmed with emotion.

"You stopped." It was a reproach the way she said it, and Brior had to hold back a laugh.

"Probably not a good idea to hit the finish line there."

"Why?" She pouted and Brior couldn't stop the laugh that time.

"We just met today. Your father might kill me. You're a virgin, and we are in a garden. Pick one."

"We're getting married anyway, and I can make a bed if that's what you want."

"Seriously?" His jaw dropped. She really did go all gung-ho when she decided on a plan.

"Yeah. Watch this." With eyes closed and her feet planted firmly on the wet grass she muttered a few words and Brior watched in shock as roots from a nearby tree sprung out of the ground. Pulsing and twisting they swayed in a hypnotic dance, forming a gorgeous headboard above a soft pallet of moss that sprouted in front of the wall. It wasn't the bed that Brior had been thinking of, but it was a bed.

"Holy shit."

"I know. And wait, there's more." She winked at him before she closed her eyes again, muttering the same words. The sound was strong before he noticed any movement but there were the roots coming up out of the ground. This time they grew into a tangled mess to block the doorway.

"Privacy." The smugness in her voice surprised him. She really did want to do this. She'd summoned a bed out of the ground and gave them absolute solitude so he could make love to her in a garden. In the rain. On a fall evening. A lesser man might have wept with joy.

"Are you absolutely sure you want to do this?"

"Brior, I have waited my whole life knowing that I would marry a man I had never met. I've met you. I like you. You've told me about life outside of this house. A surefire way to get me out. Why are you now asking questions?"

"This is moving fast. Seriously, not even a whole day."

"From all the talk from my brother and his friends, I'd figured a guy wouldn't turn down the offer of getting naked."

"I can't deny that. I'm a guy, and yes, the idea of getting naked with you holds a lot of interest for me." He stopped at the quirk of her eyebrow. He'd come to love it.

"But Astrid, I have to know you are completely sure about this. I wouldn't be a real man if I took advantage."

"A gentleman is what you are. I appreciate that. Really I do."

"I hear a but coming…"

Astrid stood, and with an ear-to-ear grin and with a few words muttered under her breath, her dress fell to the ground. Brior stopped breathing.

"But, like you said, once I've made up my mind, I don't hold back." She stood there in nothing but a pair of blue striped panties. Her breasts were small, but perky and Brior had to stop himself from drooling, and remind himself to breathe. She was petite but curvy, and had hips that were meant for grabbing onto. Brior stood and took the steps to close the distance between them before he realized what he was doing.

"You can touch me you know. I won't shatter." She may have tried to joke but her voice was thick, Brior recognized the lust, the hunger in it, and it fueled his own. With a hand that shook he traced a line down her collarbone, between the peaks of her breasts, stopping only at the line of her panties. The only barrier between them. Even though his touch was slight, she gasped.

"I promise to go slow. To take care of you. I know it's been a wicked short time, but I need you to trust me." Astrid nodded, but then cried out when his fingers left her skin.

"Give me a second." Brior dug out his wallet, praying he still had protection in it, and thanking the Gods when he found the shiny foil package. He dropped it on the low wall, before tossing his wallet to the ground. In his haste he almost ripped his shirt. It landed on his wallet. He went to unsnap his jeans but stopped.

"Have you...uh, I mean, you know how it all works right?"

The blush started on her cheeks but traveled across her chest.

"I've read books. I know, the basics. *Tab A, slot B.*"

A groan slipped from his mouth.

"I'll just keep these on a few more minutes, just in case." Brior took her hand, the heat of her skin and the cool of the rain kicked his system into high gear. What was it about her, about this whole situation that had him turned on like nothing ever had before? He tugged her hand, bringing her over to her moss bed. They knelt together, close but not touching except for their hands.

"I don't know where to start." It was a weird admission to make, but he needed to. It was important to not mess this up, and he hoped if she knew he was nervous, then maybe she wouldn't be. He'd been able to get her excited earlier; he hoped he could do it again.

"You could touch me. I like it when you do that." She was reassuring him. Telling him what to do. But her confidence fueled his. Despite his worry, she didn't seem scared at all. Nerves were to be expected, hell he was nervous his first time too.

"If I do anything you don't like, tell me to stop and I will."

"I can't imagine you would." The rain picked up a little, now more a light drizzle than a mist. A droplet of water fell from one of her nipples and something inside him broke. Bending her back slightly, to give him better access, he leaned down and covered her breast with his mouth. She arched her back, and her head tipped back, her wet hair cascading past his hands. A soft sigh escaped her, when his mouth left one breast and began paying attention to the other. A hum pumped through his blood as he feasted on her. The rain on her skin, made her slick under his hands and that made it hotter.

"You....I....Brior!"

He'd nipped at her, bringing her head back up, shock and pleasure etched across her face.

"Yeah...sorry, forgot myself."

"No, don't be sorry. Forget yourself all you want. I'm not nearly as fragile as you think."

His fingers danced along her ribs, making her draw in a deep breath. His thumbs hooked in her panties, and giving her a quick grin, he slid them down. They stuck at her knees, but Brior didn't care. With her gaze locked on his, he trailed a finger along her skin, barely grazing the springy hair he found there. His fingers slid lower, into her. Her eyes grew wide, into green pools of lust as he glided his fingers through her wetness.

"Jesus Astrid, you're so wet for me." Long, languid strokes had her breathing ragged, with sweet moans coming from her.

"I, ah.... I assume that is good." She bit it out on a moan.

"More than good."

His finger dipped into her deeper, finding her tight. Her knees buckled at the contact and she gripped his shoulders.

"Do *that* again."

Brior chuckled but did as she asked, her fingers dug into his shoulders as she whimpered. It was the single hottest thing Brior had ever seen. Over and over, slide and dip, he tried to keep his touch gentle but the noises she made spurred him on. It wasn't long till her stomach contracted, and her hips thrust against his hand. He kissed her, swallowing her cries as she had her first orgasm. The power of that, knowing he gave it to her, filled a part of his soul he hadn't realized had been lacking.

"Oh my.... that was…" She didn't finish her thought before she nuzzled her head against his shoulder.

"Good?"

"Good? That is not a strong enough word. Spectacular. Fantastic. Gorgeous. All much better words."

"I'm glad you enjoyed it." He leaned in to kiss her again, this time sweeter, taking more time. With his hand behind her neck and his mouth still on hers, he guided them down to the mossy bed. It was wet and spongy, and perfect for that moment. "You ready for the next step?" The way she shivered when he whispered in her ear had his cock jumping to life.

"Yes."

He rubbed his hand up the length of her back and down to her bottom, squeezing lightly each time he landed there. He held in the laugh as she kicked off her panties, showing him just how ready she was. He was still in his jeans. Highly overdressed.

"Let me." There was emotion in her voice but it didn't shake.

She pushed him down, then knelt over him. A Cheshire cat grin on her face as she ran her fingers across the tattoo on his rib cage, then bent over to unbuckle his jeans. She grazed her knuckles against his skin and he instinctively sucked in. She made quick work of the belt buckle and the three snaps, and Brior tried to hold it together, giving her the power. But when she hit the zipper, her fingers stroking the length of him through the material he all but jumped out of his skin.

"Let me." He batted her fingers away amid her protests.

"But I wanted to." She pouted, and damned if it didn't look sexy as hell.

"I know, but baby I wouldn't have lasted much longer and I want to make it good for you." He shucked his jeans and reached up for the foil packet.

"Can I now?" He turned to find her staring at his cock. He'd only been semi-hard until he caught a glimpse of her face.

She couldn't have looked hungrier for him than if she actually licked her lips.

"And here I believed you were shy."

"I am shy. You've corrupted me." Her hand circled him as she spoke and he let out a low groan.

"I'd argue that point but it seems stupid while you have your hand wrapped around me so nicely."

"That is an excellent point. I'm going to move my hand now, will you survive that?"

"Hello snark, that's been hiding under the shyness, hasn't it?" He'd said that last word with a screech as she tightened her grip. "I might not survive, but as long as you have fun…"

"I'm having fun." With the rain falling down over them, she had no problem sliding her hand up and down the length of him. "I like how I am able to make you grow." Her voice sounded husky, and he opened his eyes, which he'd closed in his pleasure.

"It does that." The color of her eyes changed again, almost fully black now.

"How…um, how much?"

"Not much. Don't worry, we'll fit." Close to bursting again, he maneuvered her down beside him. "Now I'm ready, more than ready actually, let's get you back to where you need to be."

She leaned into him, kissing his shoulder. "Where do I need to be?" He held her with one arm, while his other probed her center again. His fingers played, she was still wet, possibly with help from the rain.

He leaned in to whisper in her ear, "Wet and ready. I want to slide in in one stroke."

"Ahh." She gasped as he slid one finger, and then two into her.

"You're so fucking tight." He ground out the words before crushing his lips to hers. She'd taken a hold of him again and was sliding her hand up and down his cock to the same rhythm he pumped into her with his fingers.

"God. Brior, that build up. It's coming." She bit his shoulder with a cry as he pulled his fingers out. He turned away but not far as she still grasped him. He fumbled when he tried to rip open the package and then had to take her hand off him, but then he was ready. Sheathed in protection he rolled her on her back. He kissed her as he positioned himself between her thighs. Her hips rose, as he kissed her and using one arm to hold himself up he stroked her again and again. Making certain she was ready.

"This is going to hurt. I can't stop that from happening." She nodded once before she strained to kiss him. He nudged in. He went slow, trying to give her time to adjust. Despite the rain he broke out in a sweat. With her so tight, the pleasure he felt was insane. Her eyelids fluttered shut and he knew it was time. With one swift thrust he broke through her virginity, then stilled. He rained kisses all over her face and whispered apologies. The muscles in his arms bunched and jumped, straining as he held himself above her. A tear slipped from her eye but when she opened them there was no sadness.

"I understand all the fuss now." She spoke in whispers, her eyes bright with lust and magic.

"Me too." He brushed a kiss against her lips, and then he moved. Electricity snapped between them. Brior started slow, shallow thrusts to give her the right feeling but not hurt her too bad. He tried hard to restrain himself, to give her the pleasure she deserved, but when her hips began to move with him, when the snap of heat burst through and she began to meet him thrust for thrust, his control slipped. Lowering himself onto his elbows, he slid a hand down her leg, caught her thigh and lifted it to wrap around him. With new leverage he picked up his speed. He worried about her pain, but if her arched back and the noises coming out of her were any indication, then she was good.

She wrapped her other leg around his back, both of them locked together. Her hips met him at each thrust; the sound of their wet bodies meeting was music to him. The harmony their bodies made, and the humming of the air around them only spurred him on. There had never been anything like this in his life, and he wanted the explosion more than his next breath.

"It's building...Brior." She moaned his name as she came apart in ecstasy. He was close too; all it took was her dragging him down and biting the muscle that ran along his shoulder. With one last thrust he came. With his body completely spent, he snuck his hand under her and rolled till they were on their sides. With as much care as he could take, he pulled out and found a discrete place to discard the condom.

"Holy hell." There was shock in Astrid's voice, and Brior had to open an eye to see if it was good or bad.

"Are you okay? I know you're going to be sore."

"*I am fantastic*. Is it always like that?"

"Yes. Well, shit. No. Sometimes things get fumbled. Sometimes one of the people involved doesn't get into it. But mostly, yes. And...." He wasn't sure if he should bring up the magic, because surely that played into it, hadn't it? Leaning into her he paused for dramatic effect, she reacted, widening her gaze. He loved that, how expressive she was. "It can be better."

"Better?" She almost choked on the word. "It can be better than that?"

"Yes. When you know your own body. When you have more confidence. It's said, when you love your partner."

"Well then, let's fall in love."

"Wow. And we're back to no holding back." He chuckled when she slapped his arm. "No. I'm okay with it really. Before I met you I'd have said I didn't believe in love."

"And now..." Her whole body stiffened against his, and he debated finishing his sentence. But it wouldn't be fair to hold back. They'd already crossed a line.

"Now I believe in you." Her body melted at his words. Then, she tackled him. Rolling over until her body lay flush against him.

"That was the sweetest thing you could ever say. But it's us, Brior. I believe in us."

CHAPTER SIX

The next morning Brior stood outside Astrid's room. They'd agreed while they lay on their bed of moss they didn't want to wait. Astrid planned to tell her father they were getting married, whether he liked it or not. Brior was astounded by her determination.

"Are you ready?"

"As ready as I'll ever be baby." She stopped short, making him jerk where their hands had been together. "What?"

"Say it again."

"What?" He liked her bossy but he didn't understand what she was talking about.

"Call me *baby* again. Say it." A grin broke out across his face. He closed the distance between them, and with a gleam in his eye bent down to whisper in her ear.

"You like it when I call you baby? Next chance I get to have you naked underneath me I'll have you screaming while I whisper it in your ear. Over and over." He flicked his tongue along her earlobe.

She looked dazed, and started walking again without saying a word. Brior hurried to catch up to her. They walked into her father's study holding hands.

"Astrid! What are you doing in here? Where is Reggie?"

"I don't know father. I must speak to you." Mr. Black noticed their hands. His eyes narrowed.

"We will be married. I know you're unhappy with his lack of knowledge and power, but I wish to follow through on the arrangement."

"He is no one! His parents died before teaching him a thing. He works in a garage for God's sake! How will he support you?"

"You keeping an eye on me? Why would do that? Why not just not send the letter then?" Nothing the man did made sense to Brior. Mister Black stared at him, but Brior didn't back down. Though inside he was furious. If Astrid cared at all about his lack of means she didn't show it. Her grip tightened, and Brior reveled in her strength.

"He is my mate father. I do not care about his money. That is and has always been your worry. If I have to I will support us. You know that is not the issue here."

"You would waste your inheritance on some kid from America who would drag our family name through the mud? A kid who up until a few months ago was screwing Elena?"

How the hell did he know that?

Astrid stiffened beside him and Brior knew that her father had crossed a line. Too bad the poor stiff didn't realize it.

"Don't you dare talk about our family like it is the best thing on earth." Beneath his feet the ground rumbled. Tree limbs broke through the study windows. Shattered glass flew everywhere as the limbs advanced on Mister Black. "If you honestly cared about our family you wouldn't have cheated on mother. She would still be here instead of in that home you put her in." Astrid's hair floated as her powers surged. "You toss Elena's name around like she matters. She doesn't. You do not care about our family, only the order."

The tree limbs snatched him up, and wound around him. Tightening as her anger grew. "You are a hypocrite, and I will be glad to be free of this house. You will allow us to be married, tomorrow on my birthday as planned, or we will elope. I know the order would see it done."

"Temper, temper, little one. Hasn't your father taught you any control?" The woman behind the voice stepped in from the garden and Brior almost threw up.

"Elena? What the holy hell are you doing here?" Brior searched for Astrid's hand, gripping it tightly when he found it. The power that coursed through her flew up his arm, igniting him, in a way he didn't know was possible.

What is going on here? Why is the power suddenly filling me? He wanted time to figure out the whys, but it didn't look like he was going to get it.

"I've just been visiting. Why did ya miss me? I bet you did. I bet there ain't a thing that little priss could give you that I can't do better." Elena studied her nails in a practiced offhand manner.

"Don't you dare talk about her like that. She is a million times finer than you ever will be." Rage spilled out with Brior's words, though Elena was calm. Mister Black struggled against his bonds.

"So you have slept with her then." She turned to Astrid's father, an odd look crossing her face before she concealed it the mask of carelessness that Brior knew too well reemerging. "It appears that you have lost out, Mister Black. Their magic is compatible just as you feared. I expect you'll still keep up your end of the bargain?"

Compatible? Was that why he felt stronger all of a sudden, because he and Astrid were together?

"What bargain? What is she talking about father?" Astrid allowed the tree's to pull back enough to let him speak.

"Doesn't matter now, does it? You slept with the bastard after one day? I didn't think you had it in you."

All at once everyone moved. Brior went after Astrid's father provoked by the sob which broke from her throat, but Black had been let loose enough to allow him to slam Brior back with a wall of earth he invoked. Brior's breath caught as at least one of his ribs broke under the impact. He called out to Astrid but Elena had her hand wrapped in his fiancé's hair and was yanking her head back, leaning in as if about to kiss her.

"Brior!" The panic in Astrid's voice wiped out everything else. With all his energy, and most likely a good bit of Astrid's still coursing through him, he called to the earth. A root slammed up through the floor and wrapped around Elena, wrenching her away from Astrid who fell to the ground gasping.

"Elena, you bitch, don't you leave me here!"

With the wave of one hand Brior silenced the screaming Mr. Black with vines covering his mouth, and went after Elena.

"Stop running. Dammit, stop!" Brior called the earth one more time, it came to him easier now, amazing him even as he used it, and tripped her when she was trying to escape.

"It's a walled garden. Seriously? Where do you think you're going?"

"Away from this crazy family." She spun on him, dirty and angry. "Come on now, you can't fault a girl for trying to look out for herself. Can you?" Elena spat.

"I honestly don't give a flying fuck what you do, unless you bother me and Astrid again. Then I will have a problem. And those powers you wanted? I have them figured out now. I will destroy you." Stopping only inches from her dirt smeared cheek, he stared at her. "Do you understand me?"

"Yes. God, what is so special about her?"

"She's mine. That is all that matters." He muttered the same words Astrid had taught him and the tree branches broke through the brick wall of the garden. "Now you can run. Make sure you don't come back."

Without another word he turned on her, striding back to Astrid. He knelt down beside her, and gingerly checked her over.

"Are you hurt? What was she trying to do to you?"

"She's power hungry, there used to be rumors she was practicing to be a succubus, although I don't know if you can become one. All the books I've read say that you have to be born to it."

"Succubus?" He pulled her up to stand next to him, his arm around her shoulders.

"Yes, a magical woman who uses sex to siphon powers."

"Is that why she was trying to kiss you? That is what it looked like to me."

"Maybe, the connection was odd, almost as if my magic was being stolen." She squeezed her arm around his waist and he winced. "You're hurt."

"Not too bad." He nodded toward her father. "What do we do about him?"

Astrid called the vines back, and her father sagged as he gasped for air.

"Okay…okay…fine. Marry him. Throw your life away." As he spoke his voice went higher, the limbs squeezed tight.

"Thank you father. I knew you would be understanding." When she turned to leave the study the limbs disentangled, and

Brior had to keep himself from looking back when the thud of her father falling to the floor echoed through the room.

"You're scary. Remind me not to piss you off."

"Oh. I reserve that for him. I'm sure you'll be too busy calling me baby to piss me off." Astrid squealed when he picked her up and spun her in a circle. Kissing her hard before he let her go. "Let me heal you?"

"You can do that?" Was that a part of their magic he would learn too?

"If it's not bad, then yes I can." She splayed her hand along his rib-cage, under his shirt, her skin tingling against his. First there was low heat, then a shock then nothing. "Should be good as new. No more cracked rib."

"Damn, you are going to come in handy." He dropped a kiss on her head.

"You're not so bad yourself. You did magnificent in there. Your powers finally showed up."

"I'm pretty sure that you had something to do with that."

"Well then we're even. All sorted out?" Her smile was huge, and he hated to tell her the truth of his situation back home.

"About the garage thing, I don't make a lot, but I make do."

"I really do have an inheritance. I get it tomorrow. I can take care of us."

"Okay...." Brior had to think about that. The idea of having her take care of him didn't settle comfortably, but they could figure that out once they got out of the country. Maybe now he could use his powers there was a way to make that work. He could ask Betty when they got back to the states.

"There is one more thing, I live in a B & B. Though I made a friend on the plane on the way over, she might be able to help us find a new place."

"Does the B & B have a big bed?" She grinned as they walked under the doorway to her garden. She muttered the same words and the roots enclosed them. She was more calm then he was after that encounter, but he wasn't about to bring it up. Maybe she needed to go over it in her own way.

"Yes. Yes it does."

"Then everything else will work out. Now come here." A few words later and she was standing there without her dress. It was deja vu, but this time there were no panties.

You can find Sheri Williams at:
Twitter - @AuthorSheri
Fb- Sheri Williams, Author
Website – thesheriwilliams.com

Drifter's Moon
By
Michele Mohr

CHAPTER ONE

"Have you decided what you want to order, darlin'?"

I glanced up from the menu I'd been perusing for the last ten minutes and was unprepared for the massive crown of hair on the waitress in front of me.

"Umm, I'll have the cheeseburger special and a slice of whatever the pie of the day is." She filled my cup with coffee and I became mesmerized by the whirlpool of steaming black liquid.

"It's nice to see a pretty girl like you with such a big appetite." The name on the plastic tag clipped to her apron was TANYA. Her thick Georgia accent reminded me of my Granny, rest her soul.

"Fast metabolism." I saluted her with my cup before relishing the first sip. I needed the caffeine to get through the night.

"I'll have that burger up for you in a jiffy." She gave me a longer than necessary smile and pinned my order ticket to the rotating spindle. I played with my phone to distract myself until my food was ready. I noticed it was five minutes after midnight and officially Halloween. I should've been home celebrating on the couch in my pajamas watching a horror movie marathon and baking bat shaped cookies but instead I was in the middle of nowhere Georgia on a wild goose chase.

I scrolled through my email. After I sorted through a ton of online sale advertisements and other spammy things, I got to the important messages. The first one was from my boss.

Savannah,

I hope all is well in the South! I will be traveling to London this week to pick up a few objects for the New York store, but I will be available by phone/email if you need me. Happy Halloween!

Regards, Nik

I managed a store on River Street back home in Savannah called The Darker Curiosity, named after the owner and my boss Nikolas Darker. I thought the title was catchy, considering it made perfect use of his name and the items sold there were oddball antiques that had some kind of supernatural origin tied to them. Since most of the city was obsessed with the paranormal due to its own haunted history, the store made a pretty decent business. I wasn't scheduled to be back at work for another two days so why think about it until I had to?

I pressed DELETE. Next message:

REMINDER: Annual Samhain Coven Meeting
October 31st
Savannah, GA
Attendance is REQUIRED.
DELETE. Next message:

Savannah James, your presence is required at the Annual Samhain Coven Meeting
DELETE. Next message:

Your RSVP is required for the Savannah Annual Samhain Coven Meeting

DELETE
DELETE
DELETE
DELETE
Next message:

Savannah, its Adanna. I know you're getting these emails. I'm getting the READ RECEIPT!!! I need you here for the meeting so we can talk in person about your request.
DELETE

Witches were relentless, especially control freak coven leaders. I'm what my coven called a Natural Gray. It had nothing to do with my hair color, even though my eyes were gray but that was a coincidence. Anyway, I possessed the gift of white and black magic, or "gray magic." Being a witch wasn't easy, despite how cool pop culture made it look.

There were certain rules a witch needed to follow and there were consequences for breaking them. Since my powers came naturally, I'd been the envy of most other witches. I never had to study from massive ancient grimoires or sit over a cauldron and mix smelly herbs and oils together for a spell to be successful. One of the biggest components to a Gray's powers was emotion. If I intended something to happen, it happened. I rattled my own incantations off the top of my head and poof... easy magic.

Every Halloween, or Samhain as we witches called it, my coven in Savannah, Georgia, had a big annual meeting. This year, I planned to quit the team and fly solo. For a long time, I'd felt like the coven wasn't a good fit for me and parting ways was the right thing to do. They tried to enforce their rules and regulations on me because of the sporadic nature of my magic.

They thought I was dangerous, which I could be, although not intentionally unless someone pissed me off. Let's just say when I got mad, bad things happened. Good things happened when I was happy, too, but the coven forgot those times, of course. I emailed the Supreme witch to notify her of my resignation but apparently these things needed to be done in person. With today's technology, who even met in person anymore?

When the waitress slid my meal in front of me, I turned my phone off and got down to the task at hand. I hated practicing magic on an empty stomach, especially locater spells. I needed to find my scumbag boyfriend. Correction, make that my scumbag *ex-boyfriend*, Levi. He stole my necklace and I wanted it back. Well, it wasn't just any necklace; it was my moonstone talisman and my personal witch stone. Some witches used stones to guide them. With the stone not in my possession, my emotions flew off the radar. Plus my Granny gave it to me when I was a kid. She always accepted me for being different and helped me embrace my magical abilities. She passed away a few years ago, but I've always felt that her love guided me through the stone. I had to find Levi and kick his scrawny ass for screwing me over. Did I also mention the biggest emotion that drove a witch's power was love?

As I crammed ketchup soaked fries in my mouth and contemplated my shitty love life, my witchy tingles were activated just as someone sat down on the stool next to me. I hated those damn tingles because they were usually a forewarning something crazy was about to happen.

"What can I get for you, handsome?" In full service mode, waitress Tanya popped up from behind the counter.

"Coffee, black, thanks... and a cheeseburger special, Ma'am." He spoke in a slow Southern drawl. I snuck a glance in his direction.

He was a rugged, all American good ole' boy type. Mid twenties, like me, or maybe a little older. His short brown hair was styled to perfection with hardly a drop of product in it, and his faded jeans hugged him in all the right ways. He was nothing like those annoying hipster guys back in Savannah with their trendy skinny jeans two sizes too small that made their lower bodies look like a stuffed sausage. No, this one was all man, no poser, even down to his scuffed cowboy boots. After I ogled his denim clad thighs, he caught my stare and smiled. Damn, Tanya was right. *He was handsome.*

I turned my attention to my food and skated the last fry in a figure eight around my plate.

"Sorry to bug you again, Ma'am, but can I get a piece of pie, too? Whatever kind she's having." Out of the corner of my eye, I saw him point at me.

"It's pumpkin. Only kind we got today, sugar."

"Pumpkin is perfect, thanks. Can you tell me where I can get a room for the night?" She sucked in her bottom lip and poured his coffee.

"Ain't no commercial motels 'round here so you'll have to go a few towns over."

I enjoyed the first forkful of my pie before a voice from behind me chimed in.

"There used to be one just up the road a ways. No more, though. Ain't nothin' there now but cursed ground."

All American and I swirled around on our stools at the same time and bumped knees. The voice belonged to an old man in suspenders and a dirty baseball cap. He sipped from his cup and stared ahead into space.

"Hush up, Earl. Quit scaring my customers with your old spooky talk," Tanya scolded. Earl waved his hand in the air like he was swatting away flies.

I locked eyes with All American again. The funny thing was, he looked familiar. From the look he gave me, I wondered if he thought the same thing of me. My attention was drawn to his cheek, half-covered by a crescent moon shaped scar. He rested his head on his hand and covered his face as if self-conscious about it.

"What curse?" I asked.

Tanya leaned closer. "Decades ago, some loon burned down his motel to collect the insurance money but his plan backfired and he got trapped inside and died with a bunch of other folks. Some of the locals seem to think the ground where the motel used to be is cursed. Every Halloween, someone dies on that stretch of road and their ghosts are seen by drivers passing by."

"You're kidding right? Is this a Halloween story?" All American gave a half laugh and arched a brow in disbelief.

"Believe what you want. I'll be right back, y'all. I have to check on a phone order." She patted his hand and stepped away into the kitchen.

It was just as well. I had my own issues to deal with and didn't have time to get caught up in talk of local curses and ghost stories.

"So is your pie any good?"

"Excuse me?" I mumbled with my mouth full. My fork fell on my plate with a clatter. I tried to swallow fast.

"That pie you're eating. I just ordered a piece." He peered at me over the rim of his cup.

"Oh, yeah, it's delicious." I admired guys who used dessert as a conversation starter.

"I'm sorry, but do we know each other?" His crystal green irises reminded me of a deep lagoon on a tropical island, and I had the sudden urge to take a late night swim. Before I could answer him, my nerves got the better of me and I knocked my phone off the counter.

"Shit." We both reached for it at the same time and crashed our heads together.

"Ouch. Sorry, miss."

When he handed the phone over to me, another coven meeting reminder was up on the screen. I snatched it away from him as fast as I could, which caught him off guard. He tipped over his cup and splattered coffee on the front of my dress.

"Fuck!"

"Oh crap." He grabbed a bunch of napkins and dabbed the spill on my chest.

"You can stop fondling me now. I can clean it myself."

He looked me up and down.

"Fondling? Are you serious? I was just trying to help."

"Ugh. Forget it."

As I took over the wiping, the overturned cup rattled on the counter in cadence to my annoyance... and he noticed.

"What the?"

I needed to regain control before I took my magic out on innocent country folk and brought unwanted attention to myself. If only I had my moonstone.

"Excuse me, where's the restroom?"

"Straight in the back toward the right, sugar," said Tanya.

"Thanks." I sprinted to the rear of the diner.

After I locked the bathroom door, I wrapped my arms around myself and performed a breathing exercise to relax. Once I was emotionally in check, I looked at the ugly coffee stain on my favorite vintage dress. No amount of washing would get that bad boy out. I decided to take it up a notch.

I held my hands over the stain and regulated my breathing in a different direction to focus. To reach a desired result, magic was mostly about visualization and positive thinking. If you visualized the outcome you wanted, it would manifest, depending on how strong the witch was. I cleared my thoughts and imagined the dress was clean.

An aura of heat surrounded me as I activated my power. A gentle vibration flowed from the top of my head to the bottom of my feet. It bounced up again and emulated through my hands. Since cleaning a dress wasn't such a tall magical order, it didn't take long to see results. After about five minutes, the dress was as stain-free as it was before the coffee fiasco. Before I could celebrate my magical achievement in dry cleaning, a sharp noise erupted from the front of the diner. I hugged the wall.

A gunshot!

After giving my heart a minute to dislodge from my throat, I tiptoed over to the sink, pushed the stopper knob down and filled up the basin. Water was one of the four major elements and it aided a witch in spell work. Since it wasn't safe to leave the bathroom, I decided to watch what was going on up front with a little divination spell.

Inhale, exhale. Inhale, exhale. I dipped the index finger of my right hand in the sink and spun it clockwise as I envisioned the front of the diner. The water grew cloudy and fizzed to the top. Just before it spilled over onto the counter, an image appeared as if a hidden camera was filming the scene out there. I saw the gunman as clear as day. He wore a hood, but I recognized the skull belt buckle and the shifty look on his face.

Levi! What the hell was that shithead thinking holding up a diner at gunpoint?

The basin water boiled over and took away the image. I pushed out of the bathroom and was about to stomp through the swinging door when a hand covered my mouth. The scent of bleach immediately invaded my nostrils as I was pulled into a dark, tight space. I kicked my boot heels against their legs and tried to yell through the fingers pressed to my lips, but I only managed a whimper.

"Shhh, be quiet." It was All American. He held me close… *really* close. I was willing to bet that wasn't a gun he carried in his front pocket, at least not in the literal sense. He eased his hand off my mouth.

"Are you nuts? What are you doing?" I whispered.

"Stopping you from getting yourself killed by interrupting a robbery. Damn, ever hear of gratitude before attitude?"

"Levi won't kill me. If anything, he'll try to get far away from me. Knowing him, he got desperate and for some dumbass reason, he thought robbing a Podunk diner would be a good way to get a quick infusion of cash."

"Levi? You know that whack job out there?"

"Yeah, he's my ex."

"Oh, well, of course he is."

"Why did you say it that way?"

"No offense, Miss, but you just seem to have a flair for the dramatic."

"Eww, for a stranger you sure do think you know me."

"If he's your ex, and a felon, might I add, why are you following him? Are you a stalker or something?"

"No, I'm not a stalker. He stole something from me and I need to get it back."

"What did he steal?"

"My necklace."

"You want to charge out there and face off with your gun wielding ex for a piece of jewelry he probably already pawned?"

I hated to think of my moonstone behind a filthy glass display case in some seedy pawn shop.

"It's not just an ordinary necklace. You wouldn't understand."

"You're not going out there." I wiggled around, trying to find a more comfortable position. As a result, he grew hard against my ass. I'll admit I was impressed.

"Hey, Cowboy, would you mind going easy with that weapon of yours?" I couldn't tell if his sigh was more annoyance or embarrassment.

"Sorry, but what do you expect? I'm trapped in a closet with a hot girl rubbing on me while gunshots are going off."

"Which part is turning you on more, the hot girl rubbing on you or the gunshots?"

"Cut me some slack, Princess. This isn't the average day for me."

There was nothing average about what went on in his jeans, but I had no time for distractions. I had to get to Levi. When I tried to make a break for it, he locked me into the curve of his body like two cardboard puzzle pieces. The nearness of him made me imagine he held me under more pleasant circumstances.

"It's way too stuffy in here. I can't breathe."

"It's a broom closet. I'm guessing you've never hidden in one before?"

"I've spent most of my childhood hiding in one," I said.

"Huh?"

"Never mind."

"Sorry, but this was the best option for safety on such short notice."

"What a shitty night this has turned out to be." It was so tight in there I thought I would hyperventilate. I wiggled again for some relief.

"You're telling me. I'm starving."

"Dude, is food all you can think about right now?"

"Like you're one to talk, the way you were eating your pie. You were practically licking the plate, sister. It was borderline obscene." He officially rode my last nerve.

"Not all girls are salad eaters. Some of us like our carbs and sugar."

"I didn't say there was anything wrong with it. Dang."

"Whatever. I'm getting out of here."

"I'm coming with you," he declared.

"Ugh, hurry up then." I pushed down on the door handle and slinked into the hallway. It took a minute or two to adjust my vision to the fluorescent lights hanging from the ceiling.

It was quiet, too quiet.

All American tucked me behind him so he could lead the way down the hall. We peered through the little round window of the dining room door but there was no sign of Levi. In fact, there was no sign of anyone.

"Let's go. Stay close behind me."

"Yes, sir."

We moved up the main aisle by the counter but stopped within a few feet.

"What is it?" I asked.

"Everyone's gone."

"Maybe they're hiding." I took a quick look under the booths and found Earl sitting under one. He looked up at me like a scared animal.

"Here's Earl."

"The others are back here," All American called from the kitchen.

I joined him and walked up on Tanya and the cook both huddled underneath the food prep table.

"Is anyone hurt? We heard a gunshot."

"That little punk fired and missed. The bullet went through the wall."

As we helped Tanya to her feet, I decided to keep my mouth shut about knowing Levi, considering he was now wanted for armed robbery.

"Has anyone called the police yet?" I asked.

"They're on their way. You two can go. No sense in getting caught up in this mess here. Both of your meals are on the house," she offered.

I looped around and noticed the empty cash register drawer sticking out. Levi must have made off with all of the diner's earnings for the day. I felt guilty so I placed a twenty dollar bill on the counter.

"Here, take this anyway, no arguments, Ma'am."

"You're too kind, thank you, sugar," said Tanya.

All American reached for his wallet and did the same. He grabbed his burger and ate it in several huge bites before he licked his fingers clean. *Talk about obscene.* He caught me staring.

"What?" He shrugged and walked over to the vertical blinds. I shamelessly studied his ass as he leaned over the booth to peek through. What was it about this guy that had me so intrigued?

"It looks all clear outside but your psycho boyfriend could still be lurking around."

"Ex-boyfriend."

He rolled his eyes and grabbed his slice of pie before he escorted me out.

The moon was just bright enough for me to see the hood up on my old turquoise pickup truck and the mechanical guts scattered all over the gravel parking lot. The shattered glass from the windows crunched under the soles of my boots.

"That fucking son of a bitch!" The longer I looked at the remnants of sweet old truck, the higher my blood pressure rose.

"Shit. Let me guess who did this." He devoured the pie as he surveyed the scene.

"Lay off, Cowboy. It wasn't as if I could foresee this happening."

"Suuuuure you didn't."

"Oh, I assume you've had a stellar track record with women?"

"My track record isn't in question here since none of my exes just robbed and vandalized this mom and pop shop."

I circled around my truck and shed tears at the sight of all four slashed tires. I smacked the roof with both hands and kicked the hubcap, which popped off and rolled across the lot.

"No! No! No! No! No!"

The truck shook on its rims. I pulled my hands away since I had a human witness present. A witchy cover up was the last thing I needed to worry about.

"Man, you sure pissed this creep off."

"It's bad enough he stole my necklace, but now he messes with my truck? That weasel is going to pay for fucking with me! Do you hear that, Levi Perry? I wish you were dead!" A howling wind picked up from out of nowhere. I performed my breathing exercises again to make it stop.

"Look, it's late, you're upset, and it's obvious you don't have any wheels. I doubt a tow truck would even come out here this late. Can I give you a ride home or drop you off somewhere?"

"I'm too far away from home to make you take me and I don't know where I'm headed right now."

"Fair enough. I'm going to find a motel to stay for the night if you want to come along. You shouldn't be out here alone with this asshole around. It's too dangerous."

"You want me to spend the night with you… a complete stranger?"

"Relax, I meant in separate rooms, unless you *want* to share one with me?" He smirked and waited for my reaction.

"Don't flatter yourself."

"Come on, I thought we kind of got to know each other in that closet."

I realized he was joking, but it lifted some of the anger I had toward Levi and I managed to smile.

"Well, I am kind of tired." I opened the passenger side door of my poor, battered vehicle and took out my overnight bag.

"Good, then we might as well be properly introduced. The name's Jesse. Jesse King."

That name... I recognized it. He held out his hand for me to shake and a spark ignited in my palm when it met his. It looked as if he felt the spark, too... or realized his hand was still sticky with pie filling.

"Savannah James."

"Wait... Savannah from Savannah? Your grandmother had a huge wrap around porch?"

It dawned on me why he seemed so familiar. My pulse raced as I took in the sight of him.

"Jesse. It's... you."

"Well, I'll be. It must've been fifteen years since I've seen you last. We were just kids."

"Looks like you've been drinking your milk and taking your vitamins."

"Yeah, I was a pretty scrawny kid. You look pretty damn good, though, girl."

"Thanks." I wondered if he saw me blush.

When we were about ten years old, Jesse and his little brother spent a summer with their uncle. He had a neighboring house to my Granny's and we three kids became inseparable in those few months we spent together.

"It's getting chilly. Let's hit the road, shall we? We can catch up in my truck." Jesse pointed to a huge black pickup parked across from mine. He held the door open for me and smiled as I climbed in.

It was going to be an interesting night. I felt it in my witchy bones.

CHAPTER TWO

I waited for some sign of civilization along the dark road we'd been driving on since we left the diner, but all I could see was the pavement visible in the high beams of Jesse's truck. The October leaves floated on the wind, almost like they danced to some silent music I wasn't privy to hear. I shifted in my seat and tried to shake off the uneasy feeling clinging to me like plastic wrap.

"Where the hell is the next town? We should've at least seen a road sign or something by now."

"Relax, city girl. We should see something soon. Some of these country roads seem longer than they actually are."

"Maybe." I focused on the view through the windshield.

I didn't know why I got him involved in my crazy mess. I hadn't known the adult version of my childhood friend very long, but I knew he deserved better than me and my shitty relationship baggage. Maybe I should've refused the ride in the first place, but fate made me cross paths with Jesse King again and I was curious to know why.

"So, Savannah from Savannah. I didn't think I'd ever see you again."

I noticed him eyeballing my legs.

"I wrote you letters, Jesse."

He let out a heavy sigh. "I never got any letters. My dad must have thrown them away."

"Oh…how is he?"

"He died about two years ago. Heart attack."

"I'm sorry."

"A part of me isn't. You know how he was." I knew his daddy hadn't been a nice man, so I didn't push the issue.

"What about Tyler?"

He cleared his throat but didn't answer me. I remembered Jesse had done a lot to protect his little brother from their abusive father, even take the brunt of his physical anger for him. That kid meant the world to him. Their mother died giving birth to Tyler and I guess their dad resented the kid for it. No Father of the Year award for that guy.

"Jesse?"

Cold, stale air seeped into the truck. Jesse fidgeted with the heater knobs under the dashboard but I stayed focused on the road. A fast moving, heavy fog formed in both lanes from out of nowhere, and so did the woman standing in the middle. Her red hair flashed in the glow of the headlights.

"Jesse, look out!" He swerved just in time to avoid hitting her but we ended up veering off the road. The awful screech of the brakes echoed in my ears and the rough and tumble motion of the truck almost made me throw up my dinner. The truck grinded to a halt, but my equilibrium still spun me like a carnival ride.

"Shit, are you okay?" I relished his comforting touch as his fingers moved through my hair.

"I think so. What about you?"

"Yeah, just a little rattled. Where'd that girl go?"

"I don't know." A bright yellow light illuminated his face and his look of concern. We both turned forward to see the fog dissipate. It revealed a neon sign shaped like a crescent moon, just like Jesse's scar. The same shape twice in one night was considered an omen to a witch.

Under the word MOTEL, the word VACANCY buzzed and lit up on the sign, and for a reason I couldn't explain, I was drawn to it like a fly to a bug zapper. The vibrations from my locator spell were so strong I thought the ground would open up and swallow me whole.

"It looks like they have rooms available," I said.

I rested my hand on Jesse's arm to make sure I wasn't dreaming. The bulge of his triceps forced me to let my hand linger there for longer than I should've.

"I thought there wasn't supposed to be any local motels around here, according to Tanya. Looks like she was wrong."

"Yeah, maybe."

"The Drifter's Moon Motel. I think we drove straight into a horror movie."

He was right. Something was off about this place, big time, but I couldn't put my witchy finger on it. Based on the vibration strength, I knew my necklace was close. I jumped out of the truck to have a look around.

"It's here, I know it is."

Jesse followed me. "What are you talking about? What's here?"

"Come on, where are you?" I scoured the empty parking lot and stopped when the glow of the sign caused a shimmer in the dirt a few feet in front of me. I ran up to it and felt a pang of adrenaline as I picked it up and dusted it off. Victory!

"Did you find something?"

"Yeah, it's my necklace." I held it up for his inspection.

"It looks new age-y. Hey, I remember this. It's the one you wore as a kid. Your sleazy ex stole it from you?"

"Yep."

"Now I understand why you wanted to track him down across county lines."

I struggled with the clasp before I realized it was broken. *Damn you, Levi.* I put it inside my purse I wore strapped across me.

"So where is this Denim guy?"

"Levi."

"Sorry, *Levi.* Why is your necklace on the ground in the parking lot of this place?"

"That's what I'd like to know."

"Maybe he has a room here and it fell out of his pocket."

"No, his motorcycle isn't here. Besides, if he just robbed a diner a few miles away, he would skip town, not hang around to get caught. Levi is a douche but he's not stupid."

"How did you know the necklace was here when you got out of the truck?"

"Intuition."

"Right. I should have known with you."

"So you remember?" There were very few people who knew I was a witch outside the coven. Jesse, my Granny, and Levi were the exception and Levi only found out when he ran over my cat with his bike when he was drunk and I accidentally resurrected it. It was nice to be open about what I was, but Jesse and I were kids then. I wondered how he felt about it now.

"Of course I do. I even remembered the tricks you taught me."

"Which tricks?"

"Exactly. Witch tricks." His smile beamed brighter than the glowing neon above us.

"That's cute, but Jesse, I have to ask you something."

"Okay, I'm listening."

"We met when we were kids and the things I shared with you about me may have seemed cool to a ten year old, but now that we're all grown up, how do you feel about me being a witch?" I kicked the dirt with the tip of my boot, bracing myself for his answer.

"The same way I felt about it then. Why would it change?"

"I don't know, it's not like its common knowledge my kind exists."

"I've never told anyone about you being a witch if that's what you mean. You made me pinky swear on the porch over chocolate chip cookies and lemonade, remember? That's almost legally binding to a kid."

"Yeah, that was an interesting summer." My cheeks flushed at the memory of innocence long gone.

"The best summer of my life." Now I was the one who wore a huge smile. He stood with his hands in his jeans pockets and rocked on his heels.

"I'm sorry you got dragged into my Levi mess. If you want to bail—"

"Bail? There's no way in I'm leaving you here all by yourself on a deserted country road with your ex and some weird girl wandering around in the dark. Where is she anyway?" We both looked toward the road.

"Maybe she wasn't there at all, in the physical sense," I said.

"You mean we almost ran over a ghost?"

"I don't know. What other explanation could there be?"

"I think you let all that curse talk at the diner get to you." He walked around the parking lot. "Hello? Is anybody out there? Miss?"

"Shhh! Jesse, what are you doing?"

"Seeing if she's around. Maybe she's hurt or scared to come out." I wasn't sure where the girl went to or if she was a ghost or not, but I knew I didn't want to be outside anymore.

"Let's go in and get our rooms."

He nodded and followed me to the office entrance. I may have strutted a little more than necessary for his benefit.

"Check this place out," said Jesse. The lobby looked just as outdated as the outside of the motel. He tapped on the front desk bell until a tall blond man in a trucker hat and a Led Zeppelin shirt appeared.

"Hey, ya'll. Welcome to the Drifter's Moon Motel. I'm Jude. What can I do ya' for?" "We need two rooms, please," said Jesse. "Oooh sorry, no can do, my friends. All we have is one vacancy tonight."

"But your parking lot is empty," I said.

A creepy grin spread under his porn star mustache.

"Are you *sure* you two want *separate* rooms?"

"That's what we asked for."

Jesse reached for his wallet. "Let's take the room. I'll sleep on the floor if it will make you more comfortable. I can't drive anymore tonight."

"All right, my friends. Ten bucks."

"That cheap?" I pulled Jesse aside. "It kind of makes you wonder why it only costs ten dollars, doesn't it?"

"We'll take it." He ignored my concern.

"Score, my man, score." Jude winked at me. I could tell dirty thoughts went on under his greasy hat.

"Whatever. Let's just hurry up."

"Sounds like the little lady is impatient. Young love waits for no one, right?"

"We're not in love." Jesse and I said in unison.

"Hey, man, free love is cool, too."

"We're not loving anything except sleep, and even if we were, it's none of your business," I told him matter of factly. Jesse pinched my arm and glared at me. Jude continued on with his perverted, hippy sales pitch.

"Mmm, hmm. Now your room comes with all the standard amenities like TV, telephone, ironing board, coffee maker, oh and magic fingers for the bed."

"Magic fingers?" Jesse handed Jude the cash in exchange for the room key he dangled on one of those old plastic diamond shaped key chains.

"Have a nice stay, ya'll."

The exaggerated diction of those last words sent another chill through me like an ice cube sliding down my spine. When I turned around, Jude was gone from behind the desk.

I never wished I were home so bad in all my life.

CHAPTER THREE

Jesse jiggled the key in the lock until we heard a click.

"Jackpot." He motioned for me to go in first.

It was as clean inside as one would expect your average room at a dive roadside motel in rural Georgia would be. It wasn't decorated anything fancy, but the late seventies to early eighties decor was kept in theme with the rest of the place. I twirled around and flopped down on the bed.

"Is it to your liking, my lady?" Jesse teased in a poor attempt at a British accent and threw the key on the scratched-up nightstand.

"It's delightfully gaudy."

As I ran my hands across the orange floral bedspread, I wondered who or what had laid on it before me.

"Low maintenance. I admire that in a woman."

The bedding may have been questionable, but I was too tired to care. I stared at the cracks on the ceiling and listened to the gentle hiss of the ancient heating system as it attempted to kick on.

"Hey, look at this." I turned and spotted a full unopened bottle of whiskey on the dresser.

"Is that complimentary with the room? Jude didn't mention it when he ran down the list of amenities."

"It is now." He raised the bottle and saluted me.

"What was up with that guy? Did he seem a bit off to you?"

"Yeah, but we'll be gone come morning so it doesn't matter. We'll never have to see him again." He took his jacket off and tossed it on the chair in the corner of the room.

"Yeah, I have a meeting tomorrow afternoon in Savannah."

"What kind of meeting?"

"A witch meeting. I'm quitting my coven and doing my own thing. I have to be there in person to do it."

"That doesn't surprise me. You were always an independent flame." Even after all those years between now and the last time we were together, he still understood me. "When did you join a coven?"

"My Granny knew a woman in town who ran one and she brought me to meet them. She thought it would be good for me to have magical guidance."

"And you don't need that anymore?"

I didn't know how to answer that. Jesse opened the booze and took a sip before he offered me the bottle.

"Save me some. I'm going to take a shower." I needed to unwind and there was a part of me that was curious about what I would find at the other end of that whiskey bottle. I took my broken necklace out of my purse and placed it on the nightstand.

"Have fun." I'd become a sucker for that twinkle in his eyes and it scared me, especially since this entire trip was supposed to be about getting rid of excess baggage, boyfriend-wise.

I eased out of my jacket, kicked my boots off, and shuffled toward the bathroom. Before I went in, I glanced over my shoulder. His gaze was still on me. I left the door open just a crack and told myself it was because I might've overheated from the shower steam, but I knew better. As my Granny often asked me, *"Oh little Savannah, what spell are you weaving now?"*

The bathroom was clean, so I got naked and turned the nozzle in anticipation of the hot stream of water but nothing came out but a dry squeak.

"Oh come on!"

I fidgeted with the other nozzles and was relieved when water came gushing out of the faucet to run a bath. I didn't look forward to a phone call to creepy Jude to complain about not being able to bathe. I inspected the tub before I sat my bare ass in it. It passed my standards.

Shit. I had forgotten my overnight bag in Jesse's truck. Oh well, I'll just have him go out and get it later since I was already naked. In addition to the generic motel soap, I spotted a bottle of bubble bath on the counter by the sink. I opened it and took a sniff.

Lavender... the key ingredient in a love spell.

After I poured in a generous amount, I caught a glimpse of myself in the medicine cabinet mirror. Something was different. Was it my hair? It looked a little drabby as opposed to its usual chestnut shine, but that wasn't it. Oh well. I turned away from my reflection and climbed into the tub. I stretched out and dunked underneath the water to let the soothing warmth envelope me. The moment was mine. Almost.

Something slid across my throat like the movement one makes with their finger when they slide it from one ear to the other signifying sudden death.

I bolted up to the surface.

Every hair on my body stood up in the icy draft that hovered around the tub. My overactive thoughts raced in the quiet of the bathroom in competition with the echoed drip of the faucet.

"Savaaaaaaannah." A faint whisper danced in my ear. I panned around the bathroom, but I was still alone.

"Jesse?"

A few seconds later, my handsome companion stood in the doorway holding the bottle of whiskey.

"You rang?"

"Did you just call my name?"

His look of confusion told me he hadn't. He took a deep pull off the bottle.

"No. You're not falling asleep in here and dreaming, are you?"

He leaned against the door frame and rested his head on his arm. The movement made the bottom of his t-shirt rise over the top of his jeans to the point where I caught a glimpse of his stomach… and his happy trail. Did I mention I had a thing for happy trails?

"Maybe I'm just hearing things."

"You're taking a bath?" He licked his plump lips.

"Yeah, the shower part didn't work."

"I haven't taken a bath since I was a kid."

"Baths are much more enjoyable as an adult. You should try it sometime."

"I'll consider your advice, Miss James. Oh, I have something for you." He placed the whiskey down on the floor by the tub and held up my necklace.

"You fixed it?"

"Yes, Ma'am. Good as new."

"Thank you. That's so sweet of you."

I watched my moonstone charm as it floated in front of my face and landed on my chest. His hands rested on the base of my neck when he hooked it together. The chill that filled me moments before was now gone, thanks to Jesse's touch and his warm breath on my wet skin. I wondered what those hands would feel like on my body underneath the water. *Damn it, Savannah. Bad timing.* He turned to leave.

"Wait. Don't go. I could use some company." He paused for a few seconds, then sauntered in again and sat on the edge of the tub. He handed me the whiskey bottle.

"Sounds like you could use some of this, too."

"Are you trying to get me drunk?"

"Maybe." He grinned like the little boy I used to know. I wrapped my lips around the bottle and tossed it back. The whiskey ran like liquid fire down my throat, but at the same time, I needed it to take the edge off of what I'd just experienced.

"So what's your story, little girl?"

"What do you mean?"

"I mean, what have you been up to besides an awesome dating life?" I splashed him before I handed back the bottle.

"Tell me your story first."

"What makes you so sure I have one?"

"Everyone has a story, Jesse. We both know why I'm drifting but why are you?" I swished through the bath bubbles and waited for his answer.

"I finished up a job out of state and I'm on my way home."

"Where's home these days?"

"Ellabell."

"So we're still neighbors… almost."

"You still live with your grandmother?"

"I still live in that house, but I'm alone now. Granny died about five years ago of a stroke."

"I'm sorry. She was a sweet lady and was good to me and my brother."

"Yeah, I miss her every day."

"To Granny." He raised the bottle in a toast and took another drink.

"So, what kind of work do you do?"

"Independent contractor. Carpentry mostly, a little landscaping here and there."

"I'm sure your girl must be happy you're coming home."

"I don't have a girl. I wouldn't be here drinking whiskey and watching you take a bath if I did."

I silently cheered at his honorable declaration. I took the whiskey back and kept on drinking.

"Besides, we all can't have a fulfilling relationship like yours and Levi's."

"Touché, Cowboy."

"What do you do? For a living I mean."

"I manage an antique shop. Exciting, huh?"

"Do you enjoy that kind of work?"

"It pays the bills. So you never answered my question about your brother. How is he?"

"Tyler died last month." His response blindsided me. I watched his smoldering eyes gloss over with tears and I felt horrible.

"Shit, Jesse. What happened?"

"Car accident. He and I went out for a bite to eat and he insisted on using our dad's old pickup. Tyler was so proud of that truck because he got it fixed up all by himself. We inherited our dad's auto shop when he died and that was his pet project in between customers. When we left the restaurant, the truck stalled in the middle of the highway we were rammed by a semi. Tyler was killed on impact while I was thrown and rolled down a ravine. I survived and all I got was this scar as a keepsake." He pointed to his cheek. "After I buried my baby brother, I closed up the auto shop and took on as many contract jobs as I could to take my mind off missing him. I was heading back from a private job in Tennessee. I got hungry so I stopped at the diner and there you were."

"I don't know what to say. I'm so sorry."

"The weird thing is you were the first person I thought about when he died. So many times in my life I wished you were around so I could have someone, anyone to talk to, or even just be there with me. I've thought about driving to your house to see if you still lived there and how your life turned out. I'd even imagined what you'd look like when you came to the door."

"So why didn't you come visit?"

"I don't know. Maybe a part of me didn't want to impose on you. What if you were married with a bunch of rug rats? The other part of me was chicken shit, I guess. I convinced myself you didn't live there anymore so I wouldn't regret not trying."

Tears streamed down my cheeks. His words made me feel more wanted than any boyfriend ever did. I picked up his hand and held it in front of me as I had one of those "life is short so live in the moment" kind of thoughts. Maybe I should have expelled it out but I just went with it.

"Why don't you get in? There's room in here for two." His eyes widened.

"Are you sure?"

"I wouldn't offer if I wasn't, Cowboy." I held up the bottle. "Need more motivation?"

"You've motivated me since I saw you sitting at the counter in that diner tonight." He pulled his shirt off and revealed a chest that was probably sculpted as a result of hours of manual labor, not from a gym. It also looked like the perfect place to rest my head. Besides his physique, I also noticed something dangling around his neck.

"You still wear it?" I pointed to the tiger's eye charm I gave him when we were kids. He touched it and smiled.

"Off and on, when I feel I need a little something extra to get me through. I put it on before I hit the road." I gave him that necklace for protection all those years ago when he needed some magical intervention for his difficult family situation.

I watched the rest of his slow strip tease over the bottle pressed to my lips. He unfastened his belt and shoved his jeans and snug boxer briefs to his ankles.

Blessed be, he was just as beautiful naked as he was with his clothes on. While I sized him up in his birthday suit, some stray drops of whiskey trickled down the corner of my mouth and I caught them with my tongue.

"Cover your eyes," he teased.

"Fine." I pretended to cover them, but I caught another glimpse of him through my spread fingers.

He climbed into the water and slid himself all the way to the opposite end of the tub until the bubbles covered him at the waist. I lifted my legs one at a time and rested them on the sides of his to make us both more comfortable. He took the washcloth and squeezed the soapy water all over his neck and shoulders. Glory, he looked even better wet.

"Man, this does feel good."

"I told you. Just relax and enjoy it while it lasts."

We sat in silence and continued to pass the whiskey between us.

When I reached over to take it from him, my breasts popped up over the water. Jesse's stare fell to my chest and up again. I sunk back into the bath, but held his gaze. When I took another sip, I realized the bottle was empty and I was drunk. I held it upside down and shook it before I put it down on the floor.

"Uh oh, how did that happen?" he asked.

"We're both lushes."

"Hey, do you remember that time we went skinny dipping in the creek behind your house and your grandmother caught us?"

"Yeah, I've never seen her so mad. We laughed about it years later. Here we are, all grown up and naked in the water again."

"Yep, here we are." Jesse stretched his leg and rubbed his foot against my hip. I felt the effect of his touch deep in my groin. He dipped both hands in the water and rubbed my calves in small circles with his fingertips. I released a heavy breath. *Damn, he had me good.*

"I think we let the bath water get cold," he pointed out as he kept up the massage. I was so turned on, my thighs ached.

"I think it's just heating up, Cowboy." I leaned forward and slipped my hand under the surface of the water and stroked him between his legs. He was already hard when I got there. He squeezed me tighter in response to my touch.

"Damn it," he mumbled.

"Okay, that's not the reaction I was expecting." I eased my grip on him.

"No, no, I mean I don't have any condoms with me. I wasn't expecting any of this to happen tonight. I don't hook up on regular basis."

I added more points to the good guy score board I kept for him in my head.

"It's okay, it's taken care of."

"Are you on birth control?"

"Yes."

I wasn't technically on the pill but I created a fertility spell in my late teens. Burying an egg in a jar of vinegar under a rose bush in front of my bedroom on a full moon hadn't been fun, but it's been fool proof ever since.

He leaned in with an urgent kiss that released a surge of warmth throughout my body like a tiny electrical current underneath my skin. Our tongues danced and darted, exploring like the new drunken lovers we were. The force of the sensual movement made me lift my body until my breasts broke the crest of the water again. My nipples hardened when they hit room temperature. He brushed his thumbs over them and spiked another needful ache through my thighs. My body was ready for him.

Our lips broke apart and he rested his forehead against mine. I never wanted someone to be my lover as much as I wanted Jesse King right then and there.

I wrapped my legs around his waist as he lifted me onto his lap. Each delicious inch of him slipped inside me and stirred my senses into a heated frenzy. I held still as he rolled his tongue over my nipples. As my body temperature rose, so did the heat of the bath water until a heavy steam filled the room. The bubbles thickened into a lavender scented foam wall up to our chins. Jesse pulled his mouth away from my throbbing breasts and took notice of the sudden change in the water.

"What's happening?"

"Shhh... its magic," I whispered against his ear and nibbled his lobe. He curled his perfect arms around my back and held me closer.

The only sound in the room was the swishing water as a result of our quickened rhythm and the noises that escaped us in between kisses.

"I wish I could stay here with you forever, Savannah." Something about those words poked at my thoughts like one of those cheesy love songs that came on the radio, hit close to home, and took you by surprise. I gripped the edge of the tub as the intense sensation rippled through my body with spiraled warmth. I was never the silent type when it came to sex... and this was really great sex. Needless to say, my singsong echoed throughout the bathroom as Jesse brought me to my peak.

His heavy groan indicated he was right there with me. That never happened with anyone I'd been with. I let go of the tub and wrapped my arms around his neck. We held on to each other in a rocking motion as the mutual pleasure wave washed over us. I wasn't used to being held like the way he had me in his arms. Little things like that were sometimes more intimate than the sex itself. Levi never showed much affection after we did the deed. I was convinced he thought of sex as a race to see who could finish first. Let's just say I ended up the loser most of the time.

Jesse moved my stray wet strands of hair back and planted soft kisses all over my face before I tucked myself in between his neck and shoulder. The slow figure eight pattern he drew on my back helped slow my heart rate.

I was about to lapse into a total state of bliss when a smoky figure rose from the floor and whooshed out into the main room. It was quick but I knew enough from experience what I just saw.

A ghost.

I froze in my new lover's embrace. Between the whisky and the bathtub fun, I almost forgot the eerie encounter before Jesse walked in the room. A familiar pang of heaviness filled me up as I caught my breath and pulled away from him.

"Are you okay? You're shaking." He kissed my shoulder.

I stared into the dark corner of the next room, convinced that whatever I saw was still there. I recovered the moment and kissed him back on the cheek. I did a double take when I noticed the crescent moon scar was gone. My magic must've removed it when we were having sex.

"Yeah, I'm perfect... so are you. Let's get out of this tub before we prune."

As we untangled our bodies, I hoped the feeling of dread would pass. I was no stranger to the dead, as it came with the territory of being a witch. Plus based on the redhead in the road, it wouldn't surprise me if this place had its share of spirits, bottled or otherwise. I just didn't appreciate the interruption of my post bath time bliss. The dead always popped up at inconvenient times. They were kind of assholes that way.

Jesse took my hand. "Hey, I'm serious. I want you to be okay with what just happened between us." He wrapped me in a towel and held me close.

"I am. I just got a chill, that's all. This place just makes me uncomfortable. Come on, let's get to bed. I'll feel better after some sleep." I didn't share what I'd experienced. I thought it best to keep it to myself.

After we dried off, I turned the light off and followed Jesse into the room. I hoped whatever was there would just stay occupied in the shadows until we made it through the night and left this damn place in the morning.

CHAPTER FOUR

As I drifted asleep in Jesse's arms, I dreamt I was a little girl on my house's huge wrap-around porch, but I wasn't alone. I was with the ten year old Jesse and we sat cross-legged, facing each other. His face and arms were covered in bruises. He wore jeans, but I knew he had them on his legs, too. Sadly, these weren't the type of bruises a kid got from playing rough or being clumsy.

I placed my charm box between us. Every witch kept some kind of charm box, no matter what his or her age. It was filled with stones, herbs, supplies used for spells, and other things of a magical nature. That was my first one, kind of like my witch starter kit. I held up the leather necklace with the tiger's eye dangling from the end of it and clipped it on him. His bruises disappeared like they were never there. He gave me the kid version of a bear hug.

"I wish I could stay here with you forever, Savannah."

"Me too, Jesse."

I woke up with the dream still fresh on my mind. The room was freezing, so I reached for the blankets. I gave them a tug and someone tugged back, which I would've thought was Jesse if it weren't for the gentle breathing coming from his side of the bed.

"Oh real nice. You dump me only a few hours ago and you're already fucking some other guy?"

I bolted upright and saw a familiar face sneering at me.

"Levi? What are you doing in here?" He held the edge of the blanket and pulled it toward him.

"Trick or treating."

"How did you—"

"Oh, you know, I walked through the fucking wall! No big deal!" The feeling of dread was back in full force. I think I'd just figured out who my bathroom phantom was.

"Levi, you—"

"Something crazy happened to me, Van. I skidded off the road with the bike and I think I landed in a ditch or something. Next thing I remember, I'm walking up the road and I see this dump. I thought I could use the phone in the motel office to call for help since I lost my cell phone, and that hippie manager weirdo told me you were here. There's something freaky about this place."

I reached over and turned on the lamp but he disappeared. "Levi?"

"And who is this guy?" He popped up again.

I grabbed onto the blanket to avoid falling off the bed.

"Quit it!"

Jesse stirred next to me. If he woke up, I wasn't sure how he would take an official introduction to the guy I bitched about all night, let alone the fact he was dead.

"Quit what? What are you talking about?" He vanished again.

"That... you keep fading away and coming back."

"Because that's what *dead* guys do! This shit is so not cool. Fix me!"

I've told boyfriends our relationship was over before, but never that I couldn't bring them back from the afterlife. There was a first time for everything.

"I can't fix this."

"Don't give me that bullshit, Van. I heard you right before I crashed the bike. I don't know how but I did. I heard your whiny voice in my ear wishing me dead and now I am! I know what you're capable of. You did this to me now bring me back!"

His words sobered me and hit me with the weight of a cinder block. He was right. I was so pissed at him after I saw what he did to my truck that I let my emotions have the upper hand and I wished for him to die. I tried to convince the coven I was mature enough to handle my powers on my own, and the first thing I did was murder Levi using my magic.

"Savannah, who are you talking to?" Shit, Jesse was awake.

The way the muscles in his arms tightened to meet the curve of his shoulder blades made him look like an Adonis. I couldn't believe he was the scrawny little boy from my childhood who lived next door to me for an entire summer.

"Boo!" Levi taunted him before he vanished again.

Jesse flipped off the side of the bed, tangled up in the blankets.

"Are you okay?"

He grabbed the edge of the bedspread and pulled himself up.

"No, I'm not okay. Who in tarnation was that?"

"The ghost of my dead ex-boyfriend."

"I'm sorry, did you just say the *ghost* of your ex-boyfriend?"

"Don't forget the dead part," Levi pestered.

"Stop doing that!" I through a pillow at him but it passed right through him.

"What's he doing here?" Jesse asked.

"I don't know. When I have time to read through my afterlife welcome packet I'll let you know, pretty boy."

"Even dead you're trying to have the last word? Smartass." I pulled the bedspread off, wrapped it around myself, and made it across the room. I remembered I never sent Jesse outside to get my overnight bag. Even though Levi saw me naked a hundred times before, it was creepier now that he was a ghost. I put the same clothes back on.

"You're going to help me, aren't you, baby?"

"I'm not your baby anymore. We broke up, remember?"

"Oh, come on, Van. You're not still pissed at me for kissing that bartender from Stay a Spell, are you?" Stay a Spell was a bar we frequented back home in Savannah and also a popular witch hangout, among other colorful characters.

"Kissed her? I'm pissed because you fucked her in my bed, stole my necklace after I dumped you, robbed a diner at gunpoint and trashed my truck. Even if I could forgive you, you're dead, so that puts a damper on the romance, dontcha' think?"

"I took the necklace to sell it, okay? Some guy offered me a shit ton of cash for it. And I only robbed the diner to hold me over until I sold it. I didn't mean to scare those people. I'm sorry, but it wasn't a crime punishable by death, you psycho witch."

"Hey! Don't talk to her that way," growled Jesse.

"I'll talk to her however I want considering it's her fault I'm like this now!"

"Wait, wait, hold on. What guy was going to pay you for my moonstone?"

"He didn't give me his name. I met him at the bar and he mentioned he would pay top dollar for real witch stuff."

"He's probably someone who knows about the coven meeting. Plus it's Halloween and the city is crawling with shady freaks looking to score some real magical trinkets. Ugh, Levi, how could you? You're such a douche bag!"

"I may be a douche bag, but at least I'd never do another chick just hours after *you* kicked the bucket."

"Stop! Enough already," said Jesse.

"Listen, dude, I'm having a private conversation with my girlfriend here. Why don't you mind your own business and put some clothes on so I don't have to stare at your junk. And you, Van, need to try to help me instead of standing here while your new boyfriend insults me. Did you know you just fucked a witch who has the power to kill her lovers?"

"Did you know you talk a lot for a dead guy?"

"As in life, so in death," I added.

"Time is ticking here!"

"I can't, Levi. It's been too long since you've left your body. It won't work."

"Come on!"

A lump formed in my throat. Even though Levi wasn't the best boyfriend, I didn't want to see him suffer like this.

"I can try to cross you over, but that's it."

"Cross me over? I've seen you do lots of creepy shit. A little resurrection spell should be a piece of cake for a witch as powerful as you." I kind of liked the nod of confidence to my magical abilities, but resurrection spells were bad news for any witch.

"Whoa, resurrection spell? You sure have been practicing since you were a kid, huh?"

"In my defense, I've never raised the dead... on purpose."

"What about that weird cat of yours?"

"You ran over Crowley with your motorcycle and I was upset. I couldn't help it!"

"This night is turning out to be one for the books." Jesse pulled his jeans on in a huff. It made me sad to see him cover up.

"Where's my shirt?"

"Look in the bathroom where you took it off, stud," said Levi.

"You stay away from me, whatever the hell you are." Jesse hurried past him, mumbling to himself.

"It looks like the love nest is about to be empty." Levi stood there, hands on his hips in all his dead smugness.

"Shut up."

I watched Jesse's abs disappear under his shirt when he came back into the room.

"Peace out, dude."

"Fuck off, Levi. I'm not leaving without her. Come on, we'll find somewhere else to stay." He offered me his hand. As I reached for it, a rush of frigid air whipped around me. Levi grabbed me from behind and dragged me to the floor. *The son of a bitch had me in a strangle hold!*

"You're staying here with me, witchy-poo."

Before I could think of an incantation to get me out of the ghostly headlock, Jesse grabbed Levi and pulled him off me.

"Let go of her!"

Levi's grip on me was gone, and so was he. I turned over and coughed until I drooled on the carpet.

"Savannah, are you okay?" Jesse picked me up and held me against his chest. I immediately felt safe. He did that hair thing again where he moved it from my face with his fingertip and I recalled the dream about us together on the porch.

"I'm... I'm okay." Levi was sure strong for a new ghost. If I didn't know any better, I'd say he was still alive and kicking from the force he took me down with.

"Come on, let's get out of this place." He helped me up but my knees buckled.

"Easy, I've got you."

"Thanks. Where did he go?"

"I don't know, but let's not be here when he comes back."

"Good idea."

When we reached the parking lot, the neon sign flickered like a giant strobe light. Jesse froze in front of his truck and his face grew stark white.

"No, it... it can't be. Savannah, what's happening here?" The panic in his voice freaked me out.

"What is it?" I looked ahead and saw myself slumped against the passenger side window and Jesse laid face forward on the steering wheel. The front of the truck was smashed around a tree and the windshield was shattered. We both looked at each other in disbelief. "Oh no... shit fucking no."

"Either that was some strong whiskey or some major fucked up shit is happening here," he said in shaky voice.

"We can't be dead. There's no way. That tree wasn't there!"

When I tried to move, my feet locked in place like I were stuck in cement. Jesse tugged on my arms to pull me loose but I wouldn't budge. Then, every door of every room in the motel swung open and slammed shut repeatedly with loud echoed bangs. A sharp tug at my waist yanked me backward like an invisible rope.

"Savannah, no!" Jesse became smaller in my field of vision until I crossed the threshold into one of the rooms and the door shut in my face.

This night officially sucked.

CHAPTER FIVE

"Jesse!" I banged on the door until my hands turned red.

"You're wasting your time. It's not going to work," said a female voice. I turned around to see who it belonged to.

Sitting on the bed was a teenaged girl. Her long red braids swung when she stood up. As she stepped toward me, I was able to get a closer look at her face. It was the girl from the road.

"I need to get out of here."

"Oh, well sure, why didn't you say so?" Her tone oozed sarcasm.

"I'm dead serious."

She stood up with her arms crossed in a typical bratty teen way.

"You've got the dead part right. Welcome to the club."

"So it's true, you're a ghost, too."

"Ding, ding, ding!"

I glowered at her so hard that she blew over the bed and through the wall. She reemerged, but she looked different... way different. Most of the skin on her body was charred black and her hair and clothes were burnt off. Sometimes ghosts appeared as they looked in death. She shook it off and changed back to her normal self... and she wasn't too happy with me.

"Hey! What was that for?"

"Look, chick, since you're the reason I ended up like this, the least you could do is be cooperative so maybe I can find a way for both of us to get out of here."

"I've been here since 1981. If you find a way out before I do, let me know."

"And an intelligent haunting, I see." The girl shrugged at my analysis and played with her braids.

"I guess, but I prefer to be called Angie."

"I'd say it was nice to meet you, Angie, but under the circumstances..."

"I won't take it personal. Look, I'm sorry I made you run off the road, okay? Sometimes I don't see things in the living world until they're right in my face. By then it's too late."

"Okay, calm down. What's done is done. So, how did you, umm—"

"Die? I was staying here with my boyfriend the night the motel burned down. He got out alive and left me here to burn in the fire."

"What a dick."

"I know, right? Since then I've just been watching this place collect the dead and trap them here, like that new guy from the bike crash across the road that keeps hitting on me. He asked me if my carpet matched my drapes. What a pervert."

"Sounds like you met Levi. Even dead he's still cheating on me."

"*That* dude is your boyfriend? I assumed you were here with the hunk you banged in the bathtub."

"Well, who's the pervert now?" I scolded.

"There's only so many things a ghost can do to keep entertained when they've been haunting the same place for almost forty years, you know. Plus, I died before I got to do it for the first time."

"My condolences on dying a virgin."

We both flinched as a pounding noise echoed from the other side of the wall.

"Savannah, where are you?"

"Jesse?" I followed his muffled voice. "I'm here, are you in the next room?"

"I think so. I'll find you, I promise."

"Oh brother. Come on newbie, you're about to get your first lesson in Haunting 101." Angie grabbed my wrist and threw me at the wall and into the next room. *That was freaky.*

"Savannah!" Jesse ran to me and scooped me up into his arms.

"I thought I'd lost you again."

"Not if I can help it." He reassured me with a kiss.

"Eh hem." Angie stood there watching us. We broke from our embrace.

"Hey, you're the girl from the road."

"That's me."

"Jesse, meet Angie."

"We just skidded off the road into the parking lot. How could we have hit a tree and not even know?" He was pissed, but he kept his cool in front of her. To make matters worse, three ghost children chased each other around the room and through the walls. I shuddered.

"It's the curse," Angie revealed.

"Earl's curse?"

"Who's Earl?" She asked him.

"Never mind, continue."

"Every year on Halloween, someone dies on this road. Once you're dead, the motel appears like it did in its heyday so people like you who stop here to sleep or bump uglies or whatever get trapped."

I caressed my moonstone as I tried to absorb all of this.

"Curses are usually brought on by strong emotions, like anger or betrayal. If Jude's plan to burn this place down failed and killed him in the process, he's one pissed off ghost," I said.

"So we're trapped here for good?" Jesse paced the room with his hands on his head.

"Not necessarily. There may still be hope for you two."

"What do you mean, Angie?"

"I don't think you two are completely dead. I heard your heartbeats outside. You must be trapped somewhere in limbo and the curse sucked you in here. If you can get back to your bodies..."

"We can get out of here," I stated with a glimmer of hope.

"If Jude lets you."

"Has he ever let anyone go?" asked Jesse.

"No, but she's a witch. She may have the power to fight him."

"She has a point. In the tub, your magic worked when you heated the water. Can you use it to break the curse?"

"I'm not sure, Jesse. I need to think."

"She also used it to face plant me a few minutes ago. I'd say it works."

Another loud banging noise shook everything like an earthquake.

"Angie, what's happening?"

"It's Jude. He's looking for us and he's getting close!"

"What do we do now?" Jesse screamed.

"We give him an intervention." I stated with confidence.

We passed through the wall and into the next room. Standing in the middle was a man with his back turned to us. Jesse let go of my hand and stepped forward even though I tried to stop him. As he approached him, the man turned around. He looked like a younger version of Jesse with longer hair. There was no doubt in my mind of who this was, given the striking resemblance and the anguish on Jesse's face.

"Tyler?"

CHAPTER SIX

"Hey there, big brother."

"Tyler, is that you?"

"It's me, Jesse."

"How? Why are you here… in this place?"

"I wanted to find you."

"Ty, I've been lost without you, man." He reached for him but Tyler pulled away.

"Don't."

"Tyler, what's wrong?"

"Who is she?"

"This is Savannah from that summer we spent at Uncle Jack's."

"I wish I were alive to enjoy being with pretty girls like her."

"If I could trade places with you, Ty, I'd do it. I never wanted things to end up this way."

"But you let them, didn't you, Jesse? You let me die, when you swore to me you would always protect me."

"This isn't real. The wreck was an accident. You didn't cause it, Jesse. It's not your fault you survived and he didn't," I pleaded, but he just held his hand out to let me know he had control of this.

"Wow, she's still fighting your battles for you?"

"Whatever resentment you have toward me, you keep it for me and leave her out of it."

"She's the reason I died and you survived."

"No, she's not, Ty."

"It's that necklace she gave you. If it weren't for her, you'd have died with me. We could've been taking on the afterlife together as brothers all this time."

"Tyler, I… "

"Now you have the chance to stay here with me, Jesse."

The tone of his voice sent up my witch warning flag. I grabbed the bottom of Jesse's jacket to urge him not to trust what he saw. I could tell the death of Tyler hit him hard and was still a raw wound. The curse played on that emotion and I had to put a stop to it.

"No! He's not your brother. Tyler wouldn't be stuck here and you know that. This is a trick of the curse."

"Are you going to believe this witch over your own brother?"

"Stop, Tyler," said Jesse. Tears filled his gorgeous green eyes and made them look almost unnatural.

"It's funny how she can protect others but yet she scared her own mother away, leaving poor little Savannah from Savannah an orphan."

"Shut up! You know nothing about me."

"Then your own grandmother couldn't deal with you anymore so she died and left you all alone again."

"I said, shut up!" Anger radiated off me like a fever. Tyler's figure shook and screeched in violent pulses until his features became nothing but a blur. Then it wasn't Jesse's brother anymore. It was Jude.

"Damn you, witch!" A cold, gnarled wind knocked me to the floor. Jude's face was distorted and his eyes turned solid white. Whatever control he had over the curse caused a dark mold-like stain to creep all over the room. It was almost like a photograph when it's held over an open flame. As the motel changed appearance, a foul stench like burnt death hung heavy in the air.

"Savannah, look out!"

Jesse intercepted Jude before he charged at me but the creep vanished before he made contact. Jude reappeared and locked his arms around him Jesse, lifted him over his shoulders and threw him across the room.

"Jesse!"

I needed to do something to help him, but Jude was more powerful than your average ghost. After decades of pent up anger and collecting souls, he became something else, something dark and out of control.

The other ghosts gathered around and looked on. When my thoughts cleared, an idea popped in my head. Magic gained strength from harvested energy. Ghosts were trapped energy of the people they once were. I could use their presence to gain enough power to break the curse! My magic has never let me down before. Plus it was Halloween. Spells were always stronger on the sacred Sabbath. This needed to work; otherwise Jesse and I were goners.

I picked myself up from the floor and stood confident in front of Jude. As I rubbed my moonstone and stabilized my breath, an incantation came to me.

"From the North, the South, the East and the West,
This curse at hand I do attest,
Break the ties that bind you here,
Your end on earth has drawn near."

"Just what do you think you're doing?" Jude interrupted my chant and twisted my hair around his gnarly hand. I tried to focus on the spell and not the pain of my hair about to rip out of my scalp.

"Sending you to Hell where you belong, you freak of nature!"

"Nobody leaves the Drifter's Moon. Nobody! I've run this place for decades. Ain't no little witch whore gonna change things."

"What did you call me?"

"You heard me, whore. I know what you came here to do with your traveling buddy. Now you're both going to be stuck here, just like the rest of them." His sinister laugh blocked my thoughts so I couldn't remember the rest of the words.

"Oh no she's not!"

"Levi?"

He jumped Jude from behind and clung to his neck like a Velcro monkey. I never thought I'd be so happy to see him again.

"Get off me, you little shit. You won't stop me!"

"No, but she will. Finish it, Van!" I nodded at him and held my palms up to the sky.

"Earth, Wind, Air, and Fire,

Your time on Earth has now expired,

Leave this plain, your time is done,

I light your way by moon and sun–"

Jude broke free of Levi's hold and made him vanish again. Before I had time to panic, Jesse threw himself onto Jude and held him down. That pissed the ghost off even more.

"Savannah, hurry up and finish it!" As he struggled to keep Jude down, I recited the last of the incantation.

"I cross you over, hear my plea,

My will be done, so mote it be!"

Jude's face elongated and contorted into something out of a nightmare. He wailed and shook something awful before he exploded into a cold, dark mist.

Then something amazing happened. A tiny ball of light formed and grew wider in front of me. The ghosts staggered toward its soft glow as if unsure of what to do. The putrid gunk on the walls retracted and the motel no longer looked decrepit.

"Don't be afraid of it. Jude is gone now and has no control over you anymore. You're all free."

One by one, they congregated at the portal of light. There were so many of them. Men, women, even children gathered in anticipation of ending their long existence on Earth. When they walked through, an overwhelming aura of peace filled the air.

Angie was the last one to the light. She turned to me and smiled.

"Thank you, Savannah."

"You're welcome. Now go on." After she crossed over, the light grew smaller until there was no trace of it left. Jesse stood up and took my hand as the motel walls dissipated around us.

CHAPTER SEVEN

I woke up to the sun's intense rays on my face and a horrible scraping noise that penetrated my ears. The truck was moving. I was in the passenger seat as it inched away from the tree we were smashed against. The dented metal retracted to its original form and every shard of glass from the broken windshield flew up from the ground and put itself back in place. It was as if the accident never happened.

"Jesse, look." He wasn't making a sound. I turned to the driver's side and gasped for breath. He was still faced forward on the steering wheel. I unhooked my seatbelt and scooted closer to him.

"Jesse?" I placed my hand on his shoulder. Relief washed over me when he lifted his head. I reached for his face.

"Oh Blessed be! Are you okay?"

"I've been better." He groaned and pressed his cheek into the palm of my hand. "Did we win?"

"Yeah, we won."

"You did it. The curse is broken and Jude is gone ... and we're alive."

"I can't take all the credit. I had help." I smiled and squeezed his hand.

"Let's get out of here then."

"Wait. There's one more thing I need to do." I pulled my cell phone from my jacket pocket, but the battery was dead.

"Shit, does your phone work?" He took his from the cup holder and handed it to me.

"Here, it still has juice. Who are you calling?"

"I can't leave Levi's body in that ditch. He has a mother who loves him and she needs to know her son is dead. He deserves a proper funeral." I got out of the truck and walked alongside the road not too far from where Levi mentioned he crashed the bike.

"Savannah, be careful." Jesse walked a close distance behind me. I crossed to get a closer look because I wanted to see for myself that he was down there. The bike wheel was the first thing I saw sticking straight up from the ditch. I dialed 911.

"I need to report an accident."

After I told the operator where to find the crash site, I disconnected the call and let the tears loose. Jesse held me by my waist.

"I'm sorry, I just…"

"You don't have to apologize to me. I get it," he said.

"He helped me finish the spell."

"I think he cared about you more than you thought he did."

It was weird to know I'd never see Levi again. Even though he was selfish and stole my necklace in the first place, I wished him dead, which made him fall victim to the curse and led Jesse and I right into Jude's trap. Last night's events proved I still needed a few lessons in restraint of my emotions. On the positive side, I learned I could perform my magic on a significantly higher level than I knew possible, which helped the lost souls of the Drifter's Moon move on.

"I want to get out of here now." I wiped my tears on my jacket sleeve as we walked back to the truck.

"Yes, Ma'am."

"Jesse, are you okay to drive? You were knocked out cold and you could have a concussion."

"I'm fine," he protested. "Good as new, just like the truck. How are you feeling?"

"About which part?"

"Any of it, I guess."

"Physically I feel fine. I still can't get over how real it all seemed."

"And that we were dead."

"I'm sorry Jude used Tyler's memory like that."

"He used your family's memory, too. I guess we both need to work on getting rid of the scars, huh?" He rubbed his cheek and checked himself in the rear view mirror. "My scar... it's gone."

"Oh, umm, that happened in the bathtub. Sex is a powerful magic aide for my kind, even in the spirit world, apparently."

"So the whole bathtub thing... that never physically happened? We didn't..."

I caught a whiff of the lavender bubble bath on my skin and smiled.

"I think our ghosts had a great time." I said, content in the moment.

"Fair enough." He shook his head and laughed. "Damn, what a night. Let's hit the road, Miss James. You have an important meeting to get to. Time to face your coven."

I sighed at the thought of my in person resignation.

"I think I'd rather take my chances with Jude."

Jesse laughed. "Come on, it won't be that bad."

"You don't know these witches."

"Just curious, do you all dress up in sexy witch costumes at these meetings?"

"No, we don't."

"Damn, that's how I pictured it. How disappointing."

"Just start the truck," I smiled.

I grabbed my sunglasses from the side pocket of my overnight bag. When I turned around in my seat, I caught him again.

"Are you checking out my ass, Jesse King?"

"Miss James, what kind of guy do you think I am? Of course I'm checking out your ass."

I giggled and clipped my seatbelt on. "Okay, Cowboy. Take me home."

CHAPTER EIGHT

We made it to Savannah in record time. After I pled my case to the Supreme witch as to why I wanted to become a solitary practitioner, she agreed to release me from the Coven. She already knew what happened with Levi but the way I ended the motel curse proved I could control my magic after all and it earned me some witch points.

They recovered Levi's body and even ran the story on the local news in relation to the curse of the Drifter's Moon. He always wanted to be famous so I guess he got his chance. I would miss him in my own toxic way but it was time to make a brand new start. I just hoped wherever his spirit ended up, he was at peace.

Jesse picked me up after the coven meeting since my truck sat in my back yard in a heaping pile of metal now. The tow wasn't cheap either.

"Hey, hurry up in there. Halloween is almost over," he shouted from my living room. I was just about done with the finishing touches on my costume so we could start our first official date as adults. Crowley sat at my feet and looked me over in his judgmental black cat way. After I snapped and adjusted a few things, I stepped out of the hallway and struck a pose.

"Happy Halloween, Cowboy." The look on his face was validation that my costume was a success.

"Yeeeee haw."

"You like it?"

"Oh yes... I like it very much." I sauntered over to him in the sexiest way I could in five inch stilettos. My corset was maybe a size too small but it was the best the costume shops had to offer on such short notice. Since they were out of prop brooms too, I improvised and used the one from my kitchen.

"Would you like a ride on my magical broomstick?"

"It's florescent pink with polka dots."

"All the cool ones were picked over in the stores, okay?" I sat on his lap and wrapped my arms around his neck. He smelled like autumn and faded sandalwood.

"Okay, so how did the meeting go?"

"Better than I expected. They released me with the understanding that I need to be responsible with my magic. The Supreme said I could contact her if I ever need help or advice."

"Kind of like your witch parole officer?"

"Yeah, something like that. I can do this on my own. It won't be easy, but it's what I want."

"Well, you won't be totally alone. You'll have me." The confidence level in his voice led me to believe he wanted to be a part of my life.

"Do you mean that?" I played with the collar of his plaid shirt.

"Of course. You and I are connected. I couldn't leave you again if I tried."

"I have to warn you, life with me won't be easy, but it definitely won't be boring."

"I figured that out the moment I met you, Miss James."

"Which time?"

He flashed me another one of his adorable smiles, held up my oversized witch hat and gave me a long, dreamy kiss.

"Oh gag, do you two ever stop smoochin'?"

"Aaahhh!" I rolled off Jesse's lap and onto the floor. Crowley hissed and dashed down the hall. "Levi? What the fuck are you doing here? I thought you crossed over at the motel!"

"Nope! I guess I have some unfinished business left here on Earth, starting with haunting your sexy ass." He sat on the back of the couch with his feet on the cushions. "Nice outfit, by the way. You never dressed like that for me, Van."

"Really?" Jesse helped me up. "How long is he going to stick around for?"

"Only until I find a way to exorcise him."

"Forget it, you know I hate working out. Anyway, I'll leave you two porn stars alone for now. It's Halloween and I'm going out to party."

"You're dead, how are you going to pull that off?" I asked.

"Being dead is kinda cool. I've learned a few new tricks since yesterday. The hotties won't see me coming. Later, bitches." Just like that, he was gone. I slumped against the couch in defeat.

"Still want to be part of my life?"

Jesse scratched his chin. "Of course… and I think Levi is kind of growing on me."

"Don't get used to him being here. We're not keeping him."

He laughed and pulled me back onto his lap.

"So where were we?" I leaned in and wrapped my lips over his.

Was I certain what the future held for me and Jesse, my dead ex, and my new found witchy independence? No, but I was sure there'd be a lot more magical adventures in store for me. For now, perfecting my love spell was the only thing on my to-do list.

About the Author

Michele Mohr is a Connecticut native who discovered her passion for writing while living in New York City. She currently resides in Nashville, TN with her three rescue dogs and one diva cat. When she's not writing, she's talking about writing with fans and other authors on social media or binge watching episodes of Supernatural and The Walking Dead.

Follow Michele's Paranormal Indulgence blog and read her fan fiction on Wattpad
www.wattpad.com/user/authormohr

Also Follow Michele on:
Twitter: www.twitter.com/authormohr
Pinterest: www.pinterest.com/authormohr
Instagram: www.instagram.com/authormohr
Facebook: www.facebook.com/authormichelemohr

Where the Heart Belongs
By
Maria Arell

DEDICATION

To my forgiving family and friends who puts up with me and of course to the Wenches, where would I be without you?

CHAPTER ONE

Kilyn experienced the weirdest week. She opened her door on Thursday morning and discovered a package was waiting at her doorstep. The anonymous brown box lacked markings save her name and address. Late for work, she didn't have time to open it. Though curious, she valued her position at the veterinarian center, so she placed it inside the door and headed out.

As she stepped through the front door she felt a prickling on the back of her neck, the familiar feeling of a person nearby. Kilyn had spent most of her life looking over her shoulder, anticipating the worst. Inexplicably she had always been able to sense other people, especially if they were thinking of her. Growing up, on occasion, she'd felt a threatening presence. The sensation of being followed or watched. This time it felt safe. A benign guardian shadowed her, as protection against the threat. This was new and strange, but welcome nonetheless.

She had finally settled in at work. Her new place, in a new town felt almost like home. After a year, Savannah, Georgia had become comfortable. For the first time her anxiety lessened.

Growing up an orphan, she'd suffered isolation. For a girl who had lived in so many places, home was elusive. Foster families treated Kilyn like the weird kid. An introverted, lonely bookworm, who rarely interacted with others. It was a self-preservation thing, unusual things happened around her she couldn't explain or control which sparked all kinds of trouble. It wasn't until she embarked on her college education she opened up, a risk which rewarded her with a few close friends.

When she returned home later she was exhausted. It had been a busy day at work, many surgeries and worried pet owners. She was distracted from the package by an injured cat she found outside her building. It was a battered up, half-starved little thing. There was something about the cat that made her hesitate, but she couldn't just leave it in the state it was. She didn't usually take wounded pets into her home, but as a natural nurturer, she had to take care of it. Treating helpless animals was a work hazard. Kilyn had always cared for those in need. She didn't have an abundance of friends growing up, but she stuck up for those who needed saving, protecting the vulnerable.

As she tidied up her apartment on Sunday she found the forgotten package. Kilyn read, and reread the letter in her attempt to comprehend. It revealed she was not alone in the world. On her father's side a large family awaited. And her heritage was magical and elven. The letter was accompanied by her genealogy and a large, leather bound, black book. It cracked when she carefully opened it, and a small note fell out.

"This was your father's."

What is this? She couldn't make anything of it. It was all Greek to her, close written text but mostly symbols. Her hands slid over the glyphs. Her fingers tingled, but she couldn't understand the language. She read the letter once more.

"All I can say for now, is that you come from a long lineage of witches and elves. You have powers, Kilyn. Both from your mother's and your father's side."

Kilyn shook her head, put the book and letter away, and then went into the kitchen. She needed something. She searched the pantry, her relief palpable upon locating a bottle of red. She sank down on the wooden chair and took a deep gulp. All she knew about her parents was that they were killed when she was only three, in an accident. Kilyn had miraculously survived.

This was all too big for her to wrap her head around. At the same time, her past fell into place. At least the witch part. Kilyn possessed powers. She could predict the near future, healing came easy for her, and she'd been known to influence people's train of thought, altering it to her liking, not to mention what had happened with a boy from school. Kilyn shook her head, didn't want to think about it.

But elf? Seriously? That was plain fantasy.

A small meow interrupted her thoughts and the grateful cat she healed affectionately stroked itself against her legs. Kilyn picked it up and petted it softly. Progress.

"And what are we going to call you?" she asked. Its green eyes looked at her expectantly, as if the cat knew what she was saying. Kilyn realized she hadn't checked its gender yet. A quick glance and she declared: "I shall call you Doris." She smiled at Doris, who purred in her arms.

Kilyn resumed mulling the fact she had family. She had never known any until now. And what a family it was. Kilyn felt a grin spread over her face. She had a family. She belonged somewhere. She had a purpose; at least she thought she had one. Kilyn took another sip of wine. Her body hummed with excitement. She craved human company and let go of Doris, who hissed indignantly and slunk out of the room. Kilyn went to the bathroom to get ready to head out. Halloween was around the corner and she was ready for anything.

* * * *

If she had paid attention to her surroundings, she would have noticed the dark looming figure outside her building, following her movements with increasing interest. He found her fascinating. 'Spying' on her for the family was a piece of cake. Felix scouted the unknown witch for days and delivered the box, as his aunt requested. Apparently she was kinfolk, but he knew little else. He was on a need to know basis, there for surveillance and to keep her out of harm's way. Unaware of anyone else who presented a possible threat, so far the mission was uneventful.

Seeing her for the first time had been like a blow, not of recognition, but because his heart and body immediately leapt into protective mode. It was an involuntary action. He couldn't explain it. She triggered a part of him buried deep inside. No matter what happened, he was determined to protect her. Not the responsibility his aunt had charged him with.

Felix didn't usually do work like this, but aunt Violet had called in a favor. It had been a long time since he operated in the field, dealing with stray witches and their powers. This was personal for Violet, but Felix had no idea why.

He hadn't noticed anything in particular with Kilyn, until a wounded cat turned up outside her building, when she returned from work. Then the magic really spiked up. It generated a tingling sensation, a shift in the air. She was a natural, and he wondered if she was aware of what she was doing. He watched her lips move as she petted the cat, even if he didn't hear the words, he could feel the power building. Her aura turned from purple to bright turquoise, the color of healing.

To sense when magic occurred within a specific perimeter was one of his talents. He speculated that was why Violet assigned him to this project; she wanted to know Kilyn's capabilities. Kilyn, however, seemed oblivious to the power she possessed. Perhaps he was there to keep her from endangering other people.

Violet found Felix in an orphanage a long time ago. Recognizing the force that was in him, she raised and educated him. He realized he owed her his life. Before Violet's attentions he was alone, caring solely about his own survival. He didn't trust easily, having been treated bad in foster homes. Violet rescued an unsettled soul, constantly in trouble, not caring about the consequences or the people around him. She attempted to teach him empathy and openness.

"Someday, you will meet someone who will turn your life upside down, Felix, and then you'll know what I mean."

Encountering Kilyn, he finally understood what Violet meant. He ached to be with her, protect her from the evils of the world. Her white, blond hair and willowy frame spoke to his heart. Though he promised not to interfere, he realized staying away from her would be problematic.

He hugged the black leather jacket closer to his body against the October chill, lit a cigarette and drew in a deep breath. Felix had surveilled Kilyn's house since he dropped off the package. From his vantage point on the other side of the road, he could see inside her home and was dismayed she took so long to open it. He observed her bite her nails while reading the letter attached. She opened and closed her grimoire and paced the apartment. He was ready to react should she panic, this was why he was there.

He killed the butt with the heel of his boot. When she headed for the bathroom Felix gave her privacy. He knew how long her shower could take, having lived with four foster sisters, and gambled on having ten more minutes before he had to pay attention again.

Felix's instructions were clear; to remain anonymous and ensure Kilyn arrived at the coven meeting on Halloween. To judge from her reaction, that wasn't going to be easy. She was a loner who avoided talking to her coworkers. He recognized the familiar patterns of a fellow orphan. It had been ages since Violet took an orphan in, and never someone grown up.

Felix crept back into the shadows when he heard the front door open. His reverie interrupted.

* * * *

Kilyn peered into the shadows outside her building, certain she had seen something move out of the corner of her eye. She squinted to penetrate the dark alley. If she concentrated, she could barely make out a dim shadow loomed against the wall. Kilyn turned on her heel and hurried off in the opposite direction. She imagined eyes boring into her back, following her; her neck itched, yet she didn't feel threatened. It was the same benevolent presence detected over the last couple of days. When nothing followed she kept her usual pace.

A soft rain drizzled and she grimaced. Just her luck. She wrapped her cardigan tight and pulled the hood over her head. The letter mentioned a bar where she could meet fellow witches. It was a few blocks from her home, and she was excited to check it out. It exasperated her to know she'd past it a hundred times, but never realized it was there.

Outside Stay a Spell she stopped and peered through the window. The bar was practically empty. Kilyn couldn't believe she hadn't seen it before. It looked like a normal bar, nothing stood out apart from the name. She took another step closer, but lost her nerve before actually going in. Was she really ready to embrace the being the crazy letter claimed she was? Before someone noticed her, she scuttled down the street to another bar, a normal human bar, and slipped in.

It was more crowded than the supernatural Stay a Spell, but not so packed that it bothered her. She inspected the booths and tables scattered around the open space, but sitting alone by a table was more taboo than sitting by the counter. She perched on a stool and ordered a beer, shrugging off her damp cardigan.

A presence at the front door interrupted her beer. It was so overwhelming she had to turn. Its familiarity taunted her, but she couldn't put her finger on why. Kilyn regarded the man framed in the doorway and gaped.

He looked comfortable in his leather jacket; a white shirt peeked from underneath. Well-worn jeans and boots completed the look. Gorgeous beyond words. His dark eyes scanned the room as if he was looking for someone. When his gaze found her it hesitated. Kilyn held her breath, but his eyes roamed past her, without giving her more than a brightening of those dark eyes. Her stomach tightened. Kilyn chastised herself and turned back to her beer. Was she really so deprived of male attention that just a glance from a stranger, granted a very handsome and attractive stranger, sent her shivering?

The man sauntered over to the bar and settled on a stool at the other end of the counter. Kilyn tried to sneak a peek of him in her peripheral vision. He chatted to the bartender as if they were old friends.

His hair was dark and reached down over his collar. It looked impossibly soft. Kilyn's fingers itched to touch it. The whole experience her body endured was surreal. She had never been this affected by a man she had just met, or almost met, before. She had never been this affected by any man at all.

Her experiences with men were limited. Very limited. She wasn't a virgin, but it had been ages since she'd been with someone in that way. She made a face and took another swig. Was she really that lonely?

"Can I get you anything else?"

She looked up at the bartender who smiled pleasantly at her.

"Yeah, one more of these, thanks." She waved her bottle and received a fresh one. She thanked him and reached for her wallet, but he stopped her.

"From the gentleman over there." He nodded toward the man she had just been gawking at. She raised her bottle, feeling awkward, and nodded to him. Then turned back and mentally kicked herself for being such a coward. He was obviously interested, why didn't she have the nerve to play a little?

Kilyn focused on her beer instead of the mysterious man, toying with the bottle label, ripping off tiny strands of it. If he wanted something, he would have come to her. She was not giving in to curiosity or the giddy feeling in her stomach.

* * * *

Felix wouldn't say he followed Kilyn, but happened to find himself in the same bar. He tried to convince himself it was just coincidence. Surprised when she turned and regarded him intently, he tried not to stare, letting his gaze flit over her, before approaching the bar.

She looked uncomfortable, like she was unused to being in public. There was a delicate quality to her, the white blond hair all tangles, but fashionably so, and her eyes were violet. The universe suddenly revolved around her. It was a funny feeling he wasn't used to. He wanted to be there for her, care for her. Before he had only cared for himself and his family's needs.

Felix drew a hand through his hair and turned his attention to the bartender Mark. He ordered whiskey and put Kilyn's drinks on his tab. Chivalry was not dead; he smiled into his drink. He was awarded a small smile and a salute with the bottle. He nodded and smiled back. It took all of his self-control not to go over to her straight away.

Flirting wasn't something Felix did regularly. His early years had taught him to be careful and he didn't trust easily. Even though Violet had done her best to show that not everybody was bad in the world, he still had trouble opening up. Perhaps that was why he was good at his job as a protector.

He couldn't approach her about magic and her heritage. His aunt would not approve at all. He needed a plan. He gazed at Kilyn. His aunt's wishes were irrelevant. Violet wasn't there.

* * * *

Kilyn wasn't sure how to respond to such obvious interest. She couldn't look away, though he wasn't her type at all. She wasn't sure she *had* a type. He needed a haircut and a shave. Despite that, she found herself imagining how that stubble would feel against her cheek. Kilyn waved the fantasy away. Jeez, who was she kidding? Her body spoke volumes, but her mind kept trying to block out the attraction she felt. It was overpowering. She felt drawn to him like a flower toward the sun. It was insane, really.

She could do without temptation. Her body was restless, but she had work in the morning. Engaging with a man wasn't a good idea, not after the news. She went over the letter again in her mind, still unable to grasp that she had a family that wanted to meet her.

"Hi," said a silky soft voice which startled her out of her reverie.

"God! You scared me!"

He frowned, amused, but a small smile tugged at the corners of his mouth. "Well, I've never had that reaction before." The frown turned into a smile, showing off dimples, and his hazel eyes glittered at her. "I'm Felix." He held out his hand and she took it hesitantly.

"Kilyn." She ignored the tingling sensation that traveled up her arm.

"Unusual name." His eyes darkened. He really had the most fascinating eyes.

Kilyn shrugged. "I guess."

She realized how cliché her feelings were, but she could almost feel the electricity sparkle between them. The closeness of his body affected her more than she wanted to admit, and it scared her. With all that was going on right now, she was going into sensory overload.

Kilyn stalled. Conversation wasn't usually a problem for her, but for some reason she was tongue tied around Felix. She motioned to the bartender for a refill. When she reached for her purse, Felix put a hand on her arm.

"It's on me," he said.

"That's not necessary."

"I insist."

Kilyn didn't know what to say. Totally socially incompetent and shy, she realized she'd been out of the loop too long.

"Okay, thanks." She hoped that sounded casual enough. She really didn't want to lead him on, when she knew this couldn't go any further.

"I haven't seen you here before. You new in town?" Felix's look was expectant.

"I'm not new in town. Just not really the social type, I guess."

"Huh." Felix nodded, causing a strand of dark hair fall down over his face. He brushed it back behind his ear in one swift motion. "Not the sharing type, I get it."

"Not much to share." Usually men would leave after an answer like that, but Felix remained by her side.

"Let me be the judge of that." Felix swiveled on the stool and his knees brushed against her thigh. "Want to get a table?"

Kilyn glanced around the room. There were plenty of empty tables and booths that were more private than sitting at the bar. More intimate too.

"Sure," she said, against her better judgment. Sitting at the bar would have been the safe choice. She was very much in danger of letting her feelings get the best of her. She slipped down from the stool and stumbled as her heel caught on the footrest. She gasped and Felix reacted swiftly. He reached out to catch her.

"Steady there." He looked her over. "You okay?"

"Yeah, sure." Being so close to him was intoxicating. The beer she had in her system didn't help. Nor did his exquisite fragrance. It was a mixture of man, leather, cigarettes and aftershave. Yes, she was very much in danger.

He let go of her and placed his hand against the small of her back to steer her toward a small table. Kilyn relished the feel of warmth that spread from his hand and through her body. This was so unlike her. She hadn't let her emotions get the best of her since high school and that had ended badly. Raging hormones combined with what she now knew was magic powers, hadn't been an ideal combination. Still, there she sat, opposite Felix at the small table.

"You hungry?"

"No, I'm good, thanks." She gestured toward her bottle.

"So tell me about yourself," he urged, leaning forward with a glint in his eyes.

"As I said, not much to tell."

"But you're not from here."

"Neither are you." They both lacked the characteristic, southern twang.

"No, ma'am," he drawled with a crooked grin, tugging at an imaginary hat. She rolled her eyes.

"We can go on like this all night."

"Yup." He smiled and sank back against the chair.

"So what do you do, Felix?"

"I'm in the family business."

"And what, pray tell, is the family business?"

"Oh, this and that," he said with a dismissive gesture.

"Could you be any vaguer?" she asked, exasperated. "I'm a vet myself," she offered.

"Really?" Felix raised his eyebrows.

"Yes, really." Kilyn finished her beer, deciding she had put herself out there enough for one night. "And I have the morning shift so I must be going. It's getting late."

Felix shrugged. "Okay." She had expected him to object and felt strangely slighted that he didn't.

"Thanks for the beer," she said, putting on her cardigan. He rose to help her. She gave him a thankful smile and flipped her hair from the neckline.

"Better wrap up tight," he said, pulling on her lapels before tugging on her hood. His thumbs accidentally brushed her cheek as he let go. His proximity made her head spin. She stared up into his soft hazel eyes and forgot what she was doing.

"It's still raining," he said.

"Huh?" She broke out of her daze.

"It's still raining out there." He nodded toward the street. "Nice to meet you, Kilyn." A small smile played on his lips.

"You too, Felix."

* * * *

Felix watched as she disappeared out the door, forcing himself not to follow. He found her more fascinating than he'd first imagined. He didn't want to let her go, but knew he had to. He needed to report back to his aunt, tell her what he had found.

Felix exited the bar as Kilyn's silhouette disappeared down the street. His body was still aching to follow her, to touch her more than 'accidentally on purpose' as he helped her on with her cardigan. There was definite attraction between them and he was sure Kilyn felt it too. She seemed surprised when he let her go. If she only knew how much he wanted to object.

He sighed, put his helmet on and kicked his bike alive. After one last, longing glance he tore off in the opposite direction to Kilyn, towards home. To his empty apartment, his antisocial cat and a cold shower. He parked his bike outside the house and his aunt called.

"Auntie Vi," he said, trying to sound as indifferent as he could muster.

"Did she read it?" Violet never had time for pleasantries.

"Yes."

"And?"

"What did you expect?"

"A call."

"From me or her?"

"Her."

"She needs some time to absorb, I guess." Felix had no idea what Kilyn needed, but had no other information. "What would you do after reading a letter like that?"

Vi huffed. "I thought she would be thrilled."

"I'm sure she'll come around. Just give her more than five minutes. She seems a delicate type. Lonely, really. I'm sure she'll call when she's ready."

"Yes, I guess you're right. Patience is not my strongest virtue," the elderly lady said.

"Do you want me to do anything?" Felix crossed his fingers. A sanctioned intervention would be best, even if he didn't know how to tell Kilyn who he was.

"Continued observation; approach if needed." It was more of an order than anything.

"She needs guidance." Hands on guidance if he had anything to say about it. Then again, what he had in mind had nothing to do with magic. He mentally chastised himself. Kilyn had nestled her way into his brain.

"Yes, but she must come to me, I cannot intrude."

"I can," Felix said without thinking. He could almost hear his aunt's frown.

"What do you have in mind?"

Felix wasn't sure he heard her correctly, but went with it and said he would try to make contact, in a discrete manner.

"She's lonely," he said. "Having someone to talk to might help her make the right decision."

"Do you think you'll make progress in time for the meeting?"

"I'll get her there," he promised. His idea of progress wasn't likely to be the same as his aunt's, but he didn't say that out loud.

"Do your best, we need her as much as she needs us. I trust you."

CHAPTER TWO

Kilyn buried herself in work that Monday and Tuesday, trying to ignore thoughts of Felix and her new found family. Work was busy as usual and she threw herself into it wholeheartedly. No operation was too small. Seeing the smile on the owner's face when a pet was out of danger was the thing she loved most with her work. She hated when she had to tell them there was no hope.

It was a small clinic, they were only four full-time employees, but it suited Kilyn. She was appreciated for her work and felt useful, even if the days tended to be long because of extra shifts. Kilyn was only too happy to help whenever she could. She didn't have anyone waiting at home.

Tuesday afternoon found her staring at her family tree once again. The paper was old and felt fragile, she laid it out carefully on the table. It even smelled old. The ink was strong at the bottom, where she found her name along with her parents', but faded the further up the lineage she went, at least on her mother's side. Her father's seemed to be filled in at the same time as her parent's marriage. Kilyn's hands trembled as her fingers stroked the names of her parents.

Ailsa Silvrin nee Bryant, May 23, 1967 – 16 Oct., 1993. Married to Robert Silvrin, July 9, 1965 – 16 Oct., 1993.

Both witches and elves were represented. It was probably an impressive genealogy if she had known who any of the people were. The names didn't tell her anything. It was not like she had imagined so many times growing up. She had always imagined she would find her place in the world, once she knew who she was and where she came from. But nothing. No revelation, no memories sprang forth from her subconscious.

Kilyn read the letter again to find more clues but it left her with questions. She let her fingers follow the neat cursive script. Violet's phone number remained. Did she want to know the whole truth?

Kilyn could deal with being part witch, she had talents other people hadn't; she knew she was a good healer, that she could sense other people and she had been known to move objects or pushed people away by just wishing it, but elf descendant? That was something else entirely. She thought elves were imaginary, something from the world of Tolkien.

Kilyn rose from the couch and advanced on the mirror. She lifted her white blond hair, inspecting her ears. Elves were supposed to have pointed ears, right? She turned her head from side to side, but was relieved to discover she had not developed pointed ears overnight. They looked perfectly normal. There was a new guarded look in her eyes. When she thought about it though, she had never seen anyone else with natural violet eyes or bright white hair – not without the help of peroxide.

She had no one to talk to. Nobody who would believe her. She racked her brain for someone she could confide in, but found no one. She had lived in Savannah for a year but friends were scarce. Kilyn had always kept her distance from other people. For her protection and theirs. She couldn't afford to lose anyone.

The memory of the boy from high school sprang forth, unbidden. She remembered the shock and horror on her class mates' faces as the boy was flung across the room by an unseen force. Kilyn had told him 'no' several times, but he kept nagging her about something she couldn't remember now and she wanted him to get away from her. That had been when it happened. A rush of something she couldn't put into words had flown through her blood and when she opened her eyes the boy was on the other side of the room. Alive, thankfully, but beaten up from crashing into the wall.

A meow disrupted her thoughts and Doris affectionately stroked her black body against Kilyn's legs. She smiled and picked her up.

"Where did you come from?" she whispered. "Who treated you this badly?" She stroked the cat gently, murmuring soft words of encouragement, wanting her to heal faster.

She suddenly remembered those words she uttered from a memory. Her mother had spoken them when Kilyn hurt herself as a child and they always soothed her. She must have been almost three, just before the accident. Kilyn had scrubbed her knee and her mother had put a Band-Aid on and said the words as she rocked Kilyn in her lap. As Kilyn stroked Doris she realized this had been her mantra while working with wounded animals.

Kilyn wasn't ready to face Violet, but she was curious. Violet mentioned Stay a Spell and a store called Reap what you Sow in her letter. They were places magical people gathered. There was a coven meeting on Saturday.

Jeez, was she in a coven now?

Curiosity got the better of her, she was going to give it a try. Maybe she'd meet someone there to talk to, someone who could shed light on her situation. Perhaps if she knew what to expect from the witch community, she would be ready to face Violet. It was an irrational thought, but she wanted to test the waters a bit before throwing herself in.

Kilyn dressed with care. She parted her long hair into two loose braids, donned a long black skirt and blouse, and on top of that, a long knitted cardigan with a hood. Unused to the climate; it felt weird not being bundled up in late October. She put on the long pendant necklace she always wore. It was the only thing she had left of her parents. It was a silver pendant in the shape of a teardrop with a piece of amber in the middle, held fast with vines that wound round the stone and the outline of the drop. She cast one last look at the mirror, satisfied with the reflection, she left.

She tentatively stood outside Stay a Spell, unsure if this was the place for her. Squaring her shoulders, she pulled herself together, and told herself not to be such a coward.

"You can do this," she said under her breath and pushed the door open. She half expected someone to jump forward and call her bluff, to tell her she didn't belong, but all she got were a couple of uninterested glances. There was no one at the hostess booth and like the other day few patrons gathered. Kilyn stepped up to the counter and sat down.

"You're new here." The guy behind the bar regarded Kilyn.

"Yeah." She checked the drink specials and ordered one of the more adventurous choices.

"Welcome to Stay a Spell, the first one is on the house." The bartender placed a glass of green liquid in front of her. It looked positively vile and she wrinkled her nose involuntarily. "It tastes better than it looks." He winked at her.

* * * *

Felix was restless. He hadn't been able to concentrate on anything the last couple of days. Kilyn was tempting, but he didn't have a plan how to approach her. He had kept himself busy since Sunday, keeping a safe distance. He had even called his foster sisters to chat, which was something he hadn't done in a very long time. They were as surprised as himself. He realized he had shielded himself even from them who loved him the most.

He had tried to find out more about why Kilyn was so important to Violet. She finally confided that Kilyn was her niece and she'd been looking for Kilyn for quite some time. More than that she didn't want to tell him before meeting Kilyn herself.

On Tuesday evening he was out walking, for no particular reason, just a need to clear his head. It had been invaded by Kilyn. Driven by an inexplicable urge, Felix found himself outside of Stay a Spell. Kilyn was inside, sitting by the counter. He didn't have any reason to go in and he if he showed up she would know he was supernatural too. Was this the way he wanted her to find out?

Felix lit a cigarette while debating the pros and cons of going in.

* * * *

"Oh, fresh blood, I like!"

Kilyn jumped as a strawberry blonde sat down next to her.

"Is it that obvious?" Kilyn rolled her eyes.

"Totes. I'm Elvira, by the way."

"Nice to meet you, I'm Kilyn."

Elvira eyed her curiously. "Newbie, but such an old soul," she mumbled, her eyes narrowing. "What *are* you?"

Kilyn squirmed under the inspection, not knowing what to say. "I'm not sure," she whispered at last.

"Interesting." Elvira put her bag on the counter, rummaging through it, and finally presented a deck of battered tarot cars. "Let's see shall we?" She handed the deck to Kilyn with the command to shuffle it. Kilyn stared at Elvira. The girl noticed her discomfort. "Oh, don't be such a square!"

"I've never done anything like this before," Kilyn said, as she shuffled the cards carefully. They felt well used and fragile.

"Seriously?" Elvira stared at her. "Never had a reading, ever? Where've you been, living under a rock?" Elvira grinned, then got serious when she noticed the darkening look on Kilyn's face. "Oh, you mean, this whole place?" Elvira motioned with a graceful hand around the bar. "You're in here, so you must be supernatural. This place is warded against humans. You have to be magical to even notice it. Didn't you know?"

"No, I mean yes, I knew this was a bar where witches met, but I didn't know about the wards." Kilyn frowned. "I've only just found out what I am, what my alleged aunt claims I am anyway."

"Suspicious one, aren't you?"

"Well, yeah. I've been alone all my life, and now, 22 years later, I suddenly have a huge 'family'." Kilyn made air quotation marks around the word family. The tarot deck lay forgotten on the counter.

"I guess you've had that bottled up for some time."

"Yeah, I have no one to talk to about it. My aunt's letter mentioned this place. I was curious. Basically I see this as a research trip before I contact her."

"And how do you like it?"

Before Kilyn could answer, the door opened and she froze, mouth clamped shut. She knew that presence without having to check.

"Somebody you know?" Elvira was eyeing her with mild alarm.

Kilyn could only nod. If Felix could get in to Stay a Spell that meant he was supernatural. Her defenses went up.

"I have to go," she squeezed out through tightened lips, and quickly gathered her things, heading for the exit. Her escape was effectively cut short by Felix's broad frame.

"We must stop meeting like this," he said with a grin.

* * * *

Felix couldn't let the moment go. Seeing her talk to the strawberry blonde, finding out who knew what about their world, watching Kilyn's anxiety grow, he threw himself into her way again. He was sure his aunt would understand

"The heart wants what the heart wants," she had said to one of his foster sisters. Violet was a romantic soul, even if she seldom showed it.

"Felix," Kilyn breathed and looked up at him through long lashes. He relished having her so close. Her face flushed as he wetted his lips. Around them time seemed to slow.

"Fancy meeting you here," he murmured, his voice low and husky, bringing her cheeks to full flame. She bit her lip, her eyes darting around the room. Looking for what? Escape? Help?

"Stalk much?" she blurted, fixing him with those talkative eyes of hers. A petulant glint lit in her dark violet eyes.

"Maybe," he teased. Felix grinned, acknowledging the truth in her words. Her expression changed, eyes narrowing.

"I can't do this." She took a step back.

He didn't want to let her go. Her eyes transfixed him. This was bad, and he knew it. She was not supposed to be anything more than a task, someone to keep an eye on, flirting had never been included in his work. The family came first. Violet's wishes came before his carnal desires. He should distance himself.

* * * *

Kilyn took off like a frightened deer. Felix rushed after her. She felt the familiar sensation build inside her. Her emotions running amok, and so were her powers. If she didn't get out of there soon, something bad was going to happen.

"Just don't, Felix," she pleaded, over her shoulder. She was not giving in to her feral urges. Felix was everything she was not. Mysterious, dark, and alluring. Dealing with another supernatural, without knowing herself, was too complicated.

"Kilyn please." His voice rang in her ears and he took hold of her arm, making her face him. It felt like she was caught in a gentle snare. She swung around toward him.

"I can't do this," she whispered again, feeling the tears prickle in her eyes. She tore free of his grip and continued out the door, wishing he had the decency not to follow her. Kilyn had too much to deal with as it was, a romance would only complicate things.

She burst out onto the street, her heart racing with panic. She took a few steps to the side and found the wall. The rain had gone from a soft drizzle to a downpour. She didn't care. Kilyn slouched against the wall and tried to remain calm. She realized how close she had come to using her powers, could still feel her body tingling, humming with energy. Ever since she had read that stupid letter more talents were starting to manifest. She had no idea how to control them.

Kilyn decided to seek out Violet. She needed answers and help, before everything got out of hand.

"Are you okay?" Elvira put a hand on Kilyn's arm, making her look up and Kilyn nodded.

"Yes, just overwhelmed." Elvira nodded, as if she understood exactly.

"Follow your heart, it won't lead you astray. I know you're afraid, but there's no need. Not of him, at least. Cats on the other hand..." Elvira looked at Kilyn and held up the deck of tarot cards. "Beware of the cat, the cards said." Her golden eyes bore into Kilyn's as if she looked into Kilyn's soul. "Trust your heart. Here's my number if you need me." Elvira pressed a small card into her hand. Kilyn read Elvira's name followed by 'Reader and interpreter of signs and cards', then she heard Elvira's footsteps hurry away. She shut her eyes and took long soothing breaths.

* * * *

Felix stared after Kilyn. Her eyes had told him to stay away, not to follow. He should do what she wanted, but his body and soul wouldn't listen to reason. He argued with himself for a long time. It was madness, but he couldn't let her go. He had felt distress coursing through her. He needed to see that she was okay before going home.

Felix found her leaning against the wall with her eyes closed. He walked slowly toward her as not to startle her. He could sense her magic, barely under control, and he walked with caution, uncertain what she would do if cornered.

"Kilyn," he said in a hushed voice. "Are you okay?" He touched her lightly on the shoulder and she started. Finally opening her eyes, she smiled hazily.

"Who *are* you?" she whispered.

"Someone who can help."

"How do you know I need help?" She stared at him.

"Because I'm like you," he said with a hesitant smile. "Look, this is not the place to talk about it. Let's get off the street. Go someplace warm and out of the rain. You can trust me." He held out his hand. She took it, but stayed put.

"So I've been told," she whispered and something flickered in her eyes, and then she drew him toward her and planted a kiss on his lips. Startled he took a step back.

"Sorry, I just wanted to feel what it would be like."

Felix stared at her. This was a totally different Kilyn than the one he had observed over the past few days. After a beat he was back in her arms, kissing her, tasting her. A half growl rumbled through his chest as he leaned into her, pinning her against the wall. She moaned into his mouth. It spurred him on and he buried his hands in her long silky hair.

"This is insane," she breathed.

"Yes," he agreed and kissed his way down her neck.

* * * *

Kilyn relished the sensation of his lips against her neck. It had been forever since she had let anyone touch her in that way. The rain poured down, but had no cooling effect. She was on fire. She could hardly believe she'd drawn him to her. Elvira had convinced her to follow her heart, and that was what she'd done.

The concern she had seen in Felix's eyes was genuine, she was sure of that. It had lit up her desire once again, and she couldn't stop herself. Kilyn had to kiss him. For once in her life Kilyn followed her instincts and she was glad she had. Felix was an excellent kisser, gorgeous to boot. She raked her hands over his muscular back and shivered against him.

Felix let go of her, removed his leather jacket and hung it around her shoulders. It was warm from his body and she sighed happily.

"How about coffee?"

She nodded, unable to utter a sensible sentence, and let him take her hand. He led her to a small coffee shop, still open despite the late hour.

With shaking hands she tried to tame her disheveled hair and could only imagine what she must look like. Felix's hands had tousled her mane. She took the hair ties out of what was left of her braids, and shook the hair loose, combing it with her fingers. Kilyn was still shaken from kissing him, but it had felt so right. More right than anything in her life so far. Just like coming home.

After the incident with the boy in high school she had shunned intimacy, staying away from situations in fear of a repeat performance. She didn't want to feel the stares of others ever again. Her classmates looked at her like she was a freak. It had taken a new school, and several years, for her to finally work up the courage to let people close again.

Now she was part of a family? Where had they been all this time? Why hadn't they shown up when she needed them the most?

And now Felix.

Felix, who claimed he was like her, and could help. Kilyn wasn't sure she trusted him yet, but wanted to.

* * * *

Felix ordered coffee and pie for them both. Kilyn looked flushed and disheveled. Her lips were swollen from their earlier activities, and she seemed lost in thought. His heart swelled as he studied her. Suddenly, he didn't feel like the family came first, but Kilyn. The revelation hit him hard and he had to turn away from her to calm down.

She smiled thankfully when he returned with a tray and immediately took one of the cups, wrapped her fingers around it and warmed her hands.

"You cold?" he asked tentatively.

She shrugged in response and brought the cup up to her mouth, blowing on the hot liquid before taking a small sip.

"So," she said after a while, when he didn't speak. She stared expectantly at him, waiting for him to talk.

Felix didn't know where to begin. He wasn't even sure what had been in the letter. He wasn't supposed to get involved, but he was now certain he had been sent to her for a reason. And here he was, getting involved. Violet had given him leave to guide Kilyn, discreetly, this was not discreet. Making out with her was anything but. He chided himself when he thought of what Violet would say if she found out. An untrained witch could be very dangerous. He figured her powers were connected to her emotions. At Stay a Spell he could sense that she just barely contained them before rushing out.

"I think I owe you the whole story," he finally said.

"What do you mean?" Kilyn looked alarmed.

"The truth about who I am and about you too." Kilyn's eyes narrowed suspiciously. "You'll probably get a bit mad, but I hope you can bear with me."

"I know who I am," Kilyn said.

"Yes, but what are you?"

"Well, what are you? According to Elvira we both are supernatural beings, since we entered Stay a Spell."

"You got a letter from Aunt Violet, right?" Felix said. "I delivered the package. She's my aunt too." Kilyn's alarm grew.

He held up a calming hand. "Not by blood. She's the matron of the family. I'm an orphan. She found me and took care of me. But you and Violet are related."

"How do you know all this?"

"I'm her go-to guy when it comes to finding stray witches."

"How come you didn't find me sooner, why didn't she for that matter?" Kilyn glared. "Why has it taken 22 years for you guys to find me?" Her violet eyes pooled with unshed tears.

"Aunt Vi will tell you everything," Felix said. "She can explain."

"If this is your way of helping, you suck." Kilyn sat back and crossed her arms over her chest.

"I didn't want you to find out from someone else, but I wasn't supposed to interact."

"Interact? What are you? A spy?"

"More surveillance, guard, go to guy," he said, shifting uncomfortably.

"So when you said 'The Family Business', you meant *my* family business?"

"*Our* family business."

"That's weirding me out."

He cocked his head to the side, regarding her. She had a point there.

"She's only my foster aunt," he said.

"You know my family better than I do, and you're not even related to them."

Felix reached out and grabbed her hand. "Don't worry, they'll love you too," he said reassuringly, his thumb gently stroking her knuckles. Then he realized the sentence had a double meaning. He hadn't meant to give so much away.

Kilyn's eyes widened.

"I don't know if I'm ready for this life," she said quietly. Her small hand lay still in his grasp.

"You will be." He squeezed her hand. "I'll be with you all the way."

"What if I don't want anything to do with it?" Her eyes met his.

"It's not really a choice, it's a birth right."

* * * *

He was right, of course. She couldn't turn back now, running wasn't an option. She'd dreamt of this for so long, to have a family, to belong. Running from him was the last thing she wanted. Kilyn felt safe with her hand in his. Content, even. The thought of having him in her life made it easier to bear. She would consider contacting Violet. She was still angry it had taken her aunt this long to contact her. It had been a long lonely life on her own. She rubbed her face, the events of the day finally caught up with her body, leaving her dead tired.

"It's getting late." Kilyn was slow to gather up her things.

"I'll walk you home."

"I think I can manage on my own, thanks." She smiled at his chivalry.

"Please let me."

Maybe he was as reluctant to leave as she was.

"Okay, sure."

CHAPTER THREE

What had Elvira said about cats? Kilyn stopped outside her door, with her key in hand.

"What is it?" Felix asked.

"Something Elvira said," she answered, trying to remember. "Something about cats."

"Cats?"

"Yes, I picked up a stray a few days ago. A battered little thing. I call her Doris." She smiled a little, and then remembered Elvira had said to watch out for cats. It had been a warning.

"Do you want me to come in with you?"

"I'm not worried, I mean it was tarot cards, nothing serious." Kilyn shrugged with more nonchalance than she actually felt.

"Tarot is not something to take lightly, Kilyn. If she saw something about cats, let me come in and make sure everything is all right. I can sense things."

"What do you mean?"

"I can sense when magic is being used. If there's something enchanted about the cat, I'll know."

"Like a spidey-sense?" She giggled nervously. The thought of Felix in her home was exhilarating.

"Yeah, sort of."

Kilyn unlocked the door. She peered into the hallway, nothing seemed out of the ordinary. "Coast is clear."

* * * *

Felix stopped inside the door; he ushered Kilyn behind him protectively. Something was amiss.

"What is it?" Kilyn whispered, holding on to his shoulders.

"Someone's here," he whispered back.

"What?" Her voice rose in alarm.

He held up a finger in front of his mouth and gestured for her to keep behind him. He crept down the hallway with Kilyn still holding on to him. Felix liked that. She trusted him. He followed his senses through her apartment and stopped outside the opening to the kitchen. He peered in cautiously. A naked woman stood hunched over the table where a bunch of papers lay spread out.

He shot out his hand, flicked through the air, releasing his power to force her away from the table. He had her pinned against the wall as he stalked into the room. Kilyn shrieked, but he didn't look away from the woman.

"Who are you?" he demanded.

"No one," she answered, her eyes flickered between him and Kilyn.

"Stay back," he snapped, with a side glance at Kilyn who was advancing into the room.

"She's in my home, I think I'm entitled to question her," she said. She stepped up to the woman, staring at her. "Answer his question," she said. "Tell us who you are and why you are here." To Felix's surprise, the woman's green eyes glazed over. He felt the subtle shift in the atmosphere as Kilyn used her magic.

Impressive. Especially for someone so new to the craft. He kept his hold on the woman, she was under Kilyn's spell, but he couldn't be sure she wouldn't run if he let go.

"I'm Beckah," the woman whispered. "I was sent to test you."

"Test me?"

"Yes." The raven haired woman smiled. "I'm just the first wave, half breed." Her grin turned wicked and she fought Kilyn's compulsion and Felix's hold over her body. Kilyn's magic sparked and Beckah was flung out of Felix's grip, across the room. Kilyn stalked after her.

"Tell me everything I need to know." Her voice hardened and her violet eyes blazed as she towered over the smaller woman. A surge of power, different from Kilyn's, went through the room, and the woman shifted into a cat right in front of them. Kilyn gasped. Before any of them could react, the cat leapt out the open kitchen window.

* * * *

Kilyn rushed to the window, looking down, the cat was nowhere to be seen. She turned to Felix.

"What was that?" she exclaimed.

"A shifter, or a witch with shifter powers."

"Is that normal?" Her whole world had shifted from ordinary to one that contained witches and elves, for all she knew there could be vampires walking among them too. "Why didn't I sense her?" Kilyn chewed on her lip, Beckah being in her home for all this time violated her space, and that her senses didn't warn her made her second-guess herself. Alarm rose inside her. For years she'd felt watched, perhaps she had been right all along. There really was someone after her.

"Do you usually sense other people?"

"Not regularly, no, but from time to time, yes. Mostly I have taken it as a sign to skip town. It's not like when I felt you." She met his gaze, feeling shy.

"Why was that different?"

"You felt safe. But before it was threatening," she sighed and her body sagged at the realization. Felix's eyes turned dark and steely.

"I think we need to talk to aunt Violet," he said.

"Is it too late to call tonight?" She checked her watch, it was after ten.

"Let's do it tomorrow," Felix said. "But I don't want you to stay here tonight."

"I'll be fine. I doubt someone will come again tonight."

"I don't care, Kilyn. You're under my protection. I'd rather you stay with me."

Kilyn stilled. Stay with Felix? That was kind of huge, but also tempting. Elvira's words came back to her, 'Follow your heart', she'd said. What did her heart say?

"I'll take the couch and you can take the bed," Felix continued. Kilyn's imagination ran wild in a completely different direction, and it didn't involve separate sleeping arrangements.

"Yeah, okay," she finally said, hoping she sounded distracted about the cat-witch, not her naughty fantasies. "Let me just get some things."

She gathered the papers and grimoire from the table and stuffed them into her bag. Next she scanned her bedroom, selecting overnight things, throwing them into a bigger bag, along with toiletries. Felix leaned on the doorframe.

"Are you okay?" he asked.

She stopped. "I'm fine."

"Quite the power you're packing there," he observed, nodding in her general direction. Felix's eyes shone appreciatively and she felt her insides melt. What was it about this man that affected her so? It couldn't just be because of her lack of intimacy. It felt like something deeper, it was more than lust. It was a need, a heartfelt need.

"Apparently I'm a proper witch," she said, feeling proud and self-conscious at the same time.

"Are you ready? I don't think we should linger here. You heard what Beckah said, she was just a first test."

"Yeah," Kilyn said, feeling the fear rise. "God, I let her into my home!"

In two swift steps he was next to her. "You couldn't have known," he said, putting his hands on her shoulders, his thumbs caressing the exposed skin of her collarbones. She met his eyes.

"I don't know what I would have done if you weren't here," she whispered. His hand moved to cup her face.

"Don't think about that now. I was here. And honestly, I don't think you were in any danger. If she wanted to hurt you, she's had plenty of time before tonight."

She knew he was right. Beckah had been in her home for days.

"She sure found Violet's letter interesting, as well as my genealogy."

"All the better to talk with Violet." Felix placed a chaste kiss on her cheek and put his arm around her. "Come on, let's get out of here."

* * * *

The black cat landed gracefully by his feet in the alley behind the half-breed's building.

"What did you find?" he asked as Beckah shifted to human form in front of him, heedless of her naked state.

"More than I bargained for, Eike," she huffed. "That little half-breed!" Beckah's green eyes shot fire.

"What do you mean?"

"They caught me."

"What? How could you be so careless?" Eike shouted.

"Well, excuse me for doing your dirty work for you," she hissed back. "I'm here aren't I?"

"Sorry, Beckah," he said, voice softening. "You know our orders."

"She is in league with that guard witch guy who's been lurking around."

"Fuck! I had hoped to eliminate the abomination before her family found her." He groaned. This was going to be a disaster. His job had been simple enough to begin with. Just kill the half-breed and leave town. Now there were other people interested in her.

"No biggie," the shifter said, "I'm sure you'll think of something." She touched his face lightly, leaning in. "You're such a badass, Eike. One little half-breed shouldn't be a problem for you." She grinned wickedly. "Besides, you have me."

He kissed her fiercely.

"Yes, I have you," Eike said. She purred in his arms. "We have to get her before she meets that aunt of hers, though. It's bad enough she knows what she is." Beckah had proven to be a powerful ally. Not only did she volunteer to be beaten up and put herself in Kilyn's way, she'd had specific knowledge about Kilyn's aunt.

"And she's powerful too," she said. "I mean, look at me, I'm spotless." She inspected her body that only a couple of days ago had been badly beaten up. "The half-breed is an excellent healer."

She was an abomination, a half-breed and Eike's boss wanted her dead. Just like her parents for having her in the first place. Her talents were nothing to him.

"Not only is she a healer, but she's got telekinesis and mind control too," Beckah continued. "I've seen her family tree. It's impressive."

Eike heard the admiration in her voice, but he didn't care about the half-breed's bloodline. Kilyn was a disgrace to her kind and couldn't be allowed to live.

* * * *

Kilyn woke with a start. She stared wildly around before remembering she was in Felix's bedroom. Her body was entangled in the sheets and covered in sweat. She must have had a nightmare, but she couldn't remember what it had been about. On bare feet she padded toward the kitchen to fetch a glass of water. Along the way she passed the living room where Felix lay sprawled on the couch. His large body covered every inch of it. She stopped to pull up his blanket, feeling sorry for taking his bed. It couldn't be comfortable for him there. She had said as much when she saw the small sofa, but Felix wouldn't hear of her sleeping on it. Kilyn found that endearing.

She couldn't help but move a strand of hair from his face. His hand caught her wrist. She gasped.

"Kilyn?" His voice was husky from sleep.

"I was... I'm just..." she stammered. He softened his grip on her wrist and sat up, the cover fell to pool around his waist.

"Sorry," he murmured. "Occupational hazard. Did I hurt you?" His fingers caressed her wrist. Her body responded, unbidden, to his touch.

"No, I'm fine." Her breathing was erratic. She tried to keep her eyes off his well-toned torso, and not fantasize about what was underneath the blanket. "I was just going to get some water." She felt exposed in her oversized t-shirt and she tugged at the hem, trying to make it longer.

Her free hand swept a strand of hair that fell over her face. He brought her arm to his lips before letting her go. His other hand moved up her naked leg. A shiver went through her as his fingers reached the soft skin of her inner thigh. His eyes grew darker as he rose. And then his lips found hers. Kilyn capitulated. Her hands raked though his hair and down his back.

Kilyn pressed herself against him. In his arms she felt at home, safe and at ease. This was where she was supposed to be. Somewhere inside everything clicked into place. Felix was it. She knew that much. She trusted him. Kilyn threw caution out the window and just went for it. Screw the consequences. For the first time she felt like she belonged. She wasn't afraid of letting him near. He had his spidey-sense, and would surely stop her if she accidentally released any of her powers without thinking.

They fell down onto the couch. Touching, tasting, feeling. His hands found their way underneath her t-shirt and sent her blood boiling, her nipples stood erect and waiting for his touch. He looked into her eyes just as he was about to remove her t-shirt, as if he wanted her consent. Kilyn nodded slightly, tingly from anticipation. This was really happening.

"God, you're beautiful," he murmured as he removed her shirt, taking in the sight of her. She squirmed a little under his hot gaze and drew him down to her lips. She couldn't get enough of him.

* * * *

Felix was in awe of Kilyn in his arms. She was the most beautiful woman he had ever beheld. She reminded him of some woodland creature from stories of old. Willowy, powerful and stunning. He let his hands move over her skin, lightly, reverently. Kilyn shuddered and pressed against him, urging him on. He didn't want to rush. Her hands explored his body the same way he explored hers. Wanting to know every inch of her. His heart beat wildly, his breathing grew ragged.

Her hands moved to his butt, pressing his pelvis against her as her hips moved against his. It was almost more than he could take. Her hands tugged at his boxers.

"Kilyn," he breathed, between kisses. His hand moved from her breast and down to her underwear.

"Felix?" She removed his boxers, then lifted her hips to enable him to remove her panties.

"Are you sure?"

Her violet eyes stared up at him and her hand caressed his face.

"I have never been more sure about anything in my entire life."

"Where have you been all my life?" he breathed.

"Searching... waiting..." she whispered. She caressed his cheek, drew him down toward her, kissing him softly. His fingers traced her face, reveling in her delicate features. One hand snaked its way behind her neck to cup her head. Pressing her even closer he shifted to nestle between her thighs.

Before he got carried away, he rose on his knees, reached toward a small side table and produced a foil package, ripped it open with his teeth and rolled the condom on. Kilyn's hands moved up his thighs, urging him to hurry.

His hand moved down from her cheek, tracing her neck, collarbone, the swell of her breast and hip. Her breath grew shallow, and her kissing fierce. Her hips lifted off the couch, to meet him as he slowly sunk into her.

He wanted to take it slow, but she urged him on, meeting every thrust. They were perfect for each other. He couldn't do anything but let her decide the pace. She was too good to be true and he let himself get caught in the waves of pleasure that rolled over him, letting go completely as he heard her gasp and felt her tighten as she came. He cried out her name as he followed suit.

As they lay snuggling afterward he felt more content than he ever had. This was what he had waited for. Kilyn was his anchor, his home, his everything. Violet was just going to have to deal with it.

CHAPTER FOUR

Kilyn told Felix everything she knew about herself over breakfast. She was surprised she didn't feel awkward or embarrassed as the morning after a night of pleasure usually went, in her experience anyway. She hadn't spent a whole night with anyone in a very long time. But she felt relaxed and they spent the time talking and getting to know each other. Apart from her elf gene, they were quite alike.

Felix called Violet first thing. She was worried about them but seemed thrilled to meet her niece at last. Kilyn was terrified. She had no idea what to expect. Felix had overstepped his assignment just by talking to her. She found it flattering knowing he hadn't been able to stay away. Hopefully Violet would forgive them.

The tone of the letter had been gentle but precise, straightforward without any coddling. She thought Violet herself must be like that. Felix wouldn't tell her anything, but she knew he was very fond of Violet, she could hear it from the tone of his voice when he spoke of the aunt.

"I'll take you after breakfast," Felix said.

"How did Violet find you?" Kilyn asked. She popped another bit of bacon in her mouth as she waited on his answer.

"She found me when I was eight, I think. I was in an orphanage after running away from the last foster home I'd been placed in." He looked reminiscent. "Too be honest, I still don't know what she saw in that cocky little kid." He grinned.

"Did the foster parents treat you bad?" She knew what that was like. She'd been there too.

"Yeah, they realized I had talents and used me to make money and threat others. Saw me as a circus freak or something." Felix shrugged. "At first I kind of liked it. I liked being seen and what I thought was appreciation. I got a bit of the money, too. I didn't really care about other people back then. Didn't know how to." He grimaced.

"What made you leave?"

"I don't really want to bore you with ancient history."

"I'd really like to know. I want to know everything about you." She reached for his hands, and gave them an encouraging squeeze.

"It was actually when the other kids started to use me to bully other kids. I wouldn't be part of that. It's one thing to go after grown-ups that, from what they told me, had done bad things. But kids? No way." Felix looked bothered by the memory. His face had darkened and his eyes turned hard as flint.

"That was very brave of you." Kilyn's heart swelled as she looked at Felix. She tried to imagine him as a little boy, bravely standing up against the bullies.

Felix shifted in his seat under her scrutiny.

"It was just wrong."

"And then Violet found you."

"Yes, and the rest is history." He smiled and his features lightened up again and they finished their breakfast.

Kilyn was confused as to why he'd insisted she dress warm; it was hot in Savannah, until he thrust a motorcycle helmet at her. She was a bundle of mixed emotions as she sat behind Felix on the motorcycle, wind blowing in the loose strands of her hair. She felt happy, free and alive, but also fearful. She was finally going to meet her family and get an explanation as to why they had waited so long to contact her. It couldn't have been that hard, she thought. Or had they waited because of the threat Beckah had talked about? Had they thought she was safer off the witch grid? Or was it Violet's letter that had brought everything else to a head? Kilyn would soon have her answers.

* * * *

Felix grabbed Kilyn's hand as he rang the bell to Violet's house. House was probably an understatement. It was an old plantation. Violet moved there to have room for all the family. It was more of a B & B than anything else. There were always people coming and going. Felix used to be one of them but now he had his own place.

The door flung open and Violet stood in the doorway.

"Felix! And Kilyn, I presume. Welcome!" Violet ushered them into the vestibule and took their jackets. If she noticed them holding hands, she didn't act like it. "Let me look at you." She took Kilyn by the hands, studying her. Kilyn looked half bewildered under the scrutiny. Violet reached to touch the pendant that hung around Kilyn's neck, as tears spilled down her cheeks.

"Auntie Vi?" Felix said, patting her gently on the back.

"It's just," she began, looking up at Kilyn, "this was your mother's. Your father gave it to her for protection."

"You're scaring her," Felix said.

"No, it's okay," Kilyn protested.

"My darling girl," Violet said and took her into her arms, hiding her tear streamed face in Kilyn's curls. Felix watched, feeling slightly left out, but he had done what his aunt had asked of him. This was their moment. Not his.

He hadn't informed Kilyn of Violet's reaction to the news of Beckah or her threatening words about more attacks, or that Kilyn had felt watched. He didn't want her to worry. Once she was with Violet she would be safe. The mansion was heavily warded against all evil intent.

Violet led Kilyn toward one of the smaller rooms where they would be left alone and Felix was effectively shut out of their conversation. One look from Violet told him that she wasn't done with him, so he went out to the kitchen to grab a snack. He would probably be there a while.

* * * *

Kilyn stared at her aunt from across the small table. Violet seemed genuinely happy to see her. She chatted about this and that, nothing regarding Kilyn herself. Maybe she was stalling. Kilyn missed Felix and wished he was there with her. She would feel more comfortable with him by her side.

At long last a smallish girl entered through a door at the far side of the room. She carried tea and cake and disappeared after she'd put the tray down. Violet took a delicate china cup in her hands and sipped at the tea. Kilyn didn't feel comfortable enough to eat or drink.

"You have never been alone, Kilyn," her aunt said suddenly. "We have always been watching over you."

Kilyn stared at Violet.

"Why have you never said anything until now?" Resentment filled her. "Where were you when my parents died?" To her chagrin, she felt tears sting her eyes. She only had vague memories of her parents. Short glimpses of blond hair like hers, a gentle touch, soft singing at bedtime. "I know the authorities were trying to find relatives to take me in."

"Oh, honey," Violet said, she reached for her hand. "There were forces beyond our control, we couldn't get to you."

"What do you mean? What forces?" Kilyn snatched her hand away. "I was only three! I needed you! Isn't that what family is for?"

"Believe me, we wanted to, but your parents' death wasn't an accident."

Kilyn's mouth fell open. She racked her brain, trying to remember. She had been told it had been a miracle she survived. But she had no idea what had actually happened. Nobody had told her the full story.

"It was better you got adopted. They wouldn't be able to reach you then." Violet reached out to touch Kilyn's necklace again. "This has protected you until now." Kilyn toyed with the pendant.

"What happened?" she demanded.

"I don't know if this is the best time to tell you," Violet said. "There is so much else going on now. Felix told me about Beckah. The traitor!" Violet spat the word out.

"What, so Beckah is a witch? Not a shifter or whatever?"

"Yes, she is, but she's turned rogue. I knew her." Violet looked disappointed.

"So, there are good witches and bad witches, what else is new?"

"The question is, who is she working for?"

"I'm not familiar with this world yet," Kilyn said, getting serious and going into business mode. Something she'd quickly picked up from Felix.

"She didn't say?"

"I tried to force it out of her, but my compelling power isn't strong yet." Kilyn frowned. "She called me half-breed, like I was something filthy. So, this has something to do with my parents. What's so special about me?"

"You are a special breed, not filthy but made from a union of the purest of loves," Violet said with a fond smile. "Father witch, mother elf, you're one of a kind, Kilyn."

"Is that a problem?"

"Some people don't think we should mix, especially not the elves." Violet made a face. "Don't get me wrong, I loved your mother like a daughter, but elves are a very rare breed, ancient even." Kilyn's eyes widened. This was bigger than she had thought.

"So, is there a rule against socializing across species?"

"Elves are very particular," Violet said, apologetically. "Let's just say some of them are more progressive than others, like your mother."

Kilyn longed to hear more about her parents, but had to stay focused. One task at a time.

"They wouldn't mind letting witches do their dirty work?" Kilyn asked.

"Something like that." Violet smiled crookedly.

"So what do we do?" Kilyn asked. "I think I need a crash course in defending myself."

"So much like your dad," Violet commented. "First we need to figure out what powers you have. Both from your witch side and your elf side."

"I have no idea what I can do," Kilyn exclaimed. "This is all so new to me. I've known what I am for less than a week."

"But you've had these powers all along, you just didn't know what they were. You must have experienced oddities?" Violet urged. "Something you couldn't explain?"

"Yes, but…"

"See?" Violet grew ecstatic; her small body practically danced in her seat. "What happened?"

"I flung Beckah across the room," Kilyn said, grinning. "And I'm a good healer, I can also move stuff by willing it to happen." Kilyn went quiet, thinking of the boy from high school. "I need to learn how to control that. I nearly killed someone in high school."

"Don't worry, we'll teach you," Violet reassured her.

"So, how do we find who's after me?"

"We have our ways," Violet said, with a mysterious smile.

"Felix?" Kilyn asked, trying to hide the flush that crept up her cheeks.

"Among others." Violet cocked her head to the side and studied her. Kilyn reddened. Violet could see straight through her. "You seem very fond of our Felix."

"I've only just met him," Kilyn said evasively, not knowing what else to say. The strong feelings she felt for him were irrational. "Let's focus on the enemy, shall we?"

* * * *

Felix was reading through Kilyn's genealogy while the ladies spoke in the other room. The elf lineage made him curious. He knew very little of elves, and since Kilyn and Violet might take a while, he thought he'd make himself useful and search the mansion's library. He had no idea what powers elves possessed. From what he'd observed of Kilyn so far, they weren't so different from witches. One could learn to be a witch, while elves were born into it and were more naturally talented than book learned.

Elves also tended to be loners, not socializing outside of their own clans. He wondered if that was why Kilyn's parents had been killed. Elves weren't supposed to marry or fall in love with anything other than elves. Her parent's union produced Kilyn, considered by elves to be a half-breed. The more he thought about it, the more he was convinced that someone was after Kilyn because of her lineage. It made sense. Beckah said she wasn't the real threat.

Felix continued reading. Not only did elves have magical powers, but were great warriors too. Basically they were good and kind, but with time it seemed as they had separated into two different sides. One that was trying to keep their race alive by mixing with humans, and the other that wanted to stay pure and was fanatic about it. Over the years they had diminished in numbers, but the fanatics kept preaching against mixing races, hunting those who didn't share their beliefs, their kind fading as a result.

Felix compared Kilyn's lineage to a genealogy he found in Violet's old book. He thought he'd found a possible instigator. Elves were proud creatures and some very keen on keeping their bloodline pure. Kilyn's parent's marriage would be perceived as betraying those beliefs. The faction that thought elves were superior to all other races was represented in both genealogies.

Beckah must be working with an elf who wanted the line to stay pure. He checked his watch; Violet and Kilyn had had enough time together now. He gathered the books, went to the parlor and knocked quietly on the door. Violet bid him enter.

"I think I have found who might be after Kilyn," he said, sitting down on the love seat next to Kilyn. "There is a hierarchy among pure elves, so naturally there are underlings trying to work their way up."

"Okay? What has that got to do with me?"

"There is this cult who wants elves to stay pure blooded. There are too few of them left. They can't afford half-breeds."

"So this is all because of me? My parents are dead, because of me?" Kilyn rose and started pacing the room, biting her nails. "I don't even remember what happened. I only remember a white light, and then I was alone."

"Your survival 22 years ago was a mistake in their eyes," Violet said. "You were meant to die, but somehow you didn't."

"And now they're back to finish the job? I cannot be the only half-breed out there."

"No, but the only one from an ancient royal line," Felix said, tapping his finger on the genealogy he had found.

"What?" Kilyn stopped dead. "Not only am I half witch, half elf, but I'm royal too?" She sank down on the sofa again. Felix took her hands.

"I won't let them come near you."

* * * *

Kilyn wanted to believe Felix, but she wasn't sure. She couldn't protect herself and didn't know how to control the powers she had.

"Have you read your father's grimoire?" Violet asked, but before Kilyn could answer, the door burst open. They all jumped up simultaneously.

"Sorry to interrupt, Violet, but we have a breach." The man was dressed in commando gear.

"What? We are warded."

"Yes, but somehow they came through, I'm sorry, I checked the wards just an hour ago."

Kilyn watched as everybody stepped into their well-rehearsed roles. It was fascinating to see. Walkie-talkies were produced and orders were barked into them. From what she gathered they weren't sure what they were up against. In her heart, Kilyn knew they had come for her. Silently she edged toward one of the side doors, she didn't want to have innocent blood on her hands. She could stop all this by going out there and giving them what they wanted.

"Where are you going?" Felix's voice made her jump; she hadn't realized he was watching her. She should have felt him, but with all that was going on, her senses weren't attuned.

"I can't let all of these people, my family, die for me. I've only just met them. It's not right!"

"And I will not let you sacrifice yourself. Kilyn, what would I do without you?"

She stared at him.

"What do you mean?"

"Don't act like you don't feel it too. We were meant to be. I felt it from the moment I laid eyes on you," he said, an urgent tone in his voice. He put his hands on both sides of her face. "Tell me you don't feel the same." The pull of his words was strong, but she fought it.

"It's for the greater good," she said, raising her chin stubbornly.

"No, it's not. Take out the threat is for the greater good. We can't let these extremists roam free, taking down others like you. Don't you see? They have done this for ages! It has to stop! Sacrificing yourself will not end the persecution, Kilyn." Felix kissed her, urgently and passionately. Kilyn felt her knees buckle and her resolve weaken.

Yes, she felt it too. That inexplicable need to be with him.

* * * *

"You did well, Beckah," Ark said as they entered the property of Kilyn's aunt.

Beckah beamed back at him.

"I used to live here, I still know a few tricks."

"You have served us well." Ark held out his arms and Beckah gladly stepped forward to accept his embrace. Lightning shot out from Ark's hands and she fell lifeless to the ground.

Eike let out a pained snarl. "She helped you, Ark!"

"She'd fulfilled her purpose. Remember your oath, Eike, she's still a witch."

Eike fell down to his knees next to Beckah's body.

"I'm sorry," he whispered in her ear. "We knew this was going to happen. Your sacrifice will not be forgotten."

"Beckah served the elves well, Eike," Ark acknowledged.

"Yes, master, I know. Let's get the half-breed." Eike's voice was a monotone.

They moved stealthily across the large lawn. Ark performed a cloaking spell on the group, the witches would be alerted since they broke the wards, the element of surprise was gone, but this would definitely help.

Eike's heart wasn't in it. Not anymore. What he felt for Beckah couldn't be wrong, could it? He glanced over at the others. They were determined in a way he hadn't been since he met her. Love wasn't forbidden, but the men he saw had no interest in love. Eike doubted they had ever been in love. They were too scared to fall for the wrong person. He stopped short, broke off from the formation, and ran.

* * * *

"They're cloaking themselves," Felix said, alerting the others. He saw the shimmer glide over lawn from where they stood on the large porch.

"How can you tell?" Kilyn asked. She stood right next to him. Felix was happy she'd decided not to give up her life, but to try to eradicate the cult once and for all.

"I told you, I can sense magic, but I can also see through perceptive spells like these." Felix gestured toward the lawn. If she looked close enough she would see it too.

"Oh, I see it," Kilyn said.

"You are an elf too, you should recognize their spells. You should know their powers. It's in your blood, Kilyn," Felix urged.

Kilyn squinted.

"They have a focus," she said. "A stone or something to keep the spell going." She made a movement with her hand and the attackers were visible to the others.

The elves were outnumbered, but determined, their eyes fixed on Kilyn, mouths moving as if chanting. Felix shot a bolt of lightning toward the one he thought was in charge. The man fell crumpling to the ground.

"What are they chanting?" Kilyn asked.

"I don't hear anything."

Kilyn covered her ears and sank to her knees. Her pendant glowed.

"Please, make them stop," she whispered.

Felix was helpless.

Explosions burst around them, the family was fighting back, protecting their new found member. Felix glanced at Violet. She nodded. She was the most powerful witch he knew. Violet turned her attention to Kilyn, chanting, and Felix was relieved to see Kilyn's resolve return. She staggered to her feet; her jaw set and narrowed her eyes, steadying herself for retaliation. Felix contemplated the elves again. He released a blast of lightning toward them but missed. Instead he was hit by a ball of fire. Felix grunted and retaliated with another bolt of lightning. Another elf went down.

Beside him Kilyn held her pendant, her eyes closed and he could feel the magic rise within her. It was unfamiliar magic. She called upon her heritage, more elven than witchcraft. Waving her hands in front of her, toward the still oncoming elves. Then she opened her eyes to stare at the attackers.

"Be gone!" The two words were followed by a blast of air, and lightning burst out of her hands and it had the elves encircled in a way Felix had never seen before, it was like a tornado. The elves crumpled to the ground. The attack was over.

* * * *

Kilyn stared at the dead in horror. She had killed them. She felt it through her core. Even though she knew it was in self-defense, it was wrong. She sank to the floor, all of her energy gone.

"Kilyn, are you okay?" Felix's worried voice broke her daze, he kneeled beside her. She reached up and wrapped her arms around his neck.

"I don't want to do that ever again. I felt their deaths," she sobbed.

"Darling, you did what you had to do," Violet said. "And we are very thankful." Violet hugged her. "You saved us all."

Next thing she knew, Felix's strong arms were around her. He lifted her up and carried her. Kilyn was half out of it; she was battered and spent, but knew he placed her on a bed, urged her to sleep. She shook her head, but sleep overpowered her.

When at last she woke, Kilyn was alone. She felt as if a truck had hit her. She was sore all over, and when she tried to sit up she felt dizzy. Kilyn fell down onto the pillows and closed her eyes. Images from the attack came back, unbidden, and she groaned.

"Kilyn, darling, how are you feeling?" Aunt Violet's voice came through the haze. "Nothing to worry about anymore, honey." Kilyn stirred, her eyes flickering open.

"Felix?" she croaked.

"I had to make him go to get some sleep, honey. No need to worry." Her aunt patted her shoulder. "He wouldn't leave you. You have to admire his tenacity."

Kilyn took that as a blessing.

"Yeah, he's kind of a stalker," she said, smiling.

EPILOGUE

"Are you ready to enter the world of magic?" Felix asked as they stood outside the old, blue building where Reap what you Sow was situated.

Kilyn took a deep breath, looking at the entrance. Was she ready to be part of a coven? To be part of the supernatural world? With Felix beside her, she realized, she could face anything.

She smiled at a couple of kids walking by with buckets of candy in their hands. They were dressed as witches, out trick-or-treating.

"Yes," Kilyn finally said and took Felix's hand.

Links
Instagram and twitter @arellskan
Facebook: https://www.facebook.com/arellskan
Blog: http://arellskan.blogspot.com

A Stolen Spell
By
A.E. Snow

DEDICATION

To the Wenches. I'm so grateful to be on this journey with you.

PROLOGUE

Isadora Blackwood closed the book and stretched like a cat. She yawned, relishing the movement after hours sat in a dark vault pouring over pages in dim candlelight. She closed the book and ran her fingers over the worn leather. Once again, she'd spent hours in the dank, inky underground library sorting through piles of loose papers, books containing hundreds of pages of fading ink, handwritten and barely legible scribbles. She rubbed her tired eyes and dropped her pen on the table.

She checked her watch. 2 am. Samhain.

Isadora picked up four loose pages, unsure of whether or not she should include it in the folio. Those four pages held a powerful and terrifying spell. She'd been unsure if she should include the spell that allowed its practitioner to gain immense power through the acquisition of human souls. But her diligence as a historian overpowered her common sense and she tucked the spell into the book before she could change her mind again.

"Shit. I've got to get home." With a sigh, she sorted the books and documents into piles and grabbed her bag. She placed the leather bound book in the center of the table and took a last look around.

"Goodnight Blackwoods." Isadora snapped her fingers to extinguish the candles. Her footsteps echoed down the hall and the vault fell silent once again.

In the darkness, histories and mysteries swirled inside the leather-bound book. From Europe to Salem to Savannah, the secrets of the Blackwoods were recorded. Secrets and spells that not only had the power of good, but also had the power of evil.

Shadows lurked in the night outside of Fordham Hall, shades that waited, bided their time until Isadora, keeper of histories, made a single misstep and the book, and more importantly, the spell inside, could be stolen.

The vault was as quiet as a tomb in the darkness. But inside the book, the histories of one of the most powerful magical families teemed with life. The spell took on a life of its own and the dark witch who hid in the blackness outside of the Hall felt the energy pulsing from the book in time with her own heartbeat.

CHAPTER ONE

Isadora yawned as she unlocked the ornate oak doors of Fordham Hall. She'd only been gone for a few hours, yet here she was, back again to welcome the public to the historical research library of Savannah. Not that the public came in very often.

She spent more time in Fordham Hall than she did in her cozy little house. Much of that time was spent curating a massive collection of the histories of Savannah. She flipped on the lights and performed her duties on autopilot. Her thoughts drifted toward her most important work, *The Histories of the Blackwoods* which rested underneath where she stood, protected by a number of spells and charms.

The click-clack of her heels and her humming filled the Hall as she performed the opening procedures. She found her greatest happiness in the old building. Even shelving books brought Isadora joy. As she wandered through the stacks, a thin book nestled between two large, heavy books caught her attention. She touched the narrow spine and closed her eyes. Immediately, she saw the camp of the Shawnee on the banks of the Savannah River hundreds of years before going about their daily business of gathering food and supplies and cooking more than three hundred years before. Isadora's nose twitched as the smell of meat cooking wafted through the air.

Isadora smiled and moved her hand down the row to another book. This time, when she closed her eyes, she saw the ship *Anne* and her captain General Oglethorpe when he first laid eyes on the landscape that would become Savannah.

She reached out one last time to rest her fingers on the thick spine of a leather-bound book and her mind filled with a vision of the morning of December 21, 1864. The confederates were silent as their leaders negotiated a surrender to save Savannah from General Sherman's march to the sea.

Bang bang bang. She jerked out of her vision.

"Isadora! I need your help!" a voice from outside shouted.

She hurried to the front and pulled the heavy doors open to reveal her boss struggling with a large parcel. "Good morning Susanna."

"Carry this please." Susanna offloaded the heavy cardboard box into Isadora's arms and marched into the hall. At the circulation desk, she slammed her bag down on the table.

She staggered under the weight of the package and strained to lift it onto the desk. Susanna didn't speak. She took her sunglasses off and revealed puffy eyes rimmed with red. Isadora looked away, pretending not to notice. Susanna wasn't usually the crying type, but more than that, she wasn't the type to take any sympathy from others.

Susanna immediately got on the phone. "Hi Mr. Dorning. I have those items we discussed all ready to go." She purred as she stalked back into office.

When Susanna disappeared from sight, Isadora let her gaze stray to the box. One flap had popped open and she rolled her chair silently over to peek inside. Silver candlesticks glittered under the antique chandeliers. "Hmmm," she whispered and put her hand on the dull brown cardboard. Eyes closed, she concentrated on the contents. Jewelry and a lot of it, as well as an entire silver serving set. She wished she could see into Susanna's mind the way she could see into the objects.

The young librarian turned her attention from the box and got on her with morning. The library remained empty for a good portion of the morning which wasn't that odd. She sat down behind her computer and checked her email. Her lips formed a small smile when she noticed the first one. It was from Dr. Graham Hart with whom she'd corresponded for several months. He'd contacted her months ago regarding the Civil War section of her library and the correspondence had continued. She subconsciously sat up straight, smoothed her long chocolate-colored hair, and began to read.

Blessed Samhain!

Isadora had to reread the greeting several times. *Blessed Samhain?* She thought. *The only people I know who say that are witches.* Her heart skipped a beat. *Could he be...a warlock?*

She shook her head. "Wishful thinking," she said and continued reading.

> *I'm happy to report that I'm in beautiful Savannah. I have some business with Savannah State University this morning but I'm free this afternoon. I plan to stop by Fordham Hall around midday. I sincerely hope to see you them.*
>
> Best,
> Graham

She blinked several times and put her hand over her fluttering heart. She hadn't exactly admitted it to herself but she'd developed a massive crush on Graham over the course of a few months. Going so far as to look him up in the faculty directory, she discovered that he was cute, very cute. His mop of curly, messy hair looked like no one had ever quite managed to tame it and his warm brown eyes had left her knees a little weak.

Panic was her first instinct. Closing her eyes, she took several deep breaths.

"What are you doing?" Susanna snapped.

Isadora opened her eyes wide. "Nothing. Just…getting centered."

Susanna rolled her eyes. "I hope you are centered now. I need a coffee."

"Of course," Isadora said and dashed off to brew coffee for Susanna and tea for herself. She worried about Susanna. In the past few months, she'd changed. Something weighed on her but Isadora didn't know what.

The day dragged on. Every time the door opened, her gaze locked on the person who entered. But none of them were Dr. Hart.

With a sigh, she gave up and let herself be engrossed in her day's work, which involved an investigation of timeworn slave sale documents found in a trunk in an old plantation home and donated to the Historical Society by the owners who had converting it into yet another bed and breakfast.

The door creaked open again. "Welcome to Fordham Hall, Historical Research Library," she said without looking up.

"Good afternoon. Is Isadora Blackwood available?"

She raised her head and found herself staring into a pair of brown eyes. A dark red blush moved up her slender neck and turned her cheeks pink.

She cleared her throat, picked up a stack of call notices and shuffled them. "G-good afternoon," she stammered. "That's me."

"I'm Graham Hart." He stuck out his hand.

"S-so nice to finally meet you Dr. Hart," she stammered and shook his hand. When their fingers touched, a tingly feeling spread through her palm. The same tingly feeling that she always felt when shaking hands with other magic folk. Isadora's eyebrows raised in a question.

Dr. Hart smiled, one side of his mouth curling up as he nodded.

"Of course," she said again, a different connotation this time.

"I'm early, I know," he said. "I wanted to have a look around before tonight."

"Certainly." She put her hand out as if to say "it's all yours." In doing so, she knocked a book off the desk and it landed with a thud on the shiny hardwood floor.

Without missing a beat, Graham picked the book up and placed it gently on the desk as if it were a piece of gold.

Her heart swelled. "Thank you."

"Of course." He gave her another smile and disappeared into the stacks.

When she'd made the date with Dr. Hart, she thought she'd be dining with a handsome colleague who also had a keen interest in the paranormal occurrences in the Deep South. Particularly the stories that had circulated around Savannah for nearly two hundred years. She had a feeling they might be discussing something else.

"Isadora?" The voice, short and sharp, startled her out of her reverie. She sighed and turned to face, her boss.

"Yes?" She gave a pleasant smile. Trying to stay on the woman's good side wasn't easy. She didn't have a choice though as she was the only witch involved with the historical society and was solely in charge of the secret histories of the witches of Savannah and elsewhere contained in the vault. Her mother had held the same position until she died just as Isadora came of age and inherited the responsibility. As protector of the witch histories, she had access to vast amounts of knowledge and she didn't take it lightly. It was the most important thing in her life.

Susanna appeared carrying her Chanel bag and wearing a chic grey cashmere sweater. Not a single hair of her frosty blonde bob was out of place and a fresh coat of burgundy lipstick lined her lips. "I'm going to lunch. Can you get these shelved?" She pointed a manicured finger to the book cart. The head librarian found it distasteful when people actually disturbed the books in the meticulously curated library.

"Of course."

"I'll be late back." Susanna marched through the library and slammed the one hundred and fifty year old oak with a bang. She didn't feel the rules of decorum in the library applied to her.

All five people in the library looked up, startled.

Isadora sighed and reached for her tea. She frowned when she saw the empty mug with a dried up tea bag resting at the bottom. She glanced around before concentrating all her attention on the vessel. A fresh tea bag appeared inside and hot water streamed into the mug as though being poured from an invisible teapot.

Once the books were sorted, she returned them to their sections always aware of what her patrons were doing, especially Dr. Hart.

One by one, the other patrons returned their books to the circulation counter and left. Isadora added them to her cart and sorted by subject, something she found immensely satisfying. After a quick glance around the room, she found Dr. Hart in an armchair by the Civil War section, one of the biggest in the research library. She smoothed out her hair and her skirt and pushed her rolling cart into his section.

"Did you find everything alright?" she asked with a flutter of her eyelashes.

"Yes. No problem at all." Graham smiled and stood. "I have to be going, should I give this to you?" He held out the book he'd been reading.

She accepted it. "Yes...thank you." Once again, their fingers touched. This time, white sparks shot into the air. Disarmed, she dropped the book as soon as Graham let go.

They both stooped to pick it up and laughed when they both reached for it. A blush spread over Isadora's face and neck. She pulled her long hair over her shoulder in an effort to hide some of the red splotches.

Graham cleared his throat. "Shall I meet you at the restaurant? And which restaurant?"

"Stay a Spell?" She held her breath and waited. If he knew of the finest and only strictly paranormal restaurant in Savannah, it would truly confirm what she already knew.

Graham's brown eyes lit up. "See you at eight." With a toothy grin, Graham left.

Isadora watched him go with a dreamy smile. She floated back to the desk still holding the book he'd given her and leaving the rolling cart abandoned. She daydreamed about dinner with Graham. In her dream, the perfect date led to dinners at home as husband and wife with their laughter and children filling up a white farmhouse.

"Get a grip Isadora," she said surprised at herself for fantasizing about marriage and babies, not things she'd ever thought she wanted. She preferred the company of her cat, books, and tea to men most of the time. But there was something different about Graham. From the months of emails, she knew he was interested in the same things she was: paranormal events as documented by humans, cemeteries, and books.

Her gaze swept over the calendar and froze. The smile melted off her face and she groaned. "Shit," she whispered. Samhain. She had a coven meeting in half an hour. "Shit shit shit." She remembered a book from the vault that belonged to Rose. Rose needed it back and she'd promised to bring it.

Isadora climbed on a table and looked around for any patrons she might have missed. She was alone. Glancing down at her watch, she realized Susanna would be back any second. Still, she had to get that book. She dashed to the front door and locked it before running back down the length of the hall, the clicking of her heels echoing and filling up the quiet space.

Next to the Civil War section was a hidden panel, which concealed a secret staircase that led to a magical vault below. She performed the spell to remove the charms. The lock clicked signaling the spell had lifted and the way was clear. She ducked into the passage, and pulled the door gently closed behind her. The dark surrounded her and she held onto the railing as she hurried down the stairs.

Candles bewitched to stay lit, lined the walls and provided the only light in the otherwise pitch-black hallway. At the end of the corridor, the histories waited for her. Her heartbeat sped up the way it always did when she entered the hallowed athenaeum. Books and portfolios lined the room. Each one contained a piece of the histories of the oldest witch families in the world and the archives of the witches themselves. Isadora grabbed Rose's book off of the old wooden table and made her way quickly back up the stone stairs.

As soon as she got to the top of the stairs, she heard banging. "Shit."

"Isadora!" Susanna yelled, still banging and shouting from the other side of the ornately carved door.

She swung the panel shut and rushed to the door stopping only to shove the book into her bag. She arrived, breathless, a smile plastered on her face. "I'm so sorry Susanna."

"What on earth were you doing?" Susanna huffed as she shoved her way inside.

"I, uh, was in the bathroom."

Susanna rolled her eyes. "You had to bolt the door for that?"

"I didn't want anyone to come in and disturb the books."

Susanna didn't respond but rolled her eyes as she strode past.

"I'm so sorry Susanna. My appointment is in fifteen minutes," she said clasping her hands together. She told Susanna she had an appointment every month when the coven meeting rolled around.

Irritation etched itself into Susanna's face. She opened her mouth but Isadora was rescued before she could speak. When she realized who it was, Susanna's face broke out into a wide, sparkling smile. "Dr. Levin! What a wonderful surprise!" she cried.

Isadora grabbed her bag and tiptoed outside into the crisp autumn air as Susanna made an enormous deal out of Dr. Levin, the society's largest donor.

CHAPTER TWO

At 1:57, Isadora let herself in to Reap What You Sow, Rose's shop where the meetings were held. She tucked the book under the counter and ducked behind the blue curtain that blocked off the storeroom. She passed through another curtain and raced down the stairs pausing outside the meeting door to catch her breath before entering.

The witches were already gathered and she was the last to arrive. She slunk around the table and sat in her designated seat, a simple wooden chair. Adanna, the supreme witch, gave her a once over before starting the meeting. Isadora broke eye contact and stared at the table in front of her. She discreetly checked her watch. 2:01.

As the meeting progressed, a growing dread spread over Isadora leaving her arms and legs numb. She wracked her brain trying to locate the source of her anxiety. It hit her like jolt of electricity. The door. She went cold, then hot, when she realized she'd forgotten to reset the spell on the door to the vault. She wasn't even sure she'd closed it. Leaving the meeting was out of the question. She'd have to wait until it was over.

She couldn't pay attention for the anxiety. Terror filled her when she thought about the secret and dangerous books in her care, especially *The Histories of the Blackwoods*. A few loose pages ripped out of her grandmother's grimoire, held one most evil and dangerous spells in existence. One her own family had used to gain an enormous amount of wealth and power until Isadora's own mother had stolen the spell and escaped the family. Tapping her foot, she tried to will time to move faster. Finally, after what was surely the longest coven meeting in history, Adanna warned them to be careful and dismissed the coven.

Isadora shot out of her chair and up the stairs. She wished she'd brought her broom but it wouldn't have done her any good in the daylight. Instead, she removed her heels and ran down the sidewalk headed toward the other side of town.

When she arrived, she took a moment to soak up the sunlight. Light was the source of her power and she wanted to be ready for anything. When she felt full, she stepped inside. She hurried through the hall toward the Civil War section. Susanna stepped into her path holding her coat and bag. "Something urgent has come up," she said. Her usually rosy face had taken on a ghostly pallor and her hands trembled so much her keys could be heard jingling inside her leather bag.

"Okay," Isadora said in a shaky voice. Glancing back at the door, a tiny glow relief spread over her. Everything looked normal.

Susanna turned back to face her. She opened her mouth to speak and then closed it again. With a slight shake of the head, she was gone.

An older gentleman browsed the stacks. She couldn't do anything until he was gone. She stood behind the desk wringing her hands and pacing. A letter sitting on the desk caught Isadora's eye. She assumed it was Susanna's and picked it up to tuck it back in the envelope and into a drawer but the words FINAL NOTICE in red ink across the top caught her eye. Though she wasn't usually so nosey, Isadora pulled the letter out of the envelope and unfolded it.

Her breath caught in her throat. "Oh no." The letter was a final notice from the bank. Susanna's house would be repossessed if she didn't pay up. Isadora's eyes filled with tears. *No wonder she's been so nasty. I've got to figure out a way help her. But first, this man has to leave and I have to get to the vault.*

She forced a smile and marched over to the man. "Hello!" she trilled. "I'm so sorry but it's Halloween. We close early today!" she lied with enthusiasm and grabbed his arm directing him gently toward the exit. "Please come again soon. Thanks so much! Happy Halloween!" she chirped and slammed the door behind him.

She bolted the door and leaned up against it, staring toward the back of the library. Cold fear crept in around her. Fear and panic gnawed at her stomach as she took a deep breath, kicked off her heels, and ran full tilt toward the back of the hall.

Nothing looked strange in the Civil War section. The panel looked as it always had, but she knew something was wrong. There were no charms to remove and the panel popped open when she pressed on the top left corner. Before ducking into the darkness of the staircase, she glanced around at the friendly light of the hall one last time.

Her heart pounded on her way down the stairs. A thousand possibilities crossed her mind. Someone or something could be waiting for her. The whole place could be ransacked. It could be empty.

The hallway was the same. Candles still flickered in the sconces casting a dancing glow on the walls. The terrible feeling grew as she drew closer to the library.

Rounding the corner, she gasped. Books and papers lay strewn about on the earth floor; her chair lay overturned. The table had been cleared. *The Histories of the Blackwoods* was gone.

CHAPTER THREE

Isadora righted the chair and sat down in it blinking back tears.

"What am I gonna do?" she whispered to the room. She bit her lip and blinked back years. But she didn't have long to stand around feeling sorry for herself. She had to get that book back. She'd been entrusted with it, and with everything, by her mother and the witches of Savannah. Letting them down was not an option.

Jumping into action, she dashed up the stairs and out into the light.

A piece of folded parchment paper lay next to an envelope on the floor. She snatched it up. The swirly script spelled out one word. *Tonight.*

"What could that mean?" Isadora asked the empty library. She sniffed the note. Something about it seemed familiar. "Clove?" She shoved the note and the repossession letter into a drawer.

A voice inside of her berated her the entire walk home. *You should have been more careful. You should have hidden those away where no one would ever find them. You're mother tried to destroy them and you could have tried too.*

Relief washed over her when she caught a glimpse of her small red cottage. A large part of her wanted to go directly inside and crawl under the bed. Instead, she pulled back the white curtain which hid her altar, potion cabinet, grimoire, herbs, and candles. She dragged everything out into the floor and created an altar around herself.

"I guess I should try and figure out who has the book." She murmured a spell designed to help find what once was lost. She lit a match and waited watching the smoke begin to curl up toward the sky.

She concentrated on the curling tendrils of smoke while letting her vision go blurry. A face, one she didn't recognize but looked strangely familiar still, appeared in the smoke. Frowning, she squinted trying to see more. A hand with a large diamond ring put the book and four loose sheets into a folio. Then nothing else.

"Hmm." She let the candle burn but turned to her tarot deck. She cleared the energy and shuffled the cards as she concentrated on the question she would ask the cards.

Slowly she laid the cards out in a spread and flipped the first one. The Magician. Not terribly surprised, she flipped the next, The Two of Cups.

"Love?" She frowned. "Love for the Magician?" She was afraid to say it out loud, but wondered if it represented Graham. The thought made her blush. She took a deep breath and flipped the next card. The rest of the read seemed to point to her own personal power and creativity but nothing else.

With a huff, she gathered the deck, wrapped it in a piece of red silk and placed it back into the carved wooden box.

Isadora stared at her altar. After a few minutes, a thought formed in her head. The more she thought about it, the more it made sense. "Graham." she jumped up. "Dr. Graham Hart." Anger flashed in her eyes, as the pieces seemed to fall together.

She checked the clock, and noticed she had a little over an hour before her dinner with Graham. She surveyed her clothes with a frown. The whisper of a tail tickled her ankles.

"Hi there Madge," she said to her gray and white cat. "You've got to help me pick a dress."

Madge wandered off into the kitchen and began eating.

She pulled on a black silk dress splashed with colorful flowers out of the back of the closet. She'd been saving it for a special occasion. "I guess it doesn't get more special than this." It fit just right. She stepped through a mist of perfume, added black heels, and a sleek chignon. Red lipstick completed the outfit and she hoped it would be enough to thoroughly charm Dr. Hart.

"I have no idea how to charm anyone," she told her reflection. Her dark hair framed her pale face. Deep brown eyes stared back at her. "Here we go."

She cast a spell of protection around herself along with a seduction spell before gathering several amulets, which she tucked under her dress. Her clutch appeared small but was filled with charms and a potion or two. Grabbing a shawl, she stepped out into the chilly night air.

CHAPTER FOUR

Stay a Spell teemed with magical creatures and witches. Isadora stopped at the hostess station just inside the door.

"Good evening. How many?" the young witch, asked.

"I'm meeting someone actually," she said glancing around the room. "Ah. There he is." She smiled at the hostess and threw her shoulders back before making her way to a table in the back.

Graham stood while she took her seat. "You look lovely," he said.

Pleased that she had achieved the desired effect and grateful for the spell, she thanked him. "How are you finding our fair city?"

"I always enjoy visiting Savannah. It's almost as beautiful as N'Orleans."

She laughed. "Some would say it's even more beautiful."

After they ordered, Graham leaned forward. "Now that we are all out in the open. I'm dying to know what you've been working on."

"But I've told you. The paranormal histories of Savannah."

Graham chuckled. "What are you *really* working on?"

Here's my chance. She tucked a loose strand of hair behind her ear. "I'm compiling the stories of my family. The Blackwoods."

"You know, I just put it together that you are one of *the* Blackwoods."

"Oh yes. The infamous Blackwoods."

"How is the project going?"

She filled him in on the more benign aspects of her work. "It's fascinating. The Blackwoods have been present in every major magical scandal since the witch hunts in Europe. They were in Salem too."

"Salem?" He rested his chin in his hand.

"Yes. William Stoughton, the Chief Magistrate in Salem at the time, was a warlock. Did you know?"

Graham shook his head. "I didn't!"

"Indeed. He was being blackmailed by none other than Bartholemew Blackwood."

"Wow. That's fascinating." He had a sort of dreamy look in his eyes. "I'm not sure anyone has ever documented the Blackwoods so thoroughly and in one place."

For a moment, Isadora forgot about the book and the missing spell. "Samuel Parris was a warlock as well. There's a theory that at least some of the hysteria in Salem was because of Ergot poisoning which is basically an LSD trip."

Graham laughed outright. "You're kidding! How were they poisoned?"

"Bread," she said with a laugh. "Anyway, the Blackwoods were there and everywhere else. I'm not much of a Blackwood myself. I mean, I'm not evil. Some of the Blackwoods of this generation have mellowed a bit. But there are plenty left who follow the old ways."

"I didn't think you were." Graham poured red wine into both of their glasses.

She took a long drink staring at Graham over the top of her glass. The wine had stained his perfect lips and she had to pull herself together before putting the glass down. "Yes, it's been a very interesting project."

Graham asked questions about her family. She kept expecting him to slip up and say too much. They ate dinner and he never mentioned the spells at all. She supposed he might know better than to mention it. But she also knew that the spell wouldn't work for anyone other than a Blackwood so one way or another he'd need her help if he was the culprit, which she'd started to doubt.

After dinner, he cleared his throat. "I heard you had something of interest to show me." The server cleared their plates and dropped off the check. Graham slipped a few bills into the black envelope.

Her shoulders dropped. He truly didn't know. He hadn't taken the book. He didn't have the spell. A horrible dark feeling spread over her. She broke out into a cold sweat. So who did?

"Isadora? What's wrong?" Graham's brows knit with concern.

Tears pricked at her eyes. "N-nothing." Her mind raced. She tried to think of what to do but couldn't concentrate. Her chest heaved and beads of sweat popped out on her forehead.

He pushed his chair back and halfway got up. "Are you okay?"

"No."

Graham pulled her up and supported her as they made their way outside just as she started to hyperventilate.

"Oh no, oh no, oh no." Isadora wrapped herself up in her shawl to stop shaking.

"What's wrong? What happened?" Graham put an arm around her.

She stared at him for a long moment remembering the months of emails they'd sent and the secrets shared. She *knew* him and she knew she could trust him. "Will you help me?" she asked. "I need help. This thing is bigger than me."

Graham nodded. "Yes."

"Then let's go."

Back at the cottage, Isadora sat across from him. Having filled him in on the missing spell, she sat back and sighed.

"Who took it? Do you have any ideas?" Graham asked.

She grimaced. "I thought it was you."

"Me?"

"I suppose I hoped it was you. I thought I could get it back easily."

Graham laughed nervously. "Not afraid of me then?"

She didn't answer his question. "I have no idea who else it could have been."

"No idea at all?"

She wracked her brain to come up with an idea despite her acute awareness of Graham and his green eyes and messy curls.

"No." She frowned.

Graham tapped out a song on the coffee table with his fingertips. "What about someone at the historical society?"

"There's no one there that..." She let her sentence trail off. She sat up and opened her eyes wide. "Susanna."

Graham thought for a moment. "What would a human need with spells like that? A human wouldn't even know what they were."

Isadora jumped up. "I don't know why I didn't think of it before. I was being snoopy today and I found a repossession notice on her desk at work. But right under it was a note on parchment paper. It said 'tonight.' Do you think..."

"But why? Why would Susanna take it?"

She sighed and sat back down. "I don't know. Do you think she knows what it is?"

"I doubt it. Has she ever seemed interested in witches?"

Something clicked in Isadora's brain. "Or she has another motivation?"

He ran his hands through his hair. "Money?"

Shrugging, she said "Maybe." They both considered the possibility in silence.

"A Blackwood?" Graham asked.

"Who else?"

Graham stood up and made for the door. "We have to find her."

"Let's go." She dashed out the door with Graham right behind her.

CHAPTER FIVE

Halloween in Savannah raged around the two magical beings as they made their way to Susanna's mansion in the rich, historic part of town. Sugared-up children dragged their exhausted parents from door to door bargaining over how much longer they'd stay out.

In the midst of the commotion, the hair on the back of Isadora's neck stood up and chill bumps covered her arms. She glanced around but saw nothing unusual. Considering that the usual for Samhain included everyone wearing a costume.

They were halfway to Susanna's house when the professor touched her arm and whispered in her ear "I think we are being followed."

She nodded. "Agreed."

Graham turned to look behind them.

"Don't look!" She hissed. She grabbed his hand and pulled him around the corner. "Did you notice that everyone is gone all of a sudden? There are no trick-or-treaters anywhere?"

He glanced around quickly. "There's someone back there."

"Keep going. Susanna's house is a couple of blocks away. Though I don't know how we'll get there without being noticed."

Darkness, an unnatural darkness, began to fall like mist around them. "She's here." The smell of clove crept into her nose.

"How do you know?" he asked.

A memory crashed down on her. She and her mother in her grandmother's kitchen. Tiny Isadora, she couldn't have been more than three years old, held tight to her mother's hand staring up at the imposing woman who towered over her. The smell of clove permeated the air.

Her mother threw her shoulders back and said, "We're leaving. We aren't coming back."

Isadora remembered the scent getting stronger as her grandmother got angrier. "Don't bother coming back. You are no Blackwood."

Graham brought her back to the present. "How do you know it's a she?"

She shrugged. "I just do. I need some time to think."

"Wait. Look!" He pointed across the street and down the block. At the entrance of Bonaventure, the most famous cemetery, in Savannah, a crowd gathered. He pulled her across the street. "Is it a ghost walk?"

"Yes! Let's join up. We need to come up with a plan. This will buy us some time."

As casually as possible, the witch and the warlock sidled up to the small group of people gathered by the front gate. The guide, a portly young man dressed all in black with a matching fedora perched on his head, greeted them, "Hello there! Tickets?"

She opened her mouth but Graham had already produced tickets and handed them to the guide. "Here ya go! We are so excited." He winked at her, and her heart fluttered.

"You dressed up too! Love that," the guide said happily. He moved on to collect tickets from the others.

Despite the fact that they were in danger and her book was in danger and every witch she knew was in danger, she stifled a giggle.

"Everyone!" the guide boomed. The tour-goers gathered closer to him murmuring. An excited but anxious energy pulsed around them. Isadora supposed that a ghost walk on Halloween in Bonaventure was quite an adventure for the humans. "It is time. We shall now enter the realm of the dead. On this Samhain night, the veil between our world and the spirit world is lifted. Hang onto your hats people." The guide led them through the gates and into the haunted cemetery.

Lurking in the trees across the street was a witch with a vendetta.

"I'm not afraid of ghosts, but this place is spooky," Isadora whispered as they followed the group through a maze of crumbling tombstones surrounded by trees dripping with Spanish moss. It was the perfect setting for a ghost story.

"I'm not too macho to admit that I'm a little freaked out," he whispered back.

The guide stopped the tour in front of a statue of a dog. "Many visitors to Bonaventure say they've heard the Hell Hounds barking and growling. Some have even claimed to have felt the breath of the hounds. Needless to say, they didn't stick around." Everyone laughed, some quite hysterically.

Isadora surveyed the group as they moved to the next stop on the tour. The tourists, clearly enchanted and terrified, shuffled forward in their white socks, sneakers, and fanny packs.

The guide stopped briefly in front of a statue of the grim reaper. "This is a comforting image isn't it?" He chuckled, clearly loving every second of scaring the crap out of tourists. When they moved on again, she and Graham stayed behind. No one noticed their absence.

"We should get out of here," she said. "I think there's a maintenance entrance in the back."

"Should we go out front and try our luck?" He glanced over his shoulder at the angel of death. "Why would they put that here?" he murmured.

Isadora ignored him. "I think she's waiting for us there." She turned and started walking deeper into the cemetery.

Graham followed her with a groan. "I hope we make it out of here."

"Scared of ghosts?" she stepped over a stone.

Tripping over it, he stumbled. "No. I just like to be able to see where I'm going."

"Follow me." She led the way. While she too felt a little freaked out, she kept going, brushing moss out of the way. "Think of it this way: a ghost would be a very pleasant alternative to a Blackwood."

"That's true." He shivered.

Weaving their way through tombstones, they went deeper into the cemetery, the final resting place of so many. Nothing looked familiar and she started to suspect they might be lost. Tears filled her eyes as she thought about Susanna, her book, and the impending disaster. She had no idea what might happen if a Blackwood performed the spell, but she knew it wouldn't be good.

She stopped suddenly and Graham, peering into the darkness behind them, ran right into her. "What's wrong?" he asked.

"I have no idea where we are. None at all." Her voice flat with defeat.

"I thought you knew your way around." His voice tinged with irritation.

She rolled her eyes despite her tears. "I've never been here at night. Plus you aren't helping."

Graham turned in a slow circle while Isadora pulled her shawl closer around her. She wished she'd changed clothes.

A low growl filled the eerie silence.

"Did you hear that?"

"No." She said, but she had heard it. She froze, licking her lips as her mouth had gone dry. Another growl came out of the darkness right behind them. "Okay. I can't even pretend I didn't hear that."

"I realize there's nothing to be afraid of…" Graham left his thought hanging. His eyes wide behind his black-framed glasses.

Drawing in a shaky breath, she edged forward, Graham at her heel. The growl came again, closer this time. She whipped her head from side to side trying to get her bearings. "Shit." Panic and bile rose in her throat. "Am I going to be eaten by a ghost dog? I guess it won't matter so much about the book if that's the case."

"I'm sure it's fine." The tremble in his voice didn't sound convincing.

"Run for it?" She asked ready to bolt.

Before Graham could answer, a dense fog settled around them slowly at first and then all at once. He reached out and grabbed her hand. They both backed up until Isadora stumbled into a tombstone behind her. She clapped a hand over her mouth to stifle a scream. Neither spoke. They stared straight ahead into the fog, waiting. She thought she was about to come face to face with a long lost Blackwood, hungry for power.

Out of the mist, a figure moved toward them. Isadora shut her eyes and prayed to the goddess a silent but passionate prayer peppered with curse words before opening her eyes to slits. The fog parted and the figure became clear. A little girl with blonde hair and a white dress. A ghostly girl but a little girl, nonetheless.

Isadora let out the breath she'd been holding. Next to her, Graham relaxed.

"Don't be afraid," the girl said. "I called off the Hell Hounds. Though they really aren't all that scary."

Isadora opened her mouth to speak but squeaked instead. She cleared her throat and began again. "Thank you for that."

The girl smiled and peeked up at them through her pale eyelashes. "You're welcome. I'm Gracie Watkins."

She let her shoulders drop and relaxed. She smiled back at the girl. "I'm Isadora and this is Graham. How do you do?"

Gracie giggled. "It's Halloween. All Hallow's Eve. I've been teasing people in Johnson Square. Their faces turn white. It's so funny."

"Sounds like a good time." Graham found his voice.

"You look like you are going to a party." Gracie's head tilted to the side.

"Sort of. We're a bit lost though," Isadora said.

Gracie's smile faded. "There's someone looking for you."

A chill ran through her. "We were trying to sneak through the cemetery and out the back entrance to avoid that someone."

Gracie leaned in and whispered. "Do you know who it is?"

Isadora shook her head. "Not exactly."

Gracie glanced around before she spoke as though she could see through the fog. "It's not a good person. Follow me. I'll lead you out."

Graham spoke up. "Thank you very much." He smiled at the small child.

Gracie smiled back, a slow smile that started small and spread across her whole face. She waved them forward and they followed as she hovered just above the ground. The mist abated as the unlikely trio turned down a path they hadn't noticed before. Isadora glanced behind her, the path was clear but she doubted anyone could see them.

A gate waited for them at the end of the path.

Gracie turned back to face Isadora and Graham. "I'm afraid it's locked. I imagine you can take care of that though."

He stepped up to the gate and rattled the handle. Blue sparks shot out from his fingers followed by a click.

She knelt down eye-level with Gracie. "Thank you so much for the help."

Gracie put her cold hand on Isadora's face. It felt like the curling fingers of a winter morning. "You're welcome. I don't see many witches in here. Thank you for visiting." Pulling her hand back from her face, Gracie faded away with the mist. She waved at them both as they stepped through the gate and onto the street.

Isadora closed the gate and waved to Gracie but she was gone.

CHAPTER SIX

Susanna's house was dark. A single light illuminated the entryway. Unlike every other house on the street, not a single Halloween decoration adorned the white porch. Isadora peered through the stained glass door. "I guess she's not here."

"The book might be though," Graham said squinting inside.

The only thing that made the situation better was knowing that Graham, the kind professor she'd only just met but known for months, was just how she'd imagined him. He was supportive, a little shy, and easy to talk to.

She reached in the neckline of her dress and pulled one of her amulets off. "Here," she said as she gently placed it around Graham's neck whispering a spell. "You stay here. I'm going inside. If she comes home or anything happens, just hold the amulet in your hands and my amulet will glow. Okay?" She looked at her hands, surprised that they rested on Graham's shoulders.

"Okay." His gaze softened and for a moment she thought he might kiss her. Instead, he tucked a loose curl behind her ear. "Be safe. I'll be right here."

Isadora reached for the doorknob.

"Hang on." Graham positioned his hand on the doorknob and held it there. She heard a click as it unlocked. "I disabled the security system too."

She handed him her clutch and her shawl. "You should have been a thief and not a professor," she said as she slipped inside.

Familiar with the layout, Isadora moved slowly through the dark house and found herself in the kitchen at the back. A stack of bills sat on the granite counter. "Final notice, final notice, final notice," Isadora read. "There are so many of them. I thought she was loaded."

She glanced around the kitchen looking for anything out of place and noticed the empty China cabinet. "The serving set," she said remembering that fine china and silver had once called the antique cabinet home.

She put the bills back on the counter and returned to her search. "If I were an important secret history, where would I be?" She thought as she climbed the stairs.

Upstairs, she peeped into each immaculate room until she reached the last door.

The room at the end appeared to be Susanna's. A pair of red stilettos which Isadora recognized had been kicked off and left in the floor. She gazed around the room. Approaching the bed, she swept her hand across the ornately flowered duvet on the four-poster bed and eyed the dresses discarded there. Each one appeared more expensive than any Isadora owned. "Why would she-?" she thought with a frown. She rubbed the silk of one dress between her fingers.

A light bulb went off over her head. "The benefit! She's at the benefit. Of course!"

A thought crossed her mind. She silently approached the dresser where an ornate jewelry box sat. The only thing inside was a pair of small diamond studs. "Wow. It's all gone," she murmured.

She crept back toward the stairs. The front door creaked open alarming Isadora. She froze at the top of the stairs just out of sight.

"She won't be home for hours," giggled a teenage girl. Isadora recognized the young brunette as Susanna's daughter, a college student named Allison. Dressed as a "sexy witch," Allison staggered in her heels into a boy of similar age who hadn't bothered with a costume. "Let's go upstairs." This was followed by giggling, and the thump of people running up stairs.

"Shit," Isadora whispered. She backed into Susanna's room and pushed the door until it was only slightly ajar. She would just wait until they'd gone into a bedroom and then make her escape.

"Come in here," the teenager said leading the way right to Susanna's bedroom door.

"Shit shit shit," she mouthed. She whirled around to look for a way out and spied the window. She tiptoed across the plush white rug to the window and raised it slowly wincing every time it creaked. She shimmied through the window and ducked out of sight just as the bedroom light flickered on.

Isadora crawled along the roof slowly and silently until she was away from Susanna's windows and stood up. "Okay," she whispered. She took off her heels. "I can't wear heels on the roof. This whole outfit was a bad choice for climbing."

"Pssst. PSSSSSSSST" came a noise from below.

Startled, she nearly lost her balance. "Is that you?" she called softly. She regained her footing and held her heels in one hand.

"Yes." A voice answered in a whisper-yell. "I'm around the side. I heard you come out the window."

She crept along the roof edge. Luckily, latticework held up climbing roses and when she tested it, it seemed sturdy enough to hold her up. "I'm coming down." She tossed her shoes off the roof and hiked up her skirt. Getting onto the latticework was a little harder than she'd expected. When she started the climb down, she realized the roses had thorns. "Ouch. Ouch. Oh my god. Ow," she complained as she climbed down scratching her arms and legs along the way.

The lattice ended a few feet above the ground.

"Need a hand?" Graham asked.

Isadora jumped and tumbled into the grass. "I don't need to be caught," she said, out of breath.

Graham rolled his eyes. "Fine. Let me help you up at least."

She let him pull her up and hold her for a moment before she stepped away. "Well, she's not here. But her kid is."

Graham frowned. "Where could she be?"

She leaned on Graham while she slipped her heels back on. "Big masquerade ball, of course." She took her shawl from Graham and pulled it around her shoulders.

"Which ball?"

"The annual Halloween ball put on by the historical society. I hate those things." She sighed. "Come on." They slipped through the hedge and back onto the sidewalk.

"You've got hedge in your hair," Graham said pulling out a twig. She turned to face him. "And dirt on your face." He used his thumb to wipe a smudge of dirt from the tip of her nose.

"Thanks." She smoothed down her skirt and noticed a rip at the hem. "Thanks also for not looking up my dress while I gracefully climbed down the side of a house."

He laughed as a blush crept up his neck and colored his cheeks red.

"Ha." Limping slightly, she set off again. "We should have gotten a taxi for this wild-goose chase."

"Where is this big event?" He asked slowing his pace to match hers.

"Putnam House. I guess Susanna took the book?"

"How do we know she hasn't turned it over already?"

"We don't," Isadora said looking both ways before crossing the street.

CHAPTER SEVEN

Putnam House, an antebellum mansion in the historic district, brimmed with energy. "Ugh. Another thing we don't have tickets for." Isadora groaned.

"Coming up with tickets happens to be my specialty." Graham held up a pair of tickets. "That and picking locks."

"Wow. I'm impressed." She snatched her ticket out of his hand and threw her shoulders back as they approached the house.

She led the way up the stone stairs lined with luminaries, handed her invitation to the doorman and stepped into the hundred and fifty year old mansion. Though she'd been to Putnam House several times, the ballroom - all dressed in white - took her breath away as the enormous crystal chandeliers bounced light onto the revelers, the Savannah elite.

A woman in a slinky black dress sauntered by giving Isadora a look. "What was that? Do you think she knows something?"

"Um." Graham touched her arm lightly. "I think she may be looking at the leaves in your hair."

She felt around her head and pulled crunchy brown leaves out of her hair. "I guess I can say I'm going as a rose gardener."

"Except no one has that sort of costume on. Anyway, what's the plan?" He whispered in her ear, which made her shiver.

"I think we should just walk around first and see if we can find Susanna. Maybe...nothing has happened yet." Isadora grabbed a champagne flute as a waiter in a tuxedo with tails went by. "Come on."

He followed her around the ballroom. "Act like we're having fun," she ordered and then threw her head back and laughed. Graham laughed too.

She sidled by ball gowned women and tuxedoed men whirling around the room to the sounds of a jazz band as Graham trailed along behind. The ball, in full swing, had a wild almost frantic energy not unlike a party thrown by Jay Gatsby.

"Do you think the energy in here feels...off?" She turned to ask Graham only he wasn't there. "Graham?" She spun around looking for him even climbing on a chair to see over the crowd. Neither Graham, nor Susanna, were anywhere to be found.

"I gotta get out of here," she pushed her way out of the ballroom. When she ran into someone she actually knew. "I'm so sorry Dr. Levin!"

"Pardon?" Dr. Levin turned to face her.

She gasped. "Are you okay? You don't look well..." She recognized his black eyes were the result of dark magic.

"Pardon?" he asked again with a vacant expression.

She backed away slowly. Dr. Levin wasn't the only one. The band played with abandon, the music grew wild and frantic. The room suddenly erupted into chaos.

"Oh no," Isadora breathed. She shoved past the entranced revelers and out of the main hall grateful that she knew her way around Putnam Hall. She crept into one of the many parlors and shut the doors behind her.

"If I were a dark witch, where would I be?" she paced the room biting her nails. "Alright Isadora. Get it together." She pulled the amulet out from her dress. It glowed so hard it pulsed.

She squeezed the amulet tight in her hand, the wild music a distant memory and breathed deeply. She cleared her mind and entered into the stillness. You don't spend that much time on a book and not leave pieces of your soul in it. Something pulled her, tugging her. The book? Going deeper, she felt for the book in the house. "It's here," she thought. "Someplace dark and deep."

"Here goes nothing." Isadora headed toward the cellar.

CHAPTER EIGHT

The wine cellar in Putnam House stretched the length of the house and had various chambers. Isadora crept from room to room passing a few possessed partiers as she went. She attempted to look like she belonged as she made her way to the kitchen in the back of the house.

When she arrived, it was empty and dark. The entrance to the wine cellar was situated at the far end of the kitchen. She glanced around behind her once before descending the narrow staircase with no idea what might lie in wait for her. An angry relative, perhaps? A witch with vengeance on the brain?

Isadora held tight to the railing and stopped every few steps to listen. The noise from upstairs, which seemed to have hit fever pitch, made it difficult to hear anything but jazz music and the roar of the crowd. Still, she listened. Her tarot deck, tucked in the clutch she carried under her arm, called to her but there was no time.

Once at the bottom, she stopped and closed her eyes. "Here goes nothing," she whispered as she crept deeper into the cellar. The only light came from a chamber in the distance. She tiptoed, filled with apprehension, her breathing shallow.

Once again, she stopped and strained her ears but heard nothing. She grounded herself on the earth floor and let the magic fill her up. She sensed she would need it momentarily. A familiar tingling lifted up through her ankles, legs, torso, and down her arms until her fingertips shot out a spray of pinkish sparks. Centered, she strode ahead into the lit cellar.

Graham and Susanna hung suspended in the air. Both appeared asleep. Susanna's evening dress hung limply around her. Her pale silk scarf had fallen to the floor. Antique brass candelabras filled with drippy candles bounced their flickering light around the wine cellar, empty of wine.

Isadora tore her gaze away from Graham to the witch sitting down at the far end of the room.

"Hello cousin."

"Cousin?" Isadora asked, her voice cold.

The young witch, dressed all in black with long black hair cascading over her shoulders gave a chilly smile. "Our mothers were sisters." She laughed. "How is my aunt?"

"Dead," Isadora replied.

"So sorry to hear it." The young witch walked toward Isadora, her hips swaying with every step.

"I'm sure you are." She glared at the stranger. "I'm afraid I don't know your name." The book lay open on a table in front of her long-lost relative along with the spell, all four pages.

"Jonquil." She smirked.

"One of my favorite flowers." Isadora took a few steps forward. She glanced at Graham and noticed he still clutched the glowing amulet in his right hand.

The two witches stared at one another.

"Forgive me. My mother didn't tell me much about the family. Who was your mother?"

"Miranda. The middle child."

"I haven't seen any family since I was small." Isadora shrugged.

"I know. In that case, don't you think the family histories belong with...the family?" Jonquil stared right at Isadora her eyes flashing.

"I've just as much a right to them as you." Isadora stared back.

Jonquil sneered. "Your mother abandoned the family and left our traditions behind."

"Maybe it's time for new traditions."

Jonquil turned on her heel and went back to the table stabbing her finger at the spell. "How did you get this?"

"My mother took it. She tried to destroy it."

"It doesn't belong to you." Jonquil shook her head. "It belongs to the real Blackwoods."

She'd placed binding spells on the book and the spell. She had a feeling she was about to find out how well they worked. She smiled at her cousin but behind her smile, the wheels in her mind turned.

"Answer me this," Isadora began. "What did you need with my boss?"

Jonquil laughed. "It worked beautifully really. I found you and the library some weeks ago but couldn't get inside. Your charms work. You should be proud. So I set my sights on Susanna. I offered her money if she could get into the vault. At first she didn't believe that there was a vault. I knew about it because I saw it in my runes. I finally convinced her and we assumed that one day you'd leave the vault unprotected. And today was that day. Sooner than I expected and on Samhain. How perfect."

Isadora's heart sank as Jonquil spoke. She'd known it was her fault but hearing it made it worse. Still, she put on the strongest face she could muster, determined not to let her dear cousin know.

A spark of an idea lit up her mind. An old spell. She needed more time to remember. "What do you need with all of those poor people upstairs?"

Jonquil threw her head back and laughed. Isadora took the opportunity to open her clutch and pull out a small, sharp knife.

"I need their souls, of course. This spell is about to make me the most powerful witch in the country and maybe the world."

"Won't someone try to stop you?"

"No one knows where I am." Jonquil stepped around from behind the table. "By the time they find out, it'll be too late."

"Your branch of the Blackwoods sounds very special." Isadora, her hands clasped behind her back, used the knife to cut into her palm.

Jonquil ignored her. "I want you to watch. Watch how powerful I can be and how powerful this spell is. You have no right to it."

"That's true," Isadora nodded. "My mother chose the light and so have I."

Scoffing, Jonquil closed her eyes and began to chant. She too drew a knife and used it to cut into her palm.

She kept her eyes on Jonquil and brought her bleeding hand in front of her. She muttered an old Latin incantation, her mother's powerful light spell and hoped she remembered it correctly. Again and again she repeated the spell each time willing it into existence.

Jonquil held her hand up and watched the blood drip down onto the cobblestones. She continued her spell. A glow began to fill up the room.

Isadora kept her eyes on Jonquil and chanted louder. Jonquil noticed and narrowed her eyes at her cousin. The room filled up with magic like a balloon ready to burst. Isadora needed more. She stepped over to Graham and grabbed his hand. He didn't wake but his energy poured into her. She chanted with a new purpose. Jonquil, eyes closed, lifted slightly off the ground, continued her spell. Louder and louder Isadora shouted. Pressure built in the room like a thunderstorm about to erupt. Isadora concentrated all of her efforts on her spell.

A loud bang threw Isadora back into the wall. She hit her head and darkness overcame her.

Moments later, she woke feeling like she'd been hit by a truck. With a groan, Isadora forced her eyes open and blinked. Her vision came into focus and she gasped when she saw Jonquil standing behind a now awake Graham holding a dagger to his neck.

Jonquil's eyes were black "Say goodbye to Dr. Hart."

Isadora looked into Graham's eyes, which were two pools of calm. With his eyes, he encouraged her. He believed in her. She held out her hand once more. As a drop of deep red blood dropped from her red-streaked palm, she shouted the chant one last time, never breaking eye contact with Graham. She would not be responsible for his death. Another loud bang sent Jonquil flying. The knife clattered on the cobblestones and Graham darted forward to Isadora. "Let's finish this."

Jonquil stood staggering but not ready to give up.

At the same time, they sent a shower of sparks that lit up the room like fireworks. They hit Jonquil and knocked her back to the ground. Isadora dashed forward and gathered the spell and the book up in her arms backing away from Jonquil who lay twitching on the ground.

"Will she be all right?" she asked Graham.

"Yes. Unfortunately." He shot sparks out his fingertips again hitting Jonquil. "At least now she won't remember anything. At all."

Isadora sighed and slumped against the wall. She put the book down next to her feet and held up the spell. Putting her hand out, her clutch, which had flown against the wall, rose up and drifted back into her hand. She opened it and pulled out a book of matches. She struck a match and held it to the spell. Nothing happened.

"Hey. You're bleeding." Graham said and turned her hands over to hold them in his hands.

"Oh." She stared at the red streaking her hands.

Graham plucked Susanna's scarf off the dusty ground and used it to wrap Isadora's hands. "There's powerful magic protecting that spell. You placed it there didn't you?"

She nodded. "What should we do?"

"I don't know," Graham said but he smiled and pulled her toward him. "We can figure it out together."

CHAPTER NINE

Cleaning up Jonquil's mess took hours. Jonquil herself was dazed and didn't seem to have a clue who she was or where she was. Graham said that would pass eventually but he didn't know how long it would take. Isadora wiped the blood off of her and put her into a cab bound for Atlanta paying the cabbie generously to take her amnesiac cousin away. But not before she rifled through her purse and found an envelope filled with money.

They undid the spell on the crowd and slipped away as the partygoers woke up from their trance confused and disoriented. As for Susanna, Isadora performed a gentle memory-wiping spell and took her home. Her daughter came running when she heard them come in.

"What's wrong with mom?" she asked, looking a bit disheveled.

"A little too much fun." Graham beamed at her as they pulled Susanna up the stairs.

"What happened?" Susanna asked sleepily as Isadora helped her into bed still wearing her ball gown. Isadora pulled the envelope out of her clutch and slipped it into Isadora's bag.

"The benefit was a huge success," she assured her boss as she tucked the duvet around her.

"Good." Susanna smiled and dropped into a deep sleep.

Once outside, Isadora yawned. "Let's go home."

"Home?" Graham asked.

"My home. Just come on."

Graham grabbed Isadora's hand. "Wait," he said softly, his voice warm.

"What?" she asked suddenly aware of her ripped dress, arms streaked with blood and her hand wrapped in silk.

"This night...was insane and incredible." Graham took her other hand in his.

"It was," she agreed. "Thank you for helping me."

"It was my pleasure. And quite an adventure."

"I assume you want to see the book?"

"Only if you want to share it." He gathered her up in his arms, the book tucked between them.

Though Isadora felt a bit silly, she gazed into his brown eyes and got swept away.

He plucked a leaf out of her hair and then he kissed her.

A tingling sensation took over her body reaching all the way from the tips of her ears to the ends of her toes. Though the street was quiet, she heard a symphony surrounding them and felt the ground disappear beneath her feet.

When Isadora opened her eyes finally, she and Graham stood on the sidewalk in front of her house.

"Oh!" Her eyes wide in surprise. "I didn't even feel that."

"It's my specialty." Graham laughed.

Suddenly shy, she looked up at Graham through her eyelashes. "Do you want to come inside?"

Graham kissed her again. "I thought you'd never ask."

Author Links

https://twitter.com/aesnowauthor
https://www.facebook.com/aesnowauthor?ref=hl
https://aesnowauthor.wordpress.com/

Heart of a Hunter
By
Andra Shine

DEDICATION

The following is dedicated to my nana Merle Burns, and my partner Yani Shine for supporting my dream of becoming an author.

CHAPTER ONE

Ashley painted her lips as red as Snow White's poisoned apple. She scrabbled through the makeup on her messy antique dresser for the darkest of her eyeliners. She applied kohl to craft expert cat's eyes. Witchcraft worked too, but Ashley preferred the hands on approach. She scrutinized her emerald green eyes from several angles. Loneliness dwelt within.

A perfectly ordinary car accident, non-magical but cruel, orphaned Ashley at three years old, and forced her to rattle around in the family's enormous antebellum mansion, with only two aged aunts for company. She tried to make friends, but they became frightened when she used her powers around them. So she stopped trying.

Ashley blinked back tears. Reluctant to ruin her makeup she conquered dark feelings with a bright red smile. The image in the mirror was beautiful and determined. Loneliness wouldn't last a lifetime.

Footsteps echoed on the spiral staircase. Ashley's mischievous grin spread. She flicked her wrist and cast a glamor spell that changed her bedcovers from maroon to blue silk brocade. Another and the boudoir's deep burgundy wallpaper transformed, to a matching blue with ornate black filigree.

She was ready to create an up-do for her long onyx locks when her aunt Esmeralda bustled through the doorway. The elderly lady stopped and stared at the walls with eyes barely visible behind a basketful of laundry.

"Everyday a different color, I get dizzy when you change it."

"I know. Dizzy suits you."

"Can I get some help with this?" The overburdened aunt attempted to offload the laundry.

"I'm busy." Ashley's amused reflection eyed her. She shouldn't tease her aunt, but was unable to help herself. Besides, Esme adored annoying her.

"Come on, the clothes won't magic themselves away."

"Yes they will. That's the point of magic."

"All right, then. I suppose I can still do it." She dropped the basket and blinked, staring into the distance. "If I can just remember the phrase…"

She muttered something incomprehensible and waved her left arm anti-clockwise over the laundry basket. The clothes shot up, hit the ceiling and descended in a swirling tornado.

Ashley raised an immaculate eyebrow and eyeballed her aunt.

"Maybe that's not the phrase." Esmeralda failed to hide an unapologetic grin. "Agatha makes it look easy." She paused, and then rounded on her niece, her focus keen.

"Hang on, where are you going all dolled up?"

Ashley rolled her heavily made-up eyes. "Just the coven meeting."

"I may be old—"

"Ancient more like."

"—but I'm not that doddery."-

"Yes, you are."

"The coven meets Halloween. I forget a lot of things but I know Halloween is tomorrow." She gave Ashley the stink eye in the mirror.

Ashley wished her aunt wouldn't meddle. "Fine. I'm resolved to enslave a minister at midnight in the town square, using only the incredible witchy powers of my sexuality," she smirked.

"Well, you better get a wriggle on, it's nearly ten o'clock. Job like that might take a while, and with your personality, you're going to need all the time you can get."

Ashley muttered a spell and a pair of knickers that had landed on the dresser flew through the air in a loop-de-loop and fell on her aunt's head.

"Well, it's nice to see you'll have no trouble whipping your knickers off. Getting in a bit of practice I see." The old lady laughed. She removed the offending article and plopped herself on the luxurious bed amidst the clothes, rubbing at her knuckles.

Ashley chose her expensive balm, knelt in front of her archaic aunt and rubbed it into her finger joints.

Agatha, an even more elderly aunt, peeked through the doorway. "Practice at what?"

Esmeralda grinned at her sister. "Oh look, Agatha's turned up."

"With a nose that long she can't help but smell gossip," Ashley mumbled.

"Go on. Spill."

"Miss Haughty is going to enslave a minister."

Ashley thrust the balm at her aunt with a dirty look, clambered up and resumed preening.

"Ah." Agatha nodded. "That would be your sexual enslavement would it?" She cleared a spot and sat next to her sister on the bed.

"Forget it!" yelled Ashley. "You two ruin everything!" She glared at her aunts in the mirror till it cracked.

The two old ladies laughed so hard they were almost in tears.

"Lucky the wind didn't change." Agatha clutched her chest. "Honestly, the look on your face, I'm surprised I didn't wee."

"We're all surprised you didn't wee." Ashley glared at her and provoked another giggling fit.

She sighed at her uncontrollable aunts, fixed the mirror with a mumble and yanked a brush through her hair.

"Oh, don't be like that." Esmeralda poked her. "Look, upsetting a minister with sex is like shooting fish in a barrel. I'd done six by the time I was a hundred, and they didn't all try to burn me at the stake after. I'll tell you that much for free. It's old-fashioned anyway. Challenge yourself and flirt with a warlock. Or a vampire."

"A vampire!" Agatha fainted gracefully on the bed, but rather ruined the effect when she looked to see if anyone was impressed with her dramatic gesture. Ashley snorted and continued to brush her hair.

"It's on trend to seduce a vampire," Esmeralda said. "They're very sexy." She bared her teeth in the mirror, and mocked sexy poses. Ashley whirled around and waved her hairbrush at them.

"Would you two shut up? I've had just about enough of ancient, pale creatures with bad teeth and creepy talons without adding vampires to the mix. You two are quite sufficient thank you very much."

Agatha gave up her faint and reached out, Esmeralda pulled her up.

"Did I hear that right, Ez? Did she say thank you? Is Miss Haughty finally learning her manners?"

"It wasn't the right sort of thank you."

Ashley was not amused. Honestly, she couldn't do a thing without them turning it into a full-scale production. She shook her hair out, and abandoned styling it in favor of escape. With one last eye-roll at her ridiculous relatives she flounced out of the room, flicking her hair melodramatically. Then, less dramatically, had to flounce right back in again to grab her coat.

The aunts sat on the bed like a pair of sweetly smiling bookends.

"I know that look you two. You're up to something."

They exchanged blank looks, a perfect picture of innocence, albeit a rather wrinkled one. As if the picture had been scrunched up and shoved into a pocket.

Ashley watched them with suspicion; she pointed an accusing finger.

"Don't. I don't know what you're going to do, but whatever it is, just don't." She didn't trust them not to meddle in her life in extreme and embarrassing ways. Ashley backed slowly out of the door a suspicious eyebrow raised at them.

To their credit, the aunts waited until she was well out of earshot before they burst out laughing again.

* * * *

"I've a good mind to put a spell on that one, show her the trouble with throwing your sex magic around," Esmeralda declared.

"Go on, then." Agatha's mischievous eyes lit up. "I dare you. But do it right. Make her fall in love. That'll put a cat amongst the pigeons."

"You know I can't resist a good dare." A wicked smile broke out over Esmeralda's crinkly face, and for a moment she was more wrinkle than witch. She stood unsteadily, waved her hands in the air, more for balance than spell work. Then she turned around a few times, shouted a few garbled incantations then fell on the bed and started again. She rounded off the bizarre process with a chant, "*Anusin, anusin, atetin, atetin, atelin.*"

Esmeralda beamed at her sister. Agatha's expression stole her certainty and the smile faded.

"What? Wasn't that right?" Esmeralda asked.

"Well, not the first bit obviously, that was ridiculous. But the end was disastrous."

"I thought the end was good."

"You said *atelin*!"

"Surely not," Esmeralda said, she frowned and studied the ceiling as if she would find her memory hidden in the chandelier.

"I heard it, *atelin*. Right at the end, like you meant it."

Esmeralda sucked her breath through her teeth. "Well, true love then."

"Yep."

"Definitely overcooked it."

"No doubt about that."

"Not just any old love spell."

"No."

"Your actual true love spell."

"Yes."

"Not much I can do about that."

"No."

"You think she'll be cross?"

"What? That she's got around six hundred years on this earth and you've gone and called her true love to her when she's only 23?"

"Yeah, that."

"Shouldn't think so. She'll be in love won't she? People in love are idiots. She probably won't notice anything we do from here on in."

"Course not. It'll be fine."

"She'll fall head over heels."

"With that one, it'll be more like ass over tit."

Then the pair fell about on the bed cackling again.

* * * *

Ashley took her fabulous hair and makeup out for a drive. The dark Savannah roads stole silently through murky foliage, which bound a town besieged by encroaching forest. Ashley craved nightclubs and excitement. As she drove away from Mockingbird Lane, anticipation goaded her. Maybe tonight she'd finally meet someone. Not a vampire or a warlock. All the magical men she'd met were arrogant and wanted to control her. The last thing she needed was someone else telling her what to do.

Ashley cast a camouflage spell on her red Mustang. Now the law would ignore her. She floored the accelerator and blasted the radio. Fully in her element, she sang along, pitch perfect, to The Pixies 'Here Comes Your Man'.

The trees on either side of the road clawed at one another to form an ominous tunnel. The gloomy green canopy was lit by meager streetlights. The distorted shadows of the trees writhed on her windshield.

An aggressive driver, Ashley manipulated the manual gearshift and veered around the corner like a pro. The trees bore down on her as she raced towards town.

She registered movement in her side mirror. A large dark shape burst through the line of trees and bolted from the right-hand side of the road. The dim figure collided with the hood of the Mustang.

"Whoa!" Ashley swerved, but the crash was unavoidable. The body left dents as it rolled, came to a halt at the base of the windshield and obstructed the view. She peered round it and pumped the brakes, her reactions swift.

All thoughts of revelry forgotten, Ashley slowed and pulled over; careful not to slam on the brakes so the poor wretch wouldn't tumble onto the road.

Fear stabbed at her gut as she remembered another accident. Fear grew as she sprang out of the car in her rush to help. She began the first aid checks her healing tutor taught her. The bundle of limbs was breathing. He was also very naked.

Unsure if her wild heart rate was triggered by fear or excitement, his stillness pierced her core. Dark crimson splattered the Mustang's candy-apple hood. Blood. She searched for its source.

Black hair fell over his face. Ashley repositioned herself to find an angle where the streetlights would allow her to see without moving him. She pulled back his hair to reveal a perfect face, despite the thick layer of blood that ran from chin to chest. She wiped the red lips to reveal unmarred skin beneath. He looked to be in his early thirties. His mouth hung open, which exposed a clear airway. The blood, slick on his canines, was not enough to indicate internal injuries. Where was the blood coming from?

She opened his eyes with delicate fingers and attempted to discern dilation. The eyes were dark, but the light was insufficient for proper observation. She muttered a luminosity spell. The end of her finger shone. She pointed it at his eyes, no dilation, but he couldn't follow the glow while unconscious. With a shake of her finger the light dimmed.

To determine whether he could be shifted, Ashley ran her hands gently over his neck, no obvious break. Careful not to jolt it, she worked a protection spell. Once it was active she lifted his head. No head injury evident.

A shoulder graze was not enough to explain the blood on the hood of the car. No deep lesions on his upper torso, only small scratches and cuts. Though his limbs were twisted awkwardly, she detected no noticeable broken bones.

Gingerly, Ashley pushed on his flat stomach to exclude internal injuries, at last grateful for the years of lessons with healers her aunts had inflicted upon her. The acutely defined abdominal muscles were clear, except from scrapes, possibly caused by the collision with her car. He was in bad shape for a guy in such great shape.

Physically he appeared fine. He was lean, sinewy, and all muscle. His pectorals felt firm, but his thick dark chest hair was matted with blood. This explained the red stains smeared on her windshield, but she could detect no sign of its origin. He was fit and strong. His physique was clearly that of an athlete, a horribly battered athlete.

Tenacious, Ashley continued. She noticed well-formed glutes, but kept her mind on the examination. It was not easy. He was a fine specimen. There were minor cuts and abrasions on the man's strong legs, but his feet and hands wore the worst of it. They looked like he'd run barefoot for miles, and dragged his hands the whole way.

Ashley was searching for her phone to call an ambulance, when a shadow appeared. On the high ridgeline to her right, the streetlight formed an aura behind a tall man. His silhouette strained to touch her. A prickle of fear tickled her neck when she realized he stood in the same place the broken body on her hood had come from.

She had good night vision, but with the halo of light behind the man, his profile was all she could distinguish. Ashley enacted the luminosity spell again, but before completion, the silhouette raised a crossbow. She shook out the light.

"Run!" The bowman yelled.

Was the accident victim the hunter's prey? They were out in the open. There was no help for miles.

He raised the crossbow. "I will shoot!"

She rushed through a lighter-than-air spell, lifted the gory body from the hood and dashed to take cover behind the car. Careful not to harm him, she opened the back door and placed the body in the back seat. Through the interior of the car she peered into the dark, but couldn't make out the huntsman.

Ashley cowered behind the front passenger door to avoid exposure to his arrows then clambered in and over the seat. A deep breath helped her remain calm as she slid under the dashboard. She worked fast, unable to see the hunter from her defensive position.

It was faster to use magic to adjust the seat fully down. There she lay flattened against the chair, still holding the steering wheel with one hand. The other gripped the gearshift, feet on the pedals. The back window smashed, pierced by an arrow. Shaken into panic, Ashley's essence deserted her. She astral travelled over the car, and discovered this was the vantage point she needed to rescue herself and the hunted man. Now detached, the panic subsided and Ashley was able to instruct her body by remote. She let her empty vessel drive while her spirit navigated from above.

Unfortunately, that didn't permit enough concentration to identify the hunter. Not with her foot stamped hard on the accelerator, as she rounded corners at a hundred miles an hour. Her overhead perspective turned the drive into a video game, strange and surreal.

Enough bends amassed between her and the pursuer for Ashley to relax. She adjusted her seat and jumped back into her body. There was a quick jerk as the perspective changed and nausea momentarily overwhelmed her. Now that she was embodied, the wind from the broken window whipped her face and tangled her hair. She muttered the same repair spell she'd used on her mirror and the shards of glass flew back to their original position, the glass was now intact.

The grisly victim howled in pain. She watched him through the rearview mirror as he panicked and tore at the seats. In a blind frenzy he caught a fistful of Ashley's hair and wrenched her head back. Pain blossomed and spread over her scalp, she screamed with agony and rage, her attention divided between the road and the rear-view. He didn't let go.

"Get off!" She bashed her fist against his hand. The action was ineffective.

"I'm taking you to hospital," she yelled.

"No!" he screamed, "He'll find me!" He yanked on her hair.

Ashley forced out a sedative spell. Too angry to concentrate she overdid it. His body flopped, as limp as if he'd been given a large dose of morphine.

"No good deed goes unpunished." She said, and smoothed her hair. She scowled at him in the mirror. He looked vulnerable and harmless.

"Well, aren't you just a typical naked man, all action then straight to sleep."

Ashley had suffered through more excitement than she needed. She was tempted to dump him on the road and let some other kind fool sort it out. But she wouldn't risk the hospital. The man in the dark did try to kill him. She wished she were less of a sucker for a helpless victim. This one was a problem.

It was miles down the road before she fully relaxed again. She wouldn't return the way she'd come; afraid the hunter had set a trap. Instead she slowed to the speed limit, turned off the main road and travelled home the long way round.

Her watchful mansion lay in wait, like a hungry guard dog. Its broody exterior eased only by the aunts' bedroom lights, which burned in the attic level like yellow eyes. Though too far away to hear anything below the second story, Ashley didn't want to risk her aunts' attention. They would have a lot to say about her naked guest, and none of it would entertain her as much as it did them.

She shut off the engine and the headlights and let the Mustang coast into the garage.

Ashley used an automaton enchantment so she didn't have to touch the battered figure; he rose awkward and unconscious from the car. Underneath him the backseat was gross; the bloody leather would need a proper valet clean. She ignored it, cleaning was not her area of expertise.

He shuffled ahead of her like a zombie. The magical house sensed an interloper and opposed his entry. The stairs and furniture conspired to halt his progress; they defended their territory and attempted to ambush the gruesome puppet.

"Cut it out." Ashley warned her overprotective home. She controlled her burden like an expert, and made him navigate the hostile terrain to arrive in the relative safety of her room. There she allowed him to collapse on her bed. His scrapes and cuts smeared red blood on the blue silk.

Swiftly she collected her medicine kit from the closet, placed it on the bed, and unfastened its complicated locking mechanism. She mixed herbal paste in a wooden bowl and applied it to the man's wounds. Ashley whispered incantations as she worked to ensure rapid healing. His inhalations were shorter and shallower than she expected from an adult male at rest. She discovered his heart rate was rapid when she checked his pulse. There was nothing in the kit for that, so she left to collect her aunt Agatha's, more comprehensive supplies in the conservatory.

When she got back he was healed.

"That's way too fast." His pulse was still shallow and rapid. He regained consciousness while she held his wrist. He moaned and flailed around, and she let go, wary of his reaction. His violence increased, he appeared unaware of his actions. Off the bed he staggered towards Ashley, she leapt out of range and repeated the calming incantation.

The incomplete spell fizzled when he lunged and grabbed her upper arm. She yelped as he jerked her towards him. She tried to wrench herself free, but his grip was strong. He reacted like a beast and Ashley wondered if he'd suffered brain damage in the accident. He was so close she could smell his musky animal scent. He put his face close to hers, and she thought he sniffed her neck. She dug her nails into his bulging forearm, and tore the skin until he was compelled to let go.

"Just calm down, I don't want to hurt you."

He relaxed his grip. She turned to face him, and pushed against his hairy chest to force him back on the bed.

There was no resistance, but she could tell his strength was hidden under the surface. Despite his weakened state, he shouldn't have been so easy to subdue. With his coiled muscles taut, she was glad he held back, for now.

Her eyes ran over his gorgeous body, tense and waiting. She tried to calm herself, but couldn't stop her heart beating fast, and a tingle arose between her legs, despite his rough treatment. The betrayal of her own body angered her further.

"Who are you?" he asked.

"I'm Ashley; I picked your broken carcass off my windscreen and brought you home to heal you. You've attacked me twice and sniffed me! Who the hell are you?" Her jaw and fists were clenched.

"I'm Orion," he growled. He looked up at her with soulful brown eyes. Ashley ignored them.

"Why was that man shooting at you?"

"I didn't stop to ask." He avoided her gaze to examine himself. Where cuts and bruises had been, he flaunted perfect skin. There was a smear of blood on his shoulder, an arrow graze perhaps. Around his mouth, leftover blood congealed. He wiped it on his arm, casually licked it and smiled at the taste. Ashley flinched, revolted. She handed him a wet towel. Orion shrugged but accepted it.

"Who are you, little one?" Unclothed, he stared at her with no apparent embarrassment.

Indignant Ashley wanted to slap him. "Don't condescend to me. I'm Ashley Evergreen. The woman that just saved your ass." She watched, fascinated and repulsed, as he wiped away the mysterious blood.

He leered at her and she narrowed her eyes. To surrender immediately wasn't respectable, but respectable was for normal people. Anyway, she had to admit, he was hot. He knew it too. Ashley cursed herself for being so shallow and stupid and tried to cover with snarky comments. "I hope you're comfortable. That's my bed you've ruined."

Orion sneered at the surroundings and flicked the diaphanous curtains on her four-poster bed. "Certainly like your creature comforts, don't you?"

Ashley straightened the curtain. "If I'd known you were coming, I would have prepared a blanket on the floor."

"I've had worse." He regarded her with intense dark eyes and picked up a book lying on the bed. 'The Physics of Musical Acoustics,' am I supposed to be impressed?"

"By a book?"

"I'm not a big reader."

"Clearly."

"You smell good."

"It's Obsession."

"Not the chemicals." He propped himself up on his elbows, his torso tightened. Ashley held her breath, unable to concentrate on anything save his sculpted stomach. The line of hair from his chest dared her to follow its descent south. Furious at her weakness she forced herself to look at his face.

"I mean the scent below. You smell like a woman. Come here." Orion's brazen grin demanded no dissent.

The strange animalistic attraction to him dizzied and infuriated her. She advanced, confused and appalled. He reached for her, she thought to caress her, but instead he hauled her to him, her feet lifted off the ground.

His strength, especially after the accident, was inexplicable. He dragged her body over his and pushed her face down on the bed. With his other hand he struggled to pull her jeans down from behind.

"Hey!" Having dealt with her share of unruly creeps she slapped his hand away and struggled to get up. "Is that any way to treat a girl?" She wasn't so much shocked as enraged. If he thought he could paw a witch and win he had a painful lesson to learn.

The bed sank where he kneeled to position himself behind her, and she fought against him, all desire for him vanished.

"You're my bitch," Orion growled.

"Hell, no!" she shouted. The red rage rose and she resisted with all her strength. She kicked behind her and her boot connected with his balls. She was elated when a groan escaped him. She kicked again, and thrilled at his howl of pain. He crumpled and thumped to the floor. Ashley capitalized on the opportunity; she scurried away and grabbed her spell knife from her bedside drawer. She couldn't wait to turn him into something less repulsive than he already was, like a slug.

She rushed to peer over where his body had landed.

He was gone.

Ashley's heart raced. She told herself it was exertion not fear, the nausea simply residual adrenalin. Unafraid of confrontation, she'd be damned if she was going to let any man assault her and live.

Orion may have surprised her, but she had still overpowered him, and that was without her magic. Now she had her spell knife, and her wits about her. He wasn't going to escape. When she caught him, he would suffer.

Ashley held the knife in front of her as she ran out the door and down the stairs. There was no sign of him there or on the landing. The front door was open, as was the iron gate that led to the road, but on the street she stopped short. Though she searched, she saw nothing but a wide white moon in a cloudless sky and a dog running wild in the night.

"No good deed goes unpunished!" She slammed the gate. The adrenalin soured. Her body shook and she hurried inside. Once the huge, wooden front door was locked, she leaned against it and gritted her teeth. Her breathing ragged, face hot, and her anger uncontained, she turned and kicked merry hell out of the solid door until she felt the fury subside. Then determined, she charged into the kitchen. There was a black plastic sack in the cupboard under the sink, she snatched it and stomped upstairs to her room. There she yanked the bedcovers off and thrust them into the sack, then stripped the bed and shoved in the sheets for good measure.

The young witch scoured her room for unwelcome signs of the vanished brute. She ranted as she tidied. It soothed Ashley to call him every curse word she could think of and a few more she made up.

She found only the wet bloodied towel, which she stuffed into the sack with the bedcovers. When she looked around for what to do with the horrible bundle, she spied her open bedroom window and launched the lot into the garden. It could wait until tomorrow after the coven meeting. In the meantime, she wanted her space stripped of any evidence of Orion.

Her aunts kept the clean sheets in a drawer under the bed. For the first time, Ashley opened that draw and made the bed herself. She took particular care to tuck in the sheets and make everything orderly. She admired her handiwork.

"I don't know why the aunts complain about making my bed. It's not that hard." She knew she was being a spoiled brat, but it felt nice when they did things for her. They were the only ones who cared enough to bother.

She thought about telling them what happened, but she cared about them too. They would be distraught if they knew she was attacked under their roof, that's what all the guarding spells on the house were for. Besides, if she did, they'd be up all night and they were old and needed their sleep. She wouldn't have admitted it, but part of her was strangely ashamed. Of all people, this shouldn't have happened to her.

She caught her reflection in the mirror but when she faced it the mirror shattered.

"Fine, be that way!" Ashley shouted at it. She glared around her room. His presence lingered in the foul air and contaminated every filthy surface. She kicked off a dozen transformation spells. The bed, the walls, the chaise lounge, the dresser were altered. She changed the curtains, the chandelier and the rugs. From the floor to the ceiling Ashley left nothing untouched. By the time she was done, the room was no longer recognizable as the one she'd woken up in that morning.

She threw herself into the chair that replaced the chaise lounge in front of her dresser. She hated the new modern look, so she relented and transformed them both back. As an afterthought she fixed the mirror.

Ashley stared at her knitted brows, wondering why she hadn't thought to use her magic to defend against Orion. The thought spun around in her skull.

She had protected herself and she was safe, but Orion was still out there. She performed a protection enchantment on the door, the windows and the whole house for good measure.

She hesitated, but was resolute in her need to reclaim her space and feeling exhausted, Ashley collapsed, fully clothed, makeup smeared, into the well-made bed. She tossed and turned a long time before she finally drifted off to sleep, but she slept like the damned once she had.

* * * *

It was mid- afternoon before Ashley ripped off the covers and stomped to the bathroom. When the bathroom mirror cracked at her glance she slammed the wall with her palm.

"Come on!" She gritted her teeth, closed her eyes and forced herself to take a deep breath. When calm enough, she fixed the mirror with the overused repair charm. With a less murderous gaze, she studied her image and regretted mending the mirror. She rubbed the smeared kohl from her eyes, only to reveal black circles underneath. Ashley gave up and stomped back to her room. She opened the curtains, and squinted against the sunlight.

Unaccustomed to being confused or frustrated, Ashley responded to these new feelings with anger. Most problems magic fixed, but not her emotions. She hated how vulnerable that made her feel.

She threw on her traditional robes, without the usual care or attention to her appearance. How she looked was the least of her worries. She scooped her hair into a ponytail then pinned it into a severe bun. She was in no mood to fuss.

Esmeralda was clanking around on the landing.

"I know I'm late," Ashley called to her.

"Just doing a bit of dusting."

"You're fooling no one you old crone."

"That's Agatha dear, I'm the other one."

"And I'm the maiden," Ashley muttered and rolled her eyes.

Esme entered, toting a suspiciously clean duster. "You could be if you weren't such a floozy." She grinned.

Esmeralda regarded the new décor and gaped. "What have you done to the place? I swear you'd turn it upside-down just to befuddle me."

Ashley took pity on her and performed a reversal. The room returned to its usual state, the chaise and the dresser underwent enough transformations that they suffered some molecular confusion on the way. She decided to lay off the renovation, it really wasn't fair on Esmeralda, the poor dear was as muddled as the furniture.

"Happy now?"

"I'll be happy when you're ready to go."

"I am ready."

Esme cocked an eyebrow. "Like that? No makeup, all buttoned up and proper? You're not even showing off the girls, what's going on?"

Ashley sighed. "If you don't like it, you can go to the coven meeting and I'll stay here and pretend to clean." But she cast a glamor on her face so that she was at least presentable.

"Wouldn't dream of it. I'm retired. Agatha and I are ladies of leisure. We don't muck about with magic." A guilty expression crossed her face, but Ashley didn't have time to interrogate her. Whatever heinous thing she'd meddled in would have to wait.

"Get a hobby. I beg you. Whatever it takes to stay out of my life."

* * * *

The smell of dried blood in the car made Ashley gag, but she didn't have time to wash it before the meeting, so she revved the Mustang and reversed out of the garage.

"Cleaning spells, cleaning spells," she chanted as she drove, but she didn't know any. "Great. The aunts are right. I don't pull my own weight."

Tears welled, and she took several deep breaths to get herself under control. The image of Orion as he lunged at her flashed into her brain. His hand around her neck as he pushed her down. Ashley rubbed where his hands had touched her and clenched her jaw.

She sped up and shifted hard enough to grind the gears. No matter what else happened, she would learn a cleaning spell and rid her room of every last molecule of Orion, and prove to the aunts that she wasn't a burden.

She looked in the rearview at where he'd lain the night before, hot tears formed at the corners of her eyes. She drove faster.

Blind-sided by reoccurring anger, Ashley reassured herself that nothing had happened to her. She had hurt him. But her body refused to believe her. As she approached Reap What you Sow, Rose's occult shop, where the coven held their meetings, her throat was hoarse. She yanked the handbrake and the car spun, it skidded into a parking spot with a squeal of tires. Once she would have loved such a dramatic entrance, now Ashley cringed and glanced around the street to make sure no one saw.

Despite leaving late, she had arrived early. Usually she would be loud, honk the horn, make sure everyone noticed her, but this time she exited the car without fanfare and slunk into the shop.

Full of interesting smells and dangerous objects Reap What you Sow had a personality of its own. Despite, or perhaps because of her mood, it enveloped Ashley; even its forbidding dark glass case was a familiar comfort. The runes that guarded the floor warmed rather than warded her.

Instead of a quick browse, Ashley went straight to the basement, where she waited in her chair. She shifted uncomfortably on what now seemed like a veritable throne. The other witches in her coven filtered in. Rather than show off about her family seat, she sat still and quiet. Her nails dug into the wood. It was no wonder she didn't have friends here. Her constant bragging must have been insufferable.

Ashley didn't know why she suddenly craved anonymity, but now that she did, it was as if everything she'd done prior to this moment was designed to draw attention. From the overly majestic chair and her loud red Mustang, to her overblown formal robes. Now silent, Ashley realized everyone acted as if she wasn't there. She didn't know what to make of that, nothing good though.

The head witch stood and welcomed everyone, but Ashley could barely concentrate. Her mention of zombies reminded Ashley of Orion's shuffle up the stairs.

The other witches appeared engrossed but she zoned in and out, unaware of the usual dramas her thoughts focused on where her attacker was, and what she would do if she found him. She couldn't believe she'd healed him, let alone brought him home. What a fool. How could her judgment have been so bad?

And what of the hunter? Did he too have good reason to want Orion dead? Ashley didn't doubt it. She'd helped the wrong man.

When the meeting adjourned she avoided the usual catch-up conversations, and made a discreet exit. She had her own plans.

She strode to the car, frowned at the bloody back seat, and shook her head. That was careless. Here was the only place where this mess would go unreported.

"Your days are numbered, Orion," she whispered. "Savannah is my home." She hoped he was miles away and running, but she had to make sure.

* * * *

Ashley's plans required a few items. On the way home she pulled in to the local hunting shop. She sighed when she caught sight of the blood in the back seat again, but in glancing around for something to cover it saw the Ute she was parked next to also sported a tray full of bloodstains. She was in the right place.

Inside she scoffed at their Halloween decorations, which were token at best. Though tempted by the guns that lined the walls, she turned instead to the knife displays. Knives nasty, sharp and shiny, nothing like her pretty ornamental spell knife. These serrated things were for killing. She picked one up, sliced the air a few times and shivered. The man behind the counter saw the look on her face and watched her like a store detective does a hooded youth. She offered a weak smile and put down the blade.

On the left side of the aisle, fishing rods and cruel-looking hooks with colorful lures were displayed. On the right, thermals shared a rack with camouflage gear; the forest-patterned garb reminded her of Shakespeare's Puck, and A Midsummer Night's Dream, though of course love spells had nothing to do with hunters. Raised voices floated to her from the rear of the shop.

At the end of the aisle a uniformed shop assistant and a very tall man were engaged in an argument; Ashley could tell from the way they faced off. Ready for a fight, in daylight, with people nearby, she went to investigate. She continued to browse like a regular shopper but listened intently for an escalation in volume. One of the voices had a slight European accent she couldn't place.

Up close the tall man looked for all the world, like the Norse god Thor in his late twenties. He was indeed arguing, his jaw jutted out, his biceps bunched. He glared at the diminutive clerk through knitted brows, his eyes like chunks of blue ice. Though the store man stood his ground, he had his arms folded and head down like he was looking for an escape hatch in the floor.

Like Thor, the customer had a tall, wide frame, and blonde wavy hair that kissed his shoulders. In a nod to modernity, he wore a grey Marino hoodie, which his muscles attempted to split. He filled out a large pair of ripped and dirty blue jeans, with big black motorcycle boots beneath. At least six foot five, he was so large he could have worn the store without wiggle room.

A thrill ran through Ashley's frame. Her heart sped up and she stumbled towards him, her legs tugged her along. She couldn't look away.

His face was beautiful with cheekbones chiseled out of rock. She drew near like tides to the moon. The bulge of his muscles fascinated her. She reached out to touch, but snatched her hand back. The picture was wrong. All her senses told her to go to this man, but she'd felt an attraction to Orion and didn't trust intuition anymore. She concentrated on that unease, tilted her head, and stopped. Her hindbrain had noticed the barely visible crossbow, held casually at Thor's side. She tensed, like a rabbit caught in headlights.

Then a slow smile spread across her face. *The enemy of my enemy is my friend.* Warmth and happiness spread through her.

When she approached, the hunter backed away, slow and watchful. She reached out to him. "Wait. I need to talk to you."

"Please stay away from me."

Ashley couldn't believe he was defensive. "Like I really want to be talking to a nutter in a gun shop. You can't even buy something without getting into a fight."

"I am not a nutter."

"Really, and what would he say about that?" She jerked a thumb at the sales assistant, who took the opportunity to restate his side of the debate.

"You have to leave, sir. We don't allow crossbows in the shop."

The hunter and Ashley looked at the vast array of crossbows that surrounded them, being that they were in a crossbow display with a sale on. It broke the tension and they erupted with laughter.

"You know what I mean." The store clerk turned bright red.

Ashley offered a solution. "Put it in my car."

The hunter shook his head, and tightened his grip on the weapon, clearly unwilling to relinquish it, even for a moment.

"I do not know you."

Ashley grinned at the store clerk and leaned in to whisper in Thor's ear. He had to bend down to allow it.

"We have a mutual enemy. If he's the reason you're tooling up, I want to help. Tell me what you want, and I'll get it."

He straightened and looked at her, his appraisal apparent. The clerk shuffled from one foot to the other. Ashley raised an eyebrow and folded her arms. "Well? Do I look like I can handle shopping for you, or are you going to walk away empty-handed?"

The sales assistant opened his mouth but Ashley interrupted.

"Calm down, I'll handle it."

The Norse god nodded at her and handed over a list, which she snatched with bad grace.

"You can wait by the car. I think you know which one is mine."

He turned to leave. A female customer caught Ashley watching him.

"Not a bad sight from behind, is he?" the woman whispered. Ashley didn't reply, instead she shouted after the retreating hunter.

"It's the one with the bloodbath in the back seat if you're not sure!"

He paused, cringed, and then carried on.

Ashley turned to find the woman and the sales assistant wide-eyed and horrified. She smiled at them.

"It's a private joke." The small spat had helped get her spark back. She could see the car through the door of the shop, flicked a wrist and put a glamour spell on it so it didn't look like a crime scene.

Thor's list wasn't extensive: arrow bolts and a couple of knives and sheaths, one to strap on the leg, another for the arm. No specific sizes or brands were written down, so she chose the largest of everything. His legs were like tree trunks and the biceps on his arms were bigger than both of her arms put together.

She carried the bag of weapons to her car and thrust them roughly into the hands of the man who waited for her.

"Who are you and why do you hunt Orion?" she demanded.

"Not here," he said under his breath. He reached for the door handle, but Ashley refused to unlock it. Fear churned inside her.

"The last time I let a man into my car it ended badly."

A pained expression crossed his face.

"This is my fault," he said, across the roof of the Mustang. "Had I not failed in my mission you would not be endangered."

He looked so guilty she let him off the hook.

"I'm not a panda. Anyway, I didn't exactly make it easy for you. I thought you were the bad guy and he needed help."

"Orion is not as he appears to be."

"Yeah, I got that now."

"I hope you were not hurt."

"Hardly. I kicked him in the nuts. Twice."

He laughed. "You are a worthy adversary. I sincerely wish I had been a witness to that deed."

Ashley's pride produced a smile. She pointed to the coffee shop over the road. "Let's talk. Stow your crossbow." She pulled the trunk release and walked around while he placed the weapon carefully inside. She slammed the lid, and without a backward glance, crossed the road. His legs were so long he didn't have to run to catch up.

Café Diem made an effort for Halloween. Ghosts adorned the counter and skeletons hung proudly on the otherwise drab walls. Ashley smiled at the flying witch motif. Her broomstick bound sisters soared in perfect formation from the ceiling. She couldn't resist enhancing the aerobatic spectacle; and cast an enrichment charm. The witches shimmered, dipped and dived, but only in peripheral vision. The menu reflected the holiday.

"Creepy coffee for me, black, two sugars." Ashley's haughty demeanor reappeared. She was annoyed to find haughty didn't sit right anymore. Her heart wasn't in it. But she needed something to keep the hunter at arm's length, preferably the long, long length of his arms. Especially while every fiber of her foolish being screamed for her to grab him and hold him close.

She chose a corner booth away from other patrons. Aside from the holiday décor, the café was a dingy place, frequented by the blue-rinse brigade. The old style pastries and sandwiches looked hideous, but the elderly patrons were all absorbed in their cups of tea and lurid cakes, it was the perfect place to talk.

The hunter spied her; he carried over a tray with their coffees and an orange pumpkin-shaped cupcake on it. It didn't look edible, but he did. She squeezed her legs together, and shifted in her seat.

Was her body going to respond every time he was near? Her brain rebelled. It was time to grow up. Still she couldn't stop her traitorous heart's search for signs he was interested.

He stood by the table and politely waited for Ashley to invite him to sit. Curious to see how long he would stand there, she watched him. He was ridiculously conspicuous, and even the half-blind old ladies appraised him through their thick spectacles. Her pettiness embarrassed her and she nodded to the booth. He set down the tray, and attempted to climb in. The action looked awkward, the length of his legs refused to fit under the table, no matter how he tried to bend them.

"Oh, for goodness sake." She picked up her cup and moved to the table and chairs next to them so he could push his seat out as far as he needed.

Once they were both comfortable, she turned on him. "Your name and where you're from because it's clearly not Savannah."

"I am Ivar Hammond, from Sweden originally."

"Not Norway."

"Thor again?" Ivar sounded annoyed. "I do not look like this god."

"Agree to disagree." Ashley had touched a sore spot. They were getting off track.

"Why were you chasing Orion?"

"He is evil. I am not sure I can explain." He looked at her with a question in his eyes.

"Do you believe in the supernatural?"

She grinned at the irony. "Sure."

"Please do not be dismissive. Do you truly believe?"

She whispered a simple incantation. Her spoon stirred her coffee unaided. A tiny tornado materialized and carried the black liquid out of the cup; the black swirl hovered in the air. Sugar poured out of the bowl and formed a tiny farmhouse. The coffee tornado picked it up; the sugar darkened but retained its shape. Ivar held his breath, knuckles white where they clutched the table.

The danger of watchful eyes occurred to Ashley and she checked to see if other patrons had noticed. The spell abandoned, gravity reasserted itself. Coffee and sugar spilled over the table. She shrugged.

"I believe." She said.

"How did you do that?"

"I'm a witch. It comes with the territory."

"There really are more things in heaven and earth." Ivar shook his head. "Kill me now if you must."

"Settle down. All I did was spill some coffee."

"You are not evil?"

"Not last time I checked. My aunts would say I was lazy, conceited, rude and belligerent, which I'm working on. But no, I'm not evil. Don't test me, though. I've had a bad couple of days."

Ivar's shoulders dropped about three inches.

"I wondered how you picked Orion up. I thought, maybe adrenalin. Did you use your power to escape him? A woman as beautiful as you, he wouldn't leave without…" He looked away, lips tight. "I'm glad you have such power. You deserve better than Orion's treatment of you."

"Well, it was a near thing, but no, when I use my power on him I'll take my time." She wiped up the mess with a paper napkin. "Which is why I'm going to help you find him. You still haven't explained why I have to believe in the supernatural."

"I don't hunt a man, but a monster. Orion is a wolf in the shape of a man."

"A shape-shifter?"

"Shape-shifter? What other creatures abide in the light?" Horror appeared on Ivar's face.

"Just the usual, shape-shifters, witches, ghouls, zombies, spirits. There are vampires too, but they're not big on light."

Ivar's face paled, and he scanned the café.

"Oh, don't worry. None of these old dears are supernatural. Except for Rosie over there." She nodded in the direction of an elderly lady with long straggly grey hair and gnarled hands. "Poor dear, she was a banshee, but the family she screamed for died out, now she just wails a bit."

The banshee nodded back, and Ashley waved and smiled. "So, what's Orion then?"

"A werewolf."

Ashley banged a fist on the table and cursed herself for being so obtuse. She frowned. Being a werewolf explained Orion's rapid healing but not his vicious behavior.

She didn't know any werewolves, but had heard there were good ones and bad. They were like humans in that regard. A dog was only as good as its master. Then she remembered the dog that ran away the night she fought Orion, and got angry all over again.

"I'm a total idiot. I could have got him."

"It's not as easy as you think." Ivar's expression darkened.

"Why is he your problem?" she asked. "You like to hunt beasts?"

He shook his head. "I am no hunter. I was a chef.

"A chef?"

Ivar picked up the cupcake. "Food is magic, it conjures delight." He took a bite, and grimaced. "Bad example."

Ashley laughed. "And now?"

Ivar frowned. "Now I must kill Orion or…" He looked at her again.

Ashley rolled her eyes. "You've trusted me this far."

His frown deepened, and Ashley saw his internal struggle. She was patient for once. He came to a decision.

"Orion bit my sister Helena, made her a werewolf. She is imprisoned to prevent her from seeking prey. I cannot let her kill. The lore I studied says she can return to humankind."

"As long as she doesn't kill."

"Some legends say yes. Others say she must eat no meat. Stay out of moonlight. There are many folktales. I have obeyed them all. Helena waits; locked in a cell, for his death, or her own because the only thing they agree on is that her maker must be killed before she may take on human form for good.

"Why the crossbow, wouldn't a gun be easier? To use and conceal."

"Most tales say the werewolf must be killed with silver to the heart, but some more obscure myths assert the weapon must be wood. I make my own silver bolt tips so the crossbow takes care of both."

Ashley's heart went out to him. "That's quite a problem you've got there. We'd better get started."

"This is my problem, not yours. Despite your powers, I cannot condone your involvement. It is too dangerous."

Ashley would have laughed, if she weren't so insulted; she didn't need his protection. She was a powerful witch.

"I'd like to see you find him without me."

"It will be hard, but I have done it before." He looked so resigned Ashley softened.

"Look." She placed her hand gently on his. "What are you going to do? Follow the bodies?"

He looked down.

"He's a monster, but you're not. I can find him without bloodshed." She took her pendulum out of her pocket and held it out. "I can scry for him. I have his blood, and it will take me hours to find him, not weeks."

Ivar looked up at her, his hope almost tangible.

"I told you," she said. "You need me."

"I have known you less than an hour and already I am in your debt."

He placed his hand over hers and looked deeply into her eyes. "I will repay you."

Ashley was too wary to hold his gaze. "Damn straight you will. Here's the receipt from the hunting shop, there's an ATM outside. You can start with that."

Ivar grinned, squeezed her hand then reached for his wallet. "I will meet you at the car."

* * * *

Their arrival at the mansion prompted Ashley to scour the family grimoire. Ivar carried the bag of weapons, while she found a particularly vigorous cleaning spell. She ordered Ivar to fetch the bag of soiled bedcovers from the garden while she went upstairs to cleanse her bedroom.

A minute later, satisfied it was immaculate, she returned to the kitchen table to unfold a map of Savannah and its surrounds. She was smoothing it out when Ivar brought in the bag.

"It smells." He warned her.

She shrugged. "Find me a patch with blood on it."

He raised an eyebrow. "You are used to having staff?" He rifled through the bag and found the washcloth.

She hesitated, remembering Orion wiping his face, and finally she understood.

"That won't work."

"Why not? The blood is plentiful."

"But not his." She had solved the mystery of the blood with no source. The source was probably dead, the victim of a werewolf.

Ivar shuddered, put the cloth back and took out the blue silk cover. She grabbed it from him.

"I would have passed it to you, had you asked politely."

"You weren't so polite with that guy in the hunting shop."

"I tried, he pushed me beyond patience."

"Well not all of us were raised with impeccable manners."

"I'm sure you were."

Ashley didn't appreciate the rebuke and didn't hide her disdain. She could tell Ivar got the message because he delivered one of his own.

"Manners don't just show respect for others, they show that you have respect for yourself."

Ashley didn't mean to be disrespectful, merely keep him at a distance. She didn't trust herself, or him yet, and wondered if she'd ever trust a man again. The last time she helped a stranger was a stupid mistake and now she second-guessed every judgment call. But none of that was Ivar's fault.

"I'm sorry I was rude. I'm trying to be more considerate, but I'm a work in progress."

"Thank you," he smiled, "Thank you for your help. I know the reason you are in this mess is because of your obliging nature, you tried to help someone else."

"Well, let's find that someone and rip his head off."

Ivar laughed. "Agreed."

Ashley used her spell knife to cut a bloodied square from the material while Ivar studied the kitchen bookcase.

"You have excellent taste and a keen mind."

"Maybe they're not mine," Ashley said.

He rolled his eyes.

"Okay, they're mine. Most guys get intimidated when they find out I've got a brain."

"Then they are idiots. Do you mind?" He held up a history book, when Ashley nodded he stashed it in his pack.

The material cut, Ashley placed it on the map. She held the pendulum over it and intently searched for signs of the werewolf.

Ivar scrutinized the map over her shoulder as if the strength of both of their gazes would speed the search. Ashley turned to find her face close to his. Their bodies stiffened. Ivar looked to her, their lips almost touching. She held her breath, nervous; she anticipated and dreaded his kiss. He seemed about to lean in, but at the last moment straightened and moved away. Ashley breathed again, and she refocused her attention on finding Orion.

Esmeralda appeared. Had her aunt seen the near kiss? She sensed the faintest whiff of flirtation.

"Just getting myself a long, tall drink of water." The wizened witch ogled Ivar.

"Carry on, then. Don't let us stop you." Ashley fetched a glass and waved it in her face. "Faucet's over there."

Esmeralda dug her elbow into Ashley's ribs; her eyebrows waggled so much she was in danger of losing them.

Ashley sighed. "Ivar, this is Esmeralda, my extremely elderly aunt. Esmeralda, you've got what you wanted, so move along."

"Don't mind me. I like scrying. Good at it are you, Ivar? I bet you're good at lots of things."

"I try to be of use."

"I could put you to good use. You might not be in the same condition afterward though." Esmeralda winked.

Ashley laughed at Ivar's startled look in the face of her aunt's lascivious onslaught. She shoved the glass at Esmeralda. The shriveled witch just about broke her neck gawping at Ivar as Ashley marched her out of the kitchen.

Ashley tried to get back to her task but cringed when Esme yelled up the stairs.

"Agatha, get a load of the hot stuff Ashley brought home. I mean vavoom!"

Ashley shook her head. "Poor dear, she's going senile."

Ivar covered his face with his hands. "Just tell me when it's over."

"Twenty three years and counting so don't hold your breath." She returned to scrying, mortified.

Ivar paced until Ashley reached out to stop him. He covered her hand with his own, and then let go abruptly.

"I apologize, I am too eager."

He made her nervous. She opened French doors that separated the kitchen from the downstairs living room. "Go sit on the couch. It's hideous, but comfortable." She pointed to a large luxurious green and pink floral monstrosity.

"Maybe if I close my eyes—"

"I would."

"No, I mean I need sleep."

Ashley pushed him down on the couch; he relaxed back into it, and touched her arm.

"Thank you for helping me."

She nodded and placed a flowery cushion on the end of the sofa. He kicked off his boots and passed out the instant his head hit the cushion.

She tucked him in with the throw rug and brushed the hair back from his forehead. Light streamed through the windows, it touched him lovingly and danced on his golden hair. Jealously Ashley drew the curtains. She approached again, leaned in but drew back before her lips brushed his. She didn't know why he fascinated her, but knew the best thing she could do for him was find Orion. She turned back to the kitchen. Now that she'd rid herself of distractions, maybe she would get somewhere.

Again she held the pendulum over the map but instead of zeroing in on a location, it swayed toward the sleeping hunter. She blessed it, washed it, cleared it and shook it, but the pendulum persistently pointed due Ivar.

If Ashley knew anything it was that when things went haywire her aunts had something to do with it. She found them in the garden planting hemlock.

"Why doesn't my scrying work?" She glared at the pair.

"Don't know dear," Agatha replied. "Maybe you've lost your touch."

"I'll tell you who you should be touching—" Esmeralda began.

"What have you done?" Ashley read their identical guilty expressions.

"Go on Esme, it was your spell," Agatha prompted.

"You dared me."

"You'd better both come clean, before I just about have a fit."

"It was just a love spell," they admitted in unison.

"What?" Ashley roared.

"But it went a bit wrong," they said.

"Well it usually does with you two. Fix it." Ashley turned to go.

"We can't," the two replied.

"Why not?"

"It's a true love spell," they both answered.

"What difference does that make? And stop doing that chorusing thing, I've told you before, it's creepy."

"True love is tricky. Once you have love you can't magic it away." Esmeralda explained.

"I'm not going to, you are."

The aunts shook their heads.

"You're not telling me there's nothing you can do. I can't even scry straight with him around, I won't put up with being in love and powerless for the rest of my life."

"Or his, if he's mortal, that's what…?" Agatha said.

"Fifty or sixty years," Esmeralda answered.

"Not long at all."

"Find a way, and do it now. I need to be able to scry tonight."

"Why is that?" Agatha and Esmeralda shared a question and a glance.

"Never mind. Just get this spell off me. I'll be at the table, waving a useless pendulum around."

She stormed off.

* * * *

The aunts searched their spell books. Her scrying abandoned, Ashley hid in the alcove outside their rooms. She obtained information in the time-honored manner of all witches; she eavesdropped.

Occasionally one would shout they'd found something. Ashley would tuck herself further into the shadows. One witch would burst through their door and cross the hall into the other's room. Ashley would hear a heated consult, some derisive scoffs, the witch would return, and the process would start again.

They were getting nowhere.

"Alright you two. Tell me what you've got," Ashley said.

The aunts popped out.

"Nothing." Agatha said.

"Come on." Esmeralda led them into her room. Like Reap What you Sow, the room was both warm, inviting, eerie and spine chilling. Though more to see than the eye could take in, it looked like a tornado had ripped through a library. Ancient pages covered every surface.

"I've exhausted my bookshelves," Esmeralda said. To Ashley it was the ancient aunts who looked exhausted. She flopped down on the bed, and sunk into the Esmeralda shaped depression in the middle. "Any ideas at least?"

"We could kill him," Agatha suggested.

"Next."

"We could turn him into something," said Esmeralda. "You'd still love each other, but it's easier with a pet."

"Next!"

"We could turn you into something and wait till he dies on his own."

"Are you kidding me? You were two of the most powerful witches in the world and this is the best you can come up with?"

"Well, we're retired now," said Agatha.

"I want to see the spell."

"I did it from memory."

"Don't sound so proud," her sister said, "It's not like you did it right."

"Even so. Is it written down?" Ashley asked.

The aunts picked up random bits of paper, shuffled through them and finally Agatha passed her an old parchment.

"To Gain a Heart and Keep it Forever." Ashley read.

"It's metaphorical," said Esmeralda.

Agatha snatched the parchment. Her eyes lit up. "But it needn't be."

Ashley frowned, confused.

"Look," said Agatha. "If this is to gain a heart, we can reverse it, by giving one away."

"What?" Ashley was no more enlightened.

"Ah, I see," said Esmeralda. Ashley looked at her expectantly. Esmeralda hesitated. "Oh no, sorry, I have no idea what you mean."

Ashley took a deep breath and looked to Agatha again.

"If you and Ivar exchange hearts, that will break the spell," Agatha said. "Probably," she muttered under her breath.

"Exchange hearts?"

"Sure. We put your heart in his chest, and vice versa." Esmeralda understood now.

"And you've got a spell for that?" Ashley asked, before an obviously stupid and dangerous idea went any further.

"Simple organ transfer. It'll take five minutes," Agatha assured her.

Ashley sighed, and shook her head. But she went downstairs to inform Ivar that if he wanted her to find the werewolf, and not be forced to love her, he'd have to hand over his heart.

* * * *

When Ashley woke Ivar, he tried to kiss her. She pulled back.

"The aunts put a love spell on us."

Ivar groaned.

"The cure is a heart transplant."

"Of course it is."

Ashley pulled him into the kitchen, and sat him at the table for magical surgery. She settled next to him and looked more confident than she felt.

Agatha cleared away the map while Esmeralda laid out interesting and disturbing items.

"Take your clothes off Ivar," Esmeralda instructed.

"That's not necessary," her sister said.

"He didn't know that Agatha. Honestly, you spoil all my fun."

"Just get on with it," Ashley demanded. "What do we have to do?"

Agatha consulted the spell book, an enormous dusty tome written in several languages, some dead. The pictures reminded Ashley of an anatomy book. The cross sections made her queasy.

"You need to remain still." Agatha's tone was serious. "You'll both be technically dead for a few seconds, so lie on the table and we'll strap you down, we don't want your hearts to end up in the wrong place."

Ashley couldn't agree more.

"What is the difference between technically dead and dead?" Ivar asked.

"Technically? No difference, it just sounds more reassuring," said Agatha.

Ivar gave Ashley a worried glance.

"Surely Ivar's heart is bigger than mine, won't there be complications?"

"Don't be silly love, it's magic not medicine." Agatha patted her shoulder. "Lie down and be still."

"What happens if we do not finish together?" Ivar asked.

Esme's eyes lit up, but Ashley raised a cautionary eyebrow. Esme pouted but gave a serious answer.

"True love. No scrying. Honestly, why reverse it? Most people would pay good money for this spell.

"Could you give us a minute?" Ashley asked.

"Come on Agatha, the lovebirds want their private time." The aunts departed. Ashley sat on the table with Ivar's hands in hers. She looked into his eyes.

"I'm not going through life with you forced to love me, and I don't want to be forced to love you. That's not true love. I know this is dangerous, and stupid and all kinds of wrong, and if you say so, we won't do it. But Helena deserves a chance. Maybe if you're far enough away I can scry, but I don't know how far you'd have to go, because my feelings for you are so strong I don't think there's anywhere on earth I wouldn't sense you. And even if that place did exist, you couldn't get there before Orion killed again, and Orion's next victim deserves to live. If I can scry, I can find him, and you can save your sister.

Ivar nodded. "You are so brave. I am not afraid of this strange magic, I am only afraid to lose you."

"I'm scared of losing you too, but if the aunts say they can do this, they can."

Ivar nodded. "Call them back, we should begin."

Ashley laughed. "I don't have to; they're listening at the door.

The aunts had the decency to look guilty when they came in.

Agatha took rusty restraints from her kit and tied Ashley to the fasteners on the table. "I know you think it's sinister, but I bet you're glad the table used to be a torture rack now."

"Not really." Ashley replied.

Ivar climbed up next to her and allowed Esmeralda to restrain him.

Ashley watched, suspicious that her aunt was enjoying the moment a lot more than the situation called for.

The aunts chanted and the room swirled like a cheap movie effect. They placed things on Ashley's chest, her hands and feet and around her neck. Some things felt cold others warm. One was slimy. She kept her eyes tightly shut and tried to remain motionless. The hot Savannah air fled and icy fingers stroked her spine. Her chest constricted, she caught her breath. Then oblivion.

* * * *

Ashley and Ivar both gasped for breath when they stirred. They struggled against their restraints. The aunts rushed to untie them and move the dreadful detritus of the spell. Ashley clutched at her chest. She poked at her heart through her skin, it felt dislocated, her body not entirely her own. Then she realised, it wasn't.

Ivar too was troubled. He tried to stand, but fell and clutched the table for support. The look in his eyes was wild and desperate.

She turned to clasp him. He enfolded her in an intense embrace. Chest to chest their heartbeats synchronized, the dislocation disappeared. Even so, she didn't want to let go. She could tell Ivar didn't either, when she loosened her hold he drew her closer. She opened her eyes to find his gaze on her. For a long moment they stayed that way.

"It didn't work Agatha, look at them, clearly in love."

Ashley released Ivar and sighed. Esmeralda could wreck any tender moment.

"It's okay. It worked." She looked to Ivar for confirmation and he nodded. The magnetic pull towards him was gone. She still thought he was gorgeous, but that was just because she had eyes.

"Best be sure," Agatha said. "Go on, try your scrying.

The aunts gathered up the last remains of the heart transfer spell and Ashley wiped the table and set up the map again.

"What should I do?" Ivar asked.

"Boil the jug," said Agatha, "I'm gasping for a cuppa."

"I'll watch you." The incorrigible Esmeralda leered at him.

* * * *

They all sat around the table and sipped their drinks while Ashley held the pendulum over the map. She placed Ivar at the end of the table to ascertain whether he still affected her magic.

When she could tell her scrying worked, Ashley shooed the aunts away.

"Is that all the thanks we get?" Esmeralda complained.

"What are you up to?" Agatha demanded.

"Yes, and none of your business. I think you two have meddled enough for today, if we need your help we'll ask. Besides, don't you have a ton of sweets and some horribly inappropriate tricks to organize? You never know, maybe the rumors are forgotten by now and you'll get some trick or treaters."

Though they protested, Ashley closed the door firmly behind the two witches and turned back to Ivar. "Do you regret letting me help yet?"

He shook his head. "Regret is not the word. My connection with you has been more eventful than I could have imagined."

"Ever the diplomat." They'd been through a lot in a few short hours. "How about you get some more sleep. I'll let you know when I have something."

* * * *

Ashley kicked the table leg. "That son of a bitch is close."

Ivar leapt up and checked the windows. Moonlight stretched its pale fingers across the floor.

"He's not outside the house," she said.

"Where are the weirdly dressed kids begging for candy?"

"No kids come down this street. Every now and then a new kid moves into the neighborhood, but once the aunts show them the Halloween spirit, they scream and run. Last year the Halloween spirit was my great grandfather. I still think they should have waited till he was a skeleton before they dug him up; he really stank. Still, it was nice to talk to him again.

Ivar looked dubious, but didn't ask questions. He shut the curtains and delved into the bag of weapons. He strapped on knives and gathered quivers for the crossbow then affixed these with his custom silver tips. Ashley drank him in as he readied himself for action like a true hero. He caught her look and leered. "My turn now."

"I'll get my stuff." Ashley gathered up the map, the material and her pendulum.

"No, it is too dangerous."

"Like you're in charge. Anyway, there's no werewolf GPS, so get used to having me around."

She hurried to get her kit. If someone got hurt, she'd be prepared.

Ivar waited by the car. When she appeared, he looked her up and down and winked. She smiled and threw the keys to him.

"I'm the navigator."

He caught them easily and jumped in the car, then jumped out again to readjust the seat.

"You finished?"

He sighed. "You don't let anything go do you?"

"You're a big boy. You can take it."

"This is serious, Ashley. Orion is a killer."

She scowled. "I'm well aware of the kind of man he is."

Ivar frowned. "I am sorry." He turned the key and the car roared into life. "I could not forgive myself if danger befell you."

Ivar's expression contained both fear and guilt, but she had spent enough time convincing him she was strong enough for this fight. She feared for him too. They had only just met but she didn't want to lose him.

Suddenly Ashley's heart thudded, it pumped emotion through her veins. She could discern fear and anger, love and guilt. She looked over at Ivar, his face a picture of loss and confusion.

"What was that?" she asked.

Ivar shook his head. "My heart, no, your heart, it holds pain and loss. These feelings, they overpower me. They are not mine." He breathed deeply, and closed his eyes against the sensation. "Great loneliness, more than I have ever felt before."

"My parent's death." Ashley said. "So this fear, love and anger are yours?" Tears welled. "So much guilt."

"I was supposed to pick up Helena from her friend's party. I worked late, forgot the time." He avoided eye contact. "The wolf ravaged her. I found her broken body outside my restaurant. She almost reached me."

They looked at each other as the realization of their new connection became clear.

"I will experience your emotions now?" Ivar asked.

Ashley shrugged, "I've never done this before. I don't know if that will happen again."

"I'm so sorry you lost your parents. You were so young."

Ashley blinked back tears. "Come on, we've got a job to do."

Ivar pulled onto the road and drove every bit as aggressively as Ashley. He put the car through its paces as she navigated beside him. They started to see tiny ghouls and sith lords on the streets clutching bags of candy. Ashley tapped her phone.

"Are you going to live-tweet a werewolf hunt?"

"Checking phases of the moon. It might be helpful if there's a full moon tonight."

"That would be useful to know."

"A couple of days ago, but its mostly full."

"I have seen him turn to the wolf on a waning moon."

"Good." Ashley stashed her phone. Ivar sped up and concentrated on the road, Ashley noticed that he snuck quick glances at her. She removed her hairclips and the bun became a ponytail. Then she flicked back her hair, wiggled in her seat, and contrived to show a little more cleavage than before.

* * * *

About a mile from their destination Ivar pulled over. He handed Ashley the keys and climbed in the back. She flashed back to the last time a man was there. They were so different.

"So we're clear?"

Ashley handed him his crossbow.

"We're clear. Hold back until I signal you."

"And you get out of the way."

Ashley nodded "How do I look?"

"Like wolf-bait."

"Perfect."

Trees lined the road. Like rotting zombies their limbs hung heavy. They dripped Spanish Moss. The Mustang's headlights lit an empty street, the litter scattered on the roadside completed the apocalyptic image.

Ashley kept an eye out for anything that looked like a shelter. She reached the end of the road and spotted a windowless wooden shack. Beer bottles and abandoned animal bones covered the ground. This was the place.

She parked downwind and resisted the urge to check the backseat. She was more scared than she would admit to Ivar. Nausea churned her stomach. She marched up the path before she could think twice and stop herself.

The door of the dilapidated hut was a ruin, when she pounded on it the door clanged to the ground.

Orion appeared barefoot. He wore only jeans. Like a cockroach he lurked in the shadows. She glanced up, but clouds obscured the moon's ashen facade.

"What are you doing here?" he asked in his gravelly voice.

"I wanted to make sure you didn't hurt anyone else."

"What are you going to do, little girl?" Orion sneered at her.

Ashley worked a dark spell she learned from a grimoire so vile it had no name. She invoked pain and torment in Orion who thrashed around, and writhed like a hooked fish. Part of her enjoyed power over the man who had attacked her, but her cruelty shamed her and left a bitter taste.

Refining the pain spell, she forced his hands in front of him. He howled in agony and yanked his body back. His shoulders began to tear out of their sockets.

His eyes glared daggers at her. "Let me go!"

Ashley gagged him with a silence charm. The sight was so awful she ached to stop, but couldn't let Orion escape. He was too dangerous. He wouldn't stop fighting, but resisted, even when the pain must have been unbearable. Still, Ashley slapped silver handcuffs on his wrists. Smoke poured off them and welts appeared on the skin. His mouth distorted in a silent yowl. Ashley backed up and stepped sideways. Ivar should be in position. Instead of the expected arrow, Orion lunged through the gap.

Clouds made no difference, though they covered the moonlight, Orion's skin ripped, his face deformed. The change was graphic and visceral. It took only seconds, but to Ashley, frozen in place, it lasted an age. A scream stuck in her throat. Her legs shook and refused to move. It was the worst thing she'd ever seen. She held her breath watching the extremes to which Orion's body was subjected.

She couldn't look away while fur grew through his pores. He twisted and turned, back arched, his hands still cuffed together. He jerked and scratched and tore at himself.

She expected an arrow any moment but Orion was so close she knew Ivar wouldn't risk the shot. She tried to widen the gap, but tripped, and sprawled on gnawed bones. Beside her, Orion's waist shrunk. He kicked off jeans and his clawed paws raked deep gashes down his legs. He too lost balance and fell.

Ashley turned to suppress a sob when his legs broke, snapped and bent, forced agonizingly into the hindquarters of a wolf. He was a monster, but no one should suffer as he did. Despite what he had done to her, she pitied him.

She faced the hill. Ivar ran toward her, his long legs covered the distance faster than she thought possible. When she broke concentration the silence spell shattered, the pain spell was irrelevant compared to the torture Orion's condition inflicted.

Renewed howls of agony brought her attention back to the wild animal in front of her. Orion's arms were bent back, but the cuffs hindered him. He lay on his side while the bones shifted beneath his fur, howled and panted as the transformation ended. The silver cuffs dangled loosely on thin paws. Orion shook them off and in wolf form leapt up on all fours and snarled at Ashley, free to attack.

She sprang from the feral animal. It growled, snapped and lunged to bite her. From the ground she kicked out, her boot glanced off its jaw. The werewolf attacked savagely it strained to scratch and bite at her face.

Ashley struggled, fierce in the knowledge that if it drew blood, she was done. She pushed back against its chest and turned her head to avoid the razor claws. Ivar yelled her name through the wolf's snarls, its saliva dripped on her face.

She risked a glance behind her. The clouds had shifted and she could make out Ivar on one knee, he lined up a shot. The crossbow shifted to focus on its moving target.

Ashley shoved hard against Orion's furry chest; and simultaneously performed a launching spell that flung the wolf high in the air. Orion twisted, back arched to assault her.

Ivar loosed his arrow. The bolt flew above her, the sharpened silver tip found its mark, and penetrated the wolf's fur to pierce its heart.

Ashley rolled away a moment before Orion landed with a sickening thud where she had been. He shuddered in his death throes. Ashley scuttled out of the way. Transfixed by the horrible sight she didn't watch where she was going and stumbled and staggered away.

Overwhelmed by the smell of the blood, Ashley covered her nose and mouth. In death, the werewolf returned to its human form. It transformed through all the stages Ashley had previously witnessed but in reverse, this time with an arrow bolt through its heart, the blood still pumping.

Though relieved she was alive, Ashley wouldn't have wished this death even on Orion, her worst enemy.

Ivar arrived breathing hard; he must have started running before his arrow found its home. He wrapped his arms around her and turned her head away. Ashley held his rigid body until the wolf's was still. Only then, when she sensed Ivar's tension depart, did she pull back. He looked like he was trying not to sob.

Ashley was again taken over by the emotions of Ivar's heart. A rush of relief engulfed her followed by fear and love, for Helena she guessed. It was easier this time to experience the emotions, now she knew they belonged to Ivar. He was frozen in place, eyes shut. When he opened them she reached to steady him.

"It's over," she said. "I'll deal with this." She motioned to the corpse. "Call her."

Ivar dropped his head onto her shoulder. She put her arms around him and kissed him gently.

He stared into her eyes at the unspoken possibilities that dwelt within. She smiled and nodded. He took out his phone.

Ashley focused on the mess beneath her feet. The body was warm; blood flowed sluggishly from it. Ashley stepped over the corpse, careful not to bloody her boots. She crossed the threshold of Orion's lair. Inside the room was repulsive, the guttering candles illuminated bones spread over the floor. Not all of them looked like they belonged to animals. There was nothing personal or comfortable, nothing hygienic. A pile of dirty blankets in the corner stank of wolf.

"Creature comforts," Ashley quoted Orion.

She gingerly made her way over to the blankets to pick one up with finger and thumb. She dragged it to the front door and laid it down next to the body. Ashley did a transfer spell that had the corpse on the blanket in an instant, and then folded the blanket over the top.

When Ivar approached he looked happier than she'd seen him since they met.

"Everything work out?"

"Helena is human. She has been freed." He laughed and hugged her, swinging her round so her feet lifted off the ground.

"I'm glad," said Ashley, who couldn't share his joy after what she had witnessed. "But let's not celebrate yet."

He put her down.

"Care to do the honors?" Ashley indicated the body in the blanket. She opened the trunk of the Mustang and Ivar lifted the carcass inside. She shut the lid on the heap with a satisfying clunk.

"What will we do with him?" he asked.

"We'll take him back to my place." She peeled away from the shack.

"Please go the speed limit. I would rather not have a conversation with the authorities with a body in the trunk."

For the first time in her young life Ashley complied without argument.

* * * *

The house lights were on and the garage door lifted to welcome them in when they pulled into Mockingbird Lane, Ashley knew the aunts had waited up, but she still had to deal with the body. She and Ivar stood by the open trunk when the two interfering witches appeared at the top of the garage steps.

"Up to mischief are we?" Agatha stood, craning her neck to see.

"It's fine, Auntie. There's nothing going on."

"If I had a strapping man like that there would be." Esmeralda piped up from behind her sister.

"Would you leave it alone?"

"Never, I'd touch it—"

"Esme, they're hiding something." Agatha galloped down the stairs at a speed that belied her age. A gleeful Esmeralda was close behind.

Ashley shut the trunk. "It's nothing. I can take care of it."

"Don't you nothing me, Miss Haughty." Agatha waved a threatening finger. Ashley backed away in case it went off accidentally.

"Probably full of naughty things for their love tryst." Esmeralda opened the trunk with a spell that was actually accurate for a change.

Ivar gave a strangled laugh and tried unsuccessfully to look smaller. Esmeralda screwed up her face.

"Yuck. Young people today really don't know how to have a good time. Look at this, Agatha."

She looked.

"Date didn't go well then?"

"I can explain," Ashley said.

"Looks like you bagged a werewolf," Agatha said. "I hope he was a bad un."

"Maybe I don't have to explain, and yes, he was. As bad as it gets. How can you tell he's a werewolf?"

"The smell mostly." Agatha waved away the overpowering scent of wolf.

"Well done you." Esmeralda nodded at Ivar. "Killing a werewolf takes some doing."

"What makes you think it was him?" Ashley was shrill with indignation.

The aunts just laughed. "Bit too much like hard work for you I'd think." Agatha turned to her sister. "Can you imagine? Miss Haughty doing dirty work? Job like that, she might break a nail."

"I'll have you know I am every bit as responsible for this corpse as he is!" Ashley shouted.

"Yell a little louder, honey. Maybe the next street over didn't hear." Agatha patted her on the shoulder.

Ashley prodded Ivar. "Tell them."

Esmeralda waved her ire away. "Don't worry, honey. We're just teasing you. Of course we know you're capable of the vicious murder of a supernatural creature. You're a witch, aren't you? How about you two get cleaned up, Agatha and I will get rid of the evidence."

"I cannot allow you to do that." Ivar said, ever polite.

Both aunts turned on him like rabid dogs. "Allow?" Agatha shrieked.

"In our own house," Esmeralda said.

Ivar backed away, and gave Ashley a worried glance. She grabbed his hand and pulled him up the stairs.

"Better let them have their way, who knows what they're capable of."

"Besides, it's Halloween. It's practically tradition to bury a body," Agatha said.

"Or dig one up," Esmeralda agreed. "We'll put him in the family graveyard next to great uncle Crowe." She found two spades behind the garage door.

"Crowe was a rotter too." Agatha accepted a spade.

"Whatever," Ashley called over her shoulder. "Have fun." She dragged Ivar through the door. He let her.

"Come on." Ashley climbed the stairs to the master bathroom. "Let's get you cleaned up."

Ivar grinned. "You still want to be with me, even though the love spell is broken?"

"Love? Lust maybe."

Ivar's smile widened. "Your aunts will not mind?"

Ashley snorted. "They're worse than I am. Anyway, I don't want to talk about them. I don't want to talk at all."

She pushed up his grey hoodie but couldn't reach all the way. "Mountaineers could climb you," she said.

"You can climb me." Ivar helped her take off the hoodie; he almost tripped up the stairs in his haste. He reached out to squeeze her but she evaded him, laughed and ran to the top of the stairs. Her legs were no match for his. He caught up and carried her through the doorway of the blue tiled bathroom. He kissed her as they went.

"I have wanted to do that since I first saw you."

She snapped her fingers and around the room a dozen candles ignited. In the warm glow she returned the kiss. He relaxed his grip and she slid gently down his body. Pressed hard against her Norse god, she wiggled with lust. "Shut up and take off your clothes."

Instead he removed hers. She used her magic to turn the shower on and loosen the ponytail; her hair cascaded over her shoulders. He kicked off his boots.

"Do you have a spell for everything?"

By way of answer the rest of his clothes disappeared. He laughed.

"Some things I can do manually." She gripped his erection with a tender but firm hand. He shivered and moaned and thrust against her. The bathroom was cold and her hardened nipples grazed against his chest. He removed her hand for a moment to lift her into the shower.

They kissed passionately, naked and entangled. Hot water rained down on them sluicing the smells and dirt of the hunt away.

Her skin tingled. Ashley pressed herself against Ivar.

"This is what I've wanted to do since I first saw you argue with that poor sales assistant. You were so mad and so sexy."

"You are incredibly sexy no matter what you do." He pushed her up against the cold tiles.

Ivar was suddenly intense and serious. "Just because the spell is broken, does not mean that I do not love you. This is not simply a lustful dalliance for me Ashley."

"Together forever, is it?" She smiled.

"Yes. I offer you my heart for as long as it beats."

"I've already got your heart, and you have mine. For the record, the spell being broken hasn't changed the fact that I love you either. Just that this time I choose to."

He smiled. "I love you Ashley..." Ivar gave her an awkward look.

"Evergreen," she said.

"I love you Ashley Evergreen." He picked her up.

She wrapped her legs around his torso and kissed him. The room steamed up and enveloped them in a warm mist. Their bodies pressed together and their arms wrapped around each other. Ashley knew in her hunter's heart that she would never let him go.

Find this author on twitter:
@andrashocker, @andramerlyn and @merlyn_andra

Running with Magic
By
Sonja Fröjdendal

DEDICATION

To everybody who ever read one of my stories or encourage me to write and believe in what I can do. Thank you for giving me space to spread my wings, for following me on this journey. I hope you will continue to join me on my adventures in this beautiful world or words.

Sonja Fröjdendal / September 2015

CHAPTER ONE

Why would she think I need a reminder of the meeting? I have never missed one in the last twenty years, why miss one now? Guess it's one of those standard things everyone gets.

"So my lovelies, only two of you can follow to the meeting. Which two will it be? It'll be your decision to make, I don't have time for that. Need to pack for the trip." Sunshine looked at her familiars.

Considering Sunshine never missed an opportunity to do business she had a lot of packing to do. She was hoping she wouldn't encounter Teagan during this trip. He always had to be a pain in the ass. Ever since the time she left him hanging from a tree, he'd seen it as his mission to stalk her. He couldn't take a no for an answer. If he hadn't sneaked up on her that time she had been bathing in the lake, he wouldn't have ended up in the tree.

When she had solved the issues with Hamish, the ruler over all night demons, then Teagan could see her naked, hell he could touch her too then. He was the epitome of a fine demon. His skin shimmered in blue and black, drawing you closer to touch him to make sure he was real. It made her think of velvet. Shaking the thoughts off her mind, she changed her attire. Riding a dragon demanded clothes that could take a little beating. Leather pants and a tight top let her enjoy the ride without getting tangled in the harness.

As she packed the Tarot cards and Rune stones in the back pack, she made a mental list of herbs she needed to pick up at Reap What You Sow. That was one of the perks of going to these meetings, they were held in an occult shop. Only problem was Rose, the owner of the shop, sent chills down her spine. There was something about her that made most people want to walk away. Well, most people except for Adanna, the Supreme witch of the coven, she didn't seemed bothered. Sunshine had her reasons to not wanting Rose too close, she had a secret. People already thought she was a bit weird, if they knew the truth they'd really freak out. Shaking her head, Sunshine got back to making her list.

The click clack on the stone floor told her that Nikita was chosen to follow on the trip. Turning to face the wolf, she saw the candles in the hall blow out, the flaps of wings told her that Mr. Dumby was not the other companion, he'd sulk for weeks now.

"Who is following us, Nikita?"

The wolf tilted her head, her yellow eyes burrowing into Sunshine's. An image of a purple dragon appeared in Sunshine's head.

"Great! It's always nice to fly, shortens the travel time! We'll have to get your saddle out, we can't have you falling off in mid-air. Both of you will stay outside town during the meeting, normal people can't handle a wolf and a dragon in their midst."

Nikita snorted and curled up in a ball, seconds later she started to snore. Sunshine went over to the window and looked over to the stable blocks. The cave was barely visible behind the barn, nothing moved in the entrance but she still knew that Pila was inside. A little shimmer in the opening showed that something magical was hiding, only those with powers could notice but most of them wouldn't either, dragons rarely showed themselves. Pila felt safe, as she should, this estate was warded with protection spells. Sunshine's ancestors had lived in this area for centuries and no one came uninvited, no one even knew this place existed. Her friends knew she had a home somewhere around these parts of the world but they thought she lived in a small cottage, not in a big castle. Everyone in the world thought the US didn't have any castles. Yet, they existed, hidden behind the magic.

* * * *

Flying always filled Sunshine with joy, the rush of energy through her veins was making her an adrenaline junkie. Even Nikita seemed to enjoy it, though she wasn't on firm ground. Getting the specialized saddle was a good investment, she was now safe and warm. The humans thought they were clever with their airplanes. They had nothing compared to a dragon in the air. Being a witch had its perks, but not just flying, making magic was addictive. Some witches and warlocks couldn't handle it and went mad. Sunshine's great granddad had lost it, wiping out an entire village back in the 1600's. Not really something you talked about with others.

The event was recorded in a book, to be used as a warning of what could happen. The family history had its own section in her personal library, human historians would have a field day in there. Book lovers would trade a limb for the chance to get to read some of the books. Not every book or parchment had been destroyed in Alexandria.

A change in altitude warned Sunshine for the banking Pila was about to make before they landed in the woods outside of Savannah. Nikita jumped off as soon as she got released from her travel bag, stretching her legs and wandering away to search the area.

After taking off the saddle and reins, Sunshine put up camp. There was a great B&B in town but her familiars would not be welcomed. And there was no chance in hell or heaven she would leave them alone all night. Even though they could defend themselves, they could still be killed. Or stolen to be sold or used in a potion. Sunshine warded the camp with spells and charms. When Nikita came back from her tour around the camp site, Sunshine threw her backpack over her shoulder and walked into town. She would go to Stay a Spell to see if she could get any news about Teagan. It was always a good idea to know where he was.

CHAPTER TWO

On her way to Stay a Spell, Sunshine passed Reap What You Sow. She decided to pick up her order before she went to the B&B. Making a dead stop she turned around and went to the store. It always amazed her that ordinary humans didn't see the store for what it was, that they thought it was a gimmick. She had always enjoyed the smell of the store. Standing just inside the door she inhaled and let the emotions of the books and people flow over her. That was one of the few perks of being part witch and part Valkyrie. Feeling emotions of others wasn't something Sunshine did on a regular basis. That power belonged to the Valkyrie half and she didn't want to tap into that side. She wasn't a fan of taking someone's life for Valhalla, the Norse gods had to get their souls from someone else. Sometimes she had wished for different mother but that was a long time ago.

Unclenching her fists, she turned her attention back to the store. People walked up and down between the shelves. With no sign of Rose, Sunshine exhaled and went in deeper. Like a kid, she unintentionally touched the things she passed. Something she'd done all her life without thinking. She only knew that it was a good thing for the few times when she created spells. As she got closer to the counter, she collected the emotions in the back of her mind for later, her dad used them in potions sometimes.

There was a space behind the counter, except for the meeting room where the monthly meetings were, that always drew her close. She had no idea what was in there and she wouldn't dare ask Rose either, but she really wanted to know what it was. The Supreme witch would probably know but she never told someone else's secrets. Sunshine liked Adanna a lot and was glad that she was the Supreme one. She didn´t envy the position since she never wanted to be in charge of the coven.

A little noise behind her let her know that Rose was making her presence known. Without talking to Rose, she handed over the money and received the package of herbs that she had pre-ordered. That was the absolutely best thing with Rose, she never forced you to be friendly, she just let you be if that was your thing. With a little nod Sunshine left the store, she'd have to come back for the meeting but that was still a few days away.

* * * *

Entering Stay a Spell, Sunshine nodded to Seamus who stood behind the bar counter for the day, a benefit of being a regular was not having to place an order. When she sat down, her favorite drink was waiting for her. Further down the counter she noticed a young girl sipping on a drink, her long white hair was the most distinguished feature. The girl seemed nervous and unsure of why she was in there. Newbies was such giveaways, this one was no exception with her side-glances.

A hand on Sunshine's shoulder made her jump and spill her drink. It felt like she had her heart in her throat when she turned her head to face the owner. Seeing Hamish standing behind her heighten her senses and even quickened her pulse more. A cold stream ran down her spine, freezing her stiff.

"Sunshine my dear, how nice to find you here. Is everything okay? You don't return my calls. One might think you don't want to talk to me." Hamish lifted one eyebrow, cocking his head.

"If that's what you think, then why do you keep calling?" Sunshine took a deep breath.

"Because I know that you are busy and probably don't have time to return calls. So, knowing you would be in town for the coven meeting, I decided to pay you a visit. I figured it was the only option to get you to talk to me."

"I have no problem talking to you. It's the other thing I have a problem with." Deep breathing didn't calm her down as much as she hoped for. She couldn't focus enough to get her powers to work, somehow she needed Hamish to let go of her shoulder.

"I can't see why that is a problem. It's an honor, I assure you."

"I bet it is but I don't aspire to that honor. I have no feelings for you so it wouldn't be right. Take someone who really appreciate and want the privilege, someone who can make you proud." Sunshine stood up and took one step to the side, getting him to loosen his grip.

"Going somewhere?"

"Only to the ladies room. Is that a problem?"

"Oh, no. Go ahead dear. I'll wait here for you."

"We don't have anything to talk about. You got my answer and I'm not changing my mind. I'm not following you anywhere. Give up and leave me alone." Sunshine took another deep breath. Her voice started to give away her nervousness and that would be a bad thing.

"Let's say it like this. I'll leave you for now and let you finish your business in town. When the coven meeting is over, I'll send someone to pick you up for a visit to my home. If you still feel the same, you don't have to. How does that sound?"

His tone of voice made her feel patronized, like she was a small child.

"Good, let me do my thing in peace." Sunshine made sure she didn't make a promise she couldn't keep.

After kissing her hand, Hamish left Stay a Spell. She was off the hook for now. She had used the ladies room as an excuse but she went in there to cool her wrists. It usually helped her calm down. Staying focused was a necessity if the solution to get him to stop ever ought to show its face.

Back out by the counter, she found her things as she left them with the addition of a plate of hot food.

CHAPTER THREE

Teagan stretched his wings like normal people stretched their arms or legs when they woke up. Growing up he'd hated his wings, even in the magical world they were unusual. His siblings all had black leather wings, Teagan, on the other hand, had wings covered in feathers that shimmered in blue green. Now, in the ripe age of 365, he liked them. The color made him blend in in the forests and the seas, the feathers kept him warm in the cold.

Taking a deep breath he stepped in under the waterfall, letting it drench him completely. His thoughts wandered freely while he did the earthly thing of getting ready for the day. He needed to make sure to bump into Sunshine during this week, she'd avoided him for too long. That freaking dragon of hers was an excellent flier, she escaped his attempts to tail her every time. He would go to Rose's shop and see if he could find something to track that familiar of Sunshine's without being caught of course.

With a big flap of the wings, to shake of the water, he flew away to find his soul mate. The problem was to get her to agree they were soul mates, she was a bit pig-headed when it came to things out of her control. One of the things that made her perfect for him, she wouldn't just go along with everything he said. The other demons, especially the female ones, thought he would harm them if they didn't do what he wanted. His annoying sister had spread that rumor when they were just spawn, for the laugh of it. Teagan's dad had done everything he could do make sure it stuck, he had been afraid that they would think Teagan wasn't a real demon.

* * * *

Landing outside of Savannah, Teagan disguised his wings by folding them tight against his back, humans always seemed to freak out when they saw something that wasn't normal. A small shift in the atmosphere showed that someone had used magic somewhere near. Sunshine was the only witch he knew that didn't care much who knew she was around or what she was. A peace of mind came over him and he walked in to town. Her tracks were easy to follow, her energy signal was strong this close to Samhain.

On his way through town, he noticed a young woman coming out from Stay a Spell in a rush. It looked like she was shaking. Teagan slowed down to see if anyone followed her out, he didn't have to wait long before a young man came through the door. Their body movements made it look like they argued inside, whatever it was seemed to be forgotten quickly since they started kissing in the alley.

Teagan had no interest in watching others make out so he entered Stay a Spell. He wanted to get a drink before he ran into Sunshine, not that it helped to keep his cool around her. He knew she would be in town considering the time of year. She never missed the coven meetings and this one was extra important if he figured it out right.

The feeling that pulsed through his body when she touched him, when she was really pissed off was exhilarating. He needed that rush the way humans craved drugs. He now knew what it was like to be an addict. Nowadays she didn't have to touch him, it was enough to see her, like now by the bar, to remember it.

He was out in deep water and his family wouldn't be happy about it when they found out that he was in love with a witch. Too bad he couldn't keep it a secret, a downside to be a magical being, everything came out in the open sooner or later. Especially if you were a demon, they all knew if you kept something from them. Teagan walked to the bar and sat down beside Sunshine.

"Finally decided to join me?" Sunshine didn't turn her head when she spoke.

"I didn't want to intrude while you ate."

"Why are you here? Can't recall that we have a meeting."

"Can't a bloke talk to a gorgeous lady without a reason?" Teagan prodded at her.

"Sure they can, but you are no ordinary bloke and I'm not a lady. What are you up to?" Sunshine turned and stared at him.

"I have no ulterior motive other than I just want to talk to you." Teagan was mesmerized by her eyes that always seemed to hold the world in them.

"Seriously, Casanova. I'm not buying that bullshit! You always have a reason for talking to me, what do you want?" Sunshine hit him hard on the shoulder. It snapped him out of staring.

"Seriously, I don't! Can you stop hitting me every time we meet? It might have been cute in the beginning but now it's just making you look like a bitch." Teagan glared at her, rubbing his shoulder.

"Hmm, not sure I buy that but I'll lay off for now. So how's your family?"

"Why do you want to know about my family? You don't know them, do you?"

"Well, if we're going to be friends I should learn to know them." As she cocked her head, her long, blond hair flowed over her shoulder.

"My family are demons just like me, nothing to know." He couldn't figure out what she was after.

"And your other friends? You never mentioned them."

"What about them? They are not the right people for you to know." His frown got more noticeable.

"Are you saying that I can´t defend myself?" The wrinkle between her eyes got visible, showing her irritation.

"That is not what I´m saying."

"So what are you saying then?" Her face acted as an open book, showing her frustration over not understanding.

Teagan didn´t really know what he was saying so he grabbed her and pulled her close. As he kissed her, he got goosebumps all over his body. She tasted like honey, she smelled hyacinth. Her skin was smooth as silk when he caressed her arms. As he kissed her, he knew there was a price to pay. Sunshine didn't take kindly to beings that overstepped her boundaries. She would explode. He better be long gone when she did and that meant he had to be on the run the second he let her go.

CHAPTER FOUR

It was two days after the encounter in Stay a Spell and Sunshine was still simmering from the kiss. Thinking on the kiss and why Teagan kissed her worked her up. She hoped he didn't have an ulterior motive behind it. The kiss had created fireworks though, in more ways than one. Luckily Cook was a witch with a protection spell on her establishment, the place would have burned down otherwise. Teagan had run out quickly afterwards. Who knew demons were such cowards. She tried to focus yet again on what she was doing, trying to make her center herself.

When the cauldron boiled, she threw in the herbs she got from Reap What You Sow. It was quite handy to have an occult shop in the area. Made it so much easier to make spells and potions when she didn't have to collect the ingredients herself. Rose always got the good stuff Sunshine had to hand it to her, and she was a freaking magician. Even if she wasn't a witch.

The last things Sunshine needed for the spell were the bottled emotions she collected in the shop. Stirring them in would get her emotional, it always did. It was the downside of working with emotions. The spell would be stronger with them in so she didn't mind much.

"So, this is where you hide when you leave town?"

Startled, Sunshine dropped the bottle in the cauldron. Slowly she turned around to face him, that voice could only belong to one person.

"How did you find me and what are you doing here?"

"Well, you´re not that hard to follow when you are upset. You leave a trail of puddles of magic when you let things get the better of you."

"You followed me! What the hell!? Are you insane?" Her magic rushed to the surface. Telling someone off while concocting a potion wasn't the smartest thing, but she didn't care. It really hit her in the face when she messed a potion up. Especially if she made a potion to reinforce a spell. She could almost feel her face change as the potion hit her face.

Sunshine stared Teagan down, she was close to the boiling point. He had pissed her off already earlier in the morning, albeit he didn't know that. Having a spell backfiring in the face making her look like a horse's ass was not the way to get on her good side.

"What the HELL did you do that for? Are you TRYING to piss me off? Because if you are, you´re doing a damn good job." The chill that ran up her spine was a dead giveaway that her eyes would get more golden. If she didn't watch out, she would blow something up.

"If you can´t keep your temper in check, how the hell am I supposed to?" Teagan waved his arms in the air, growling the words out. "A simple question have you going all Frankenstein's monster on me. I only asked you why you wouldn´t make our arrangement permanent? What is it with you and relationships? Did poor little witchy get trashed by her Daddy who didn´t care?"

"How dear you drag my Dad into this? You have NO idea who he is or what he has done." The air around Sunshine shimmered and exuded heat. She didn´t want to stay any longer. Slowly she elevated into the air.

"Oh, no you don't! You don't run away from me!" Teagan spread his wings and flew up to her, grabbing her arms tight. "Trust me Sunshine, I mean you no harm. If not me, trust your heart, it won't lead you astray."

Sunshine stiffened up and glared at him. "Why did you say that? What do you mean with that?"

"It's something my Dad used to say when I was a youngster. Trust your heart, Son, it won't lead you astray. So far it never has." Teagan seemed to assess her reaction eagerly.

"Your Dad?"

"His name is Hamish."

"Hamish? That's your Dad? Well, that would explain a lot now, wouldn't it? Freaking Hamish? Why not complicate things even further?" Sunshine pushed away from Teagan and landed. Still steaming over it, she was leaving small fires in her wake.

"You know my Dad? How can you know him?"

"For heaven's sake, Teagan! Everyone knows about Hamish. If you are someone with powers that is. Working with magic, you sooner or later come across him and his minions."

"Sunshine? Can you stop walking around or at least put out the fires you're making?

"For crying out loud!" She waved a hand and the fires were out.

Teagan ignored the big wolf who came into camp and closed in close to Sunshine.

"Can you tell me now what made you mad at me this morning at outside Reap?" Keeping her in his arms soothed him and he noticed her breathing slowed down.

"You said I needed help! Really, am I that kind of woman that needs help? It pissed me off."

"I don't think you need help. I offered to help because that's what friends do, they help each other even if they don't have to. It's not pity, it's love. If my offer insulted you, I beg for your forgiveness."

"You love me, and I'm supposed to believe that? Okay, can we talk about this later? I can't handle this now, I have your Dad to deal with."

"Sure. Why do you say that? Deal with my father?"

"Hamish wants me, for himself as a partner." Sunshine shuddered.

"Why? Do you want him?" The shock was vivid in his voice

"I don't know, all he said was that I would light up his house with my presence."

"So you don't like him?"

"No, I don't like him."

"Good. You're my mate and I don't want to have to fight my father for you." He raised his hands defensively. "Don't blow me up or put me on fire, hear me out first. Ever since the first time I saw you, I've known that you are the one for me. That I had to have you by my side. Can you for once stand still long enough to feel something?"

* * * *

"Of course I can. I have found you intriguing since I saw you the first time three years ago. My heart skips a beat, my blood rush threw my veins when I see you or think of you. Why do you think we have this chemistry?" Sunshine laid her hand over his heart making the energies surrounding them change colour and intensity.

Teagan leaned in and kissed her gently, holding her face softly but firm. She liked the feeling. Wanting more, she pulled him closer. His moan thrilled her. Nikita nuzzling her way in between them, pushing them apart.

"What?" Sunshine couldn't mask her irritation.

Nikita whined and looked toward the other side of the open field. Both Teagan and Sunshine turned their heads. Five demons stood watching. All dressed in the same clothes that Teagan wore, showing that they came from Hamish's halls.

"What do you want?" Teagan took, a step forward, placing himself in front of Sunshine. When he spread his wings, she was hidden from their sight.

Clenching her fists, she braced herself for the impact the fist would make against Teagan's back. Annoyed because he was patronising her again, until she remembered he liked her. She really needed to get her temper under control. He just wanted her to be safe because he loved her, she would do the same thing for anyone she loved.

"We're here for you, Teagan. Your father wants you home, you're late. You have betrayed your father, by claiming his bride and have to pay the price."

By the sounds Sunshine could tell that one demon was coming closer. She took a step to the side, showing herself.

"You boys want to play? Let's play. I can't let Teagan have all the fun." Grinning from ear to ear, Sunshine made herself battle ready by letting all her emotions rush to her hands. Teagan changed position and she gave him a reassuring touch on the arm.

The remaining four demons charged like one, using the advantage of having wings to come from above. Just as one of them got close to her, Sunshine unfolded her own wings and took to the sky. The sound of turmoil from Teagan fighting two demons made her dive back down. The surprise of not having the advantage of wings were clearly shown on the demon's face that attacked her.

"What? You thought demons and angels are the only beings with wings?" Blowing him up with a fire ball was very satisfactory, the other one saw her powers and tried to flee. He didn't get far before she blew him up too. It didn't take long before Teagan killed the last two demons.

"You have wings?" Teagan's eyes looked like they were about to fall out.

"Yeah, so?"

"You never told me."

"It's none of your business. Or at least it wasn't but I guess I have to be honest. I'm not only a witch, I'm also a Valkyrie."

"Your Mom is a Valkyrie?"

"Yes, my Mom is a Valkyrie. You didn't think it was my Dad, did you?" She smiled wickedly.

"No, but it could have been a distant relative down the ancestry line. And you tell me this just now?" He paced up to her like the predator he was.

"Yes, I'm telling you this now, but only because you just asked. You shouldn't have secrets from your friends or your partner. Or was that just a lot of bullshit from you?"

"I never talk bullshit, as you say. I meant every word I said. I want you as my partner but I'm not going to rush you. I love you and can wait, not too long though."

"Okay. I like you too, maybe even love you." Her wicked smile grew wider.

He stared at her, closing in.

"Why do you smile like that? What are you up to?"

"Just this…" Sunshine tackled Teagan and kiss him fiercely. The built up tension exploded quickly making it feel like she was on fire. She could almost imagine the flames rising from their bodies, scorching everything close by.

When they emerged for air, a few minutes later, the clearing was on fire. Sunshine pulled away and threw herself on the burned ground, breathing heavily.

"That is what I call chemistry. No wonder things catch on fire."

Teagan chuckled and took a deep breath as he threw himself down by her side. "Yeah, it can´t be that you are a fiery personality. Can you put the fires out before the forest burns to the ground?"

A one-handed wave fixed the fire problem.

"Perhaps it's my fiery persona, but that won't help me get rid of Hamish. Your father wants me and he's sending goons to pick you up. Someone will be smart enough to stay in the shadows and spy on us. Are we going into hiding, which I know is something that we don't want to do, or do we go head on and enter the lion's cave?"

"We do neither, no hide or seek. We go on with our lives as before. If someone seek us out or finds us, we deal with it then. Why worry before we know anything? Seems like a waste of time, don´t you think?" He turned to his side and kissed her nose. "Are you going to fix your face or keep it as it is, as a reminder?"

"My face?" Sunshine gingerly touched one cheek.

"Crap! You destroyed my potion sneaking around like that on me."

"I did no such thing. You got scared and dropped the bottle. It´s not my fault if you don´t have a ward system up when doing magic."

"Hmph." Sunshine got up on her feet's and chanted a reverse spell. She watched Teagan's face while doing so, she wanted to know how he would react. This was the first time she did magic on purpose in front of someone who wasn't a witch. His face showed curiosity.

"How does it feel when you do that? We can't do magic like that, at least not me."

"It feels normal, nothing weird or anything like that. So you can't do any magic at all? But other demons can do magic."

"I'm a night demon, even if I show myself to you at any time of day, my realm is dreams usually. I'm a demon of nightmares. I'm not the only one but we have different zones so to speak. No one will work in my zone, not with nightmares anyway." He winked at her.

"Yeah, I figured that one out myself considering all the demons at Stay a Spell."

"Was it an important spell or potion you were working on? Do you need to find a new bottle with whatever it was?"

"No, I can get it from here if I need to. It was bottled emotions and we have lots of that around, don't you think? The potion its self was something I was going to do just in case I needed it against Hamish, I'm not very good at making potions. As you can tell."

"So are you going to make it again?"

"I don't think I'll need it now that you are around. I just have to make sure we have Pila with us and the demons will hopefully stay away. If not, she'll help with the fighting. When did you start following me?"

"I followed you because I wanted to know where you live, which I still don't know, and to see if I could get you to understand that we are made for each other. I started following you a few days ago, when you left Savannah."

"You do know that this following me business is sounding a little like stalking, don't you?"

"Yes, it seems like stalking and I wouldn't have done it if it was someone else."

"Why follow me then?"

"Because I knew you would likely kick the living daylights out of me if you felt any danger of sort." He was now shaking from his suppressed laughter.

"So if I had been a delicate flower, you would have courted me?" She raised one eyebrow.

"Yes, I would have. You miss a lot when you are a capable woman."

"Hmm, I might be a delicate flower. You don't know that."

"Really? That comes from a woman who was pissed off at me because, I quote, I don't need help from any one." He couldn't hold in his laughter any longer and let it out.

"Eh, shut up!" She said but couldn't help but laugh herself too.

CHAPTER FIVE

After his offer of help had been turned down, Teagan watched Sunshine clean up the mess after the exploding potion and the demons. He hadn't grasped that she actually agreed to be his partner, without trying to kill him first. To this day, three years after the first time they met, he remembered the feeling of her touch and what she wore. That day it had been a bright green dress with yellow flowers on it. A couple of days ago it was a rainbow coloured one and today it was a red one. He had never seen her in anything dark and gloomy. She didn't fit the profile of a witch according to the books and movies in the human world.

He had to figure out a way to keep her away from his father. Teagan's mood sank as he thought of his father. Hamish would change her to fit in his world, change the thing that drew him to her. Mold her the same way he did every female he lured in. Sunshine would not cave in easily, she would break and her soul would die. Most beings in the magical world would be scared to learn she was half Valkyrie. Too bad his father wasn't one of them, he would only see that as another reason to make her his. Sunshine might believe that the dragon Pila was enough as protection but she didn't know his father.

"Are you ready, lazy?" Sunshine snapped her fingers beside his ear.

"Who are you calling lazy? Why should I help you clean up your mess?"

"Oh, really? It's my mess now? What happened to the demon who said friends help each other? Especially since it was your father's, aka your, friends or family members that we wiped out?"

Seeing her smile like that and joke with him only reaffirmed his desire to protect her.

* * * *

Landing on the courtyard outside the castle of Sunshine's home was an eye opener. It was huge, perched high up on a mountain cliff. It was impregnable. He knew nothing about her family. Would they accept him, being a demon and all?

"Never seen a castle before, sweets?"

"Not one this big and this high up. I guess your family built it originally?"

"My great, great, great what-ever ancestor thought his family should be protected from the humans and their fears. Luckily for him, he had a huge family that could help him build it. Of course, they used magic to make it easier and faster to build it. He was no moron and he didn't want to risk his daughters because they didn't have a good place to hide."

"So they all married witches and warlocks or were their spouses tolerant people?"

"No, no, some of them were humans. Not all of them knew about the magic though. They were kept out of loop of everything unless they needed to be safe from protection. If you want to, you can read about it in the library. There have always been historians in my family, everything is recorded for the future. Let's get inside now, you need to meet the family."

"Your family?"

"You thought I lived alone?"

"I didn't think at all on your living conditions." Sweat trickled down his spine. Meeting the family when they'd just decided to be a couple wasn't really what he wanted to do today.

"Come on, little coward. It's just Dad and my Aunty at home, maybe my sister and her husband. I don't think my brother is back from his trip to Europe yet so his family won't be here." The twinkle in her eye gave her away.

"You're just messing with me. Do you really think I will turn around with my tail between my legs and run?" Teagan pulled her close and kissed her.

"You don't have a tail." She put a hand between them.

"You think I'd bail on you?"

"Nah, you aren't that much of a coward. But don't worry, if you survived living with Hamish all these years, you'll survive a meeting my Dad." The smile he loved was visible again.

"If you say I'll survive, let's do this and get you packing so we can get you to that coven meeting." He felt his smile mirroring hers.

* * * *

"Sunshine, have you read all these books?" Teagan stared wide-eyed around the library.

"No I haven't, not yet anyway. There is a section in the back with the Latin books I haven't got to. My Latin isn't good enough for it and I've been busy with other things." The muffled voice came around a corner making it a little hard to understand what she said.

"How many books does this library contain?"

"I'm not sure. Dad said something about doing a shopping spree the last time he was home. I don't know how many new books he bought and all that. But if we don't count that, there is a few millions of books in here."

"The books you are looking for now, are you going to use them at the meeting or are you lending them to someone? Aren't you afraid they'll get damaged or get lost?"

"We have more than one copy of the books I'm giving away. The one that looks like it's over grown with lava is a beginner's guide to be a witch. One witch from the coven needs them. She'll be at meeting so I said I'd bring them and save her the trip out here. She doesn't have a dragon."

"Not many people do."

"I'm spoiled. I thank Dad for that."

"Thank me for what, sweetheart?"

"Dad!" Sunshine threw herself around the neck of the man who entered the room.

The dark haired man was tall, even if he didn't reach Teagan's six foot, five inches, with broad shoulders. A human might get intimidated by his strong presence but Teagan was a demon and few people frightened him. *So that's where she gets it from, all the love.* The sensations filled the room and his heart, he realised he never had a choice. A demon has no defence against love.

"What are you thanking me for?"

"Just that I got a dragon to ride."

"I see, well you always wanted one so why not."

"And how many parents would give their daughter a dragon as a gift?"

"True, my dear. Who is you friend?" He turned his attention to Teagan.

"I'm Teagan, sir. Your daughter's mate."

"I'm Max. Mate you say? You hide your wings well but I guess you're a demon of sort?" Max shook Teagan's hand with a firm grip.

"A night demon."

"One of Hamish's brood then. Doing his bidding or can you think for yourself?"

"I think for myself, sir. I'm not in my father's lead."

"That's easy to check." Max snapped his fingers and stared into Teagan's eyes.

"Dad! Why do you have to act like this?" Sunshine glared.

"Because you never brought one home before and that tells me you mean business. I don't want you getting hurt."

Teagan saw and heard them but couldn't move or talk. He could feel the sweat drizzle down his face. His heart beat pounded in his ears. He also felt another presence in his head, poking around like it was looking for something hidden. It was an odd feeling and he hoped it would be over soon. Max stared into his eyes the entire time while he delved deeper into Teagan's mind. All of a sudden the intruding presence was gone and Max smiled warmly.

"He is a keeper, sweetheart. He has his flaws and he has done terrible things. But his love for you is pure and I think you will have a good influence on him. Being a demon won't be an issue, you'll just have to understand that he will protect you at all cost. You'll probably have lots of head-butting but if you both communicate, it won't be anything to worry about."

* * * *

Flying was something Teagan had done all his life. Doing it on the back of a dragon was totally different. He had taken a deep breath when they landed outside of Savannah. The experience was not on his top ten list, not that he would tell Sunshine that. She'd probably scorch him.

"Are you ready to go in to town? The meeting starts soon and I have to be there in time. I also have the book delivery, you know."

"Just waiting for you to do your wards around the place for Pila. Sorry that I can't help you with that."

"It's something I've done since I was a toddler, I can do it in my sleep."During the walk into town, Teagan noticed a bunch of signs that hinted that something was wrong. He hadn't heard a single bird chirp since they left camp. Walking with a witch that was one with nature should have kept them singing. Not too far from town they encountered four demons blocking their way.

They stared at Teagan, and two of them took a few steps closer. "Teagan, we can do this the easy way or the hard way. Which way do you want it?"

"Well, I would prefer you leave me alone but I guess that's not an option. I'll take the hard way then. Wouldn't want to spoil the fun for my girl. Ready, my dear?"

"I'm ready, love. Let's do this." As Sunshine got ready to throw a fireball at them, she found her arms tied down to her sides. Four more demons stood behind her and held tight, preventing her from helping Teagan fight. He was surrounded by demons but he didn't need the support.

Teagan and Sunshine were outnumbered but he trusted the Sunshine would take out most of them with a few spells. He had always enjoyed messing around with the other demons. They were proud and he took advantage of their mistakes. This time though they fought with determination and didn't back down. His brothers didn't play fair, several attacking at the same time. Teagan started to take as many hits as he gave, making it difficult to fight. Teagan felt like a fool, he should have known that his father would ambush him.

Between hits, Teagan noticed that Sunshine was still restrained. He pulled all his effort to his wings and knocked a few demons out when he flew over to Sunshine. He pulled her to him. He kissed her, getting her energies to flame and burning the demons holding her. With their backs against each other, they fought off the remaining demons, feeding off each other's strength.

"I have an appointment. Do you mind if I finish this off?" Sunshine's tone was filled with irritation.

"Be my guest."

"Good. Then duck."

Teagan hit the ground seconds before a huge fireball burned the enemy to cinders. It was a good thing that his witch could put out fires as good as she made them. There were no real danger to burn down the forest.

"Are you okay, love? Did I burn you?" She knelt beside him, stroking his cheek with her fingers.

"You didn't hit me with it. Your aim is impeccable." Teagan brushed the dirt off his clothes as he stood.

They held each other for a few minutes, glad that they were still together and in one piece. A little singed at the edges and some cuts but nothing major.

"Did they hurt you?" Teagan pushed her away and examined her to see if she was injured.

"They didn't touch me, except when they restrained me. I think your Dad has them too well trained for that. Would they dare to hurt the next queen?" She raised an eyebrow.

CHAPTER SIX

"Are you sure you're not going to stay in the shop during the meeting?" Sunshine put a hand on Teagan's arm.

"Yes, I'm sure. Some of witches are new ones and they might not have met any demons before. I don't want them to feel uncomfortable. I'll be around making sure it's safe."

"Do you really think your Dad would be so reckless to attack a shop full of witches? He isn't stupid. A fool, yes, but not stupid. He'll wait until we are by ourselves before doing it again. Can he afford to lose more demons?"

"He has millions of lower level demons to use for his handy work. He doesn't care if he loses a few thousands as long as he gets what he wants. How do you else think he has stayed the master of them for all these years? He won't back down in a hurry. Not as long as he thinks he will get what he wants."

"Well, he won't get me no matter how many demons he sends. There is no way in hell, or heaven that that will happen. You don't have to worry." Embracing him made her believe in her own words.

"I'm more worried that he'll kill you or put you in one of the prison caves if you don't do as he wants." Teagan hugged her more tightly.

"Let's make a deal. I promise not to leave the shop without company and you go to Stay a Spell during the meeting? Okay?"

"It's a deal. I don't trust my father, so please follow the deal." He looked her sternly in the eyes.

"I promise I'll stay safe. As safe as I can, you know me." She smiled.

"Yes, I know you by now." A smile lingered in the corner of his mouth.

"I'm going in now since I've got to get these books to their new owner. And I want to see if Rose has any books about demons, need to find the tricks to keep you in line." The corner of her mouth twitched as she said it.

"well, there is one. Some Norwegian author wrote about a family of witches and talents. My uncle Tamlin is mention in it. He fell in love with a human and chose humanity and mortality. Dad never talks about him. Anyone who mentions him is executed or sent to the cave. Not even Grandma talks about him."

"Good! I'm not the only one with family secrets."

"I thought you liked to be the black sheep in the bunch."

"Sure, I have no problems being that with my friends but when it comes to my love life, I prefer my partner being my equal in every way." She winked at him.

"I agree on that part, love. Have fun in the meeting and I´ll see you later." After a tip-of-the-nose-kiss, he nudged her in the direction of the shop door.

She entered the shop and turned to wave at him, knowing he´d be standing there until she was safely inside. This Halloween would be a really great one. She made her way behind the counter and went down the stairs to the meeting room.

Links:
www.twitter.com/FrjdendalSonja
www.facebook.com/sonjafrojdendalauthhor
www.writingwenches.com

Magical Shift
By
Kay Blake

DEDICATION

I dedicate this one to you, the reader. Thank you so much for reading and I appreciate you. To My Witchy Wenches Coven, thank you so much. Rebekah Ganiere, you are so awesome. Tami Lund, Jennifer McMullen Ray and Andra Jenkins. I thank you for critiquing for me. You three made my story better and I love you guys to pieces. Thanks for your help.

Love you all

Kay

CHAPTER ONE
October 30th

    I grimaced as the signs of another headache appeared. My temples were killing me. Pain throbbed around like a beating drum. They've gotten worse the past few days. Ever since my nana passed, their frequency had increased, now they were debilitating.

    I did everything Nana taught me to try to get rid of the headaches. Her herbal medicines and special brews were magic. Most times they worked. They always made me feel better, no matter my ailment. Today not so much. Her remedies were one of many things I missed about her.

    Most times when I had an extremely bad headache, something bad would happen. The day my dog died when I was younger, I had the worst headache and when I came home from school, Nana told me what had happened. It was the same for a week before the most important person in my world was taken from me. In my eyes the worst thing that could ever happen to me already did.

    I glanced out the kitchen window. Darkness obscured the sky, patches of light peaked through the horizon. Perfect for my morning run. Taking a sip from a bottle of water, I glimpsed at the picture on the mantel. I picked it up to wipe the dust off it. In it, I sat on Nana's lap, a huge smile plastered on my face. I didn't have the same chubby cheeks, but my dimples were still there. My body now slim and toned. My cheek bones high. I looked very much the same, but yet more grown up.

    At the age of five, my parents died and Nana raised me. She was everything to me, my mother, my father, and my best friend too. Man, I missed her.

Placing the picture back down, I picked up the picture of my childhood friend Sabrina. I found it going through Nana's things. We were two peas in a pod. Inseparable actually. Everywhere we went it was Paige and Sabrina. One day she stopped coming over. Nana told me she wouldn't be living with her aunt anymore, but she never mentioned why. I had no way of contacting her. Nana absolutely refused any contact with Sabrina. She was like talking to a brick wall when I asked about Sabrina. At first it hurt, but eventually it eased. Sabrina crossed my thoughts many times over the years.

I pulled my shoulder length wavy brown hair back into a messy ponytail and stepped outside. A cool breeze hit me and I shuddered. It was colder than usual for an October morning in Savannah, Georgia. Usually at this time of year, my brown skin would bronze, the color left over from the summer sun.

I inserted my ear buds and started my IPod. The woods near my home were made for peaceful runs. Nana used to warn me about going into the woods alone. She always had fearsome stories about what went on in there. As a child, her stories fascinated me. She would insist there were dangers in the woods, and forbid me to go in. I wouldn't know what was in there since even as an adult, I never wandered too far in. Nana had powers that I didn't.

Me? I received my powers a year ago at midnight. At first I thought I'd lost things, my keys and my sunglasses. Then later I'd find them in different places. By the time I arrived at the Halloween coven meeting, I had realized that I was accidentally moving things around. At first it seemed fun, but after a while, I grew frustrated because I didn't know how to control the telekinesis. I'd find my hairbrush in the fridge and the flour would end up in the linen cupboard. Glasses would be broken on the hall floor. Almost a year and endless practice later I have a greater degree of control. Nana would've made sure I learned it all, but I think I did pretty well for someone who had to figure it out on her own. Although when I'm angry or tired, I still tend to do things more unintentionally than not.

My usual route took me around the edge of the woods; a circuit that ended back home. I could take the road on the opposite side, but that led into town. Now that Nana had passed, I had been going further in, not when the run was so peaceful and the forest so close to my house.

I paced myself as I ran past the trees. Pink's upbeat tunes dazzled my eardrums. I reveled in the sense of freedom running gave me, even if it was only for a moment.

Nana often called me her special little girl. She said there weren't many of us in the black culture. I came from a long line of witches and I inherited the powers I got. It skipped generations. Many of the other black witches my nana had known in her lifetime learned their occult knowledge from books and spells.

I kept up my pace until the feeling I wasn't alone in the woods crept up on me. I took one of the headphones out and scanned my surroundings to see if I could spot something. My intuition was usually right. I turned around a few times, seeing nothing, I placed my earphones back in. Lately, I have been feeling like I was being watched. Most times the presence didn't feel threatening, and other times it did. Maybe Nana was warning me away from the woods from beyond.

The hairs on the back of my neck pricked up and I picked up the pace. I could hear all of Nana's past warnings in my head, but I needed my daily run like I needed coffee. It was my fix.

My senses tingled again. I spun around again this time certain that I wasn't alone. I didn't want to deal with the abnormal today.

I was isolated by my abnormality. Okay, yes, I had the coven. The coven, a sacred place with friendly enough witches, but they weren't my nana. I had always been an awkward girl. I guess kids didn't know how to relate to a girl who lost her parents. It was school and then home for me. That was until I met Sabrina. Sabrina was the only girl to talk to me and become my friend.

I stood up on my tippy toes to see if I could get a better look through the trees. Not that it helped much, I'm so short, but it couldn't hurt. Looking to my left, I caught sight of a pair of what looked like blue silver eyes and I shrieked. I moved around and strained my eyes, but the trees made it impossible to see. Counting quietly, I kept running hoping that my instinct was wrong, that is was just my imagination working on overdrive.

I forced the worried thoughts from my mind and tried to concentrate on the things I had to do today. As a personal trainer who worked from home, I could work my schedule around my clients. I loved the enthusiasm my clients felt whenever we would meet up. Their dedication was a big plus for me.

Reaching the end of my normal route, I turned to head back home. Little beads of sweat rolled down my face. Suddenly I wanted nothing more than to be at home.

* * * *

I waited in the woods as I have been doing for many weeks with barely any sleep. Mentally and physically I was exhausted. She stopped several times to search the area so I knew she saw me. She seemed jumpy and nervous, but she continued her run. At one point I was sure she noticed me, but maybe she thought it was a wolf in the forest. She didn't outright run away screaming, but she did yelp a little.

I had been followed. I knew the other presence in the woods and she wouldn't let up. There wasn't enough time to get into a confrontation with her. She was more powerful than I expected her to be. I was attacked and pain shot up my body. I howled when my flesh tore, but I had to get to Paige. My legs were beginning to give out on me, so I crawled. Each time I moved took more effort than the last. The pain unbearable. I reached Paige's door and realized I had beat her here. Seeing the entrance, I dragged myself inside, changing unbidden. All my determination was at its breaking point and all I saw was darkness welcoming me in.

* * * *

I was only about ten feet from my front entrance when a strange sound hit my eardrums, so loud it overpowered the music from my IPod. Both whimpering and growling filled the air.

Unsure if the sounds I heard came from my house, I crept forward, and realized my door was open a little.

Pink faded as I took my headphones out, I cautiously looked around, ready to run or fight. Ill prepared for an attack, I slowly opened the door. My speed, might not be enough if I was outmatched and I still didn't trust myself enough to use my powers. Besides even though I mingled with humans, I had to keep my powers hidden.

Shit. Shit. Shit. I peeked my head into my entryway knowing that an intruder could be anywhere in the house. The knives were in the kitchen and they were the only weapons I had, but there were a lot of places for someone to hide on the way there.

Maybe, I can bring the knives to me from here. No that wouldn't work. With my luck trying me trying to bring the knives with my telekinesis would come with the blade first at full speed. My telekinesis made my life very complicated at times.

I moved in further into the entryway trying to get closer to the kitchen. I was able to get a few steps from the kitchen when something grabbed me and I screamed. I kicked out and immediately the grip released. I fell to the floor. A loud thud came from behind me. Scrambling to get myself up, I turned around and there lay the most athletic – and naked – man I have ever seen. He lay on his stomach.

Oh my God. These kinds of things only seems to happen to me.

I raced to the kitchen, grabbed one of the knives and rushed back to the man lying on my floor. He was lying face down and his head laid to the side. Reaching down apprehensively, I pushed his long black hair away from his face and got a good look at his strong jawline and goatee. His skin was tanned. He could be the bogeyman my nana warned me about so many times in my youth.

Dropping the knife to the floor, I rushed to help him. Checking his airways, I realized his pulse was good. I didn't see anything broken, though he was cut. Luckily Nana taught me a lot about medicine. As long as he was comfortable he would be fine. There was still a small part of me that was nervous about this man who seemed more asleep than anything else. Something about him was certainly different, but what was still unknown. There was also something familiar about him, but I couldn't peg my finger on what it was that seemed like I knew him at some point or at least seen him before.

Paranoid? Maybe, but how else could I possibly be? Strange things happened to me all the time. If you asked people outside of the magical realm they would tell you they considered me odd.

Turning his body over slowly, I noticed an expression of discomfort graced his features. A nasty red scratch grazed his cheek. There was some kind of brand that was on his left arm. It covered his shoulder, and went down right above his elbow. His body looked strong. I admit, I was a bit scared, but something inside told me I needed to help him.

Positive that my floor couldn't be comfortable, I thanked my lucky stars that my couch converted to a bed. More than likely I could heal him myself. From what I gathered he didn't need a hospital. He didn't even need stitches. I could heal him myself. Deep down I knew if Nana had found him when she was alive, she would help him, no questions asked. She had a heart of gold.

I took a deep breath, moved him onto the bed. I hoped I didn't hurt him in the process. I struggled as I dragged him to the couch. Getting his top half on the couch first, I took a deep breath, and pulled his lower half up next. If I hadn't appreciated being fit before, I did today.

He had a long nasty gash on his chest. Not enough to require stitches, but still raw. I winced. It looked painful. I got up and went to my attic. There were different enchanted herbs my nana had left me and up until now I really had no use for them outside of those that helped with my headaches. All the adrenaline pumping, I didn't even realize that my headache had disappeared.

I picked up some comfrey and some fresh parsley my nana would use to reduce swelling and the discoloration bruises usually left. I rushed down to the kitchen, ready to start the brewing process. I also grabbed some bilberries that could be used in a tea.

Keeping the knife with me, I took turns to stir the brew and watch the living room. I called my clients for the day and rescheduled. How could I explain why a man lay naked on my couch?

After twenty minutes the brew was made; I pulled out my small wooden bowl and mashed the concoction into a paste.

With the paste in one hand, and warm water in the other, I walked over to the man who lay on my couch. I placed the items on the floor and kneeled by his side. I used the warm water to clean his wound. His chest moved up and down steadily, which was a good sign. I applied the paste and made sure it all absorbed into his skin. Turning my attention to his cheek, I applied the herbal paste there, too. Handsome wasn't enough to describe him. I knew I should be afraid of him, but I wasn't. I placed the blanket over him and let him sleep.

CHAPTER TWO

Shortly after noon, the handsome stranger finally woke up. I watched from across the room as he stood. He moved around the room and peered through each of the windows, I wondered what he hoped to see as I watched him. At first I couldn't be sure if he noticed my stare, because he didn't react, but was still in all his naked glory. His body was absolute perfection. He sniffed the air and his shoulders dropped, his demeanor changed from hyper alert to relaxed. He caught my eye and with one quick motion he wrapped the blanket around his torso.

He touched the now faint mark on his chest and then gave me a look that sent exciting chills down my spine. I guess Nana's enchanted herbs did the trick. I didn't know anything about him, yet for some reason, I sensed I could trust him.

His face was serious and his beautiful blue eyes pierced through my soul. He stood a foot taller than me and I wondered what it would feel like to have those massive arms around me. I knew if that blanket didn't cover him, I would admire what lay underneath. I was a twenty two year old woman and men say they find me attractive, but I haven't been laid in eight months, so could you blame me for being horny?

"I'm Kean." His deep voice interrupted my fantasies.

"I'm Paige." I glanced down at the floor, and tried my hardest not to look at the bulge barely hidden by the blanket.

"Paige. Thank you for not leaving me on the floor."

"My nana would roll in her grave, if I wasn't hospitable."

"Your nana?"

"My grandmother. Well, my late grandmother. She always taught to try to help those in need, and considering you were lying in the middle of my floor, I assumed you needed help.

He smirked and my heart pounded so fast, I thought it would beat out of my chest.

I averted my gaze. I didn't want to be rude, but the longer I stared at Kean, the more I knew I would jump his bones. I could already feel the tingles start and all of that from his smirk.

"Uh, I cleaned up your wounds. The one on your chest seemed pretty nasty," I said, looking at him again thoughtfully.

He glanced down at his chest then back at me.

"Thank you. This now just looks like an old scar;" he said.

"You're welcome. Your wounds scared me a little at first."

He gave a slight nod and glanced at his chest again.

"May I ask if you have any clothes for me to wear? Not to say I don't like to be free at times, but I don't want to make you uncomfortable." He gave a small smile and winked.

"I have some of my father's old clothes in the attic. I haven't really gotten around to looking thorough all it, but I think there should be something that can fit."

I quickly went up the stairs. My attic stood in the middle of the hall on the ceiling. Pulling the cord, I opened the attic door. As a kid, I hated coming up here. Walking up the stairs that were rickety at best, I smelled all too many familiar scents. It was like Nana was still alive. A tear slipped down my face.

There were tons of boxes, but I found the one I was looking for behind some old childhood toys of mine. Nana was such a hoarder. Getting the box I needed, I headed back to the stairs and threw the box of clothes down the stairs.

Once I was back downstairs, I handed the box to my guest. When he took the box from me, it took everything from me to not stare too hard at his muscles.

If only he could wrap those arms around me.

"Uh...let me show you the bathroom." I quickly walked out and he followed me. His gaze burned through my back. Once we reached the bathroom, I opened the door and pointed to the towels and other essentials.

"I figured you wanted to take a shower. Take as long as you need. I'll be downstairs if you need me. After we can talk."

"Thank you."

I made my escape and closed the door.

Once downstairs, I plopped down on the couch and closed my eyes. His scent lingered in the air. Twiddling my fingers, nerves, and curiosity filled my thoughts about the stranger that showered upstairs. I wondered where he came from. How did he find me?

Kean's shower was short, when he walked in wearing the clothes I had brought him it brought back memories of the man who used to own them. My father was also tall, and Kean towered over me. I quivered inside. He had on a form fitting black tee and the blue jeans my father used to wear when he took me out for ice-cream. His long black hair glistened from being wet and his blue eyes gleamed.

"Thanks for the clothing, the shower and everything else you've done since I've been here," he said

I wonder what he's thinking. Better yet, how did he end up in my house?

"No problem. I'm sure you're hungry." I could feel his gaze on me as I opened the fridge door.

"I have steak, but it's frozen, so dinner might be a while. Would you settle for a quick trip into town and we can get something to eat?"

Kean looked at me and gave a small grin. "That will be fine, Paige."

"Before we do that, I have some questions for you."

"Sure, ask away, he said.

"What happened to you? Why were you laying on my floor?"

"Honestly, I don't know."

"You don't know?" I gave him a look of disbelief.

"No. I didn't get a chance to get a good look at it. All I know was I was attacked and I ran. I ended up here."

The answer he gave didn't satisfy me, but I didn't push. Being attacked by something you didn't see was a lot to go through.

"So you are?" I asked.

"I told you my name already," he said with a small smile.

"You know I didn't mean that. Better question, what are you?"

"Don't you mean who?"

"No, I mean what. Something about you is different. Most people don't run naked and you smell different too. Not human necessarily." My brow furrowed.

"Seeing that you were able to make me like brand new, I am sure you don't go around spilling your guts to someone you barely know," he said.

He was right. I was around humans all the time and none of them knew I was a witch.

"I can understand that," I said. I thought for a moment.

"Don't you think I deserve some kind of explanation about why you ended up in my home and on my floor?"

"You do," he said with a serious tone.

"Do you plan on telling me, or is giving me one word answers the route you're going to take?" I asked, my eyebrow raised.

"I knew your grandmother."

"You did? I don't recall her mentioning you, and I don't know about you at all. I'm pretty sure I would remember someone like you," I said skeptically.

"Your grandmother, or Ms. Alecia as we called her, always treated me and my family with kindness. I met her when she healed one of my cousins. She was picking some herbs by our house on the other side of the woods. He got into a pretty bad accident, but we couldn't go to the hospital. There was no way too explain what really happened. After that my mom and Ms. Alecia became friends even though she wasn't a witch like her." He had a hint of a smile on his face. Nana usually caused that reaction in people.

"That sounds just like Nana. She always wanted to help someone."

"She helped my family tons of times and now I am returning the favor or trying too."

"How exactly do you plan to return the favor?"

"By keeping my promise to her."

I didn't get the vibe that he lied to me and his eyes stayed on me the whole time.

"She was a wonderful woman;" I said wistfully.

"I'm starved. Let's go into town," I said.

Grabbing my purse and jacket, we headed out.

We headed to Stay a Spell on River Street. I loved this place. Cook made amazing food and this place catered exclusively to the magical community. We found an empty booth and sat. I noticed the stares of the other patrons on Kean. I suspected it was partially because I did not usually frequent this place with a man on my arm. It could also be because Kean was sexy as all hell.

Cook stopped by briefly and gave a warm smile. Her food was always superb. Cook was also an excellent judge of character.

We ate in comfortable silence for a while. I watched his jaw work as he chewed the perfectly medium rare steak thanks to Cook.

"This is really good;" he said in between chews.

"That's one of the reasons I love Cook. She has the magic touch in the kitchen."

I took one more bite and then placed my fork on the plate. "So…" I continued. "Are you planning on telling me exactly what you are?"

"What?"

"Stop trying to dodge my questions. What are you? My nana, though kind, stuck to the magical folk, so that means you fit that category."

"So what are you, some kind of a werewolf?"

"A werewolf?"

"Yeah, a werewolf. I don't know, it kind of fits you."

He chuckled.

"No. I'm a shifter. A werewolf needs the moon to change, and I can change at will."

"Can you shift into anything?"

"I can, but I prefer wolves."

"So, that's why you were naked earlier?" I asked, feeling my cheeks heat up.

"Yes, that's why."

"Hmm"

"Hmmm, what?" he asked, his brow raised.

"I am trying to figure out how Nana ran into a whole family of shifters in the first place."

"As, I mentioned earlier, we lived on the other side of the woods and many of the stuff your grandmother used was around our home. Growing up a shifter, you are unlikely to have much control in animal form. That was how my cousin got hurt. If it wasn't for your grandmother, my cousin would have died. She saved his life. My family and I owe her so much. We promised her that we wouldn't come near you. She also told us if we saw you in the woods to let you know. We fixed things around the house and she made sure you was never there. I started watching out for you when she started running near the woods."

"Nana kept me busy. She said idle time led to trouble, so I kept busy. Dancing, singing, you name it."

"You sing?" he asked again his eyes gleaming with a smile.

"A little. Not too much anymore." I shrugged.

Kean placed the fork on the now empty plate.

"Today has been too bizarre," I said.

"I promise I will tell you all I can when we get back to the privacy of your home."

I nodded. I wasn't sure how to take what he said

I finished my food and we sat in silence. My thoughts were all over the place. I wanted to know why would this handsome man had come into my life out of the blue. And why did I have the strange urge to keep him as close as possible.

After we finished eating, we decided to take a walk around River Street. River Street, the magical community hangout was known for the shops that littered the street.

"Outside of randomly popping up in girls home, what do you do?" I asked jokingly.

"I'm a mechanic."

"A car guy huh?"

He shrugged.

"Yeah, I have a thing for engines and seeing a car go from nothing to something is one of the best feelings in the world," he said.

"Interesting. I pegged you for the guy who wrestles bears in the woods." He stopped for a moment and laughed loudly.

"I've never heard that one before. Good one."

"I aim to please;" I said mockingly. "Do you have a girlfriend?" I asked him.

"I did. Not anymore"

"Is it someone I know?"

"You did. Once."

What could that possibly mean?

"Meaning?" I asked.

He sighed for a moment. "Do you have any significant other hiding around?" he asked completely ignoring my question, his voice casual.

"Nope. I haven't had a boyfriend in a long while. Though Nana tried fixing me up with many people before." I laughed and shook my head.

"Was it that bad?"

"No, for the most part. I just hate being set up with guys and knowing that I would do something that would result in never getting a phone call again. She insisted on playing matchmaker and I loved Nana, but that drove me insane."

Kean laughed.

"Your grandmother was quite a woman. Sometimes it felt like she was out grandmother too. I miss her;" he said with a sad smile on his face.

"I know what you mean. I miss her every single day."

We continued to stroll and window-shop. This was the first time in a long while I had the company of someone that didn't grace my television screen, and I liked it. Not too long during our stroll, my temples begun to hurt.

"My headache is returning;" I said with a grimace.

A quick flicker of worry passed across Kean's face. He looked out across the road and his body language changed. He froze and no longer relaxed, he gently but insistently tugged on my arm.

"I think we should get you home, Paige." He tried shuffling me to the car.

"What's wrong? What are you looking at?" I looked around to the location he was looking at, but saw nothing. I didn't understand why the sudden rush to get home.

"You will shortly," he said. "Assuming we get back to your place in one piece."

CHAPTER THREE

"You're what?" I shrieked at Kean as he sat across the kitchen table with his blue eyes pleading with me to understand.

"Paige. This is something that I have to do and I am going to do that the best way I know how. After all your grandmother has done for us, I made a promise that when the time came, I would protect you." he said. His gaze searched mine.

"Aren't bodyguards supposed to let the person they're guarding know that's what they are doing?"

"Yes, but —"

"But what? You should've told me in the beginning, when I first asked you." I lost my temper and as usual reeling myself back in would be difficult.

"I did mention that I watched you."

"Yeah you did say that, but you didn't say it was kind of like a job for you. That you and Nana had agreed to this. You still haven't told me why!"

The dishes in the kitchen started to shake. Kean looked around and then at me. I've always been lousy at controlling my magic when I'm angry. Nana used to tell me this would prevent me from ever fully understanding my powers. I tried hard to work on that, but Nana's recent death had made my emotions and my powers more unpredictable.

The silverware that lay in the drain board begun to float around, and the chairs both Kean and I were sitting in started to rise. My stomach churned and my nerves were on a roller coaster about to take a plunge down a deep hill. My stomach knotted, and I was lighter than normal.

To raise Kean while he sat was no easy feat. The chair flying startled him.

"I know you are angry. This has to be blindsiding you. Please, calm down."

I took several deep breaths to relax. Everything that floated crashed down to the floor. Though I knew this was all my doing, I jumped at the noise it made. My head snapped back and I steadied myself with the table. Kean was completely unfazed.

In a flash, he stood next to me. He put an arm around me, and immediately I was comforted. Gently he touched my face and without a break in eye contact he kneeled in front of me. I stared at his ice blue eyes and realized, that despite everything he'd told me – and everything he hadn't – I wanted to throw myself at him.

"Paige, I know this sounds crazy. I got hurt on the way here. I partially failed my job since I should've came here and told you all of this sooner. I guess she, I mean they, got wind that I would be on my way to help you. I didn't mean to scare or alarm you. All I know is I need to be here at least until Halloween has passed and then if you want, I will leave. You have my word."

I sighed. "So Nana asked a shifter to protect me?"

"She mentioned that you might need my help sooner rather than later. I had to put a lot of the pieces of the puzzle myself."

"And it's got something to do with Halloween, and a woman?"

His eyes narrowed. I was right, but he didn't or wouldn't reply. I realized the eyes that watched me were the ones I sensed while on my run this morning. Those sexy, ice blue eyes. Many times I sensed something, but I never saw anything, so I brushed it off.

"You were following me earlier, weren't you?"

"Yes. I have been for weeks." He confirmed what I thought.

"Weeks?" I laughed sarcastically. "I'm glad no one felt the need to tell me anything about any of this. Nana should have told me this especially since it concerns me."

"I know it's crazy. I should've told you sooner. Your grandmother said you would tell me to go away," he said apologetically.

I couldn't argue with that. I usually handled things on my own. If I did things myself, and failed, I had no one else to blame, but myself. It was my motto and it has worked for me.

"I got wind of some things that made me come here. Otherwise I would have stayed where I was, watching you from afar, but making sure no harm came to you."

A huge part of me was confused about everything he said. Yes, my nana said I was special. One day, at the age of seven, she came into my room to see my toys flying around. I vaguely remember, she said that by the smile on my face, none of it fazed me.

After that I couldn't do it again. Not even if I concentrated. Nana told me I had to stop thinking about it so much. After realizing I had to wait to fully get my powers and still had to practice to perfect them, I gave up did the typical things people my age did. School, work, minus the friends and partying.

My life was simple and I liked it that way. Now all of this was beginning to be too much.

I rubbed my temples again and grimaced.

"Sorry. I lost my cool. This is a lot to process," I said.

"I can only imagine how it feels to be left in the dark. My parents were always pretty forthcoming about magic and shifting."

He leaned against the table. "You know, I have seen a lot of things in our world, but you are the first person I've met that could do what you just did."

"Really?"

"Yeah. I mean there are some pretty strong shifters. Witches, too, but being able to move things with your mind at that force, even without focus, is pretty damn cool."

I shrugged.

"I can tell you know there are way cooler powers out there."

"That's true too."

"I am going to check the perimeter of the woods and your house. I really don't want to leave you alone, but I can't protect you if I don't check to make sure everything is safe."

"I don't think I want you to go, Kean," I said softly. I surprised myself with my words, but that didn't make them any less true.

"I don't want to go either, but I have to. If only there were two of me. It'll be easier if I shift and run. I can cover more ground quicker and then come back to you."

It warmed my heart that he didn't want to leave. I watched him walk out the door and sighed.

I stood to take the picture of Nana and me off the mantle. As a child, things were much easier. No, I didn't have my parents, but Nana made up for it in more ways than one. After she died, I felt alone. I glanced at the picture of Sabrina and me. For a brief while I had a friend, then she too disappeared. I decided I would find out what happened to her, starting tomorrow. Since Sabrina left the best way to describe what my life has been is lonely. But the small amount of time I spent with Kean, the loneliness didn't loom so large.

Nana, I miss you.

I brushed my fingers over the picture and closed my eyes. For a moment I could feel her presence. A tear dropped on the picture and I wiped it off. Placing the picture back on the mantle, I pushed back my thoughts and my lonesomeness.

Later that evening, I sat in Nana's old rocking chair on the back porch, twirling a few strands of hair as I listened to the rain tap on the tin roof. The overhead light dimly showed some of the shadows on the back porch. The thunder rumbled and shook the walls, and I shuddered. Today I had been overwhelmed. One of those days where there was too much to handle.

Kean returned, as promised, and I glanced over my shoulder when he stepped into the entry behind me.

"Are you okay, Paige?" he asked.

"Yeah I'm okay, I guess. Actually no, I'm not okay. Why won't you tell me who wants to hurt me? And why wouldn't Nana tell me either?"

"I can't, I promised her. Try not to worry about it, if you can. Thinking too much can drive you batty. Believe me, I know," he said softly.

"Wouldn't you be worrying if someone dropped this kind of info on you?"

"You're right, but it won't change things."

I stared at the rain beating down around my house. Kean sat next to me on the swing.

Despite my confusion and nerves, I couldn't help but be attracted to Kean. If he made a move, I don't think I would tell him no. In fact, I knew I wouldn't. More likely, I'd suggest he take me right here on this chair. I was a ball of wound up emotions.

I leaned my head on his shoulder and he froze and then I felt him relax.

"I'm sorry," I mumbled.

"Don't be sorry." His fingers traced the outline of my face. I stared into his eyes and momentarily I was lost in them.

He leaned in hesitantly and pulled my face closer to his. I leaned in and closed my eyes, and I placed my lips on his. Slow at first, his lips brushed against mine like the light flutter of a butterfly's wings.

My heart raced and I pressed against him harder. He responded. His arms wrapped around me and he drew me closer. He ran his fingers through my hair. I sighed into him as I hungrily kissed him.

Never breaking the kiss, he pulled me onto his lap with ease. He slowly moved away from me.

"You're gorgeous;" he said holding my face.

And all of a sudden I became shy. My palms felt sweaty and my stomach tightened with nervousness.

He kissed me again with purpose. It shot sparks through me and immediately between my thighs ached with wetness.

I pulled at his shirt wanting to feel his skin, needing to get closer to him.

I removed his shirt to reveal his muscular chest. I placed tiny kisses on him, working my way from his stomach, up to his chest. I traced my finger over the faint scar. He grabbed at my shirt and immediately it tore.

"Shit. I'm sorry about that."

"It's only a shirt. Don't worry about it."

I saw the imprint of his erection through his jeans and I had the urge to touch it. I pulled at the button and tugged the zipper down. His erection was huge, but I couldn't wait for it to fill me.

I felt bold, if only for a fleeting moment. I placed my hand on his package and let my fingers trace the outline of the imprint. I wanted him badly, it had been a while.

I was too hot and bothered. His small touches to my breasts and his lips were driving me mad.

"Take me upstairs. To my room."

"As you wish." He gave a devilish grin and picked me up.

He carried me up the stairs, as we approached the door, he kicked it open.

Gently placing me on the bed, he paused momentarily. "Do you have condoms?"

"Yes, in the first drawer on the dresser right there;" I said and pointed at the vintage blue dresser. He opened the door and grabbed one out of the box.

Turning back to me, he kneeled and pulled my jeans off slowly placing small kisses on the way down until my clothes were all the way off.

His gaze roamed my body.

"Is something wrong?" I asked hesitantly.

"No. Red on a woman gets my blood going. It looks really sexy against your skin, baby."

He gently tugged at my panties until he slipped them off. A twinge of shyness had me reaching down to cover myself.

"Don't do that. I want to see you. All of you."

I did what he asked.

Suddenly, his lips were on my clit and he begun flicking his tongue across. I jerked a little as the pleasure and tension mounted.

He licked more intensely. I let out a loud moan and squirmed. His strong arms pressed me down on the mattress as he continued lapping my juices like a delicious dish. I tried to pull myself away all the delight he gave me, but he continued to hold me down. I moaned and tried to keep myself still as he slowly tortured me with his tongue.

"Kean...Um...I'm coming." My legs tightened around his head. Spasms of pleasure radiated from where he continued to torture my clit, not giving me a moment to catch my breath. He kept slurping and licking and I thought right then and there I would die.

"I need it now, Kean. Now!" He said nothing as he rolled the condom over his erection. Placing himself over my opening he slowly put it in and we both sighed together.

Gritting his teeth, he started to move.

"Fuck," he muttered. "You have no idea how good you feel."

We moved together, picking up the pace. He kissed one breast and massaged the other with his hand. He pounded into me and I accepted it, breathless from the pleasure that coursed through my body.

My legs begun to shake as the fire which coursed throughout my body foretold an approaching orgasm. "Kean." I moaned out his name and all but fell apart.

"I like the way you say my name," he whispered.

I wasn't able to say a word, as he pulled out and flipped me over. I clung to the headboard on my hands and knees. He positioned himself behind me and entered me with such force, I trembled. He pumped hard and fast. I moaned and he grunted and cursed slamming into me. His hands gripped my ass and he seemed to be losing all control.

The shadows grew longer and each thrust push me further and further over the edge. "Kean. I don't think I can take any more. It's too much." I buried my head in the covers as an orgasm tore through me. I screamed his name over and over. He muttered something I couldn't understand and he growled as he came. He leaned his forehead on my back. His breaths heavy, he pulled out and laid me on top of him front to front. That topped any other sex, I ever had. Developing feelings for him wouldn't be wise. I barely knew him. But I knew that what I was feeling wasn't going to go away, and if I decided to let him go, it would be hard to.

CHAPTER FOUR
October 31st

I had two clients today who agreed to work out together. I usually didn't take clients on Halloween, but after yesterday's cancelations I had no choice. I had to be open to them being here today.

Usually, I practiced my magic on Halloween it was much stronger than any other day, so spells came to me much easier.

I popped two Tylenols and rubbed my temples. The headache came back with a vengeance, even worse than yesterday. I didn't have the time to brew up any of the special remedy I normally used. My clients waited for me in my workout room-cum-living room. Thanks to Kean, and his strong muscles, my living room was rearranged. Now, I could accommodate them both in my living room rather than the basement. Besides, the air system ran in my living room and our workouts tended to get very sweaty.

After asking Kean to wait upstairs, I did several work out exercises with my clients. A little more than an hour later we ended and I watched as they left my home in good spirits.

I started putting my living room back in order when Kean came back down to help me.

"Watching you move these things around is making it really hard not to ravish you right there," Kean said, his voice husky.

I laughed. "Oh really? I asked shaking my butt a little.

He laughed.

Kean finished helping me arrange my living room and we shared looks. As much as my body wanted him on the spot, I knew that if I did, I would never make it to my coven meeting.

I headed into Rose's shop around two in the afternoon. Rose owned an occult store where all the coven meetings were held. Customers stood around looking for items to purchase. Teenage girls looked at some of the love spell displays. I smirked. Not too long ago, Sabrina and I did the same thing. We would fawn over the love spells when we were about twelve and thirteen saying one day we will have the perfect guy and a love spell surely could help. At the time Nana said I was too young for any of that, though once I was older, it didn't stop her from trying. I remember one time Sabrina and I have one of those conversations and Sabrina be very angry with Nana because of her firm no. That seemed so long ago.

Kean said he would wait for me after the meeting. I knew he wouldn't go far. He seemed extremely protective. I told him I'd be fine and I would meet him at the house, but he insisted on accompanying me to the meeting.

I wanted to tell Adanna that I had Kean with me, but we all knew that she struggled with coven meetings. I didn't want to upset her. I had nobody else to tell because I wasn't that close to anyone else. I was a loner most of the time. Though Kean fit under the magical creature category, the coven meetings were secret and were only for the coven members.

Walking past the blue curtains, I headed down the stairs. Even though I've been to two coven meetings without Nana the stairs spooked me. They always did. I hoped as the years passed, I wouldn't get such a spooky vibe.

Once inside I took a seat in my designated chair. Everyone had a chair unique to them. My chair had cat paws in place of standard chair legs. The seat was high and cushioned, with white stripes running across the arms.

Adanna walked in with a handsome man behind her. He didn't say much during the meeting. She told us we should report any strange activity and the usual "to dos." I wanted to tell her what Kean said about someone wanting to hurt me, but she seemed to have a lot on her plate. Besides, nothing had actually happened yet and maybe nothing would. Kean could be blowing this whole thing bodyguard thing out of proportion.

The meeting itself bored me. Adanna brought up the same things from topics before and told us that if we saw anything that can put us at risk with humans to let her know.

Kean waited for me after the meeting, as he promised. I smiled and headed to him, eager to be near him.

"I can't wait to get home and relax, unless there's something you want to do instead?" I asked, looking at Kean expectantly.

"What do you usually do on Halloween?"

"Honestly, as cliché as it sounds, it's me in front of the television watching horror movies. I don't go to Halloween parties anymore. It's kind of hard to explain if something randomly starts floating around."

Kean laughed. "That bad, huh?"

"The last time I attended a party, one of the college guys tried to grab me and I got angry. I sent him flying back against the wall. Lucky for me, everyone was too drunk to remember what happened or to believe what he said. So I decided until I get a better handle on things, no parties for me."

"Makes sense," he said thoughtfully.

"Perfect sense;" I said.

"Well, how about we head to the market and I'll pick up some ingredients for dinner and dessert?"

"That sounds like a pretty sweet idea." I smiled widely.

Kean prepared dinner as I sipped wine. He showed skill as he chopped ingredients. In no time my kitchen smelled divine. "Where did you learn to cook?"

His blue eyes roamed my face and then he grinned. "I may have bared it all to you the first time we met, but us shifters have our secrets too." He winked.

I laughed. "Point taken, but I'm sure you can spare a secret or two about learning your culinary skills."

"My mother always liked trying out different recipes and I used to watch her cook. She danced and sung while doing so. It was one of the perks of being in the kitchen with her. Everything about food, I learned from her."

"That's so sweet. Nana was amazing, but sometimes I wish I could have those kinds of memories about my parents," I said.

We swapped stories of growing up as we chowed down on the spaghetti and beef dish he created. He was always getting into mischief. Climbing trees, and getting into scuffles with the boys growing up. He was a loner by choice, but very close to his family.

Taking the last bite of my food, I sighed.

"If you keep cooking like this, I am going to have to move you in here."

"Is that so?"

"Every bite I took leaned more and more to a yes," I said grinning.

He laughed.

After dinner, we took the brownies with us and retired into the living room. One of my favorite movies, "Dawn of The Dead" was coming on. I snuggled close to Kean and he wrapped his arm around my shoulders as we snacked on brownies.

Toward the middle of the movie, I noticed the air felt too thick. I struggled to breathe. I began to feel unsettled. I shifted uncomfortably. Kean looked at me, concerned.

"What's the matter?"

"I don't know. I feel a little sick. It's like I can't breathe."

"Do you want to lie down?"

"No. I think I may need some air. I'll be right back."

I headed to the front door. Kean following close behind me. When I opened it, there stood the shadow of a man and someone I hadn't seen in a long time. I gasped.

Kean's body tensed beside me. He let out a low growl. I still felt too sick to acknowledge it. A violent wave of nausea crept up my throat and I backed away, shaking my head, trying to keep the contents of my stomach from coming back up. The further away I got the better I felt and I realized the source of my sickness was in front of me.

Kean stepped in front of me, protectively.

"You?"

"Yes, me. Who did you expect, the tooth fairy?" The woman stepped inside, followed by the large man.

What the hell was going on?

CHAPTER FIVE

I stared into the face of Sabrina. The malice in her eyes contradicted that at one point we were good friends. The man who stood behind her, loomed over my home. He snarled and clenched his fists. It all started to make sense. This was the person Kean was protecting me from. But why?

From the corner of my eye I noticed Kean sizing him up.

Kean stepped in front of me protectively.

"Sabrina? What are you doing here?" I asked perplexed.

Sabrina walked a circle around us, her black hair swung as she moved. Her bodyguard stood there blocking the front door. I began to feel sick again and tried to shake it off.

"You mean to tell me lover boy here didn't tell you anything about me, my darling Paige?"

I looked up at Kean, confused.

"What does she mean by that, Kean?" I glanced back at Sabrina. The sick feeling in my stomach got worse. Whatever spell she had cast was getting stronger.

She stepped back in front of me, rage blazing in her eyes.

"Kean here used to be my lover. I told him how much I hated you and your family. I told him I needed his help to get rid of you. He didn't agree. So he left. I guess he wasn't loyal after all. I thought dogs were supposed to be loyal."

Kean gritted his teeth and his gaze pleaded with me. I couldn't even begin to understand why he didn't say any of this before. I didn't have the time to question him.

Sabrina's bodyguard stepped closer and Kean placed his hand I front of the man. The man gave a chilling laugh and knocked Kean's hand off of him. Kean grabbed him and was rewarded by being flung behind me. I winced. Part of me wanted to make sure he was okay, but I couldn't. I had bigger fish to fry.

"Why, Sabrina? What did I ever do to you? We were friends."

"Friends is such a loose word. We were friends once, until I asked your grandmother to help me learn witchcraft like you. My family told me I terrified them, and they sent me to live with my aunt.

"I know that you lived with your aunt. That was how we met."

"Ding ding. One hundred points for you Paige. I bet your grandmother didn't tell you I asked her to help me or tell you why you no longer saw or heard from me."

I said nothing. Nana never did give me a straight answer about Sabrina being gone, but Nana did that sometimes. Though I never understood why.

"And this concerns me how?" I backed up. I needed to clear my mind, but everything she told me made it hard too.

"I have always been fascinated with witchcraft and spells, but I didn't have any witch blood in me or magic. I knew witches had covens and I asked your grandmother to allow me to learn, so I could join. She told me my heart was filled with too much hate and too much rage. I mean you would be if you had parents like mine. She said I didn't know how to forgive or to not let anger control me. It wasn't my fault that my parents couldn't deal with me. She declined to teach me. Then she sent me away. Time and time again I would ask and her answer would always be no. She had no problem teaching it to you and telling everyone who would listen how proud of you she was. She made me sick." She closed her eyes for a moment and then sighed. "Eventually, I started to despise her. After studying and practicing on my own for a long while, I came back here and met your boyfriend over there."

"She was right. My nana always had an inkling about people. If she said you weren't a good fit to learn, I can guarantee she had good reason. "

"Oh, please. My nana was always right," she mocked me. She rolled her eyes and sneered. "Your nana was an old bitch and she's lucky to already be dead. I can settle on getting rid of you. You aren't even good enough to be in a coven, and once your coven sees how easily I can defeat you, they will welcome me in with open arms. With a coven backing me, I can be more powerful than I am now. This will be like taking candy from a baby. "

I could hear the glasses in the cupboards shake as her words hit me.

"I can guarantee they would tell you you're crazy," I spat.

"I think we all can be a little crazy at times. You lost everyone that ever cared for you just like I did. Your parents, your grandmother, and Kean will leave you too, just like everyone left me. He doesn't even respect you enough to tell you the truth, just like your precious Nana."

I hadn't been this furious in a while. I had always been a good friend to Sabrina and now she stood in my home, threatening to hurt me because Nana wouldn't let her be a witch? Because she couldn't control her rage. I knew about trying to control your anger. But Nana's decision was something I had no control over or any knowledge of. Then to throw in my face the death of my loved ones, she was going down.

Kean seemed to still be done. Focusing all my energy on her bodyguard, I lifted his body up and forced him out of my home.

I can't believe I just did that.

Shock filled me. I've tried to control my magic for so long, but until now, it never worked.

Kean staggered a bit as he got up and then he shook it off. He glanced at me and then looked outside.

"I'll deal with him," he said and rushed outside.

That left me alone with Sabrina.

"You're better than I thought," she sneered.

I glared at her.

"No matter. I can still beat you."

Mist began to fall around me, blinding me. I queasiness overwhelmed me and my skin burned. Sabrina had a great teacher. I was surprised. Patience and Sabrina didn't mix. It amazed me that she was able to master this kind of ability without having magic in her bloodline.

I closed my eyes and counted down from ten, cleared every feeling and every notion from my mind. Mist still filled the room, but I could feel her energy and it was all I needed. Using my magic to lift the vase off the table behind me, I flung it toward her head. Her concentration broke.

"What the hell?" she yelled and the mist slowly cleared. I used my magic to make her levitate. I had her midair, her arms and legs straight, like boards protruding from her body. Focusing further I used my magic to bind her. I had noticed that she needed her hands to cast, and if she couldn't use them, she wouldn't be able to harm me.

I made her spin round and round. I didn't want to hurt her. However, I did want her to leave me alone and go back to the hole she crawled from. I was hurt. I thought we were great friends at one point. I guess it was because I didn't know better.

"Paige," she yelled. "Put me down. Put me down." I kept my main concentration on her, but shifted just enough focus to move some of the knives so they floated around her. I needed her to be frightened enough to leave. I didn't have the heart to badly injure or kill her. One of the knives cut a lock from her hair, the hair spun toward me.

I heard the scuffle going on outside and then it all came to an end with what sounded like a sickening thud. I hope Kean was okay.

I sensed the beginnings of a headache coming on, and I had used too much magical energy. But I needed to send a message to her. I caught her hair spinning in the air and I took the red hair tye from my hair and wrapped it around hers. The look in her eye told me she knew I was binding her powers.

"Sabrina, I want you to take your friend and leave. Don't ever step foot near my house and don't ever set foot back into town. Leave and never come back. I will enlighten my coven about your actions and I can guarantee no other decent coven would want a vengeful witch like you. Even if you've mastered your manipulations. Even if you ever manage to escape my binding charm."

Sabrina appeared both dizzy and startled. Finally, she nodded. I released the magic and she dropped to the floor. My breathing heavy and my head pounded.

"Now go," I said as I steadied myself. She climbed to her feet, a glare on her face, but fear in her eyes. She dusted herself off and strode out of the house quickly.

A few moments later, Kean rushed back in, and my strength and legs gave in to the blackness creeping into my mind.

I woke up in my bed, Kean's blue eyes looking at me. He had some bruises on his arm, but nothing serious. My body ached for once the pain in my head was not too bad. It was the smallest headache I had in a long time.

"How long have I been out?" I asked.

"Six or seven hours. You were exhausted."

"Thanks for putting me in bed."

"I recall you doing the same for me not too long ago." He winked.

I smiled, and then winced. "Tell me something, Kean. Is everything she said true? You two were dating? She wanted to hurt me and you to help her do it?"

His shoulders sagged and his forehead creased. He sighed heavily. "I'm sorry I didn't tell you. I really hoped she didn't make good on her threat. Yes, it's true."

"You didn't think to clarify who wanted to harm me when you knew she knew who I was?"

"I know it sounds stupid. She fooled me. The sweet girl I met had way too much hate, and anger. All the time. I didn't even she even knew you at first. One day she mentioned she started ranting about being hurt and not good enough. At first I thought maybe she was just trying to blow off some steam. Her plans sounded too malicious. She even went as far as to mentioning kidnapping. Once I realized who she was and that you was the one she wanted to harm, I had to leave her. I know I should've told you, but I didn't think you would believe me."

I nodded. What he said made sense. I was too forgiving at times. Too trusting and if he told me this, I would've told him to leave and forget I existed. Thinking about it now all the times my Nana would change the subject or when Sabrina seemed upset with me, it all made sense. I wanted to forgive Kean, but right now everything seemed too much. I couldn't help, but still be angry.

"Kean." I sighed. "I need a little space. I'm on information overload, and I can't pretend this doesn't bother me. I'm not good at hiding my emotions."

Kean's gaze pierced mine. He wanted to say something. It was written all over his face. A small part of me wanted him to refute what I said, but I knew he wouldn't. I also knew my emotions still felt too raw.

"I want to make sure you relax and then I'll leave. I promise."

I nodded and closed my eyes. The bed shifted as Kean sat down. A large part of me didn't want Kean to leave. But I knew if I didn't allow myself time to gather my thoughts, I would hold a grudge against the man who somehow in this short amount of time had my heart in a pitter patter.

I drifted to sleep as his hand closed around mine. Darkness covering my dreams.

EPILOGUE
Three Weeks Later

I pulled up in front of a modest house. Trees surrounded the front of his home, and I could see a small lake in the backyard. It took some time going through Nana's things, but I finally found Kean's address.

He hadn't spoken to me since the night he left my house. I knew I asked him for space, but a small part of me wished he had tried to reach out anyway. I had given myself time to weigh everything that happened, and my heart wanted to see if anything could grow between us.

Stepping forward, I lifted the brass knocker and let it fall against the wooden door. I heard some rustling and then the door opened. There he stood, shirtless, his chest wet with sweat and his long hair tied back.

"Paige?"

"Hey, Kean." I could hear the nerves in my own voice. I shifted my weight around with my feet.

"Come in." He stepped aside and I walked into his living room. I expected the typical bachelor pad, but I was surprised by the surroundings. His space was much neater than I expected and there were some real homey qualities about it that I liked. The furniture had a mothers touch to it. The walls had plenty of family photos, but the two I noticed were the two of Kean evenly spaced from each other. One was a picture when he was a little boy, and the other one quite recent.

"Your house is nice." I wanted to make small talk because all of a sudden I felt my heart drop into my stomach. Usually I could express myself easily, but now, after practicing what I wanted to say, nothing came to my lips.

"You came here to tell me about my home decor?" he asked.

I wish I could read his thoughts. His eyes showed no emotion, his expression blank.

"No. I...Why didn't you call me or come to see me?"

"You told me not to," he said quietly.

"You didn't have to listen, you know."

He smirked and took a step toward me. "I know you're a bit of a firecracker, and as cute as you are when you're mad, I didn't want to see any dishes flying past my head."

I pouted and then smiled. "Okay, so you have me there. I need to control my temper better. Honestly, I missed you like crazy. I know the whole thing with Sabrina wasn't your fault, but I didn't want to hear any of that at the time."

"Okay."

"That's it? Okay?"

"Okay as in I understand why you asked me to go away." he said and turned to walk away.

I groaned softly and watched as he walked his frame leave the living room. I heard some rustling, and moving around, but when he didn't return right away, a small panic entered my mind.

Maybe he doesn't want to talk right now. Or worse maybe he's not interested in me anymore.

Trying to hold in the tears threatening to fall down my cheeks, I turned to leave.

"Leaving me again, Paige?" he asked with a small grin on his face. He put a tank on and his blue eyes watching me with amusement.

"No. I...I don't know. I don't want to bother you."

He laughed. "Did I say you were bothering me?"

"No, but—"

"But what?"

I shook my head. In one motion he stood in front of me.

"Paige, you are my firecracker and that's one of the many things I love about you."

Smiling, I snuggled against his chest. "I missed you."

"I missed you, too. I would love if you stayed for a while."

"I think that can be arranged."

He lifted me up to plant a kiss on my lips, and I kissed him back greedily.

Staying for a while didn't seem like a bad idea at all. Maybe even for the rest of my life.

You can follow this New Yorker on Social Media. Pick your poison. (You can follow them all if you want)
Here they go
You can follow me on Social Media
Twitter: @ AuthorKayBlake
Instagram: @AuthorKayBlake
Pinterest: @AuthorKayBlake
Blog: www.authorkayblake.wordpress.com
Facebook: http://www.facebook.com/authorkayblake
Tsu: http://www.tsu.co/authorkayblake
Goodreads: http://www.goodreads.com/KayBlake
Amazon: http://www.amazon.com/Kay-Blake/e/B00K5WCK38

Hope to see you there
Kay

Thank you for taking the time to read Bewitching Desires. We hope that you enjoyed your time with us in the Savannah Coven. Please take a moment to show us some author love by leaving a review on your favorite retailers. Amazon, Barnes and Noble, Ibooks, Kobo, and GoodReads.

Have a wonderful Day!

Rebekah, Tami, Niki, Jennifer, Danielle, Sheri, Michele, Maria, A.E., Andra, Sonja, Kay

Made in the USA
Charleston, SC
07 October 2015